Someone Like You

Tracy Corbett started writing in her late twenties. As well as writing novels, she's written several short stories, pantomime sketches and magazine articles. Tracy describes her writing style as modern tales of romance, with engaging quirky characters, who overcome adversity, grow as people and conclude in satisfying optimistic endings. When she's not writing, she enjoys amateur dramatics, gardening and music. She works part-time for a local charity.

Tracy Corbett

SOMEONE LIKE YOU

1⊘ CANELO

First published in the United Kingdom in 2021 by

Canelo
31 Helen Road
Oxford OX2 0DF
United Kingdom

A CIP catalogue record for this book is available from the British Library.

Print ISBN 978 1 80032 331 5
Ebook ISBN 978 1 80032 330 8

Look for more great books at www.canelo.co

Printed and bound in Great Britain by Clays Ltd, Elcograf S.p.A.

1

Prologue

A low mist shrouded the gravestones. The trees were bare, their twisted branches like wizened fingers reaching up to the sky. All was quiet, the cemetery abandoned. The damp kept mourners away.

The hearse crept past two ornate pillars guarding the entrance of the East London Crematorium, its low engine noise masked by the rattle of jangling bridle reins. Hooves tapped rhythmically against the concrete pathway as the horse-drawn carriage led the procession.

Lilith Monroe rubbed condensation away from the window and blinked away the onset of tears as the hearse slowed to a halt.

Rows of headstones stretched ahead. Grand statues of cherubic angels, contrasted with simple carved wooden crosses. Some graves were adorned with an abundance of flowers, others lay neglected, their eroded inscriptions covered with moss.

It was an eerie sight. Made more poignant by the grim weather.

The hearse door opened.

A Victorian-attired funeral officiant bowed his head and offered Lilith his hand. She accepted the gesture and exited the hearse, regretting her decision not to wear

I

gloves. It was bitingly cold. The frost had yet to melt away and her hands were feeling the effects.

Buttoning up her black coat, she followed the funeral officiant to the main chapel doors, where she was instructed to wait until the pallbearers had unloaded the coffin.

Silence filled the misty air, broken only by the occasional rattle of bridle reins as one of the horses whinnied and shook its head impatiently.

Lilith glanced at her hands, white from the cold. Her warm breath was visible against the cold January air.

She bowed her head when the wreath of white roses bearing the word 'Granddad' was removed from the glass carriage and placed on top of the dark wooden coffin. Strands of limp mousy hair escaped from its clasp, and fell against her pale cheek, the dank air making it even more lank than usual.

Four pallbearers lifted the coffin and positioned themselves in front of the chapel doors.

Lilith removed the folded handkerchief from her pocket and moved into position behind the coffin.

The chapel doors creaked open.

'In The Bleak Midwinter' began to play.

Slowly the pallbearers moved forwards, the coffin balancing on their shoulders.

Lilith had experienced some desolate moments in her twenty-nine years on the planet. This was right up there. She'd lost her mother when she was four years old. She'd never known her father, and she had no brothers or sisters. She'd spent the majority of her adult life caring for two elderly grandparents, both of whom were now gone. Bleak didn't come close to describing how she felt.

But although life hadn't been easy, she'd made the best of her situation. She'd had a good relationship with her grandparents and she'd been a happy child. She'd embraced what little family she'd had, and she had enjoyed being part of a loving unit.

But the good times had faded once old age and illness had taken its toll on the older generation, and it had been a long while since she'd felt anything close to happy. Yet it was only as she followed the coffin between the rows of empty pews that the reality of her solitary existence truly hit home. She was alone. Painfully alone.

The hymn rose in its crescendo, haunting and melancholic.

She looked around the vast chapel. There were only three mourners: her grandparents' elderly neighbours, Mr and Mrs Black. And Amir from the local Post Office.

No distant relatives. No friends or work colleagues. Her granddad had outlived them all.

Standing ahead was another solitary figure. The vicar. A silver-haired woman, with a soft lyrical voice and thick-framed glasses, the perfect requisites for a member of the clergy.

Her grandparents hadn't been regular churchgoers, but they considered themselves to be religious, so a Christian ceremony had seemed fitting.

The vicar offered a consoling glance as the pallbearers neared.

Lilith's attempts to stay in control were waning. It was an effort not to dissolve into a crying puddle on the floor. Not helped by the haunting music, or the frosty chill, nor the sight of the coffin being lowered onto the platform.

The shake in her legs reverberated up her body, making it hard to balance on her low heels.

Clasping the front pew, she slid onto the bench seat, knocking the kneeling cushion from its hanger. The chapel seemed to close in on her as she struggled for breath, making her feel dizzy. She should have eaten breakfast and not allowed her grief to interfere with the need for sustenance. She was paying the price now.

As the final chords of 'In The Bleak Midwinter' faded into the rafters, the vicar approached the ornate wooden lectern and opened a large Bible. Behind her, the illuminated stained-glass image of Jesus cast her in a soft glow.

Adjusting her glasses, the vicar paused before beginning her sermon, taking a moment to make eye contact with the congregation. 'Praise to the God of All Comfort,' she began, her voice enhanced by the microphone attached to the lectern. 'Who comforts us in our troubles, so that we can comfort those in trouble, with the comfort we ourselves receive from God.'

Lilith closed her eyes. She didn't feel comforted in the slightest.

Far from it. The only life she'd known had ended. Her family were gone. Her daily routine of caring for her granddad and nursing him through crippling arthritis and dementia was no longer required. What the hell was she going to do with her life?

There would be no daily visits from the care team while she was at work. No frequent discussions with the GP about her granddad's medication, and no curling up on the sofa to watch *Pointless* together, even though her granddad no longer knew the answers.

A work colleague had commented that she was finally 'free'. It was a burden lifted. She'd been unshackled from the relentless responsibilities of caring for an elderly relative.

But Lilith didn't see it that way.

She felt untethered. Cast adrift. Orphaned and very, very much alone.

The vicar finished her opening sermon and beckoned for Lilith to join her at the lectern. 'We will now hear from Royston's granddaughter, Lilith.'

There seemed little point using a microphone to address three people, so Lilith stood by her grandad's coffin, resisting the urge to reach out and touch it, fearing her voice would fail if she did.

She turned to the congregation and removed the poem from her coat pocket. The paper shook in her hand, the folded crease marks blurring the words. But she knew the verses well enough to recite them by heart.

When she'd finished reading 'Gone, but Not Forgotten', she returned to her seat.

She'd spoken too quickly, garbled her words. But it was hard to remain composed when a crushing weight was pressing against her chest, making it hard to breathe.

The vicar resumed her sermon. 'Thank you, Lilith. What a beautiful sentiment. Memories are indeed a precious gift. They allow us to keep the person with us, treasured in our hearts, as we move on with our lives. Gone, but not forgotten, as the poem aptly reminds us.'

Lilith covered her mouth, trying to stem the noise threatening to escape. Why was it that British culture didn't allow for grief wailing as other cultures did? Why was she expected to grieve quietly and in a dignified manner? She didn't feel like being dignified. She wanted to scream and yell at the cruelty of it all.

But she couldn't do that. It wasn't the done thing.

Instead, she suffered in silence as she listened to the vicar speaking about her granddad, relaying stories from his time in the Navy and his career in the Post Office. She talked about his forty-five-year marriage to his beloved wife, Julia, and the loss of their only daughter, Hannah, aged just twenty-seven.

Lilith swallowed past the ache in her throat. Now wasn't the time to be thinking about her mother. Keeping it together was hard enough as it was.

Thankfully, the vicar moved on to a lighter topic and began talking about her grandparents' love of music. In particular, their joint adoration of Elvis Presley.

The mention of Elvis made Lilith smile. Her earliest memories were of listening to Elvis records and watching his films. Her granddad used to impersonate him, while her grandma would watch the crooner embroiled in a punch-up with the film's baddie and proclaim, 'Elvis is such a good fighter – he never loses.' Funny that.

They'd bought every single one of his albums and had even visited Graceland for their Ruby wedding anniversary.

Lilith remembered her granddad crying when they'd played 'Love Me Tender' at her grandma's funeral twelve years ago. It had been 'their song'. The song they'd danced to at their wedding in 1965.

And here she was again, about to bid goodbye to her granddad with another Elvis classic.

The vicar peered through her glasses at the CD machine on the lectern. 'Let us now enjoy Royston's favourite Elvis song. Dedicated to his beloved wife, Julia. "The Wonder of You".'

Lilith braced herself for the inevitable wave of emotion she knew would engulf her. It was the song her grandparents had sung to each other, and the song her granddad had chosen to be played at his funeral today. There was no way this wasn't going to hurt.

So it was something of a shock when the distinctive opening chords of 'Jailhouse Rock' filled the chapel.

For a moment, she froze, stunned into silence. Too dumbfounded to react.

As her senses returned, she glanced at the vicar, expecting to see a horrified look on her face – recognition that she'd selected the wrong track. But there was no indication that she'd realised her mistake, only a slight look of puzzlement at the Monroe family's odd choice of funeral song.

Lilith turned to Mr and Mrs Black.

They flinched as Elvis, 'began to wail, in the county jail—'

Amir from the Post Office looked at her as if to say, 'What the…?'

What the… indeed.

Even the pallbearers looked uncomfortable. Their sideways glances and hunched shoulders indicated they were trying not to laugh. She couldn't blame them.

As the chorus rang out and Elvis serenaded 'everybody in the whole cell block', Lilith noticed the funeral officiant making his way towards the lectern. The discreet slicing motion he made across his neck was met with a confused expression by the vicar.

It was only after he'd whispered in her ear that she lunged for the CD machine.

The music cut off abruptly.

An awkward pause followed.

A red-faced vicar then sheepishly approached the microphone.

'I do apologise,' she said, looking crushed. 'There seems to have been an error in the CD track selection. You may have gathered that my musical tastes favour more classical tunes, rather than popular modern music.'

Modern? Elvis had been dead for forty years.

'Please accept my sincere apologies.' The vicar wiped her forehead. 'Let's try again.' She lifted her glasses and squinted at the CD machine. 'We will now hear… "The Wonder of You".' She made a show of pressing play.

If 'Jailhouse Rock' had been the most inappropriate song to play at a funeral, then 'Return to Sender' had to be the most appropriate.

For the first time in a very long while, Lilith laughed. Really laughed. As in… hysterical–uncontrollable–shouldn't-be-laughing-but-can't-help-it kind of laugher. Her sides hurt. Her face hurt. She couldn't stand upright. She clutched hold of the pew, doubling up as she tried, and failed, to compose herself.

Forget wailing, this was worse. She was almost snorting. It was agony. Her body was in torment. Conflicted between heartbreaking grief and bellyaching hysterics.

But it was okay. Because she knew her granddad would be laughing, too. He would have loved this. Her grandma, too. They'd asked for 'The Wonder of You'. Instead, they'd got a medley of Elvis hits.

She could see the vicar looking at her, puzzlement on her face.

Lilith didn't care.

She couldn't have planned a more fitting goodbye if she'd tried.

She waited until the song had played out, and her heightened emotions had settled, before approaching the lectern.

The vicar frowned. 'Is everything all right, my dear?'

'I'm fine, Vicar. But I do have one request.'

'Of course.' The vicar looked concerned. 'Whatever you need.'

'Any chance we could hear "The Wonder of You" before we leave?'

The colour drained from the vicar's face.

Chapter One

Two months later…

Lilith dismounted her bicycle and secured it to one of the railings outside the ironmongers. Not that anyone was likely to steal her ancient pushbike. It was hardly a desirable item. What with its flaky paintwork, rusty wheels and old-fashioned basket attached to the front, it looked more like a museum relic, than a reliable mode of transportation. But needs must.

Maybe she'd add 'get new bike' to her wish list – along with the other life decisions she was now free to make since she was no longer a full-time carer.

She dug out a tissue and wiped her eyes.

Trying to put a positive spin on her situation was exhausting. However hard she tried, it didn't stop the grief undermining her attempts to move on with her life.

Checking that her bicycle was secure, she removed her shopping bag from the basket – which currently contained various condiments for her elderly neighbours, Mr and Mrs Black – and checked her surroundings.

North Haringey was a bustle of heavy traffic and irritated shoppers. Cars were parked bumper to bumper, their exhaust fumes filling the grimy London air. Drivers leant on their horns, pausing in their frustrations as a police car sped by, its blue lights flashing.

Lilith checked her directions. Retro Reds Beauty Salon should be a few doors down.

She walked along the busy pavement, slaloming her way around the animated shoppers, not knowing what to expect from the salon that her work colleague had recommended. Taye was an extrovert, his black skin inked with tattoos and his hair shaved into an intricate design. But he'd assured her this was the perfect place for a 'reinvention'.

And she was in desperate need of an upgrade.

But then the doubt crept in and she began questioning whether she really wanted to do this. Maybe it would be safer to stick with her current look? But this just depressed her even more. Her current look was so nondescript she was almost invisible – a point proved when a passer-by bumped into her as though she wasn't standing there.

She found the salon and stopped outside to study the fancy artwork painted on the window. Unlike the other shops lining the street, Retro Reds Beauty Salon was a blast of vibrancy. It looked glamorous, funky and quirky. All things she most definitely was not.

Had she made a mistake in coming here? But how else was she going to kick-start her new life? Drastic action was called for. And this looked like the kind of place where 'drastic' would be on the menu.

Ignoring the trepidation she felt, she opened the door. A loud bell announced her arrival, preventing an unobtrusive entrance. The sight ahead made her blink. Maybe she needed to wear the sunglasses she'd just purchased ready for her holiday.

Black and white chequerboard tiling covered the floor. The walls were painted turquoise and covered with prints of glamorous 1950s pin-ups. A baby-pink sofa sat to one side, contrasting with bubblegum-pink cushions.

A stylist was blow-drying a woman's hair. The stylist was wearing a turquoise top and pink circle skirt, a match for the decor. Her arms and legs were decorated in tattoos and her long bouncy hair was a vivacious red. The client's hair was… green.

Panic started to encroach. Lilith wanted a makeover, sure. But this wasn't the transformation she had in mind. No way could she carry off green hair. Her pale complexion couldn't take it for a start – she'd look jaundiced.

She lunged for the door, aiming for a quick getaway, when a woman's voice said, 'Are you my eleven-thirty?'

Lilith paused, her hand on the door handle. Stay… or go?

Come on, she told herself, for once in your life take a risk.

She took a deep breath and turned. 'I am, yes. Lilith Monroe.'

'Cool.' The woman came over, a sexy sway to her gait. She was the epitome of glamour. Her hair was bright copper, styled into ringlets and pinned up on one side. She wore a white camisole over a lime-green bra and a tight-fitting canary-yellow skirt.

Like her colleague, her arms and legs were covered in decorative tattoos and were accentuated by a pair of killer heels. 'You're Taye's mate, right?' She smiled. 'Can I take your cardigan?' She snapped her pink bubblegum against her bright red lips as she perused Lilith's sad knitted cardi complete with baggy elbows. 'Nice shopping bag,' she said, as if feeling the need to compliment her client in some way. 'Bold print.'

Lilith's insides fluttered, as they always did when someone complimented one of her designs. 'Thanks, I made it myself.'

The stylist's perfect eyebrows raised in surprise. 'You did?' Her eyes travelled curiously over the rest of Lilith's drab attire, grey jeans and scuffed trainers. No doubt wondering how someone so plain could create something so colourful and vibrant.

Lilith often wondered the same thing.

Removing her cardigan, she handed it to the stylist, who gestured to a mint-green chair. 'Take a seat,' she said, discarding Lilith's cardi. 'I'm Ruby. I run this place with my partner, Red.' She nodded to the other stylist, who looked over and smiled.

Lilith sat down and faced the mirror, which was framed with rows of illuminated spotlights. The bright lighting drained her of all colour. She looked transparent. Positively ghostly.

'So, what can we do for you today?' Ruby leant on the back of the chair and studied Lilith's refection. It was quite intimidating to be scrutinised in such a way.

In contrast to Ruby's glamorous appearance, Lilith looked like a sad excuse of a woman, with her sallow skin and dull, murky eyes.

But then she reminded herself that's why she was here. It was time for a reboot.

The last few years caring for her granddad had been torturous. There'd been no let up from the daily worries or struggles of coping with his failing physical health. And no respite from the fear that his Alzheimer's would result in injury – or worse. When she'd come home from work one day to find him drying washing in the microwave, she'd known full-time care was required. He was no longer safe to be left alone. And without any other family to support her, it was left to her to protect and care for him.

But in doing so, she'd neglected her own needs. Forget personal grooming and regular trips to the hairdressers, she'd barely had time to wash and dress each day. Everything had been put on hold. Her career. Her social life. Her love life. She'd sacrificed it all.

Not that she was complaining. But her situation had changed now. And like it or not, she needed to change with it. Starting with her appearance.

'I'm not exactly sure what I want,' she said, meeting Ruby's gaze in the mirror. 'I was hoping you could suggest something.'

Ruby smacked her gum. 'I'm guessing nothing too drastic, right?'

'If by drastic, you mean dying my hair a primary colour,' she glanced at the green-haired woman a few seats down, 'then no. But I was hoping for something a little more… I don't know, vibrant? Something more defined and less…' she pointed to her lank hair, 'insipid?'

Ruby looked mildly intrigued. 'Are we cutting it today?'

'Yes, please. I mean, it needs it, right?'

'Hell, yes.' Ruby cleared her throat. 'Sorry, what I meant was, it could definitely do with styling.'

'You don't need to worry about offending me. I'm aware my appearance is shocking. Do whatever you think is necessary.'

Ruby smiled. 'Well, all right then.'

She walked around the chair, viewing Lilith from all angles, lifting her hair and tutting when she saw the state of her split-ends.

'Okay, so I'm thinking a choppy bob, cut above your shoulders, with long chunky layers to give it body and a sweeping side fringe. You have great bone structure, a heart-shaped face. So cutting your hair below your chin will accentuate your cheek bones and jaw line. At the moment, your features are masked.' She scraped Lilith's long hair away from her face. 'All this needs to go.'

'Okay. If that's what you recommend.'

'Colour-wise, I'm thinking a dark copper base, with a mixture of lighter blonde and chocolate lowlights to add depth and make your eyes stand out.'

'My eyes?'

'Warmer tones will make your eyes pop. They're green, right?'

Lilith nodded.

'Pretty. And your skin is good.'

'Are you kidding me? It's deathly pale.'

'But it's clear and even, so you can take a strong hairstyle. The right colour will do wonders for your complexion. Do you wear make-up?'

'Not usually, but I've just bought some new stuff from Boots. My old stuff had virtually dried up.'

Ruby tilted her head. 'You're serious about this change, aren't you?'

'You sound surprised.'

Ruby shrugged. 'Most people have decided who they are long before now.' She reached for a gown and tied it around Lilith's neck. 'It's rare for someone of your age to embrace a big change.' She began sectioning off Lilith's hair, securing it with a clip. 'Not that you're old, you're what, mid-twenties?'

'Twenty-nine.'

'Right. So by that age, people have normally found their groove. Most people are creatures of habit. We stick to what we know.' She pointed at herself. 'Take me, for example. I've looked this way since I was fifteen.'

'You have?'

Ruby nodded. 'Stuck in my ways. It's brave of you to want to change. Good for you.'

'Thanks.'

Ruby patted Lilith's shoulder. 'Back in a sec. I need to mix up the colours.' She sashayed off, blowing a huge bubble of gum and bursting it with one of her pink talons.

Despite the stylist's encouraging words, the reflection staring back at Lilith in the mirror still looked sullen and morose. No amount of hair colour or make-up was likely to change that.

Not that she was expected to be all happy all the time. She was still grieving. Mourning the loss of her granddad. It would be odd if she didn't feel sad.

But in truth, she'd been grieving for her granddad long before he'd actually died. Once Alzheimer's had taken hold, the sense of loss had kicked in.

The wound had been created the first time he couldn't remember who she was. A wound that had deepened with each stage of deterioration. From losing his ability to talk, to making grunting noises when he watched TV. Finally, he had no longer smiled when she entered a room. It had eaten away at her. Dented her confidence and had affected her ability to cope.

Consequently, when he'd eventually passed away, the first emotion to hit had been relief. His suffering was over. It was only in the weeks that followed that relief had been replaced by grief. A deep ache that refused to shift. And had magnified as she'd packed away his clothes for the charity shop and tried to find a home for all their furniture.

She'd wanted to keep some of her grandparents' belongings. In particular, their collection of Elvis albums and the old gramophone they'd played them on. But where would she keep them? She had no succession rights to the local authority flat, and although the council had given her six months' notice to find alternative accommodation, the likelihood was she'd end up renting a single room in a shared house somewhere. She doubted her new housemates would welcome a fifty-year-old gramophone.

But parting with her grandparents' stuff had been hard. Like giving away her past. Her life. Leaving her feeling untethered and unsure what to do next.

She dug out a tissue. Tears still surfaced easily.

Small steps, she told herself. Don't try to work everything out in one go.

She knew she wanted a more fulfilling career. And that one day she desperately wanted a family of her own. But for now, she needed to concentrate on repairing her self-worth, which had taken a bit of a battering.

Ruby returned pushing a trolley laden with bowls of coloured liquids. 'So…' she said, picking up one of the brushes. 'Can I ask what brought about this desire to reinvent your appearance?' She removed one of the clips and began pasting on the dye mix. 'I'm guessing something happened to make you want to change. Break-up? Divorce?' She paused. 'You don't have to divulge, it's just that being a hairdresser is a bit like being a counsellor. Clients often find it therapeutic to open up about their troubles.'

'So Taye tells me.' Lily smiled. Her work colleague was one of life's 'sharers'. He divulged everything.

Ruby grinned. 'I hope he told you how discreet we are? Nothing said inside these four walls ever gets repeated. We never breach confidentiality.'

'He did tell me that, yes.'

'Good. It's very important that our clients know that. Otherwise they'd never open up, and we do love our gossip. Don't we, Red?'

The other stylist glanced over. 'Positively thrive on it. Don't hold back. Otherwise it makes for a very dull day for us.' She winked at Lilith and returned to finishing her client's up-do – which was looking very fancy, even if it was green.

'As I was saying.' Ruby combed through the colour. 'It's a common reaction for women who've been cheated on to want to improve their appearance. You know, make the bastard realise what he's missing, and all that. Which I can totally understand,' she said, rolling her eyes. 'We've all been there. Right?'

Actually, Lilith hadn't. Her broken heart hadn't been caused by a man. Well, not a man she was romantically involved with.

'What happened? Catch him in bed with your best friend?'

Lilith shook her head. 'Nothing so dramatic. My granddad died.'

Ruby sighed. 'Aw, that's sad.'

'He was a big part of my life,' she said, feeling the need to explain, although why, she wasn't sure. 'My mum died when I was four. I was brought up by grandparents. He was my only remaining relative. I've spent the last ten years caring for him.'

'Oh, sweetheart, that sounds grim.'

'I didn't mind. I was happy to do it. But it didn't leave much time for anything else.' She glanced down at her scuffed trainers. 'Like buying new clothes, or make-up. I only had my hair cut about once a year, and even then the hairdresser used to come to the flat. She cut my grandma's hair, so she wasn't very modern.'

'Ah, that explains it. Still, you're here now.' Ruby wiped a spill of dye from Lilith's hairline. 'And look on the bright side. From now on, you can focus on you. The world is your lobster, as my other half would say.'

Lilith laughed.

Ruby tore off a strip of clingfilm and wrapped it around Lilith's hair. 'What's the plan? A new look is a great start. But what next? Travel? Adventure? Excitement?'

'All of the above, I hope.'

'Good for you.' Ruby set the dial on the timer. 'I'll check on you in twenty minutes. Cuppa?'

'Yes, please.'

When Ruby had disappeared out the back, Lilith reached down for her shopping bag.

She'd made the bag the week after the funeral, an effort to occupy the long winter evenings and keep her mind from dwelling. She had hoped that handling the deep rich fabric, embroidered with different-coloured swirls, might cheer her flagging spirits. It hadn't worked. Not much, anyway.

Everyone had warned her the weeks afterwards would be the hardest. When life had returned to normal for everyone else, the loneliness would kick in. They'd been right. So, she'd turned to the one thing that gave her comfort – sewing.

Her grandma had taught her to sew as a young child. Being a bit of a loner, Lilith had been happy to spend hours in her bedroom making things. Dresses for her dolls. Scarves for her granddad. Even a duvet cover for her bed. She'd progressed to making full-sized clothes when her grandparents had bought her a sewing machine for her ninth birthday. She'd made all sorts of garments, rarely using a pattern, and created a colourful array of bizarre outfits. None of which she'd ever worn – she'd just liked making them.

She left school at sixteen, having won an apprentice-ship at Clothing Connexions as a pattern-cutter. The factory was within walking distance of the flat and her grandma had said it would be a good skill to learn. It was hard work and not exactly glamorous, but Lilith's plan was to apply to fashion college once she'd completed her apprenticeship. After all, if she was going to achieve her dream of becoming a costume designer, she needed to prove herself a skilled seamstress first.

Sadly, her grandma had died shortly after she'd started work. Her granddad hadn't coped well, and his health had started to deteriorate almost immediately. Lilith's plans had been put on hold. She simply couldn't abandon her granddad in his time of need.

So here she was, thirteen years later, and still working in the same clothing factory, for the same draconian boss. No nearer to achieving her dream of becoming a costume designer.

Lilith shook away the thought and opened her shop-ping bag, taking a moment to admire her brand-spanking-new passport. A shiver of excitement made her skin tingle.

She removed the holiday brochure from her bag and traced her fingers over the picture on the cover. A white sailing boat, cutting through deep blue waters, the sun casting the holidaymakers on deck in a warm glow.

Ruby appeared behind her. 'Planning a holiday?'

'All booked,' she said, still not quite believing she'd taken the plunge. It felt indulgent and reckless. But exciting too. Like a real adventure. 'I fly out next Saturday. Two weeks in the Caribbean.'

'Lucky you! Looks amazing.' Ruby placed a mug of tea on the counter. 'Girls holiday?'

She shook her head. 'Just me.'

Ruby startled. 'You're going on holiday on your own?'

'Yes. Is that strange?'

'Err… I guess not.' Ruby's expression indicated it most definitely was. 'It's a brave thing to do.'

Was it? She didn't feel brave. She was just trying to kick-start her life. She hadn't had a holiday for more than a decade, not since leaving school. And except for that one week in Majorca when she was fifteen, she'd never even been abroad. She was trying to make up for lost time.

And besides, she didn't have anyone she could go on holiday with. She was close to her work colleagues, Dottie and Taye, but they both had families of their own. They wouldn't want to holiday with someone from work, would they? And she could hardly invite Mr and Mrs Black from next door.

No, waiting until she'd made new friends and sorted out her career could take months. Years even. Waiting was not an option. It was time to take the plunge – even if she was petrified.

So, she'd used fifteen hundred pounds of the seven thousand pounds her granddad had left her to book the luxury all-inclusive Caribbean holiday. She'd allocated another five hundred pounds for spending money, and for updating her appearance, and then had set aside the rest for relaunching her career when she returned from her holiday.

It was a sound plan. One her granddad would approve of. The right balance between indulgence and planning for the future.

The timer buzzed, making her startle.

Stage one of her makeover was complete.

No turning back now.

Chapter Two

In the decade since becoming a parent, Will Taylor had frequently been shoved headfirst out of his comfort zone and into some pretty excruciating experiences. From dealing with dirty nappies, to toddler tantrums in the supermarket, to being forced to partake in the Dad's Race at the school sports day. It was all mortifying stuff. But being dressed as Pierrot the Clown, complete with black beret, trouser braces and white face paint, was by far the worst experience so far.

But what else could he do? It was his daughter's eleventh birthday and she was having a Parisian-themed birthday party.

It wasn't like his daughter asked for much. In fact, Poppy rarely asked for anything. She was a sweet-natured contented little girl who, compared to some of the girls in her class, was a dream to parent. The fact that she was a little shy was the least of his worries.

The birthday party had been her grandparents' idea. An effort to persuade their timid granddaughter to socialise more. Poppy had agreed to the party, but on the proviso that it was family only. In the end – thanks to some sweet talking by her adoring cousin, Zac – Poppy

23

had agreed on a compromise. Family, plus three school friends.

Will should have felt relieved. After all, dressed as a clown, he wouldn't have wanted the whole world to witness his humiliation. But today wasn't about him. It was about encouraging his beautiful – sometimes shy – little daughter to celebrate her birthday with people, and not spend the day in her bedroom playing with her dolls, as she'd wanted to do.

He rubbed his temple, forgetting he was covered in white face paint.

'Stop that!' his sister said, marching over. 'You'll smudge your make-up. Honestly, the kids are better behaved than you.'

'What have I done now? I'm just standing here, minding my own business.'

'Exactly.' Gemma glared at him – which would normally be intimidating, but not so much when she was dressed as his sidekick, Columbine. 'It's what you haven't done. Hiding in the corner with your arms folded is hardly setting a positive example to your daughter, is it? We're supposed to be encouraging her to socialise. She's not going to come out of her shell if she sees her dad skulking about in the shadows.'

'I am not sulking.'

'I said *skulking*.' Another glare. 'And who're you trying to kid? You're taking the whole mournful mime act to another level. Why don't you join in with the games?'

'I wouldn't feel comfortable.' He glanced over to where his twenty-one-year-old nephew was currently administrating beauty treatments to the four girls, putting on a comic French accent and declaring them all, '*magnifique!*'

'Zac doesn't seem bothered.'

'Zac's a natural extrovert. He enjoys dressing up.' Hence his flamboyant French Dandy costume, complete with frilled shirt, silver cummerbund and knee-length breeches. A look that hadn't allayed his brother-in-law's fears that his son favoured 'messing around' with make-up to pursuing a nice sensible career in IT. 'Plus, he's closer in age and doesn't pose a threat.'

Gemma swung around to face him. 'A threat? What do you mean?'

How could he explain that being the single father of a young girl wasn't as straightforward as when you were part of a couple. He still felt uncomfortable hanging around the school gates, even though he had a legitimate reason for being there. He avoided hosting playdates at his home for fear of someone accusing him of doing something untoward, and he declined all requests to act as a school chaperone. The one time he'd accepted, he'd spent the entire trip trying to avoid being hugged by a tearful girl who'd been picked on by another child. Hugging his own daughter was acceptable. Hugging other people's daughters wasn't.

Single mums didn't seem to face such scrutiny. But as a single dad, he definitely did. Which was unfair, but it was the reality of his situation.

Consequently, there was no way was he about to assist Zac in applying face masks to four eleven-year-old girls and decorating their nails with glitter. 'It's better if I let Zac run the show. After all, it is his job. Why would I interfere when they have a trained make-up artist to pamper them?'

Gemma looked unconvinced. 'Feeble. But you may have a point.'

'Big of you.'

'It doesn't mean you can't join in and be useful.' She leant closer, her white powdered face turned up to him. 'Everyone else is running around like blue-arsed flies.'

She was right.

Will's dad was blowing up balloons and attempting to twist them into sausage dogs, his French onion seller outfit a far cry from his former work uniform as a Police Chief Inspector.

In contrast, his mum looked in her element as she loaded the long dining table with buffet food, adding pink cupcakes to the stands and sprinkling them with icing sugar. As a former Head of a primary school, dealing with pre-pubescents wasn't something that fazed her. She'd even made her own costume, converting a French flag into a makeshift dress.

Even his normally dour brother-in-law was making himself useful. Chris was in charge of the music, over-seeing the playlist and ensuring Billie Eilish featured regularly – even though he doubted his brother-in-law knew who Billie Eilish was. Chris wasn't a fan of popular culture. He liked the opera, maths equations, and rarely wore anything other than a suit. Today he was dressed as wartime Napoleon – which although not exactly suitable for a pre-teen birthday bash, was at least French.

Gemma nudged him in the ribs. 'Go and offer the mums a drink.'

Will cringed. Oh, God. Not 'the mums'. He risked a glance over to where the three yummy mummies were huddled in front of the backdrop of a Parisian cafe. 'Do I have to?' But they caught him looking over and smiled, waving in unison like an elite synchronised swimming team. 'They'll eat me alive.'

Gemma's hands went to her hips. 'Ignoring the fact that you're being incredibly sexist and judgemental, not to mention completely up yourself, have you even spoken to them?'

'Yes. And it wasn't fun. And before you accuse me of being sexist, I overheard them discussing what they'd like to do to me.' He checked no one was listening. 'Believe me, there was nothing respectful about it.'

'Yeah, well, it's only to be expected.'

'Meaning?'

She sighed. 'You're a widowed dad. You're reasonably young. You're good-looking… in a feminine sort of way, and you run your own company. Even as your sister, I can see that's an appealing package.'

'"Appealing package?" Now who's being sexist? And what do you mean, "I'm good-looking in a feminine sort of way?"'

'Well, you know, you're not all buff like the twenty-somethings you see down at the gym.'

'Excuse me? I'll have you know I work out.'

'You're not exactly Magic Mike, are you? You're more…' She tapped her lip in contemplation. 'Jude Law-esque. You know, all boyish and dimpled, rather than manly and chiselled.'

'Oh, that's not judgemental at all!'

'I'm just saying, you've been on your own for eight years. Maybe it's time you got back out there and started dating.'

'I date.'

'Oh, please. That is not dating. That is fu—'

'Keep your voice down.' He attempted to cover Gemma's mouth. 'You want the whole room to hear? Including my ten-year-old daughter?'

'Eleven.'

'Excuse me?'

'Your daughter is eleven. Cute little thing? Small for her age? Has her dad's grey eyes?'

'I know who my daughter is.'

'Yeah, well, she's eleven.'

'Only just.'

'Either way, she's growing up fast and you need to stop living in the past. Or at least, start dating someone age-appropriate.' She patted his chest. 'Now, go and offer those lovely mums a drink. You never know, one of them might be the woman of your dreams.'

Except that was an impossibility. The woman of his dreams was dead.

He had no intention of engaging with 'the mums', but he was sick of squabbling with his sister, so he headed in their direction.

The pair of them had been the same as kids. Bickered constantly. Gemma was five years older and liked to be in charge. A situation that continued to cause grief, as Will was now technically her boss. She'd taken over as Financial Director for TaylorMade Events a few years back. And despite being very good at her job, she didn't like taking orders from her younger brother.

Will headed towards the mums in the pretence of topping up drinks, a ruse to stop his sister nagging. He knew her desire for him to 'find love again' came from a good place, but it didn't make it any less annoying.

He crossed the dining room, wondering if it would be inappropriate to pinch a can of beer from the fridge? The fruity pink cordial his mum had made earlier didn't appeal, and he'd rather stick to water than endure the sickly strawberry milkshakes that were also on offer.

He searched out his daughter, which wasn't easy amongst so much pink clutter. His parents' normally rustic open-plan farmhouse in picturesque Chobham, was currently filled with balloons, fairy lights, ribbons and feathers. There were cut-outs of the Eiffel Tower dotted about, along with trays of sweet treats. A three-tier cake perched on a stand covered in white icing and topped with a giant pink poodle.

He wouldn't mind if Poppy looked like she was enjoying herself, but her smile was a little forced, and it soon faded when she thought no one was watching.

Unlike her three friends, who'd turned up wearing pink chiffon dresses, complete with black and white accessories, pink lips and nails, Poppy hadn't been keen to dress up. She'd only relented when her cousin had intervened and swapped the party dress Will had bought for her with a sophisticated 'French artist' look. Zac had rolled up the sleeves of one of Will's navy suit jackets and teamed it with a stripy top and blue beret. He had also used the pink sash from the party dress to make a neck scarf. He'd then drawn on a moustache, given her bushy eyebrows, and rouged her cheeks. Poppy had loved it.

Will knew why. She was in disguise. His daughter was the proverbial wallflower.

He'd often wondered if she would have been this shy if Sara hadn't died. Was it a lack of a mum that had caused such timidity? Or was she always destined to be an introvert? He'd never know.

Poppy had barely been two when her mum had died. A freak skiing accident. Not even a bad one at that. Well, that was how it had seemed at the time. Just an awkward landing and an innocuous bump on the head. It was only later in the evening when Sara's headache had worsened that they had called a doctor. A precautionary measure – not because they'd genuinely feared anything was seriously wrong.

And then she'd lost consciousness. One moment she was alert and chatting, the next she was unresponsive. A brain scan showed extensive swelling. An operation followed to relieve the pressure, after which she was placed in an induced coma. Hours turned into days, days into weeks. But she never regained consciousness. With no possible chance of recovery, the decision was made to switch off life support. A decision that would haunt him for the rest of his days.

Something touched his ankle, jolting Will from his thoughts.

He glanced down to see a small hand poking out from underneath the white tablecloth.

Checking no one had noticed, he crouched down and lifted the tablecloth. 'What are you doing under there?'

'Hiding,' his daughter said nonchalantly, as though this was perfectly normal behaviour for the birthday girl.

'Don't you want to hang out with your friends?'

She shook her head.

He suppressed a sigh. 'Have you eaten anything?'

She shrugged. 'Not really.'

It didn't surprise him. Poppy didn't like people watching her eat.

'I'll get you something.' He stood up, never sure how to handle situations like these.

Should he force her to rejoin the party? Or let her be? If only Sara was around to guide him.

He fetched a paper plate and added a sausage roll, a handful of Skips and a cheese spread sandwich. An overload of additives. She probably wouldn't sleep a wink tonight. Still, it was her birthday.

He added a frothy pink cupcake. Let the kid enjoy herself.

One of the mums spotted him and wagged her finger. 'Too many carbs,' she chastised playfully. 'You'll ruin that nice figure of yours.' She made a point of checking him out, her eyes travelling down his chest, her head tilting to one side so she could admire his backside.

He probably should feel flattered. Violet's mum was an attractive woman. Bubbly, sociable and clearly interested. But she was also part of his daughter's world, and he wasn't about to risk becoming the latest school gate gossip.

And it wasn't like he fancied her. In fact, he couldn't remember the last time he was interested in a woman. Not in a meaningful way. His sister was right, he had occasional hook-ups, but never with anyone he really liked. In fact, his dalliances were with women he specifically *didn't* like. Which was probably an issue he needed help with, because although he didn't need a shrink to tell him he was deliberately avoiding relationships, he certainly did need someone to explain to him why.

He smiled at Violet's mum, whose name he couldn't remember, and nodded to the plate. 'For Poppy,' he said, moving away before he got trapped in conversation.

He waited until she'd resumed chatting with the other mums before ducking down and shuffling under the table, squashing himself into the gap. He handed Poppy the plate of food. 'Eat up.'

She took the plate. 'Thank you, Daddy.' She had her mum's smile. Wide and disarming. 'Crisps *and* cake?'

'It's your birthday. I'm indulging you.'

She took a bite of sandwich, leaving a mess of cheese around her mouth.

He used a napkin to wipe it away. 'Are you having fun?'

She nodded.

Why didn't believe her?

'Are you excited to play with your smartphone later?'

'I guess.'

Hardly a convincing answer.

He'd bought her the phone because general consensus amongst the other parents was that eleven was about the right age to get one. Starting secondary school without one would alienate her from the other kids. They'd all be scrolling through various social media sites, exchanging messages, video clips and selfies, and she'd be left out.

Plus, she'd be going to school by coach, so from a safety point of view he wanted to be able to contact her. It didn't make the decision any less daunting, though.

He'd insisted the guy in the shop show him how to manage parental controls, a feeble attempt to protect her from cyber-bullying. But it still scared the shit out of him.

But his worrying would be a moot point if she wasn't into the phone. Her expression when she'd opened her present indicated that she wasn't thrilled. She'd been polite and thanked him, because she was a well-mannered child who wouldn't want to upset her daddy, but he knew her well enough to know she was disappointed.

This feeling was compounded when she'd opened her second present, the Fashion Angels Crafting Kit, and an expression of pure joy had lit up her face. Now that was a present she liked.

He guessed not all eleven-year-olds were ready to venture into adulthood. He shouldn't push her. His baby girl still preferred dolls to technology, and pets to boys. And he was totally okay with that... most of the time.

Still, it wouldn't do any harm to try and sell her the virtues of the phone.

'You'll be able to send me messages from camp,' he said, trying to sound excited. 'And photos, too.'

She stopped chewing. 'Do I have to go to Wales?'

He experienced a sudden sinking feeling. 'I thought you were excited about your school trip?'

Her eyes lowered. 'A bit... but... I... I don't want to be away from you for so long.'

His chest contracted. 'It's only two weeks. And think how much fun you'll have. You get to go pony-trekking, kayaking, and camping in a treehouse. You'll be with all your friends, and nanny and granddad will be staying in a hotel close by, so you can call them if you need anything.' He reached for her hand. 'And now you have your phone, you'll be able to call me and tell me all about your activities. How cool is that?'

Her forehead creased into a frown. 'But you'll be in the carbon.'

'Caribbean,' he corrected. 'And yes, I'm going on a little holiday, too.'

'But that's miles away. My teacher says it's in another continence.'

'Contin*ent*.' Bless her. 'And yes, it's part of North America.'

Tears pooled in her eyes. 'What happens if I get sick?'

'Oh, sweetie, that won't happen. And if it does, then nanny and granddad will look after you until I get home.' He squeezed her hand. 'I promise you, if you get sick, I'll be on the first flight home. But that's very unlikely to happen. I doubt you'll even miss me. You'll be having too much fun.'

She launched herself at him, knocking the wind from his lungs. 'Violet says I need a new mummy. She doesn't understand why I don't have one. And... and neither do I.'

Oh, Christ. Not this again.

He tried to compose himself. 'Sweetie, we've spoken about this. I'm sorry you don't have a mummy. I wish you did. More than anything, I do. But it's not like a job vacancy. You can't advertise for a replacement. That's not how it works.'

She clung hold, her skinny arms wrapped around his neck. 'Violet's mummy said she thinks it's odd that you don't have a girlfriend.'

Does she now? Bloody woman. He'd be having words with Violet's mummy.

'You're the only woman in my life,' he said, rubbing her back. 'You know that. And we do okay, don't we? We have fun. You have lots of people looking out for you, and who love you. We don't need anyone else. We're a team. Right?'

'But what if something happens to you on holiday? I'll be all alone. An orphan, like in the *Annie* film we watched.'

His daughter sure knew how to lay on the guilt. 'Nothing's going to happen to me on holiday, sweetie. I promise. Now come on, stop crying. It's your birthday. You should be enjoying yourself.' He patted her back, trying to soothe away her concerns, meanwhile praying that she didn't back out of her trip.

It would be the first solo holiday he'd had since... since... well, he couldn't remember when. His teens, probably. He'd holidayed with his family as a kid, with mates as a teenager, and then with Sara. They'd met at university. Married at aged twenty-two and had had Poppy a year later. Holidays since Sara's death had been child-friendly, involving kids clubs and waterpark activities, in family resorts, where everyone was in bed by nine.

He was thirty-four. He'd been a full-time solo parent for more than eight years. He'd started TaylorMade Events shortly after finishing uni and had been working like a dog ever since. What with trying to build his company and parent Poppy, there'd been little time for anything else. It had been an onslaught of work and child-rearing. Nappies and then playdates. Meetings with clients, interrupted by horseriding lessons and gymnastics classes. There'd been no respite. Just the occasional day off when Poppy's grandparents or his sister had taken over.

He was grateful for his family's help, he couldn't have done it without them, but he'd never wanted to impose. Poppy was his child, his responsibility. And if he was honest, a part of him had wanted to keep her close. He couldn't bear the thought of losing her, too.

Did that make him selfish? A bad parent? He wasn't sure. Maybe his insecurities had made her clingy and afraid to be away from him.

Oh, God. He'd caused this, hadn't he? His anxiety had dented her confidence. He should cancel his holiday. He was naive to think Poppy was ready to be away from him for two weeks. What had he been *thinking*?

Poppy released her hold and sat back, smudges of white on her cheek.

He wiped away the face paint with his thumb. 'If you don't want to go to Wales, you don't have to.'

'Really?'

His heart sank. 'Really. I'll cancel my holiday.'

Her little face lit up – and then dropped. He could almost see the clogs whirring as she mulled over the problem. She ate a crisp. Licked her fingers and then moved to sit on his lap. 'Will you call me every day from the carbon?'

'Caribbean. And yes, of course, I'll call you every day.'

'And will you face-chat me?'

'FaceTime. Yes. I'll send you video clips too, if you like.'

She seemed to consider this. 'And they definitely do pony-trekking in Wales?'

He nodded. 'I've signed you up for the course. You get to go on hacks every morning. Imagine that? Horseriding every day, not just Saturdays.'

Her brief smile wavered. 'And if I get sick you'll come home?'

He kissed the end of her nose. 'Promise.'

With a deep sigh, she said, 'Ohkaaaay then.'

'Okay?'

She nodded. 'I'll go to Wales… and you can go to the carbon.'

He felt the relief wash over him. 'Thank you, sweetie.'

He was going to the carbon! …Christ, she had him at it now.

He needed this. Time away. A break from parenting. A break from work. Time to clear his head and recharge his batteries. No one could say he hadn't earned this, or that a two-week holiday on a beautiful Caribbean island wasn't long overdue.

So why did he feel so bloody guilty at leaving his daughter behind?

Chapter Three

It was the sudden heat that startled Lilith as she got off the plane at Punta Cana airport. Like a hairdryer blowing into her face. The draft from the huge engines messed her newly-styled hairdo as she descended the steps onto the tarmac.

Unlike Gatwick, there was no bus to take her to the terminal and no air-conditioned walkway to keep her cool. She had to carry her hand luggage across the open expanse of airfield towards the main building, all the while fanning her face and failing in her attempts to keep cool.

The thatched building ahead didn't look like an airport terminal. It looked like a giant beach hut. The area in front was awash with greenery, filled with exotic plants and palm trees.

A prickle of excitement ran over her skin. Or was it panic? Like it or not, her adventure had begun.

As she entered the terminal building, she was hit by a wave of noise. The inside looked like a barn, with exposed beams and bare flooring. It was filled with people, all talking and shouting, pushing baggage trolleys around the vast space.

She queued at the Customs desk, where a solo official didn't look in any rush to deal with the horde of visitors arriving.

Lilith – or rather, Lily – as she'd renamed herself for the duration of her holiday, removed the hotel brochure from her shoulder bag. The adults-only Luxury Bahia Resort boasted a beachfront location, three infinity pools, and four à la carte restaurants. Activities on offer included various boat trips, nightly discos, and a range of spa treatments. Talk about luxury.

She smiled to herself. Her previous self might have felt insecure at the idea of flaunting herself in front of strangers. But new-and-improved 'Lily' was hellbent on enjoying herself.

After all, she didn't know anyone here. She'd never see any of these people again, so what did it matter if she let her hair down and threw caution to the wind? Exactly.

And it was better to regret something you'd done than something you hadn't done, as her grandma used to say. Which was good advice.

Let's just hope she felt the same way in two weeks' time.

Talking of letting her hair down, she touched her bare neck, enjoying the sensation of her shorter hairdo. It was as though some of the weight she'd been carrying of late had been cut away along with her hair.

The stylist had been spot on. The warm copper tones accented with blonde highlights had done wonders for her complexion. When she'd arrived home from the hairdressers, she'd spent twenty minutes staring into the mirror admiring her reflection. Boosted by her new look, she'd immediately gone shopping and bought a suitcase full of new outfits, including colourful beachwear and revealing bikinis. She'd even knocked up a couple of sexy evening dresses on her sewing machine.

It was only when she'd tried them all on that she'd panicked slightly. They were very risqué. Well, probably not for most women her age, but for someone who'd spent the last decade in jeans and hoodies, they felt positively scandalous.

Shy, timid, Lilith Monroe would never wear such outfits. But new-and-improved 'Lily' was relishing the opportunity to be brave and adventurous. Even if new-and-improved Lily was also a bag of nerves.

The queue ahead moved and she shuffled forwards.

Wearing her new white sundress and jewelled sandals had felt ridiculous in the cold wet of London, but she was now grateful she'd stuck with her summer outfit. The heat was stifling, enhanced by the mass of bodies filling the terminal. Huge fans whirred above, doing their best to ease the oppression of the heat.

She fanned her face again, relishing the thought of diving into a cool swimming pool later.

The queue shifted ahead and she reached the cubicle and presented her passport.

'Welcome to the Caribbean,' the official said with a laid-back drawl. 'Enjoy your stay.' He handed her passport back.

'Thank you, I intend to.' She moved into the main area and searched for the screens showing which conveyor belt her luggage would be on.

She wasn't a seasoned traveller, by any stretch of the imagination. She wasn't sure which was more daunting: Gatwick, with its multitude of screens and string of departure gates, or the antiquated Caribbean airport, with only three conveyor belts and mass of holidaymakers all vying to read the blurred text on the solitary screen.

By the time Lily reached the correct conveyor belt, the crowd of people was three-deep, preventing her from getting near the moving luggage.

Thankfully, she'd tied a red ribbon around her suitcase, a tip from Taye, so she could distinguish her suitcase from all the other black cases being tossed around the conveyor belt.

Some people waited patiently, checking their phones, or chatting to their travelling companions. Others jostled to the front, eager to get their holiday underway.

Lily waited, figuring the crowd would quickly disperse once everyone had collected their luggage and headed outside to the waiting transfers.

And then she spotted her suitcase.

She moved forwards, hoping to grab it. She squeezed through the tight gap in the people around her – but she wasn't quick enough, and the case was gone before she could reach it.

Oh, well. It would come around again soon enough.

An opening appeared further down in the conveyor belt crowd, so she moved into it, accidentally treading on a man's foot. 'I'm so sorry,' she said, glancing up at a good-looking man wearing dark shades. 'I do apologise.' She felt her face flush.

'No worries,' he said, reaching out to steady her. 'You okay?'

'Yes, sorry.' She stepped away, slightly flustered by the warmth of his hand touching her arm. It spoke volumes about her lack of contact with the opposite sex that a man touching her arm could create such a buzz in her blood. Talk about repressed.

He offered her a brief smile and returned to typing on his phone.

She fanned her face, the heat in her cheeks no longer solely down to the warm weather.

And then the crowd surged again and Lily was jostled out of the way as a couple in front swung their bags off the conveyor belt, and nearly took her legs out from under her in the process. Baggage claim was dangerous stuff. She needed to keep her wits about her.

Her suitcase reappeared, trapped beneath another bag at a funny angle. Keeping her eyes locked on her luggage, she waited until the bag was almost level before reaching forwards.

She managed to catch the strap and tugged hard, but the bag was too heavy to shift off the moving machinery. She found herself being dragged along, almost running to keep up with it.

She tugged again, but the bag caught on the edge of the belt. Instead of falling backwards with her bag in tow, she fell headlong onto the conveyor. She landed with a thump, banging her knees on the metal.

'Let go of the bag,' a man yelled from behind her.

She looked up and realised she was about to disappear through the rubber flaps at the end of the conveyor belt. Oh, hell.

She let go of the bag, but there was no way she could get up.

Then a pair of hands grabbed her by the waist and lifted her.

She was now airborne, travelling backwards through the air, unable to do anything other than yelp. Overcome by momentum, they continued flying backwards until they hit the ground with an almighty thud.

The man underneath her let out a loud groan as they landed. Which wasn't surprising, as he had taken the full force of her body weight.

It was hard to move. She felt like a cockroach stranded on its back, unable to turn over. The man continued to moan as she tried to roll off him. Her elbow connected with his ribs. Her sandal scraped down his bare shin and her head clocked his chin as she flipped her body over.

'Please stop moving,' he groaned.

She did. Except she was now on top of him. Face down. One arm either side of him, her chest pressed against his, one knee balancing precariously between his legs.

She blinked, her brain taking a moment to catch up with her eyes. It was the man whose foot she'd trodden on. The good-looking one. Now minus his sunglasses, she saw he had a pair of disarming blue-grey eyes. Goodness.

'I'm so sorry,' she said to him – for the second time in as many minutes. 'Are you hurt?'

'I will be if your knee moves any higher.'

Her knee. Right, yes, it was in a rather delicate place.

Come to think of it, their entire position was delicate. She was lying on top of him, her body pressed against his, their faces inches apart. This was not an everyday occurrence. Not for her, anyway. Still, no one could say she wasn't shifting out of her comfort zone.

'How do you suggest we extricate ourselves without causing further injury?' she said, aware of the warmth radiating off him. He smelt faintly of aftershave and peppermints.

'I'll lift you,' he said, and then hesitated. 'If that's okay?'

'Sure. I mean, I don't have any better ideas.'

They were surrounded by an audience. People had gathered to watch. Some enquired if they needed medical attention. Others stared, enjoying the floorshow and filming the commotion. Great. No doubt the footage would be uploaded to various social media sites before the day was out.

And to think she'd thought buying revealing bikinis was scandalous? It was nothing compared to this.

The man's arms encircled her body again, and holding tightly, he gently rolled her off him.

Talk about smooth.

When their bodies had locked together, something rather alarming had happened to her insides. Dormant nerve endings jumped to life, and her body felt like it was awakening from a deep slumber, as if to say, 'Well, *hello* there.'

The man got to his feet, wincing.

Oh, dear. He didn't look particularly happy. But then he offered her his hand and pulled her upright. 'Are you hurt?'

She shook her head. 'You?'

'Nothing broken.' He rubbed his chest. 'I hope.'

'Thank you so much for rescuing me. It was very brave of you.'

He laughed. 'Hardly.'

'It was. I mean, I nearly disappeared down the luggage chute.'

His face relaxed into a smile. 'True. It wouldn't be the best start to your holiday.'

'No, I could've been knocked unconscious, loaded back on the plane and returned to the UK without so much as having had a single Pina Colada.'

He grinned. 'That wouldn't do.'

'No, indeed.'

But then Lily was distracted by shouting. 'Miss! Miss, I have your bag!' She turned to see one of the porters dragging her suitcase behind him. 'I rescue your bag!' he said, grinding to a halt. 'I take you to your transfer, yes?'

'Oh, right. Yes, thank you, that would be helpful.' She turned back to the man who'd helped her. 'Thanks again for your help, Mr... err?'

He picked up his bent sunglasses from the floor. 'Will.'

'Mr Will... Right. Sorry again for squashing you... and your sunglasses.'

He had a wry smile on his face. 'No problem. Enjoy your holiday.'

'You too.'

'This way, Miss! Come. Transfer this way.' The porter ushered her away.

She glanced back to find the man still watching her, a puzzled look on his face. She could hardly blame him. Poor man.

Not quite the start to her holiday she'd imagined. But at least she and her luggage were in one piece.

The porter led her outside to a waiting coach. The engine was running and she realised she was the last passenger to board. The driver gave her a filthy look as she made her way down the aisle and took the last remaining seat at the back.

Thankfully, the transfer time was only twenty minutes. She couldn't see much out of the windows, just the occasional palm tree flashing by.

They made two stops at other hotels before reaching The Luxury Bahia Resort.

As the coach drove up the long winding driveway, her excitement intensified.

The hotel looked amazing. It was huge, with signs for a golf course, tennis courts, and a fashion boutique. Not that she needed any more clothes. She'd already spent her allocated amount.

She exited the coach and went to collect her suitcase. A hotel porter had already unloaded it and was carrying it to a waiting buggy. 'You check in, Miss, and then return to me so I can take you to your room. Yes?'

'Oh, okay.' She headed for Reception. It all seemed very efficient.

The lobby was huge with a high ceiling and marble floor. Several grand chandeliers hung down from the white ceiling, adorned with gold accessories. Talk about opulent.

Having checked in, she returned to the waiting buggy armed with her room key, complimentary vouchers for the disco and an invite to welcome drinks in the bar this evening.

She climbed onto the buggy's rear seat, and almost fell off when it pulled away. What was wrong with her today? It was probably a lack of concentration. She was so busy admiring her surroundings, she wasn't paying attention to what she was doing.

Facing backwards, she could see the hotel in all its glory as they drove off. And boy, what a sight. Plants with huge leaves lined the pathways. Palm trees every-where, their trunks bare, with an abundance of gigantic leaves sprouting from the top, like bottles of exploding champagne.

The buggy stopped outside a two-storey building. The driver jumped out and beckoned for her to follow. He led her to a wide entrance, flanked by two large potted plants, and wheeled her suitcase towards a lift.

He showed her to her room on the first floor, deposited her suitcase inside, and thanked her when she tipped him. She'd never tipped a bellboy before. That was something else she could strike from her wish list.

She laughed when she saw her room. It was bigger than her grandparents' flat. It contained a queen-sized bed, with a cabinet either side, and a large padded headboard attached to the wall. A huge flat-screen TV hung on the wall opposite. But the best bit was the air-conditioning. The room was wonderfully cool, a welcome relief from the oppressive heat.

She went into the bathroom and looked in awe at the walk-in shower cubicle and double sink.

Returning to the bedroom, she headed for the seating area at the end, where a sofa, two chairs and a small writing table sat in front of a set of French doors, leading onto the balcony.

She pulled back the voile curtains and slid open the doors. The heat hit her immediately, so she closed them behind her.

Leaning on the balcony, she stared at the view ahead. It was mostly palm trees, so tall they extended way past the height of the building. In between the gaps, she could make out the blue of the sea beyond. The sound of crickets and the smell of coconut washed over her. She breathed deeply, savouring the moment. She was in the Caribbean.

Laughing, she returned to the French doors, intending to shower and go for a swim at the beach, but the doors wouldn't open. She tried again, pulling on the handle, but they appeared to be locked.

Strange. She looked over the edge of the railings, hoping to see a passer-by that she could call down to for help. But the pathways below were empty. What to do?

She tried the doors again, just to be certain, but they were definitely locked.

Damn.

Could she climb down? She assessed the drop below. Dense foliage clung to the walls of the building, thick and sturdy, like a fairy tale beanstalk. It was too far to jump, but climbing down was an option.

It was that, or wait for someone to randomly walk by. But that might be hours. And she'd be burnt to a crisp by then in this heat.

Resigned to her situation, she tucked her dress inside her knickers and climbed over the edge. The first part was relatively easy. She was lulled into a false sense of security, imagining herself ground level in a matter of minutes.

Unfortunately, as her body weight tugged on the foliage, it began to come away from the wall. By the time she'd realised she was in danger of falling, it was too late to abort her plan. She was stuck. No way up, no way down.

And then a man's voice said, 'Bloody hell, what are you doing?'

She was so startled she almost lost her grip. 'Err… I… I locked myself out. I'm trying to climb down,' she said, too scared to look away from the wall.

'I can see that. Stay there,' he called.

She was hardly likely to go anywhere, was she?

She heard dragging metal and various banging noises below.

Further grunts were followed by a voice saying, 'Can you move further to the right?'

'Your right, or mine?'

'Your right,' he said, his voice sounding oddly familiar. 'And they're both the same.'

'Oh, right.' She lifted her arm and glanced down. Heavens. It was conveyor belt man. He was standing on a table below.

He obviously hadn't realised it was her until that moment either. His frown eased into a smile. 'You're kidding me?'

'Hello again.'

He shook his head. 'You sure know how to make an impact.'

'Is that a compliment?'

'I'll let you know.' He lifted a chair onto the table. 'Are you always this accident-prone?' he asked, climbing on top of it.

'Not normally. At least, I don't think so... Maybe I have jet lag?'

'Maybe.' He sounded amused. He was now right under her. 'I'm going to reach up and put my arms around you, okay?'

'Okay... What do you want me to do?'

'Nothing. Don't let go until I tell you to, okay?'

'Wouldn't dream of it.' She wasn't stupid. Evidence aside.

When his hands touched her bare legs, she jolted. Bloody hell.

He must have sensed her discomfort, because he said, 'Sorry, but I can't see much. Your dress is in the way.'

'Don't mind me,' she said, her voice high-pitched and strangled.

His hands were now squeezing her waist. That wasn't the worst of it. Oh, no. His face was pressed against her bum cheeks.

Not humiliating at all.

'Ready to let go?' he asked.

'Have you got me?'

'I guess we're about to find out.'

'So what's the plan?'

'Well… either I catch you and lower you to the chair… or I drop you and we both fall off the table.'

'Right. Not a great plan then?'

'I could always leave you here and ring Reception for help?'

'That could take ages, and I can't hold on for much longer.'

'Then we're stuck with my plan.'

He was right.

Oh, well. Here goes. 'Good luck.'

He gave a half-laugh. 'You too.'

She let go.

Time seemed to slow.

What followed was a lot of swearing – by him. And screaming – by her.

They both grappled for balance. The chair below wobbled and slid away. They jolted downwards another few feet.

More swearing from him.

More screaming from her.

And then there was a loud crash as they ended up lying on the table in a very similar position to earlier. Him on his back – her lying on top.

He groaned in pain.

Oh, crikey. Had she killed him? But then she realised he wouldn't be groaning if he was dead.

'I'm so sorry,' she said, clambering off of him. 'Are you okay?'

'I'll live,' he said, trying to sit up.

'That's twice you've rescued me now. You're a real hero. You deserve some kind of medal.'

His laugh turned into a cough. 'I definitely deserve something.'

'Do you need any help? A glass of water? A doctor?' She helped him off the table.

'I'm fine.' He rubbed his stomach. 'Are you okay?'

'Me? I'm fine.'

He stilled and looked at her. Those eyes again. The intensity made her belly flip.

She swallowed awkwardly. 'Thanks to you,' she added, suddenly feeling guilty for standing there uninjured while he was in pain. And then she clocked his expression. 'Why are you looking at me like that? Am I bleeding?' She checked for injuries.

'Not blood, no. Err… your dress.'

'My dress?' She looked down.

The front of her dress was devoid of buttons and was flapping open like a badly erected tent. Worse than that. Her new lace underwear was on full show, leaving nothing to the imagination.

'Oh, good heavens.' She clutched at the loose material. 'Right… well, thanks for your help. Time to go. Sorry about injuring you… again. My bad. Must try harder, and all that.' She ran for the French doors, not realising they were closed, and smacked straight into them. *Ouch*.

'It's easier if you open them.' He limped over and used his key card to unlock them.

'Right… yes, good to know. Helpful.' She rubbed her forehead. 'Essential, I'd say.'

'You okay?'

'Absolutely peachy. Couldn't be better. Top of the world. Firing on all cylinders.' She yanked open the doors, cringing when she saw the perfect imprint of her lip gloss on the glass.

'I'll ring Reception and ask someone to let you into your room,' he called after her.

'Thanks. Room 212. The one right above yours.'

'That much I'd figured. Bye, then.'

'Bye!' She ran from the scene, overwhelmed by heat, humidity, and humiliation.

Her breath came in short bursts, her skin prickled with burning shame. Had she lost all semblance of sanity? What was wrong with her?

When she reached her door, she slumped down against it.

So much for a new and improved version of herself.

'Lily' was proving to be an unmitigated disaster.

Chapter Four

Will accepted the offer of another beer from the waitress and settled back against the sunlounger. He rarely drank during the day back home, consuming excess amounts of alcohol only happened on the odd occasions he met up with his uni mates. Being a parent required him to remain sober at all times. But for two blissful weeks he was free from his responsibilities and he could let loose. Besides, he needed something to help him unwind.

He closed his eyes, relishing the feeling of the sun heating his skin. He could hear the vibration of humming birds in the surrounding bushes, accompanied by the low throb of reggae music emanating from the poolside bar.

A sudden burst of laughter made him open his eyes. A group of lads were throwing a ball in the pool, their coordination skills hampered by alcohol and the drag of the water.

An overzealous throw saw the ball fly in the air and hit a woman perched on one of the submerged stools surrounding the bar. The lads apologised profusely, their remorse interjected with hysterical laughter.

Will took a gulp of barely chilled beer and smiled. He didn't mind the beer being warm, or the drunken antics of the lads enjoying what looked like a stag trip. He was just glad to be finally relaxing.

It was the second day of his holiday, but it was the first time he'd been able to properly unwind. A long journey on Saturday, followed by a sleepless first night and the anxiety over leaving Poppy, had left him restless. When he'd finally managed to get some sleep, he'd been plagued by a bad dream.

In the months following Sara's death, dreaming had been a nightly occurrence. Over time, the dreams had subsided, but it was only in the last couple of years that they'd stopped completely. Or so he'd thought. But the images that filled his head on Saturday night had been as vivid as they had been eight years earlier. Sara lying on a hospital bed, looking serene and unblemished, the extent of her injuries hidden from view. Nurses tending to her, apologising for hurting her when they'd administered injections, even though she couldn't hear them. Their attentions then turning to him, consoling him when he collapsed in a fit of sobbing, offering him food, water, a listening ear.

The dream ended the way it had done in real life, with the doctor asking him about organ donation, followed by the heartbreaking realisation that his wife was never waking up. Will had woken with a jolt, sweaty and hot, shaking from the recollection.

Consequently, his first day in the Caribbean hadn't been as relaxing as he'd hoped.

He'd reasoned this was due to missing Poppy. He was bound to be out of sorts. So he'd FaceTimed his daughter, only to discover she was coping a lot better without him, than he was without her. Her first day at camp had been fun and apparently she loved the cabin she was staying in. So much for her not wanting to go.

Despite feeling reassured that his daughter was okay, Will had still drunk himself into a stupor at lunchtime, and spent most of the afternoon in his hotel room asleep.

Thankfully, he'd woken this morning feeling more buoyant, less anxious, and determined to enjoy his holiday.

He'd spent most of the day by the pool, people-watching. In particular, the woman who'd left him bruised and confused on Saturday night. Lily, as he now knew she was called, had arrived at the pool looking like something from a fashion magazine. Big floppy hat, huge sunglasses, and a sheer sarong tied around a skimpy bikini. He'd been mesmerised… along with most of the other men around the pool.

But the elegant and polished appearance slipped when she became entangled with the sunlounger and managed to bang her head on the parasol above. This was followed by knocking over her drink, tripping over her bag, and forgetting to remove her hat before entering the pool. The pièce-de-résistance was watching her attempt Zumba.

The exuberant entertainments officer had spent twenty minutes drumming up business for his class, encouraging the holidaymakers to join him by the pool and 'get those hips moving.'

Will had declined. He was content to leave his hips where they were – stiff and resting on the sunlounger. But Lily had been persuaded to join the class. She'd looked embarrassed at first, hesitant and uncoordinated, a step behind everyone else, like she had absolutely no concept of what Zumba was. This feeling was compounded when the instructor stood behind her and encouraged her to thrust her hips forward. Her expression was priceless.

It was a puzzle as to why she'd agreed to join in. Like she was forcing herself to 'have fun'. But whatever the reason, it made him smile. She was certainly entertaining to watch.

Following the exertion of the class, she'd collapsed onto her sunlounger and had remained there since, relaxed and sleepy, soaking up the sun, just as he was.

For some inexplicable reason, his eyes kept landing on her. He could argue that he was simply intrigued. After all, this was the woman who'd nearly disappeared down a luggage chute and had almost fallen from a balcony. Feeling curious about her was only to be expected. But her aptitude for mishap wasn't the only reason he felt drawn to her. There was an aura around her that he found... attractive. And he couldn't remember the last time he'd found a woman attractive. Well, he could, but there'd been no one serious since Sara.

Sure, he'd met women he found physically attractive. But never anyone who... how could he describe it... *fascinated* him?

Her outward appearance was current, but there was something about her manner that was slightly dated. Even when she'd been squashed on top of him Saturday night on the balcony, she'd been incredibly polite, profusely apologetic and had used quite formal language. As if she was from a bygone era.

She'd called him a 'hero', for God's sake. He'd been called a lot of things in his thirty-four years, but never a hero.

He glanced over. She was preparing for a swim, untying her sarong and letting it drop to the ground. *Jesus.*

He wasn't the only one watching. Although at least he was being discreet, unlike the stag lads who were openly gawping.

She ambled towards the pool, a vision of sophistication, but started hopping about as the hot concrete burnt the soles of her feet. The serene illusion was shattered.

Yelping, she stumbled back to her sunlounger to retrieve her flip-flops.

He smiled. It was probably intrusive to be watching her, but he couldn't help it. She was good value.

Recovering her composure, she tried again, sashaying towards the pool as if she hadn't just burnt her feet. She slid out of her flip-flops and lowered herself into the pool, failing to hide her reaction to the cold.

He suppressed a laugh as he watched her swimming lengths. Well, not lengths… widths. And not really swimming, more a hybrid of doggy paddle and trying not to drown. Either way, she was definitely entertaining.

And then something caught her eye. She paused by the edge of the pool, and he followed her gaze to the middle-aged woman seated by the bar – the one who'd been hit by the ball. The woman was unsuccessfully trying to climb off the bar stool.

As if in slow motion, the woman pushed herself off the stool and instantly disappeared under the water.

Will's first reaction was to laugh. The woman was completely pissed.

But when she didn't immediately re-emerge, he realised the situation wasn't funny.

Lily was now splashing towards the woman, shouting something about 'needing a lifeguard', but it was lost amongst the noise of the music.

Will looked around for a lifeguard. One was seated by the neighbouring pool, but looking in the opposite direction. There was no time to alert him.

Will got up and raced over to the pool, trying to ignore the heat burning his feet. And to think he'd laughed at Lily. He'd made the same mistake.

Without hesitation, he dived into the pool. Luckily, he was a strong swimmer and reached the bar within seconds. He ducked under the water and grabbed the woman's shoulders, dragging her to the surface. She immediately began coughing and spluttering, flailing her arms about.

'You're okay,' he said, trying to calm her down. 'I've got you.'

She gasped for air. 'Help! Help!'

Lily held onto the woman's arm, helping keep her afloat. 'It's okay, Mrs Hayden. You're safe now. Just try and relax. Breathe slowly.' She obviously knew the woman. 'That's it. Well done,' she said, in a soothing voice. 'You see? Drama over.' She turned and smiled at Will. 'And you said you weren't a hero?'

The force of her smile hit him hard in the solar plexus – but that could just be the weight of Mrs Whatshername's kicking him in the gut. 'I didn't do much,' he said, easing the woman over to the pool's side.

'Are you kidding me? You saved her life.' There was no irony in her voice. It was like she was being perfectly serious. 'Like I said, a real-life hero.' Her smile went up a notch and he felt a little light-headed. Must be a lack of oxygen.

Thankfully, the lifeguard then appeared and helped pull the woman from the water.

'Don't leave me!' The woman clutched hold of Lily.

'I'm not going anywhere, Mrs Hayden. Let's get you up to your room, shall we? I think you could do with a lie down.'

'I do feel a little queasy,' she said, sounding morose. 'It must've been something I ate for lunch.'

More likely something she *drank* for lunch, but Will didn't feel it necessary to point that out. 'Do you need a hand getting her upstairs?'

'No, I can take care of her. But thanks for the offer.'

The lifeguard eased the woman onto a waiting buggy and they drove off, Lily comforting the woman. He was left standing by the pool.

He needed a lie-down after all that effort.

He headed back to his sunlounger, where he spent the rest of the afternoon drifting in and out of sleep. He occasionally found himself smiling as an image of Lily filled his head. And then he felt guilty because another woman should be occupying his thoughts.

The only female he should be focused on was Poppy. But then, wasn't the idea of this holiday to take a break from the stress of parenting? Exactly.

He stopped beating himself up and headed up to his room to shower and change.

At eight p.m., he headed down to the buffet restaurant, and afterwards found a quiet spot at the terrace bar to enjoy his beer.

The best part about being abroad was getting to be outdoors at night. There were very few occasions back home when it would be warm enough to sit outside in cargo shorts and a short-sleeved shirt. But here it was still unbelievably warm, the humidity broken only by the occasional gust of breeze and faint movement from the giant fans whirring above.

The terrace was romantically lit, with tealights lined along the walls. Lanterns hung down from the thatched awning above. He'd deliberately chosen an adult-only resort, feeling the need for a more grown-up environment. He'd figured a hotel full of kids would only make him miss Poppy more. But the flipside of choosing an adult-only resort was that it attracted couples. Honeymooners, in particular, and those wanting a more intimate and romantic setting.

There were a few groups, like the stag party from earlier. But there weren't many singletons. Which meant he felt both conspicuous and incredibly lonely.

He knocked back his beer.

The terrace lights suddenly switched from low-key to pulsating. The atmosphere changed as the space was lit by flashing blue and red lights. Soft melodic music shifted into a thumping beat. Then a DJ appeared behind a mixing desk wearing headphones and announced it was, '*Paaaarty* time!'

Will swivelled on his stool to watch the outdoor space fill with people. It was as if someone had opened a floodgate. The once quiet space now vibrated with noise.

A group of women danced together, as did a few couples. Even the stag lads – who looked half-cut were moving – albeit like a scene from *The Inbetweeners*. But they were all put to shame by the staff and locals, who made dancing look as easy as breathing, their bodies grinding to the music effortlessly.

And then he spotted Lily.

She was wearing a long clingy red dress with a split up one side and strappy stiletto shoes that she could barely walk in, let alone dance in. It didn't stop her. She moved about enthusiastically, her big circular earrings bouncing beneath her bobbed hairdo. It was an odd sight. Sexy, yet funny too. She reminded him of one of the bionic Fembots in Austin Powers.

He doubted she meant to be funny. But somehow, he suspected she wouldn't care. She didn't look focused on anyone else, she was just having a good time. Good for her. It was an enviable quality.

Two songs later, she discarded her shoes and carried them over to the bar.

It was only after she'd leant across and yelled, 'Another Pina Colada, please,' to the barman, that she spotted Will. 'Oh, hello.' She perched on the stool next to him. 'Fancy bumping into you again.'

'Literally.'

She frowned and then realised what he meant. 'Oh, you mean, because last time I *literally* bumped into you?'

'Twice.'

'Three times, if you count today by the pool.' She smiled and once again he felt something shift in his chest.

'Ah, but that wasn't your fault. I can't hold you responsible for Mrs Whatshername nearly drowning. How is she, by the way?'

'Sleeping, last time I checked. She's in the room next to me. We got chatting at breakfast this morning. She's here celebrating her divorce.'

'Is that a thing?'

'Apparently so.' She shrugged. 'It's all the rage. A way of turning a negative into a positive. They were married for forty-three years, before he left her for his thirty-year-old physiotherapist.'

'Ouch.'

'I know, cliché, right?' She smiled when the barman handed over her cocktail. 'Ooo, thanks.'

'No wonder she was knocking back the booze.'

Lily removed the umbrella from her drink and tucked it behind her ear. 'It's sad, really. But she's brave for coming on holiday alone. It isn't the easiest thing to do.'

'Tell me about it.'

She seemed surprised. 'Are you here alone?'

'Yep. You?'

She nodded. 'All alone. But determined to have a good time.' She raised her cocktail glass. 'Here's to flying solo.'

He clinked glasses with her. 'I'll drink to that.'

She took a huge gulp of drink.

He tried not to focus on the sight of her red lips sucking on the straw.

'What brings you on holiday on your own?' she said, coming up for air.

'Nothing as dramatic as celebrating a divorce.'

'Oh, you're not married then?'

He stilled. When a woman usually asked him that question, she was making a play, ensuring there were no obstacles preventing her from propositioning him. But Lily wasn't flirting. Or if she was, she needed lessons.

'I'm not married,' he said slowly, which was true, but it didn't ease the twinge in his chest.

'Sorry, none of my business.' She waved her hand about, looking genuinely mortified. 'I'm not normally so nosy. The alcohol must be affecting my manners.'

He smiled. 'Yeah, it can do that.'

'I don't usually drink,' she said, taking another gulp of Pina Colada.

'You don't? Why's that?'

Her forehead wrinkled, as she considered her answer. 'Lack of opportunity, I guess.'

'Busy life, huh?'

'It has been, yes.' There was a sadness in her expression that was at odds with her party girl demeanour.

'Do you have a demanding job?'

She blinked. 'I guess so… Or rather, I did.' And then she shook her head, her smile returning. 'Let's just say, life at home is crazy busy.'

'Tell me about it.' He lifted his glass. 'Hence the opportunity to let loose.'

'Indeed.' She took a huge mouthful of cocktail, her eyes almost watering as the alcohol hit home. She definitely wasn't accustomed to drinking. No one used to alcohol would be knocking back a potent cocktail with such gusto.

'I'm guessing you're not married, either?' he said, and then wondered why he'd asked that. 'Sorry, I'm the one being nosy now.'

She didn't look offended, or react like he was coming onto her. She simply shook her head, dislodging the paper umbrella from behind her ear. 'No, not married. Free as a bird, as they say. No ties.' But despite her jovial tone, an air of sadness surrounded her.

'Me neither,' he said… and then he flinched.

Why had he said that? He had ties. Boy, did he. She was about four-feet tall and was the centre of his entire world. But mentioning his eleven-year-old daughter would only lead to questions about Sara, and Will wasn't up for that. This holiday was about taking a break from his life. He didn't want to see the look of sympathy on Lily's face when he admitted he was a widower. Or have to recount Sara's death, or talk about the struggles of being a single parent. He just wanted to be treated like a single bloke on holiday with no baggage. Was that so much to ask?

Lily slid off her stool. 'Would you like to dance?'

He shook his head. 'I'm a terrible dancer.'

'Good, so am I.' She took his hand and led him onto the dancefloor.

Laughing, he let her. Partly because it felt mean to refuse, but mostly because it cut short their conversation about personal lives.

Thankfully, the dancefloor was packed, so his lack of rhythm was masked by the mass of bodies surrounding them. But the tight space meant they kept knocking together, the gap between them narrowing as the floor-space filled with more guests.

'You're worse than I am,' she yelled.

He smiled. 'I did warn you.'

He never normally danced, he was too self-conscious. But there was something about being abroad with strangers that enabled him to let go of his inhibitions. Well, that and the several pints of beer he'd consumed.

He wasn't drunk, but he'd had enough alcohol to soften the edges. No one was judging him. They weren't even looking at him. It was liberating. He spent his whole life being judged. Or that's how it felt. Was he being a good father? Was he paying the bills? Was he keeping the house clean? Was he satisfying Poppy's emotional needs?

Everyone felt the need to constantly 'check up on him'. How was he doing? Did he need more grief counselling? Why hadn't he remarried? Or at least started dating?

It was an endless stream of questions, designed to be helpful and caring, but in reality were a constant reminder that he was 'being assessed'. Like everyone was waiting for him to stuff up.

It was nice to be free from all that. No scrutiny, or whispered conversations and concerned glances in his direction. He was invisible. Normal. And no one was speculating about him dancing with a hot woman. Or cared that he lacked coordination.

It was bliss. And fun.

After a while, the music switched tempo and became slower, more sensual. The crowd began pairing off, moving together as they selected a partner. Once again, the locals displayed how it should be done, as their bodies fused and their hips locked in erotic fashion.

'Well, I'm not attempting *that*,' Lily said, her eyes widening as the man next to them bent his partner over backwards. 'I'd dislocate something.'

He liked her self-deprecating humour.

He shrugged. 'Maybe they stretch beforehand.'

'They must at least do yoga,' she said, taking his hand, her other one encircling his waist. They were in what could only be described as a 'ballroom hold'. Not exactly fitting for the occasion, but he went along with it, mostly because it was nice to be held.

He couldn't remember the last time he was this intimate with a woman. One-night stands didn't count. There was nothing affectionate about hooking up with someone you'd just met. It was primal, selfish. An easy way of satisfying an itch.

But dancing with another human being was… romantic. It allowed time to savour the moment, to feel, to look and to absorb. A chance to really notice the other person, rather than not remember anything about them the next morning.

By his own admission, he hadn't exactly behaved very gentlemanly of late towards the opposite sex. The only consolation was, he could categorically state, was that none of the women he'd hooked up with had felt any differently about him.

As odd as it felt to be in such a formal hold, it was nice too. Lily fitted snugly against his chest. Her hair was soft and her sway matched his. They might be uncoordinated as separates, but together they were completely synchronised.

The music changed to an uptempo number. Damn. He'd been enjoying himself.

'Drink?' she yelled, releasing her hold.

He nodded and they made their way to the bar.

'I'm thirsty,' she said, fanning her face.

'I'll get these. What'll you have?'

'Pina Colada, please.'

He ordered their drinks.

She perched on a barstool. 'Thank you. You're very chivalrous.'

Chivalrous? He couldn't help smiling. She was cute. And funny. And just a little bit odd. 'It's an all-inclusive bar.'

'Oh, right. Yes, I'd forgotten that.' Her look was sheepish. 'It's still nice of you.'

The barman handed them their drinks and Lily drank most of hers in one go, sucking the creamy liquid through the straw as though it was a milkshake.

'You really were thirsty.'

'These are so tasty,' she said. 'I'd never had a cocktail before this holiday.'

'You hadn't?' Where had she been all her life? 'What do you normally drink?'

She looked embarrassed. 'Err... well, a little wine every now and again. Oh, and a dry sherry at Christmas.'

'Sherry?'

'Is that uncool?'

'No... just a little unusual.'

Her face fell. 'You mean, old-fashioned.'

Ah, so she knew she was somewhat outdated. He felt bad. He hadn't meant to tease her. 'They say sherry is the next gin. It's making a comeback. You're ahead of the game.'

She smiled. 'That's complete tosh. But it's incredibly sweet of you.' She moved closer, her hand leaning on his thigh. Her face was inches from his. She had green eyes, he noticed. Pretty.

And then the atmosphere seemed to change between them. Gentle banter dropped away, replaced by a growing heat. Her hand squeezed his thigh, her pupils dilated and her green eyes, no longer a picture of innocence, displayed a look of pure wanting.

Well, *hello*, things were getting interesting.

He wouldn't have put her down as someone who'd move this fast. Not that he was complaining. His body certainly wasn't. She was gorgeous. If she was up for it, then so was he… But then she lost her footing and slid off the stool, almost landing in his lap. Crap. She was pissed.

He caught her before she hit the floor. 'Whoa, how many have you had?'

She screwed up her nose. 'Three… maybe four. Is four too many?' She tried to stand up, but veered to the left. 'Definitely too many.'

He tightened his hold. 'What do you need? Water? Coffee? A lie down?'

'A lie down, I think.' She tried to stand upright. 'Sorry about this.' She held out her hand, inviting him to shake it. 'It was very nice meeting you again. Thank you for a lovely evening, but it's time I called it a night.'

He ignored her outstretched hand. 'There's no way I'm letting you walk back to your room in this state.'

'I'll be fine—'

'You can barely stand.' He slid his arm around her waist. 'Lean on me. No arguments. I'm taking you up to your room.'

He half-carried, half-dragged her away from the bar and across the lobby.

She was floppy, warm too, and giggling. 'You smell nice,' she said, burying her face in his neck.

She certainly knew how to distract a guy.

'And very handsome. Has anyone ever told you, you look like Jude Law?'

Only his bloody sister.

'I bet he doesn't smell as nice as you.'

He laughed. 'I don't envy the hangover you're going to have tomorrow.' He pressed the button for the lift.

'I'll drink plenty of water before I go to bed.'

Somehow he didn't think that was going to help.

She looked at him, one eye shut. 'On a scale of one to ten, how drunk am I?'

He gave her a rueful look. 'Eleven.'

'Oh, that's not good. How drunk are you?'

'A four… maybe five.' He stopped outside her door. 'Where's your room key?'

'My womb key? Oh, you mean my *room* key.'

Right. Cause he was the one slurring.

'Here.' She removed it from inside her bra, dislodging the strap of her dress.

Bloody hell.

Thank God he wasn't more drunk. His resistance was being tested to the limit.

He took the key card and opened the door.

'Lean on me,' he said, carrying her over to the large bed. 'You'll feel better once you're lying down.'

'I'd feel better if you were lying next to me.' Her arms slid around his neck. 'Or on me, even.' She looked him straight in the eye. 'Would you like to lie on me?'

He wasn't sure whether to laugh – or say, *what the hell*, and kiss her. And if she'd been one of his meaningless pick-ups, he would have done. But it was clear she didn't know what she was saying… or doing. Even if she did, she'd regret it in the morning.

Besides, he had his own heart to think about. He could imagine one night with her and he'd be smitten. She was sweet, funny, endearing and—

She kissed him.

Just like that.

No warning. No chance for him to extricate himself. No preamble. Just kissed him.

And try as he might, he couldn't back away.

Why? Well, for one thing, he didn't want to hurt her feelings. She wasn't accustomed to kissing random men, he was sure of that. He didn't want to dent her confidence by rejecting her. Also, he didn't want her to feel awkward in the morning. She'd be mortified.

Oh, who was he kidding? He didn't back away because he didn't want to back away. Simple as.

As kisses went, it was right up there. Passionate, warm, enthusiastic and extremely hot. His body had gone into spasm. His legs were shaking. His head spinning. Every nerve-ending in his body was urging him on, willing him to 'lie on her' as she'd requested.

Boy, did he want to.

But he couldn't do it. It'd be wrong… even though it felt really, really right.

He gently pulled away. 'Lily?'

She tried to kiss him again. 'Yes?' Her voice was soft and breathy.

He held her at arm's length. 'You've had too much to drink. It wouldn't be right.'

Her other dress strap slid off her shoulder and her slinky dress slipped below her strapless bra. 'You don't want to stay the night with me?'

Hell, yes. One hundred per cent, yes.

He closed his eyes, trying to dispel the image of her breasts. 'Not tonight,' he managed – although how, he didn't know. 'Come on, lie down.' He eased her onto the bed and covered her in a sheet. 'Sleep tight, pisshead.'

She smiled. 'You really do smell nice.'

'Go to sleep.' He kissed her forehead and left the room… before he did something really, really stupid.

Chapter Five

Thursday, 18 March

Lily checked she had her sunglasses, hat and purse, before leaving the hotel room. It was a ten-minute walk to the sailing centre, so she didn't want to forget anything that might scupper her planned excursion.

She'd woken this morning determined to do something more adventurous and not spend another day laid up in bed. It was such a waste of her precious holiday. She was supposed to be having fun and exploring the tropical sights, not recovering from the effects of too much alcohol.

The whole of Tuesday had been lost to a god-awful hangover. She'd never felt so ill in her life. She couldn't even lie out on the balcony. Her eyes hurt, her skin hurt, even her hair hurt. She'd barely eaten anything, and even drinking water had made her retch. Lily was never getting drunk again.

Now, as she exited the lift into the main lobby, she checked the coast was clear and almost ran from the hotel, praying that she wouldn't bump into Will.

If dealing with the physical effects of having been paralytic had been painful, it was nothing compared to the humiliation of remembering her inappropriate behaviour on Monday night. As the memories had slowly returned, her sense of shame had deepened… Which was why she'd spent yesterday at a neighbouring beach and had avoided the pool area at the hotel. She absolutely did not want to bump into Will. Not when she'd practically accosted the poor man.

She couldn't remember her exact words, but she had a vague recollection of asking him to 'lie on her'. Oh, good God. She stopped walking and covered her eyes. Had she really said that? Worse, she'd *kissed* him.

Groaning, she continued towards the beach, head down, sunglasses on, hoping to remain inconspicuous.

Talk about brazen. Not to mention stupid, and dangerous, and naive. What had she been thinking? Supposing he'd turned out to be an axe-wielding murderer? She could be lying dead now in a pool of blood and it would be her own stupid fault.

Well, maybe not entirely her fault. After all, murderers had to be accountable for their actions, but she certainly hadn't put her safety first. Something she wouldn't be doing again.

Thankfully, if Will was of the murdering persuasion, he'd kept it hidden Monday night. He'd been the perfect gentleman. Kind, thoughtful, and respectful. He'd helped her to her room, checked she was okay and then left… which was entirely the right thing to do.

She should be grateful that he hadn't taken advantage of the situation, or responded to her request to 'lie on her'. She stopped again, the thought making her cringe again.

Why had she said that?

Except, she knew damn well why. Just because she'd willingly sacrificed a social life to care for her ailing granddad, it didn't mean she was happy about denying herself such things. She was human, after all. She had needs, same as the next person. And it had been a long time since she'd had the desire or opportunity to address those needs.

Throw in a handsome man, who appeared to be charming, funny and sane, and no wonder she'd got carried away. Who could blame her?

But maybe it wasn't as bad as she feared? Maybe she'd only thought about propositioning him and hadn't actually acted on it? But that was wishful thinking. She'd definitely humiliated herself. She'd thrown herself at a man she barely knew. End of.

Of course, there was another plausible explanation for him rejecting her advances, other than chivalry. And that was that he just didn't fancy her. A highly depressing thought.

Lily reached the beach and paused to savour the view ahead.

It was glorious. The white sand was peppered with sunloungers, each one shaded by a thatched parasol. Further down the beach Zorbing was taking place. Holidaymakers were encased inside giant plastic bubbles, rolling across the sand, and being shunted into the water.

A local man was selling fresh mango. He ambled along the beach with his basket of fruit and a giant knife. She'd been slightly alarmed when she'd seen him yesterday, until she'd witnessed his dextrous culinary skills in peeling and slicing the mango. It was quite an art and the fruit had tasted heavenly.

She headed for the sailing centre, a makeshift wicker hut containing various water devices. Further out to sea, she could see the Geotubes protruding from the water, an effort to redress the effects of climate change. The large bags of biosynthetic tissue helped to calm the waves and prevent the fine sand being dragged out to sea. They looked like beached whales at first glance, but they were perfectly safe, and served an important purpose.

A man appeared from the hut. 'Hello, Miss. You want to join us for sailing?'

She lifted her sunglasses. 'I'm booked for kayaking. Lily Monroe.'

'Ah, yes. Miss Monroe. Like Marilyn, yes? Only prettier.'

Charmer. He was a fibber, too. Still, it was all part of the service. The staff were enthusiastic, complimentary, and unfailingly friendly towards all the guests. It might be an act, but it felt nice, and it helped her to feel more included.

The downside was, it was hard to refuse them when they 'encouraged' the guests to partake in the hotel's activities. As she'd discovered this morning when she'd agreed to take part in a competition entitled 'Wipeout'. Why she'd succumbed, she had no idea. She wasn't sporty, or competitive, or even vaguely coordinated. Consequently, she hadn't made it past the first obstacle before she'd landed headfirst in the water and had ended up covered in bruises.

The sailing instructor beckoned her towards the hut. 'Have you been kayaking before?' His laid-back gaze travelled over her non-sporty purple fashion shorts and lilac vest top.

'Never.'

'Are you a strong swimmer?'

'Not really.' She frowned. 'Is that a problem?'

'Nothing in life is a problem, Miss.' He grinned and handed her a lifejacket. 'But the currents are strong. You need good muscles.' He flexed his impressive biceps. 'Like me, yes?' He winked at her and laughed.

'Indeed.' She glanced down at her skinny white arms.

Impressive muscles, she didn't have. She had what her grandma had described as a 'delicate frame'. Which was the polite way of saying she was 'weedy'.

'We pair up novices with a more experienced sailor,' the instructor said, pointing to a bright yellow boat. 'We have two-seater kayaks, see?'

'Okay.' It was probably safer that way. 'Will I be sailing with you?'

'This man here. Come, I introduce you.' He led her over to the boat. 'Hey, man.' He nudged the guy, who turned around.

Oh, good God. It was *Will*.

The instructor grinned. 'Pretty, yes? I choose well.'

Will did a double take when he saw who he'd been lumbered with.

She knew how he felt.

She gave him a feeble wave. Hardly the most sophisticated of greetings, but it was all she could muster.

He was wearing navy swim-shorts and a White Stripes T-shirt. His baseball cap and sunglasses covered most of his face, but she knew it was him. There was no mistaking those shapely arms. Or legs. Or the dimple in his chin.

She mentally slapped herself. Objectifying a man based on appearances wasn't cool.

But tempting as it was to turn and run off, she knew it was pointless. Running on sand in flip-flops was only marginally less humiliating than kissing him, and would only result in her landing face-down in the sand.

'We get you in the water, yes?' The instructor lifted the front of the boat.

Will lifted the rear and they carried it down to the sea.

Resigned to her fate, Lily followed them.

So much for a nice relaxing afternoon on the water. The next two hours were going to be excruciating.

Having lowered the boat into the water, the instructor went to help another customer.

Avoiding eye contact, she went to step into the boat, when Will appeared in front of her. 'Your lifejacket is the wrong way around.'

Of course it was. She couldn't even get that right.

'The straps fasten at the front,' he said, swapping it over for her. 'May I?'

'Be my guest.'

His arms brushed against hers as he slid the straps around her waist and secured them at the front. Her body betrayed her by breaking out in goosebumps.

'I haven't seen you at the pool for a couple of days,' he said, not making eye contact.

'Err… no, I went to the beach yesterday,' she said, feeling guilty, even though she had no reason to feel that way. She didn't owe him an explanation. It was up to her what she did on her holiday. 'I wasn't avoiding you, or anything,' she added, and then silently cursed. Why had she said that? Of course she'd been avoiding him.

He smiled. 'It never occurred to me that you were.'

'It didn't?' She felt her cheeks flush.

His eyes lifted to hers. 'Is there a reason you'd feel the need to avoid me?'

Was he serious? 'No… I mean, yes. It's just… I had rather too much to drink on Monday night.'

'Did you?' He returned to straightening her lifejacket. 'I didn't notice.'

'You didn't?' Who was he trying to kid?

She waited for him to remind her of her inexcusable behaviour, but his expression didn't change. 'I had a bit too much myself. I don't remember much. I hope I didn't do anything I shouldn't have?'

She realised he was letting her off the hook. He could have easily teased her, or relayed the full horror of her humiliating proposition, but instead he was pretending he didn't remember. 'You were the perfect gentleman,' she assured him.

'Good. I'd hate to think there was any awkwardness between us.' He gestured to the boat. 'Shall we?'

'Okay.' She accepted the offer of his hand and stepped into the boat. 'I'm guessing you've done this before?'

'A few times. Not recently.' He handed her an oar.

'I hope I don't slow you down.'

'You won't.' He pushed the boat out until he was waist-height in the water. 'These boats aren't designed to go fast. It's all about relaxing and enjoying the experience.'

'Sounds nice.' The kayak rocked when he climbed in and she grabbed the side, fearful of being tipped out.

He glanced back. 'You okay?'

'All good.' Lily forced a smile. 'What do I do now?'

'Paddle to the right. I'll paddle to the left. Shall we head over to the shipwreck?' He pointed directly ahead. 'Astron Wreck. It's a famous local landmark.'

She nodded. 'Lead the way.'

He began paddling.

The water was clear and blue and calm. There wasn't a cloud in the sky, which meant there was nothing to soften the glare of the sun. Her skin felt hot and tingled from the intensity of the heat. She was glad of her hat and the fifty-factor sunscreen.

The sea became choppier once they'd sailed past the Geotubes, the boat fighting the waves. Lily tried to follow Will's rhythm, but she battled to stay balanced.

Rowing clearly required core stability, another attribute she didn't possess. But true to his word, Will kept a slow steady pace, and for the most part she was able to match his stroke.

'Did you enjoy Wipeout this morning?'

Oh, God, he'd seen that? She inwardly cringed.

He winked at her over his shoulder. 'Looked like fun.'

'I assure you, it wasn't.' The memory came back, fresh and raw of being bounced from an inflatable tube into the air and belly-flopping into the water. 'I nearly drowned.'

He laughed. 'Why did you take part?'

Good question. 'I'm forcing myself to try new things.'

'And why's that?' He sounded curious.

How much to reveal, she wondered? 'I feel the need to be more… adventurous.'

'Nothing wrong with that. Good for you.'

They'd reached open water. The sea had darkened in colour, morphing from a pale blue into a deep turquoise. It was beautiful.

'I know what you're thinking,' she said, watching the way the sunlight sparkled on the water.

'And what's that?' There was a hint of amusement in his voice.

'That I'm not the adventurous type. And you're right. I'm not a natural risk-taker. I'm not even sure myself why I agreed to take part.'

Maybe it was simply a need to try and make up for lost time. An effort to cram into a two-week holiday a lifetime of experiences. If so, she was likely to do herself an injury. She was not cut out for physical exertion.

'Maybe I was hoping I'd discover a hidden talent,' she said, dragging her oar through the water. 'And that beneath my very un-sporty exterior, there would be a warrior goddess waiting to be unleashed.'

He laughed. 'But there isn't?'

'God, no. I fell off the first obstacle. Which might not have been so bad if a woman twice my age hadn't gone after me and completed the course.'

Smiling, he said, 'At least you took part. I chickened out.'

'Very sensibly.'

The shipwreck came into view. From a distance it looked like a rusty lump of metal. It was sunken into the water, one end protruding.

'So if you're not sporty, what do you like doing instead?'

She focused on the ripples of water caused by the kayak cutting through the water. 'Sewing, mainly. I love anything to do with fashion. I make a lot of my own clothes.'

'Impressive. Where did you learn to sew?'

They neared the shipwreck. She could see its mast poking up, weathered and beaten. 'My grandma taught me. We used to watch period dramas on the telly and try to recreate the costumes. We'd draw sketches and then make patterns using old bedsheets. She'd then take me to the weekly jumble sale at the church hall and we'd buy old bits of material to reuse.'

He stopped rowing, allowing the kayak to float closer to the sunken vessel. 'Sounds like fun.'

'It was.'

The waves were choppier by the shipwreck and she had to hold on to the side of the kayak. She could see barnacles attached to the rusty orange metal and faint writing on the side of the shipwrecked boat.

Will shifted to half face her. 'You say, used to? Isn't your grandma around any more?'

She shook her head. 'She died a while back.'

'Sorry to hear that.'

The boat rocked as a splash of wave caught them off guard.

'Seen enough?' He must have noticed her concerned expression.

'Yes, thank you.'

He pointed behind her. 'We could head over to those rocks and then work our way back to the beach.'

'Good plan.' Relieved, she began frantically paddling. She preferred it when the sea was calmer.

He moved the kayak away from the shipwreck. In no time they were safely away from the choppy currents, and she was able to relax a little.

Will slowed his stroke rate and they returned to moving at a leisurely pace through the water. The occasional splash was a welcome relief against the heat of the sun. Her skin appreciated being cooled off.

It was quiet and serene out on the water and Lily felt the tension leave her body, expelled by the tropical surroundings and exertion of rowing.

A few moments later, Will said, 'So you're creative then?'

'As opposed to academic, you mean?'

He laughed. 'I didn't mean it like that.'

'Well, you're right. I was always better at the arty subjects at school. Never ask me to work out a maths sum without a calculator. I'm rubbish.'

'Me too.' He glanced back. 'Hence why my sister became my accountant. She's a maths wizard.'

'Your accountant? Are you self-employed?'

He nodded. 'I run an events management company.'

She stopped rowing. 'Wow, that sounds very grand.' She felt a little intimidated. After all, she worked in a factory. 'What kind of events do you manage?'

'All sorts.' He continued rowing, the muscles on his shoulders working overtime. Not that she was looking, or anything. 'Product launches, conferences, festivals, parties. Even a few award ceremonies.'

Goodness. She was in a kayak with a real-life entrepreneur. 'Sounds like hard work?'

'It can be. But it's fun, too, and you get to meet some really interesting people.' He nodded to the rocks. 'Shall we stop here for a while? I don't know about you, but my arms are tired.'

She doubted they were. He was stopping for her benefit. He could probably hear her panting. She unzipped her bum bag and removed a small drinks bottle. 'Water?'

He took the bottle. 'You came prepared.'

She considered telling him she also had plasters, antiseptic cream and paracetamol, but figured this would make her sound like a bit of a loser. At the very least, it would make her look uptight, and not the chilled confident woman she was aiming for.

'How did you get into events management?' she asked, retrieving the bottle from him.

He shifted position so he was facing her and dangled his feet in the water. 'I did a business degree, then worked briefly in travel and tourism, before moving into hospitality.' He circled his feet in the water, turning his face up to the sun. 'Both industries gave me a good grounding for events management and taught me two valuable lessons. Firstly, I knew I couldn't face doing the same job every day, I'd get too bored. And secondly, I didn't have the right attributes for reporting to someone else.' He gave her a rueful smile. 'I'm not good at taking orders.'

She squinted at him. 'So you started your own company?'

He nodded. 'TaylorMade Events. Blending magic with logic,' he said, using his hands to sign-write. 'Corny, huh?' He laughed. 'Oh, well, too late to change it now.'

She watched him tilt his head further back and close his eyes. He was starting to tan. His light-brown wavy hair had flecks of blond around the temple. The faint hairs on his arms and legs had lightened in the sun. He looked healthy, and relaxed, and tantalisingly good.

She shook her head. She seriously needed to cool off.

She took a sip of water – except, she missed her mouth and spilt the contents down her front. Served her right for gawping. 'Do you employ loads of people?' she asked, hastily brushing away the spilt water.

His eyes still closed, he shook his head. 'Only four permanent staff. Me, my sister, and two designers.' He opened his eyes. 'Everyone else is hired project by project, depending on what we need.'

When he smiled at her, she felt slightly flustered. The kayak wasn't big, and there wasn't anyone else around. It was very intense, in a stranded *Blue Lagoon* kind of way.

She fanned her face, suddenly overheating. 'You're obviously very passionate about what you do. It sounds like you're successful, too.'

'I guess we've been lucky.' He looked out to sea. 'We've been through some tough times, too.' For a moment, he seemed lost in his thoughts. She watched his face cloud over. Then he snapped himself out of it.

'It must be nice to be your own boss, though?' She trailed her fingers through the cool water.

'Most of the time. But it has its issues.' He opened his arms. 'Like trying to take a holiday, for example. No work, no income.'

'Ah, yes. Tricky.'

'What do you do?' He focused his gaze on her, his eyes appearing more blue than grey today. 'I'm guessing something to do with fashion?'

She blinked in surprise. 'Why do you say that?'

'That red dress you had on the other night was quite something.' An undecipherable look flickered across his face. He shook it away. 'It looked designer.'

It did? Goodness. 'Well, it wasn't. I… err… I made it myself.'

'Really?' He looked fascinated. 'So you are a designer then?'

She opened her mouth, fully intending to correct him and say that— No, she wasn't a designer, she wanted to be, but she currently worked in a clothing factory. But what came out was, 'Yes, I'm a designer.' Now, why had she said that?

The smile he gave her made her insides flutter. 'Do you work for a fashion house? Or your own label? Bloody hell. I'm not sharing a boat with a famous name, am I?'

Her cheeks flushed. 'I assure you, I'm not famous.' Far from it.

Guilt nudged her in the ribs. Oh, God, where was she going with this? Talk about digging herself into a hole. But it would be mortifying to admit that she was a nobody. He was such a high-flyer himself that she couldn't bring herself to admit to earning minimum wage and spending her days cutting patterns.

And besides, wasn't the idea of this holiday to reinvent herself? She fully intended to kick-start her career when she got home, so she wouldn't be lying... much. She was just embellishing a little. Imagining what her life might be like, rather than dwelling on what it was currently like. And it wasn't like she was ever going to see him again, was it?

'I design for the stage mostly,' she said, hoping that having made costumes for her school play twenty years ago, that this counted as 'stage design'. 'With some TV work, too,' she added, figuring that as the nativity play had been videoed and had since been added to YouTube it also counted. Talk about stretching the truth.

'What TV shows have you worked on?' He sounded interested.

Oh, hell. 'Err... not many. Nothing you'd have heard of. Very little, in fact... And mostly abroad.' The hole she was digging was getting deeper. It was time to switch topics. 'Wow, look at the fish.'

He followed to where she was pointing.

Never had she been so glad to see a school of fish.

Thankfully, it proved to be a good distraction.

Their colours were vivid, and they looked almost luminous as they darted about, changing direction and diving deeper. But the fish would only divert Will for so long. She needed an escape. 'Maybe we should get moving? In case the tide turns, or something?'

He gave her a puzzled look. 'Have you had enough?'

'I have. Silly me, I forgot to put on sunscreen. I think I'm burning.' She rubbed her arms and winced for effect.

His eyes grew wide. 'You're not wearing sunscreen? Bloody hell. We definitely need to get you back.' He swung his legs into the boat and began frantically rowing.

Shame and guilt battled for prime position within her. Why had she lied?

But she knew why. Because sometimes lying was easier than admitting the truth.

Over the years when people had asked her if was okay, she'd told them she was fine, even though she wasn't. She would smile when she was sad, and she would mask her tears when she was unhappy. Why? Because no one really wanted to hear the truth. They were asking out of politeness. It would have been indulgent to moan or complain about her lot. Especially given what her granddad had had to deal with. So she'd lied. She'd pretended she was okay, when she was anything but.

She'd even lied to her granddad, editing the information the doctor had given her about his health for fear of upsetting him. Did he really need to know he was on 'borrowed time'? Or that a 'Do Not Resuscitate' order had been added to his medical file? She didn't think so.

Sometimes the truth was too painful. Sometimes lying was the kinder option.

Although in this case, if she was being honest, it was because the truth was too shameful. There was no way she was about to start relaying the sadness of her life to a hot bloke she'd met in the Caribbean who ran his own flipping company. He'd run a mile. And who could blame him?

No, a little pretence was called for. Nothing harmful, just something to boost her confidence and allow her to keep up the pretence of being a successful, happy, confident adult.

And anyway, was it really lying? After all, she *did* design clothes. She just didn't get paid for it. And that was just semantics.

Who was she trying to kid?

But saying she was a 'designer' out loud had been empowering. It had filled her with pride. She'd liked the way it had sounded.

There was no doubt about it, when she returned home she was going to become a proper designer. Definitely.

Excellent plan.

In the meantime, she just had to keep up a little white lie, try to avoid the topic of her work life, and keep on rowing until they reached the safety of the beach.

Piece of cake.

Chapter Six

Will took a deep breath and smiled. He couldn't remember the last time he'd felt this relaxed. The sky above was cobalt-blue, the golden sand below was soft and warm. The only sound was the lapping of the waves caressing the shoreline and the faint music coming from the bar further down the beach. He felt boneless, his body devoid of tension. No doubt helped by the absence of daily chores and the effect of two beers.

He rolled his head to one side and watched a gecko dart across the sand towards a palm tree. Its splayed legs and deft claws gripped the bark as it disappeared up into the foliage.

He rolled his head to the other side, and his smile increased at the sight of Lily lying on the lounger next to him. She looked as relaxed as he did. She was reading a book, her ankles crossed, one arm tucked under her head.

He allowed his gaze to travel the length of her, from her flushed cheeks to her lightly tanned skin, and ended up fixated on her pink toenails. She wore a turquoise-patterned sundress over a matching bikini. The dress had fallen open, revealing her shapely legs, causing his gaze to linger a little longer.

He'd spent most of the last two days in her company. On Friday, they'd met for lunch at The Olive Branch and then relaxed by the infinity pool, occasionally visiting the heated whirlpool, which had been both incredibly soothing and alarmingly distracting. The warm bubbles and fragrant aroma were the perfect antidote for unwinding. But the intimacy of the space, combined with the sensation of Lily's warm skin sliding against his, had left his senses feeling alert and heightened, not subdued.

Yesterday, she'd treated herself to a day at the spa, so he'd walked into the local village and bought Poppy a cuddly iguana and a cute shoulder bag with a giant parrot embroidered on the side. He'd met up with Lily in the evening, and they'd enjoyed a meal at the hotel's à la carte restaurant. Lily was easy to talk to, self-deprecating and funny. They'd talked about films, and he'd discovered her taste ranged from 1930s horror movies to 1950s musicals. Her favourite actor was Jack Lemmon and her favourite film was *Benny & Joon*. And whereas there was nothing wrong with her choices, they weren't exactly current. The last film she'd seen at the cinema was *Black Swan*. It was like she'd been absent from the world for more than a decade and was frantically trying to catch up.

But despite her slightly dated persona, there was nothing artificial about her, even though at times she looked uncomfortable, like she was battling between wanting to let loose or moderate her behaviour. She was an eclectic mixture of worldly wisdom and childlike innocence. And he was fascinated.

The evening had ended with a walk along the beach. Conversation had flowed easily, which was just as well. If it hadn't, they might have registered the soft moonlight and star-filled sky and realised the setting was incredibly romantic. As it happened, they'd ended up joining the other guests at the foam party on the beach, which was about as far from romantic as you could get.

The music was incredibly loud. Strobe lighting had lit the area, and a huge gun-like contraption blasted everyone with foamy suds. Within half an hour, they were soaking wet and covered in soap. The dye from Lily's red dress had leaked, streaking down her arms and legs, making it look like she was bleeding. It was funny and surreal and weirdly sexy. Which was crazy. There they were, dancing on a beach to Shakira, laughing as they had sunk into the soft sand and slipped all over the place from being sprayed with foam. There should have been nothing sexy about it. It wasn't logical.

But her wet dress had clung to Lily's body, leaving nothing to the imagination, and their suddy hands had slipped over each other as they'd tried to stay upright. That alone had played havoc with his ability to behave himself.

Not that he'd allowed anything untoward to happen. He might have registered the sexual nature of the situation, but Lily hadn't. Far from flirting with him, she'd just been enjoying herself. Dancing, laughing, and squealing when she was sprayed with foam.

There was only one moment when the atmosphere had changed. And that was when they'd left the beach and stopped by the pool shower to rinse off. As they'd stood under the running water, bathed in moonlight, wiping foam and red dye from each other, the laughter had faded into a moment of stillness. Their eyes had locked. Their hands had entwined. And their bodies had touched. As the moment intensified, their faces drew closer... but just as their lips were about to touch, sudden laughter had broken the moment. A group of drunken partygoers had appeared from the beach and had staggered up the pathway.

Dripping and messy, Will and Lily had jumped apart and returned to their hotel block, where they'd parted company with a brief cheek kiss, the only intentional intimacy they'd shared all night.

He hadn't minded. It had been a lovely evening.

But he'd be lying if he said it hadn't left him wanting more.

As if sensing him staring, Lily glanced up from her reading.

'Good book?' he said, trying to cover being sprung watching her.

'Not bad.' She pushed her sunglasses onto her head. 'The baddie is about to get his comeuppance. I hope the hero saves the day.'

'Disappointing if he doesn't.'

'She.'

'Sorry?'

She smiled. 'The hero is female.'

'Ah, right. My mistake.' He shook his head. 'Under-lying sexism. The bane of women's lives, eh?'

'Tell me about it.' She rolled her eyes. 'It's just nice to be able to relax and read. I can't remember the last time I finished a book in two days.'

'You don't read much at home?'

'I do, but it tends to be when I'm in bed. After two chapters I'm usually asleep.'

'The busy life of a designer, eh?'

She glanced away. 'Something like that.' She covered her knees with her dress, as if needing to distract herself. 'Do you read?'

'Not much.'

89

The last book he'd read was one of the Harry Potters, and that was read out loud to his poorly daughter when she'd been laid up with a stomach upset. He'd enjoyed reading to Poppy when she was small; it was one of the few things he'd felt confident doing as a parent, but now she'd outgrown the need to be read to. He was redundant. Maybe he should start reading more? But when would he have the time?

Thoughts of Poppy reminded him he still hadn't mentioned his status as a 'widowed father'. Guilt flooded through him, as it always did when thoughts of his home life filtered into his brain. Keeping Poppy a secret made it seem like he was ashamed of her, and he wasn't. Far from it. As painful as it had been losing Sara, he'd never for one second regretted having Poppy. She meant everything to him. So why not mention her?

Well for one thing, it would seem weird now. He couldn't just casually drop his eleven-year-old daughter into the conversation, when for the past week he'd not said a word. It would make him look like he had something to hide.

And besides, there was no need to mention Poppy. She was no one else's business but his. He'd come to the Caribbean for a break. Not thinking or talking about his homelife was doing him the world of good. Poppy was having a great time at camp, and he was relishing the opportunity to focus on his own needs and be selfish for once. Was that so wrong?

'So, what are your interests, apart from planning events?' Lily asked, breaking into his thoughts. 'I'm guessing golf?'

He frowned at her. 'Why golf?'

'Isn't that what most men of your age group enjoy?'

'Are you implying I'm old?'

'Of course not… much.'

He feigned looking indignant. 'Thanks!'

'If it's not golf, what is it? Metal detecting? Building model railways? Topiary?'

He laughed. 'How old do you think I am?'

'Eighty-four.'

He nudged her foot. 'Cheers.'

'But you look good for an octogenarian. You're ageing well.'

'Good to know.' He rolled onto his side. 'I feel eighty-four when I play football. My knees aren't as accommodating as they used to be.'

'You play sports?'

He nodded. 'Just not golf.'

He was stretching the truth somewhat. He hadn't 'played' sports for years. These days he was an observer, not a participant. It had been years since he'd had the time to do anything other than visit the gym twice a week. Even then, it was often a rushed session, as he needed to get home to Poppy.

'What else apart from sport?' Her chin balanced on one hand as she studied him. 'Do you have any other pastimes?'

Sure. He had all sorts of pastimes. Playing with dolls. Making up pretend games. Running around the local park, dressing up as Pierrot the Clown… But none of these he could admit to.

'Dinner with friends,' he said, even though this was another thing he rarely did any more. 'Meeting up with uni mates.' Another thing he hadn't done much of over the years. 'And travelling. I've been to some amazing places.' Which was entirely true… but again, just not recently.

Her face lit up. 'Really? I'd love to travel.' And then her cheeks coloured. 'What I mean is… I'd love to travel *more*.' She made a scoffing sound. 'Of course, I've travelled. It's not that I haven't been anywhere… but there are loads more places I'd love to visit.'

'Where—'

'Where have you been?' She cut him off before he could ask the same question. 'Where were some of your favourite places?'

He sensed Lily wanted to keep the conversation focused on him. Okay. A little strange, but he was happy to oblige. 'Bali was a favourite.' He'd gone there on his honeymoon. 'And Florida. Goa. Italy. Brazil.' All the places he'd visited with Sara. 'And Switzerland.'

He wasn't sure why he'd said Switzerland. Zermatt *had* been one of his favourite destinations – until the accident. It was now tarnished with painful memories that meant he'd for ever associate the place with the loss of his wife.

'Did you go skiing in Switzerland? I've always wanted to ski.' Lily sounded wistful.

He didn't answer. He couldn't.

'Not that I'd be any good,' she said. 'I'd probably crack my head open.'

He turned away. For a moment, he struggled to breathe.

She touched his arm. 'Sorry, have I said something wrong?'

He forced a smile. 'Of course not. I'm a bit squeamish, that's all,' he lied, trying to compose himself. 'I was imagining all that blood.'

'Oh… right.'

He doubted she believed him, but she let the matter drop.

They fell into an uncomfortable silence. Will lost in his thoughts.

He saw Lily glance at him, probably wondering how she'd put her foot in it, and he felt bad for her. He was being unfair. He'd chosen not to tell her about his life, so he couldn't be upset that she'd struck a nerve.

Deciding he needed to lighten the mood, he swung his legs around off the lounger. 'Okay, time for a swim. Fancy joining me?'

She closed her book. 'I do.'

'If you're feeling brave, how about a banana boat ride?'

'No way.' She stood up and unhooked her dress straps, letting her sundress drop to the floor. He was suddenly eye level with her exposed midriff, his face so close that he could see the outline of her ribs.

He looked away and told himself to get a grip. It wasn't like he hadn't seen a woman's body before. What was wrong with him? He was acting like a schoolboy with a first crush.

'Have you seen the speed of those things?' Lily said, oblivious to his distracted state. 'It's a wonder anyone survives.'

Will stood up and forced his gaze away from her curves. 'What happened to being more adventurous?'

'There's being adventurous, and then there's acting plain crazy.' She slipped her feet into her flip-flops. 'Anyway, if you think I'm going to humiliate myself while you sit laughing at me on the beach, think again.'

'As if I'd do that. I was going to do it with you.'

She shielded her eyes from the sun, looking at him suspiciously. 'You were?'

'It looks like fun.' He grinned at her. 'Tempted?'

She glanced out to sea, screwed up her forehead in contemplation, and then looked back at him. 'Okay. You're on.'

He was shocked. 'You're going to do it?'

'What's the worst that can happen?' She held her hand up. 'Actually, don't answer that. I don't want to know.' She stepped into her sundress and wiggled it back up her body.

He tried not to stare.

'Let's go, before I chicken out.' She fastened her bum bag around her waist and they made their way down the beach to the sailing centre.

He hadn't expected her to say yes. She was full of surprises. Part fearless, part mouse.

She nudged his arm. 'What's so funny?'

He turned to her. 'Pardon?'

'That is not the expression of an innocent man. What do you know that I don't?'

He was struggling not to laugh. 'Nothing.'

'Fibber.' She pinned him with a glare. 'Have you done this before?'

'I have not.' Which was true.

'Why do I feel a *but* coming…?'

'There's nothing, I promise.' He took her hand to give it a reassuring squeeze. 'Trust me, this is going to be fun.'

'Yeah, but for whom?'

Her indignant expression made him laugh, but then he realised he was still holding her hand. Why had he done that? It had been an impulse. An excuse to stop her escaping. But now he was stuck. He could hardly just let go. That would seem rude, like a rejection. But continuing to keep hold of it felt too intimate. Like they were a couple. And they definitely weren't a couple.

Holding hands was something people in a relationship did. It felt like a betrayal to Sara to hold another woman's hand.

The familiar feeling of guilt re-emerged.

He used the excuse of reaching the sailing centre to let go.

'There's a group on a banana boat now.' He pointed to the yellow inflatable contraption on the water. 'Doesn't look so bad, does it?'

She watched the boat bumping along the water, the participants bouncing around as the speedboat changed direction. 'I guess it looks okay,' she said, until the speedboat swerved and the banana boat flew in the air, dislodging all four passengers. She gasped. 'But that doesn't!'

'It's part of the experience.'

'What, face-planting in the water?'

He laughed at her disgruntled expression. 'Light-weight.'

'Need I remind you, I've already nearly drowned once this holiday taking part in that wretched Wipeout game.'

He gave her an admonishing look. 'You're backing out?'

'No—' She fiddled with her bum bag. 'I'm merely reassessing my options.' She looked around, as if searching for a way out, and then pointed to a blue inflatable sofa-seat, bouncing gently at the water's edge. 'That looks safer.'

He didn't have the heart to tell her the outcome would be the same. 'Fine by me. I'll book us in.'

Ten minutes later, they were kitted out with lifejackets and protective helmets and were wading into the sea to reach the inflatable craft.

He watched Lily tuck her dress into her bikini bottoms and climb onto the sofa-seat. 'Need a hand?'

'I can manage.' She gripped the straps and tried to pull herself onto the craft. 'At least, I think I can.'

He watched her flounder, and resisted the urge to help. He'd been sexist once already today, he didn't want to repeat his blunder.

She resorted to jumping onto the seat, but bounced straight off and disappeared under the water.

He pulled her up. 'Careful, there.'

'Ugh, salty,' she said, spitting water from her mouth.

'Look on the bright side.'

She wiped her mouth. 'Which is…?'

'You're wet already, so it doesn't matter if you end up in the water.'

'That is not a bright side. That is a reason to quit and head back to the hotel for a bath and cocktail.'

'I thought you were off cocktails.'

'After this, I may reconsider.' She climbed onto the sofa-seat and dragged herself towards the back.

He tried really hard not to stare at her backside as he climbed onto the inflatable sofa-seat in front of her.

The driver of the speedboat yelled for them to, 'Buckle up and hold on!'

'Thank God these things come with a seatbelt,' Lily said, fastening the strap. 'At least we won't end up in the water.'

In theory.

The driver gave them a questioning thumbs-up, to check they were ready, and then sped off.

There was a few seconds' delay before the slack in the rope tightened. When it did, the inflatable sofa-seat jerked upwards and they were thrown backwards.

Lily screamed.

Will laughed.

They both grappled to hold on.

The boat bounced along the water, throwing them upwards. To one side. Then the other.

He'd thought the crash helmets were a tad overkill. How wrong he'd been. Their heads banged together every few seconds as the chair turned one way, then the other.

Lily was screaming, her eyes firmly shut, her body being tossed around like a rag doll.

One large bump saw her fly upwards and land on him.

Ouch. So much for the seatbelt, it had snapped open.

He groaned when her elbow dug into his stomach.

'S— so— sorry!' she yelled, trying to get off him.

'Don't worry about it!'

And then the boat changed direction and she head-butted him again.

'This is not fun!' she yelled, making him laugh.

He lost his grip and fell backwards. 'Christ, no!'

She started laughing. 'It's hell!'

'I agree!'

'You said it would be fun!' Water splashed into her face making her squeal.

He slipped further down the inflatable. 'I lied!'

The boat ahead suddenly jerked sideways. Far from being secured by the seatbelts, both gadgets failed, and Will and Lily slipped free from the straps and flew in the air.

Oh, crap.

The only thing he heard as he hit the water was Lily screaming.

He sank underwater, the force of the landing over-riding the lifejacket's ability to keep him afloat. He kicked his way to the surface and looked frantically for her.

She emerged a few seconds later, flailing her arms about.

He swam over. 'It's okay, I've got you.' He pulled her towards him, and then realised she wasn't drowning, she was laughing.

'Well, they were rubbish seatbelts,' she said, her arms encircling his neck.

'Sorry we ended up in the water.'

'I'm not.'

'You're not?'

'I couldn't have taken a second more of that torture.' She held onto him, her eyes locked on his. 'If he hadn't thrown us off, I was ready to jump.'

'Not a fan, huh?'

'Put it this way, I'd rather sign up for Zumba and Wipeout combined, than endure that again.' She looked around for the speedboat. 'Please tell me it's over?'

'The driver's indicating for us to get back on.'

She tightened her grip. 'I am not getting back on that thing.'

'Okay, we don't have to,' he said, laughing. 'Which leaves us with two options. Either get towed back to shore, or swim? Any preference?'

'Swim. Definitely, swim. My nerves are shredded.'

He smiled. 'Are you going to let go of me?'

'No.' She squeezed him harder.

'Helpful.'

'Is… is that a problem?' Her teeth had started to chatter.

'Now why would you think that?' He shook his head, resigned to his fate. 'Climb aboard.'

'Thank you.' She twisted her body so she was behind him. 'My hero,' she said, hugging him tightly.

'Yeah, right.' He twisted to look at her. 'Secure?'

'Very.' She smiled and for a moment he stopped breathing. Her face was next to his, their cheeks touching… And he was expected to swim like this?

He was a strong swimmer, but he'd never attempted breaststroke with a woman attached to his back before. It wasn't the physical exertion that was the problem, it was the distraction of feeling her warm breath against his ear. Her arms encircling his chest. And her body resting on his.

Will's heart contracted, filling him with a sense of acute loss. However much he tried to avoid intimacy, his body craved it. He missed laughing with someone, cuddling up on the sofa to watch a film with someone, and sharing a bed with someone.

Most of all, he missed loving someone. And being reminded of that hurt like hell.

Once again, he was torn. Torn between wanting to throw her off his back, and torn between wanting to turn around and kiss her senseless. But if he did *that*, he might never stop. And that was a risk he wasn't willing to take.

Chapter Seven

Friday, 26 March

Being awake at four a.m. might be a strange experience for some people. Not for Lily. In the last months of her granddad's life she'd regularly been up during the night, taking him to the toilet, or changing his bedsheets. Some nights he'd be so distressed and in such discomfort that she'd had to sit with him to calm him down. Panic attacks were common when death was looming, apparently. A person would often experience a deep sense of foreboding, which in the early hours of the night could be extremely frightening. For both of them.

So it wasn't uncommon for Lily to watch the sun slowly rise and witness the moment when night morphed into a new day. But the dismal sunsets in North London were nothing compared to the magical spectacle of the Caribbean.

She'd never seen anything more beautiful in her life, or seen such vibrant colours. The pale sand below was cool against her skin, no longer warmed from the hot sun. The long stretch of empty beach bled seamlessly into the inky-blue of the sea, where the waves caressed the sand like a lover. Shafts of coral light shone so brightly it was like the sky was on fire. The glow flared upwards, streaking the sky, fading into purple and ending with a wash of indigo. It was breathtaking, hypnotic, and incredibly romantic.

As if sensing the wonder radiating off of her, Will squeezed her hand, his thumb circling her palm. The movement was slow and sensual, reminding her of the intimacy they'd shared just a few hours before. Like she needed reminding.

She'd spent almost the entire last four days of her holiday with Will. They'd eaten together, sunbathed together, and gone sightseeing together. They'd even shared a couple's massage, something that had contributed to last night's intimacy. It was hardly surprising. The romantic setup was designed to evoke the senses. Why else would the room be scented with lavender, lit with candles, and have soft music playing in the background? The sight of Will lying on the bed next to her covered in little more than a flannel, his bare skin drenched in essential oils, had sent her hormones into a frenzy.

Judging by the way he'd returned her watchful gaze, Lily was pretty sure he felt the same way. His dilated pupils had been fixated on her as the masseuse had kneaded the back of her thighs. It had left her in no two minds about where his thoughts were headed. Or hers. The end result had been inevitable.

It had started on Monday with a trip to the local golf club, which was a sort of 'in joke', following her teasing Will about his sporting prowess. Turns out, he wasn't lying when he said he couldn't play. But his wayward aim was a lot better than hers. She had barely managed to hit the ball, let alone putt anything. Consequently, after much hilarity, and also annoying the other golfers who were trying to play seriously, they'd returned to the hotel for a swim.

On Tuesday, they'd spent the day at the beach and booked one of the wicker pods for dinner. The pods were built on stilts and were extended over the sea; they looked like they were floating above the water. The interior had long bed-like cushions as well as a dining area. It wasn't surprising that after they'd eaten jerk chicken and refried beans and ordered mojitos, they'd ended up lying side by side watching the sunset.

The occasional touch of hands, legs and feet, had led to hand-holding, followed by Will's arm sliding under her neck, supporting her as they'd cuddled.

And then they'd kissed.

It had started out with a look that had lingered, followed by unconscious leaning, as if drawn together like magnets. Their lips had touched, tentatively at first, as if exploring the idea, posing a question for the other to answer.

Lily's enthusiastic response seemed to be enough to reassure Will that his advances were welcomed, and the kissing switched from soft and restrained, to deep and frantic. A situation that only ended when the pod bed had moved beneath them, and they had realised their exuberance was in danger of causing a structural collapse.

By the time they'd exited the pod, their heated exchange was cooled by the waves splashing against their legs as they'd headed for shore. A look had passed between them as they'd paused by the hotel lift, both knowing that if they resumed kissing it would result in only one outcome.

Despite both agreeing that parting company would be the best action, it was evident that neither had wanted the evening to end. Not that she didn't want to take things further. Boy, did she. Big time. She just needed a little more time to build her courage. This was a huge step. For her, anyway. Thankfully, Will had understood and was happy to go at her pace.

But if nothing else, the sense of building anticipation had made for a thrilling Wednesday. Whether it was swimming together in the infinity pool, or enjoying the bubbling warmth of the whirlpool, they'd held hands, kissed frequently, and looked to anyone watching like a couple in the throes of a passionate affair.

They'd talked, but not about anything significant. They were both happy to steer clear of real life and focus on the nonsensical. They compared what superpowers they'd like to have, and played guess-the-backstory of the other hotel guests. They'd talked about TV, films, music, and food. Lily knew that Will was pro-Marmite, but anti-shellfish. He was an early riser, but never went to bed before midnight. He wore boxer shorts, but hated socks. His ambition was to trek across the Sahara Desert.

They'd discussed it all. A range of topics which covered everything, except reality. Or life, back home. Something Lily was relieved about, especially as she'd lied about her job. She would deliberately avoided any topic that might lead her back to admitting that she wasn't a costume designer after all, but only a lowly pattern-cutter working in a miserable factory, for an equally miserable boss.

In the space of just two weeks, a whole new Lilith Monroe had been invented. A less tense version, someone who was more alert and who slept better than her previous counterpart. And it wasn't just the physical change. Lily felt emotionally calmer, too, like she'd shifted from a place of misery, into experiencing moments of pure happiness.

She wasn't naive enough to believe her grief had miraculously disappeared. It was a respite. A reprieve. She was existing in a bubble, shielded from the real world and sampling the hedonistic delights of life, without the mundanity of her normal existence.

She still felt a little untethered, like an astronaut who'd been cut adrift from her space shuttle. But whereas before it had felt like she'd been sucked into a black hole and her future had looked uncertain and scary, she now felt like gravity had shifted and she was slowly drifting back down to Earth, ready for the start of phase two of her life.

The hard part lay ahead, but this holiday had given her the confidence she needed to change her path. She had tried out a new version of herself. Tested the water. And seen a snapshot of what, and who, Lilith Monroe could be. A woman who was funny, unafraid, uninhibited and entertaining. She was no longer invisible. And she'd *liked* it.

Thursday had started with a coach trip to the opposite side of the island, where they'd boarded the Capitan Gringo yacht, along with a load of other tourists, and had headed for an uninhabited island.

They'd sat on the deck, admiring the views and exchanging enigmatic smiles, before the yacht anchored next to a hidden cave, were they'd all been kitted out with snorkelling gear, ready to explore.

The idea of venturing into a darkened cave would have had the old Lilith running for the hills. But new and improved Lily didn't want to regret missing out on an adventure, so she'd overridden her nerves and lowered herself from the boat.

And she was glad she had. Walking in flippers might be cumbersome and challenging, but swimming in them was a revelation. Once she was submerged, she felt like an elegant dolphin cutting through the water with ease and poise. The sea was pale turquoise, and so transparent that she almost didn't need to plunge her face into the water to see the luminous swarms of fish below.

Snorkelling was fun. Her bravery grew, and she followed Will over to the cave entrance. But her courage was tested to its limits when she realised she had to dive below the water and swim through a gap in the rockface to enter the cave. But she steeled herself, took a deep breath and ducked under the water. Unlike Will, who negotiated the narrow entrance with ease, she had to cling hold of the rocks and drag herself through the gap to the empty cave. She emerged through to the other side slightly panicked. But she'd made it, and it felt good to have overcome another fear.

An hour later, they'd reboarded the yacht and were taken to a secluded island for a BBQ on the beach. Here they ate kebabs and drank papaya juice, and then followed this up with a nap. Lily drifted off to sleep in quiet contentment, listening to the lap of waves, with Will stroking her arm.

They'd arrived back at the hotel around seven p.m. and met up for dinner a couple of hours later. The gap had allowed her time to formalise her thoughts. Things were heading in a certain direction, and she needed to be sure she was okay with that before venturing out for the evening.

Decision made, she'd applied make-up, doused herself in perfume, and selected the floaty silver dress she'd been building up the courage to wear.

Will's expression on seeing her had been worth the effort. His grey-blue eyes had widened as she'd descended the steps, his gaze skimming over her bare shoulders and hovering where the dress dipped below her cleavage.

It had felt provocative to wear such a dress, and slightly scandalous. Definitely something old Lilith would never have done... which was all the motivation she'd needed to sashay up to him and kiss him, allowing her lips to trail across his cheek and savour the sensation of his shiver. It was heady stuff. Intoxicating. She could get used to feeling this empowered.

Dinner had been a flirtatious affair. They'd dined in a secluded tent, with billowing white fabric that shielded them from the sea breeze. They'd eaten mashed pumpkin and fried plantain and drank enough alcohol to soften the edges without tipping them into inebriation.

The evening had ended with a moonlit walk along the beach, an extended kiss, and Lily boldly inviting Will to join her in her room.

Will had smiled, gently touched her cheek, and asked if she was sure. Her firm reply of, 'Very sure,' had evoked another smile. He'd taken her hand and they'd silently walked back to the hotel, exchanging seductive glances along the way.

They'd stopped to kiss a couple of times, building the tension, which soon over-spilled into a frantic groping session in the lift as it travelled up to the first floor.

They'd stumbled from the lift still kissing, bouncing along the wall, until they'd reached her door. More fumbling followed, as she'd struggled to unlock the damn thing without breaking their kiss, and they'd eventually fallen into the room.

At this point, things had slowed, almost as if they'd both registered the choice ahead. A rushed moment of lust, or an extended night of enjoyment? Tempting as the first option had been, she was glad they'd opted for the second. It allowed her time to memorise every touch, every lingering kiss and every sensation her body had experienced. Despite her only wearing two items of clothing, Will still managed to take his time removing her dress and undies, seemingly wanting to enjoy each moment as much as she did.

By the time they were lying on the bed naked, they were both shaking and she'd lost any semblance of shyness or uncertainty. What followed was beautiful, sensual, and extremely intense. As though it wasn't merely sex. It was something a lot more.

For her, it was a release of years of frustration and heartbreak. A re-entering of the adult world, where she could pursue her own dreams and ambitions and desires. It was about finally being able to let go and just 'feel'. She was allowed to be selfish, to take something she wanted, with no guilt, and no one judging her.

What it meant for Will, she didn't know. And she wasn't about to ask.

Sitting here now on the beach as dawn broke on Friday, the last day of their holiday, he looked almost wistful. But he hadn't looked that way last night.

There were times when he'd looked as absorbed as she was, his face displaying pleasure and a wanting so strong she felt consumed by him.

But there was a moment when his face had clouded over and he'd buried his face in her neck, as if hiding whatever emotion had surfaced. Her skin felt damp and Lily wondered if he'd been crying.

But then Will had noticed her questioning frown, and had kissed her with such intensity that it had squashed any concerns she might have had. He'd wanted this as much as she did, of that she was certain. Whatever demons he was trying to outrun, he wasn't voicing them out loud, and she was fine with that. She hadn't wanted anything to spoil their perfect night.

And it had been perfect. Tender. Intimate and loving. He was considerate, experienced and completely attentive. Every inch of her had been caressed, kissed and enjoyed, and she'd been left feeling thoroughly ravaged and extremely content.

Affectionate cuddling had followed, a joint shower, and then drifting in and out of sleep in each other's arms.

Just before four a.m, he'd nuzzled closer and asked if she'd wanted to watch the sunrise with him. It had seemed the fitting way to conclude the evening.

But it also marked the end of her holiday. And as such, the end of her romance and the reinvention of Lily. This time tomorrow, she would be back in rainy Haringey, surrounded by her grandparents' dated furniture, facing a return to work on Monday.

The thought was enough to kill her afterglow.

And so here they were. Sitting on the beach at dawn. Both uncertain as to how to say goodbye.

'I've had the most amazing holiday,' he said, as if reading her thoughts. 'I'm sad it's over.'

'Me too.' She leant into his shoulder, relishing his warmth. 'I wish we could stay another week.'

'Or month.'

'Or year.'

They both laughed.

He laced his fingers into hers. 'Not sure my work colleagues would be very happy.'

'Mine either.' She rested her head on his shoulder and watched the sun emerge from behind a shaft of pink light.

'I wasn't expecting this.' He glanced down at her, his expression earnest and a little sad. 'I wasn't expecting... you. This. Us. It's taken me by surprise.'

She knew the feeling. But was it such a surprise? After all, she'd come to the Caribbean looking for an adventure. And she'd found one. She just hadn't expected it to be Will Taylor.

'Thank you,' he said softly, kissing the top of her head.

She raised her chin to look at him. 'What for?'

He paused, as if deciding how much to say. His arms rested on his bent knees, looking down at the sand, shaking his head. 'Before this holiday, I was... I don't know... stuck, for want of a better word. I needed to move on, but I didn't know how. Being with you has broken down a barrier I didn't know I'd erected.'

Cryptic. He'd been running away from something too, had he? He'd kept that bit quiet. But then, so had she. And she wasn't about to starting prying now, not when they were about to part company. What was the point?

'Nothing about these last two weeks has been hard work,' he said, staring out to sea. 'It's been fun and easy. I can't remember the last time I laughed so much, or felt so relaxed. You've been like a tonic. And I know it has to end, but I want you to know, I'll treasure these moments with you for ever.'

She swallowed awkwardly. 'Wow, that's heavy.'

He barked a laugh. 'Sorry. It's just that my life has been difficult of late. I feel like you've changed that. So, thank you.' He leant forward and kissed her. 'You're an incredibly gorgeous woman, Lily Monroe.'

She smiled back at him. 'You're not so bad yourself.' It was a flippant response to such a heartfelt admission, but what could she say? That he'd changed her life, too? That nothing was ever going to be the same from now on? She couldn't do that.

Why? Because she'd pretended to be a successful, confident, and competent woman who had her life and career sorted. If she admitted now that she was none of these things, and that she'd merely been 'pretending', then it might taint what they'd shared. He would think less of her. And she couldn't bear that. This holiday had gone a long way to restoring her battered self-esteem. No way was she about to sully that by revealing the truth. She'd held it together this long, all she had to do was see it through until the end… which was now.

The time had come to say goodbye.

She broke eye contact and moved away. Touching him right now wouldn't be helpful. 'I don't know about you, but I'm not keen on emotional farewells. I wouldn't want a big scene at the airport or anything.'

He frowned. 'What are you suggesting?'

'We say goodbye here. Now. We end this on a positive note, with a stunning view to remember and an unblemished memory to cherish.'

'Right.' He blinked rapidly. 'Good plan.'

She had no idea how to react, or what to say. But it wasn't like they had an option, was it? There was always going to be an expiry date on their liaison. It didn't make leaving him any easier, though.

'Thank you for your company during these last two weeks,' she said, her voice barely a whisper. 'It's been wonderful. *You've* been wonderful.' She had to force the words out, the pain in her chest was crippling. 'I hope you have a safe flight home, and good luck with your events business.' She stood up, brushing sand away from her shorts. 'Goodbye, Will.'

He caught her hand before she could walk away. 'Wait a sec.' He got to his feet and pulled her close, his watery eyes searching her face. He looked pained and conflicted. Tormented even. He opened his mouth as if to say something… but then sighed, and shook his head. 'Goodbye, Lily. Take care.'

'You too.' She reached up on tiptoes and kissed his tearstained cheek, trying to memorise his scent, the curve of his jaw and the way his wavy brown hair had been lightened by the sun.

Without a backwards glance, she turned away and walked down the beach. Away from Will Taylor. She fought to hold back tears and she resisted the urge to turn and run to him, hold him, and never let him go.

But he wasn't hers. He never had been. He'd been on temporary loan. A gift. A moment of unadulterated pleasure.

It wasn't love, even though it felt like it. How could it be? She didn't know him, not really. And he certainly didn't know her.

He'd met *Lily* Monroe. Enigmatic, mysterious costume designer and temptress, who wore revealing clothing, and didn't baulk in the face of adventure.

But underneath the bluster and pretence, was her old true self. A quiet, sad and lonely woman, who had no career prospects, who was alone in the world, and who was about to be made homeless.

A broken heart was the least of her worries.

Chapter Eight

One month later...

Lilith had been back in the UK for four weeks. Four long agonising weeks that had felt like four years. So much for feeling rejuvenated and empowered to change her life. The moment she'd stepped off the plane at Gatwick the fog of grief had descended. It was like the Grim Reaper had been awaiting her return, and was now taunting her for believing she could overcome her struggles and emerge the other side stronger and happier. But no. The sense of loss she'd felt prior to heading off to the Caribbean still consumed her, only now it was magnified by missing Will. The holiday bubble had definitely burst.

She scrunched up the letter from Haringey Council which reminded her she only had two months left before she had to quit her local authority property, and chucked it at the bin. It hit the rim and landed on the worn mottled brown carpet. Typical. She couldn't even get that right.

She manoeuvred herself around her dressmaker's dummy, which was standing in the centre of the tight living space. The half-finished cobalt-blue dress looked out of place against the drab surroundings, the bright colour stark against a background of beige woodchip wallpaper and dark-wood furniture. Making the dress had been a feeble effort to lift her low spirits. An attempt to recreate the vibrancy of her Caribbean holiday. It hadn't worked. If anything, it had deepened her sadness, adding to the tightness already constricting her chest.

Lilith hoisted her rucksack onto her back and collected her bike from the cramped hallway. It didn't help that she was surrounded by constant reminders of her granddad. The flat still looked the same. It smelt the same. It felt the same. It was as though her Granddad would appear at any moment, balancing on his walking frame and ask for a cup of tea. Her grief was reignited every time she stepped over the threshold, and it wasn't helping her move on. Maybe being forced to move home was a blessing in disguise. It might shift her out of her slump.

As she closed the door behind her and wheeled her bike down the pathway, she glanced back at the terraced bungalow. It had no character. The brickwork was bland, the windows tainted by condensation, the brown paint-work dulled and flaking. But the thought of leaving still made her chest hurt. Whatever its fault, it had been her home for more than two decades. Leaving would be a wrench.

Mrs Black appeared from next door carrying a bag of rubbish. 'Morning, love. Off to work?'

Lilith forced a smile. 'Yes. At least it's stopped raining.'

Mrs Black shuffled down the pathway in her bright green slippers. 'And it's Friday, so you've got the weekend to look forward to.'

'This is true.'

Her elderly neighbour leant against the rickety shed for support. 'Anything nice planned?'

'House-hunting, most likely.' Lilith balanced her bike against the shed. 'Here, let me help you.' She took the bag of rubbish from her neighbour.

'Bless you. The wet plays havoc with my arthritis.'

Lilith dumped the rubbish in the wheelie bin. 'I received my formal notice to quit this morning.'

Mrs Black gasped. 'Oh, love. I'm sorry. We're going to miss you.'

'I'll miss you, too.' She helped her neighbour retrace her steps up the pathway. 'But these properties are designed for older residents, not the likes of me. There'll be someone who needs it more than I do. It wouldn't be fair of me to stay.'

Mrs Black patted her hand. 'But it's your home. You've lived here most of your life.'

'I know. But I need a fresh start. It'll do me good,' she said, with more enthusiasm than she felt. 'And it's not like I'll be gone tomorrow. I'll be around for the next couple of months.'

'You make sure to stay in touch. You're like family to us.'

'Thank you, Mrs Black. That means a lot.' She smiled at her frail neighbour, as she was hit by another wave of remorse. Who would do their shopping for them? Or carry out errands with her not around? It made her sad to think of them struggling alone.

Maybe she'd have a word with the council before she left and see if they could provide some support for the couple. 'I'd better be off to work, I don't want to be late. My boss is a stickler for timekeeping.'

'Of course, off you go.' Mrs Black squeezed her hand. 'Have fun,' she called out, as Lilith headed back down the pathway.

'I will,' she lied, mounting her bike. Fun wasn't a word she ever associated with work. Torture was a more fitting description.

Pushing away from the kerb, she did her usual unsteady wobble, before she got control of the bike and headed up the hill. Her thighs complained as she peddled harder trying to ascend the incline until she reached the top and could free-wheel down the other side.

She wasn't a huge fan of exercise, cycling to work was a financial necessity. She'd never partaken in sports or gone to the gym. Any free time she'd had had been used to design and make clothes, even as a child. But she supposed cycling the mile to work and back every day was good for her lungs. Plus, it allowed her to blow off steam.

Why her grief had intensified over the last four weeks, she couldn't fathom. Tears had come easily, as did the ache in her chest. Her plan to improve her flagging spirits by jetting off to paradise for two weeks had spectacularly backfired. Instead of sticking to her proposed schedule of relaxing, swimming, and soaking up the sun, she'd stupidly partaken in a holiday fling. And then she'd exacerbated the situation by falling for the blessed man. That hadn't been a smart move.

Lilith was startled when a car horn blared from behind. She swerved into the traffic, distracted by thoughts of Will Taylor. At this rate, she wouldn't need a new place to live, she'd be joining her grandparents six feet under.

Waving an apology at the driver, she concentrated on riding her bike. She panted as she negotiated another hill and tried to avoid hitting a car door that opened in front of her.

She hadn't meant to get so involved with Will. It had crept up on her. One minute she was enjoying his friendly banter, the next she was staring into his hypnotic grey eyes and removing her clothes.

In that moment, it had seemed like the most natural thing in the world. The perfect antidote to a multitude of ailments. The need to be touched. The need to stop thinking. To feel something other than loss. She'd felt sated afterwards, caressed, loved, even. And it had felt good.

Boy, had it felt good.

She just hadn't realised the feeling wouldn't last, and that instead of them parting company with good memories and no regrets, their separation would leave a gaping hole in her chest that you could drive a bus through.

Initially she'd reasoned that the sadness would quickly fade. Once back in the UK all thoughts of Will Taylor would be forgotten. After all, it had only been a two-week romance. How attached could a person get in a fortnight? It wasn't logical to pine over a man she barely knew. But logic didn't seem to be winning over. Yearning was the dominant emotion, and that wasn't helping to lift her spirits.

Her place of work came into view as Lily entered the grimy industrial estate situated behind the high street. The roads were busy, filled with commuters. The fumes from the buses and trucks clung to the spring air, creating a haze of grey that dulled the sunshine and made her cough. The smell stung the inside of her nose. London air was not conducive to healthy breathing.

Work was another factor contributing to her low mood. Despite all her good intentions that she was going to launch her career as a costume designer the second she returned to the UK, her resolve had deserted her when faced with impending homelessness.

It wouldn't be sensible to jump ship until she'd secured a new home. Plus, she'd applied for the team leader role where she currently worked. A promotion would mean more money, more experience. A step closer to achieving her goal of becoming a designer. Running a costume department would require people-management skills. Skills she currently lacked. Maybe if she had six months' team leader experience under her belt, a company might be more inclined to take her on.

That was what she kept telling herself, anyway. As an attempt to kill the niggling voice in her head that kept pointing out she was making excuses. Procrastinating. Being a feeble coward.

Whatever the reason, the desire to be bold and 'get out there' had disappeared. And she was gutted as hell.

She secured her bike to the railings outside Clothing Connexions and made her way inside. The building was a large generic oblong, identical to the other units on the estate. Only the large sign hanging above the doorway differentiated it from the tile centre next door or the kitchen wholesalers opposite.

Her mood dipped further as she touched her security pass against the clocking-in machine and realised she was late… again. That wouldn't help her promotion prospects.

Speeding up, she dumped her rucksack in the lockers, and raced towards her workstation, praying her line manager wasn't on the prowl. But luck wasn't with her this morning.

'You're late,' he barked, when she skidded through the double doors.

She tried to look apologetic. 'Only by a couple of minutes,' she said, raising her voice to be heard above the whir of sewing machines. Ahead, rows of tables were filled with an array of tape measures, scissors, pattern paper and metres of unrolled fabric. Behind the tables were dozens of workers, all wearing their signature blue tabards. It was a familiar sight, one she'd seen virtually every day for the last thirteen years.

Her boss folded his arms across his wide chest. Keith Long – aka Darth Vader – often stood by the entrance like a security guard, ready to pounce on any unfortunate workers who dared show up late. He was wearing his usual tan-coloured steward's overalls with his Shop-floor Manager badge. He resembled a 1970s TV cop, with his dated green tie, slightly too long unkempt hair and one-too-many-beer-belly-paunch.

He checked his watch. 'Three and a half minutes, to be precise.'

'I'm sorry, Mr Long. It won't happen again.'

He produced a notepad. 'That's the fourth time you've arrived late for work since January of this year.'

He was keeping track? 'I know, and I'm sorry, but—'

'The company will not tolerate poor timekeeping, Miss Monroe.'

'I appreciate that, but—'

'One hour's pay will be deducted from your salary.'

'An hour's salary?' She felt the colour drain from her face. 'That's not fair.'

'The company cannot be expected to pay for workers' non-attendance.'

'But a whole hour's pay? I was only a couple of minutes late.'

He gave her a hard look. 'If you refer to page nine of your employee handbook, you'll note that as your line manager, I have the authority to deduct an hour's pay for repeated offences of poor timekeeping.'

A few colleagues were watching the exchange. Some giving her a sympathetic smile. Others looking grateful it wasn't them getting it in the ear.

'But I've worked here for thirteen years,' she said, baulking at the unfairness of her situation. 'Until January of this year, I'd never been late for work before.'

'But you've been late four times since,' he said, tapping his notebook. 'Four times in four months. That is not acceptable. Consider this an official warning.'

'Is that really necessary?'

'You've failed to take notice of the verbal warnings issued on three previous occasions, so perhaps this time you'll take heed of my words.'

Technically, he was right. She had been late a few times. But it was hard to focus on work when your personal life was disappearing down the toilet.

'I also noticed your workstation wasn't cleared away last night. Yet another infringement of the standards expected of our employees.'

She frowned. 'I cleared away my workstation. I always leave it immaculate.'

'Not on this occasion. Your tabard was left on the table.'

Her overall? *That* was his gripe?

'Please ensure it doesn't happen again, or there'll be grounds for a second official warning.'

She was too stunned to speak.

He pointed to her workstation. 'Your shift started six minutes ago.'

There was no point arguing. He'd never retract from a decision. He was too afraid of losing face with the other workers. He ruled by fear and intimidation. Compassion wasn't a characteristic Keith Long possessed. It didn't matter that her life had been upended four months ago.

That sleep still evaded her or that she had to drag herself out of bed each day and force herself to function. All that mattered to her boss was that she showed up for work on time and produced her quota of patterns.

She went over to her workstation and picked up her tabard. The tabard she usually placed in her locker. But not last night it seemed. She'd slipped up again. And boy, was she paying for it.

Dottie and Taye appeared.

Dottie Walsh was seventy-three, grey-haired and heralded from the Home Counties. Taye Malik was forty-seven, originated from South Africa, and spent his weekends deejaying at an East London nightclub. The three of them made for quite an unusual friendship.

Dottie rubbed her arm. 'Are you okay?'

She shrugged. 'Not really.'

'Have you had any breakfast?'

'No time. I overslept.' She sighed. 'The perils of not falling asleep until four a.m.'

'I'll fetch you something from the canteen.'

'You don't have to do that.' Lilith searched the room, hoping her boss wasn't still loitering. 'I don't want you getting in trouble with Keith.'

'I can handle Keith.' Dottie gave a dismissive wave. 'If he asks where I am, tell him I'm having bladder problems. It's my age,' she said, with a wink. 'Works every time. He gets so embarrassed, he doesn't say another word.' She headed for the canteen.

'I see Darth Vader was being his usual charming self?' Taye raised a perfectly trimmed eyebrow. His shaved afro hair currently sported intricate patterns, and his clothing was always on trend. Unlike her. He scanned her drab grey sweater and faded black jeans.

'Don't start,' she said, feeling self-conscious. 'I didn't sleep well.'

He held up his hands. 'I wasn't going to say a word.'

'Liar.'

He smirked. 'At least your hair looks good.' He fluffed up her bob. 'Although it could do with more volume. Do you use mousse when you blow-dry?'

Mousse? She could barely afford bread this month. But today was payday and she was due overtime, so maybe she'd treat herself to some fancy hair products this weekend. She'd used the last of her styling oil on holiday. 'Sometimes. If I'm going out.'

Not that she went out. Her work colleagues knew some of her troubles, but not the depths of her situation. And she wanted to keep it that way.

She went to pick up her wage slip and tore open the envelope, hoping to distract Taye from focusing on her appearance. She didn't need him to tell her she looked woeful. She was painfully aware of the fact.

It was a shame, because on holiday wearing vibrant clothes had felt liberating and perfectly in keeping with her surroundings. But once back in dismal Haringey, her desire to be flamboyant had disintegrated, along with her tan. The bright revealing clothes that in the Caribbean had looked evocative and sexy, now looked ridiculous. Like she was trying too hard. Being someone she wasn't – a fraud.

So the new clothes had been packed away, and Lily had returned to wearing her old stuff and not bothering to style her hair, much to Taye's disappointment.

In truth, she shared his disappointment. It felt like all the progress she'd made in the Caribbean had evaporated. Her self-esteem was back to being rock-bottom. Long gone was the adventurous spirit that had propelled her to try kayaking, Zumba and snorkelling. She was back to being drab, sad, and feeling wholly untethered. New and improved Lily had well and truly disappeared.

And then she saw her payslip total. 'You're kidding me?'

Taye frowned. 'Problem?'

'I haven't been paid any overtime.'

He looked over her shoulder. 'Are you sure?'

'Look.' She showed him the wage slip.

'They must've made a mistake. Did you log the hours?'

'Definitely. I was relying on that money to use as a deposit when I move house.' She didn't want to dip into any more of her nest egg. That cash was safely tucked away, ready for the launch of her new career – which at that moment was looking like a distant fantasy, rather than an achievable reality. But things might change. Especially if she could secure the promotion she had applied for.

Keith Long appeared. 'You don't appear to have started work, Miss Monroe?'

'I'm sorry, but there's a problem with my pay. I haven't been paid any overtime this month. Please may I go to Accounts and sort it out?'

'There's been no mistake. I declined to authorise overtime this month.'

'But *I* was paid overtime,' Taye said, sticking up for her.

Keith gave him a disdainful look. 'Is this your workstation, Mr Malik?'

'No, but—'

'Then return to your work, please. This matter doesn't concern you.'

'But, I—'

'Would you like a verbal warning, Mr Malik?'

Taye mumbled something under his breath and returned to his workstation.

Lilith turned to her boss. 'Why didn't you authorise my overtime?'

'Overtime is payable at the line manager's discretion.'

'I know, but you've never refused to authorise it before.'

'You've never been repeatedly late before.'

'That's an entirely separate issue.'

'I disagree. You cannot expect the company to pay for extra hours when you've failed to work your regular shift hours. Perhaps if you arrived on time, you wouldn't need to work extra hours to complete your workload.'

She couldn't believe what she was hearing. 'I've been late four times. Each time by no more than a few minutes.'

'It adds up.'

'Not to eighteen hours, it doesn't, which is the overtime I've accrued this month. Overtime which you asked me to do, if you remember, to ensure we met the deadline for the Karen Millen order.'

'An order we would've fulfilled on time if you'd completed your regular hours.'

'That's not true.'

'Are you accusing me of lying?' His gaze narrowed, waiting for her answer.

She needed to tread carefully. She didn't want to put her promotion chances at risk. 'No, but I think I've a right to challenge why I haven't been paid for the extra hours I worked.'

'And I have the right to refuse paying for those extra hours.' He checked his watch. 'It's now thirteen minutes past your shift start time and I've yet to see any work being done. And you wonder why you don't get paid?'

He turned to walk off, but then paused. 'By the way, the team leader role—'

She mentally crossed her fingers. 'Did I get it?'

'Unfortunately not.' He walked off.

'Why not?' she called after him.

He ignored her.

A wave of rage raced up her spine. She was the obvious person for the role. She was experienced and dedicated. There was no one better suited. Why hadn't she got it?

Dottie appeared by her side with a takeaway carton and a coffee. 'Here, get this down you. But don't let Keith catch you, you know what he's like about consuming beverages at workstations.'

But Lilith was too angry to drink. 'I didn't get the team leader role.'

Dottie looked shocked. 'Why not?'

'He gave it to his son, that's why not,' Taye said, coming over. 'I just overheard Barbara from Accounts talking about it.'

'That little twit?' Dottie looked outraged. 'He doesn't know a tuck from a dart.'

Lilith clenched her fists, fighting the urge to scream. 'He gave the promotion to his son? A twenty-year-old kid who's been here less than a year?'

Taye shrugged. 'Looks that way.' He touched her arm. 'You okay?'

'No.' She shook her head. 'I'm not.' She fumbled to untie her tabard, indignation burning within her.

Taye's eyes grew wide. 'What are you doing?'

'Quitting,' she said, screwing the tabard into a ball.

'Is that wise?' Dottie glanced around, no doubt checking Keith was out of sight while they tried to talk their friend out of making a huge mistake.

But it wasn't a mistake. It was destiny. The universe was intervening to give her the kick up the backside she needed. 'I want to be a designer.'

'I know, lovey. But you're also about to be made homeless.' Taye's arm went around her. 'This isn't the time to be quitting your job. Find a place first, get another job, then quit.'

Tears pooled in Lily's eyes. 'I can't.'

'Why not?'

'Because I'll never do it. There'll always be a reason to stay. An excuse. The voice in my head will undermine me and tell me to give it one more year, or hold out for the next promotion. But I'm never going to get that promotion, because Keith won't allow it. He's got something against me.'

'He's jealous of you,' Dottie said. 'He knows you're more skilled than him. You should be running the shop floor, and he knows it.'

'It doesn't matter what the reason is. I don't want to be shop steward, or team leader, or even continue as a pattern-cutter. I've stayed here because it suited me. It was close to home, it allowed me to care for Granddad. It didn't push me out of my comfort zone. But my life has changed. I need to change, too.' She searched her friends' faces. 'Do you honestly think I should stay here?'

Dottie and Taye exchanged a look, then shook their heads.

'Me neither.' Lily threw her tabard on the table. 'This morning I felt trapped. I was consumed by grief, frozen into carrying on with my sadness, unwilling to be challenged. Scared to try something new. But this has reminded me that I want more. I *need* more.'

'But wouldn't it be better to have a plan in place first?' Dottie rubbed her chest. 'This is all so sudden.'

Lilith shook her head. 'Not really. I've wanted this for ever, I've just never been able to act on it before. But now I can. There's nothing stopping me. And I *do* have a plan. I'm going to spend the weekend writing my CV and sending out samples of my work in the hope someone is willing to offer me an apprenticeship.'

Taye looked unsure. 'So not a great plan?'

She lifted her chin, aiming for an air of defiance. 'I disagree. I think it's an excellent plan… and so does Lily.'

'Lily?' Taye looked confused. 'Who's Lily?'

'Me,' she said. And then overcome with the moment, she climbed onto a stool and addressed the whole room. 'I am Lily! And I am going to be a costume designer!'

If she expected rapturous applause, it didn't come. Instead, she was met with a sea of puzzled expressions and complete silence.

Oh, well. She didn't need anyone else to believe in her. She believed in herself.

Kind of.

Chapter Nine

Sunday, 2 May

As Sunday mornings went, it was pretty typical. The bells from the local Windlesham church were ringing to announce the start of morning service. The low hum of lawn mowers hung in the air like swarms of bees invading the village, and the faint waft of Sunday roasts drifted in through the open bedroom window, merging with the heady scent of cut grass.

Will liked the outdoors. Relaxing in the garden with an occasional glass of wine was as pleasurable as travelling to exciting destinations abroad. Whether it was savouring the tranquillity of a quaint English village, partying in a bustling city centre, or exploring a remote area of conservation, there was always something to enjoy.

His business was thriving. It had been for a few years, so eighteen months ago he'd been able to reward the fruits of his labour by buying an idyllic cottage nestled in a quiet country lane in picturesque Surrey. He'd been won over by the original inglenook fireplace, low-beamed ceilings and thatched roof. Sara would have loved it. She'd always preferred vintage to modern. Shame she'd never got to experience the delights of village life.

The cottage had cost a fortune, mortgaging him up to the hilt. But it was worth it on days like today. Compensation for the long hours he worked, the sacrifices he made. Recompense for the sadness he'd experienced in his life.

It was just disappointing that his daughter didn't seem as happy as he'd like her to be.

Poppy blew on his pink nails. 'Pretty,' she said, admiring her handiwork.

Having his nails painted wasn't high on his list of enjoyable pastimes, but who else could Poppy practise on? She had no siblings, no mother, and rarely wanted to join her friends on a playdate. Will had been tied up with work all week, and most of yesterday, too, so spending a few hours with his daughter playing dress-up seemed like the least he could do.

'Nanny and Granddad will be here soon. Aunty Gemma and Zac, too,' he said, as Poppy untwisted a tube of red lipstick. 'Are you excited to see them?'

She nodded, aiming for his lips with the lipstick.

He braced himself. He was already wearing blue eyeshadow and pink blusher. He hadn't shaved this morning, so the blusher made him look like he had a rash, rather than glowing healthy cheeks.

Poppy's face was a picture of concentration as she applied the colour to his lips.

He couldn't help smiling.

She was wearing a pale blue top, denim skirt and pink trainers, the colour a match for her bedroom. His daughter might be shy, but her taste in decor was bold and beautiful. Two of the walls were painted pale pink, two dark pink. She'd chosen white voile curtains, matching the canopy above her bed. A huge fluffy rug covered the wooden flooring. Cuddly toys lined her bed, the shelving was packed with colouring books, reading books and a large photo of Colin the Rabbit.

Although his daughter was traditionally girlie when it came to decorating her room, she bucked conformity when it came to naming pets. Her tortoise was called Pete, and the frogs in the pond were Brian and Roger. Her wish was to one day own a dachshund named Doris. So far, Will had resisted getting her one – his work hours weren't conducive to caring for a dog – but he knew it was only a matter of time before she wore him down.

Next to the photo of Colin was a photo of her mum. It was natural for Poppy to want a reminder of her mummy, and he'd never shirked away from talking about Sara when Poppy asked, even if it was painful. He'd kept the stories light and funny, focusing on the good times they'd shared and how much Sara had loved Poppy. But it was hard when he was frequently asked, 'why did Mummy die?' Will had always answered Poppy honestly, as the grief counsellor had instructed him too, but the words never got any easier to say.

Now, Poppy reached over to blot his lips with a tissue. The texture of the lipstick was horrible, thick and creamy. Not like Lily's lipstick, which he hadn't minded tasting at all.

Thoughts of Lily twisted his gut. Partly, because he felt guilty for yearning after another woman when his dead wife was smiling at him from the bookshelf. But mostly because he still missed Lily. He should have fought harder. Persuaded her to give him her contact details before they parted. Convinced her somehow that their brief holiday fling didn't have to end, that it had the potential to develop into something meaningful.

Instead, he'd let her walk away. He hadn't contradicted her when she'd said she didn't want an 'emotional farewell' and had wimped out. Why hadn't he admitted that he'd fallen for her? Told her that he'd just experienced the most amazing two weeks of his recent life and he wanted to continue seeing her?

Because he'd bottled it. That's why.

He didn't trust what he was feeling was real. It couldn't be. It wasn't logical or sensible. It was a fling. A holiday *romance*. No way was it the 'real thing'. How could it be after just two weeks?

There hadn't been anyone serious since Sara. He hadn't wanted there to be. Relationships were painful and complicated, and would mess with his calm orderly life. Letting someone else close would tip the balance and shatter the fragile dynamic between him and his daughter, and create a ripple that would create mayhem and disorder.

No, walking away was the right thing to do.

So why was he still yearning after her? Why was he panicked at the thought of never seeing Lily again? Why was he constantly imagining what his life might look like with her in it?

It didn't make sense.

'Finished!' Poppy startled him from his thoughts.

He blinked away thoughts of Lily and smiled at his daughter. 'How do I look?'

'Weird,' she said, scrunching up her face. 'Scary.'

He glanced into the full-length mirror attached to the wardrobe. Scary was an understatement. He looked like a cross between a bad drag queen and a psychotic clown.

'It's better than last time,' he said, searching for a positive. 'Your make-up's fine, it's me that's the problem. I'm a terrible model.'

'True,' she said, making him laugh.

He stood up, his knees stiff from sitting on the low stool. 'Cousin Zac will be here soon. You can practise on him. He looks better in make-up than I do.'

'Will you leave the make-up on so I can show Zac? He can tell me what I did wrong?'

'No, sweetie. There's no way I'm hosting a family BBQ looking like this.' He loved his daughter, but he drew the line at public humiliation.

She looked dejected.

He tugged gently on her French plait. Braiding hair was another skill he'd acquired since becoming a single dad. His talents were endless. 'Come on, everyone will be arriving soon. Are you going to help me set the table outside?'

'I guess.' With a sigh, she packed away her make-up box and tucked it inside the cupboard.

It was strange, really. He'd expected her to start experimenting with make-up herself at some point, but she showed no signs of being obsessed with her appearance, unlike some of her friends, who already looked like miniature women. He guessed he should feel grateful. He couldn't imagine it was going to be an easy situation to deal with.

He went into the bathroom and washed his face, scrubbing at his eyes, lips and cheeks, trying to remove all traces of make-up. After he'd dried his face and checked he hadn't missed anything, he headed downstairs. The doorbell rang just as he reached the hallway. He opened the front door to discover his brother-in-law looking grim.

'Hi Chris.' Will glanced over to where his sister and nephew were exiting the family's silver SUV. 'Anything wrong?'

'*I'm* fine.' His brother-in-law's tone indicated it was everyone else who was the problem. He handed over a bottle of expensive wine and stepped into the hallway, heading for the kitchen. 'I assume we're eating in the garden?'

'That's where BBQs are normally held,' Will called after him. He was hardly going to have a BBQ inside, was he?

Gemma arrived at the doorway, Zac a few paces behind.

His sister kissed his cheek. She was dressed in jodhpurs, ankle boots and a checked shirt, the archetypal country-casual attire. 'The Happy Hamiltons have arrived,' she said, her tone dripping with sarcasm. 'Are Mum and Dad here yet?'

'Not yet. What's up with Chris?' He stood back to allow his sister inside.

'The usual.' She nodded to a dejected-looking Zac. 'He's been on at Zac again.'

'What about?'

'His clothes. His piercings. His tattoos. His chosen career—'

'What's wrong with his career?'

'It's not for boys, apparently,' Zac said, joining his mum in the hallway. 'I'm a disgrace to the Hamilton name.'

Gemma sighed. 'Your father never called you a disgrace.'

'Yes, he did. He just never said the words.' Zac gave his uncle a half-hearted grin. 'Nice nails. What's for lunch?'

Will glanced at his hands. Shit. He'd forgotten to remove the nail polish. 'Burgers, sausages and chicken kebabs.'

'Sounds cool. Where's Poppy?'

'Upstairs. Can you get her for me?'

'Sure.' Zac ambled upstairs, his lithe frame accentuated by tight black jeans and a slim fit T-shirt. He wore a battered leather jacket and his black hair was styled into a quiff, while his guy-liner made his blue eyes pop. He was a good-looking lad, striking. Talented, too. Shame his father couldn't see that.

Gemma inspected his nails. 'Poppy?'

'No, I did them myself,' he said, rolling his eyes. 'Of course it was Poppy!'

'All right, keep your hair on. Someone's grumpy this morning.'

'I wasn't until you arrived.'

'Oh, please. You've been grumpy since you got back from your holiday.' He startled. Had he? 'For someone who claims they had a great time, you'd never know it by your mood. What's wrong?'

'Nothing's wrong,' he said, a tad too defensively. 'Holiday blues, probably. Work hasn't been easy since I got back.'

'It never is. You don't normally let it get to you.' She tapped his chest. 'What gives, Bro?'

'Nothing. And don't call me Bro. You're not a US rapper. You're from Surrey.'

'Just trying to stay down with the kids.' She raised her hand for a high five.

He ignored her. 'Well don't. It's embarrassing.'

Zac appeared downstairs.

'Where's Poppy?'

'Playing with her dolls. She didn't want to come down.'

Gemma tutted. 'You need to fetch her, Will. You mustn't indulge her by allowing her to stay isolated so much.'

'Yes, thank you,' he snapped. 'I'm well aware of that.'

Gemma raised her hands. 'I'm just saying.'

'Well, don't.' He didn't need his sister pointing out his shortcomings.

'Chill, guys. I'll fetch her, okay?' Zac ran upstairs, clearly unwilling to get embroiled in another family argument.

Will was saved from further criticism on his parenting skills by his parents' car pulling into the driveway.

He used it as an excuse to escape Gemma and went out to help his dad carry in the pasta salads his mum had prepared.

'Hi, Mum. Hi, Dad.' He kissed them both. They were dressed in their Sunday church best. 'How are you both?'

'Good, thanks.' His dad closed the car boot.

'Are you okay, love?' His mum handed him two large bowls. 'You look tired. Are you sleeping okay?'

'I'm sleeping fine,' he lied.

'And Poppy?'

'She's fine too.' He forced a smile. 'Head through to the garden. The rest of the clan have just arrived.'

Will followed them into the house, pleased to note that his daughter had now emerged from her bedroom. She greeted her grandparents with a hug, and then ran off to play with Colin the Rabbit. Not exactly sociable, but at least she was outdoors with everyone.

Zac joined Poppy at the end of the garden, and made an effort to keep his little cousin amused. He was a good lad.

Chris was by the BBQ. He'd lifted the lid and was fiddling with the controls, eager to take charge of the cooking. The archetypal control freak.

Will headed over. 'You're my guest, Chris. I don't expect you to cook.'

'I don't mind.' By which Will knew that Chris meant: I'd rather do it myself, so it gets done properly.

But Will wasn't in the mood to pander to his brother-in-law's pedantic standards when it came to barbequing. 'Why don't you open the wine?' he said, engineering an excuse to keep Chris out of his hair while he cooked. 'There's a bottle opener on the table.'

Chris reluctantly stepped away from the BBQ. 'Zac tells me you've offered him work on another project?'

'That's right.' Will fired up the gas BBQ. 'Should be a good one.'

Chris didn't look convinced. 'A summer fête?'

Only Chris could refer to The Royal Windsor Festival as a 'fête'. 'It's a celebration of nine hundred years of Royal residency at Windsor Castle,' Will replied, as he adjusted the heat on the BBQ. 'It's a huge project. Our biggest to date. We've had to overcome competition from a dozen other companies to win the contract. Arranging an entire festival is no mean feat and we're taking on dozens of extra staff – caterers, carpenters, security, you name it. Not to mention an independent film production company. Zac's in charge of hair and make-up for the actors involved in the tour guide film. This is a big step up for him. Me, too.'

'Right.' Chris glanced in Zac's direction. 'Not my cup of tea. But my son seems keen enough.'

Poor Zac. Will wondered how the kid felt about being the source of such disapproval. 'It's good to know he's excited about the project. Zac's an essential part of the team. We're lucky to have him.'

Chris decorked the bottle. 'You don't need to pacify me.'

Will frowned. 'What makes you think I'm doing that?'

'You only hire Zac because he's family. Let's not pretend it's for any other reason. Maybe if you didn't encourage him to mess about with all this hair and make-up stuff, he'd see that he needs a proper career. One in which he'll be respected and valued. And one that enables him to earn a decent wage.'

Will was dumbfounded. 'You think I only hire Zac because he's family?'

Chris's eyes searched out Gemma, who was setting the table with her mum. 'Well, don't you?'

Did his brother-in-law think that's why he hired Gemma, too? 'Chris, TaylorMade Events is a very successful business.'

'I know that.'

'And it's because of the people we have on board working for us… which includes Gemma and Zac.'

Chris nodded. 'It's good for Gemma to have an interest, a side project to keep her occupied.'

'A side project?' Was this guy for real? Will picked up a glass and held it out so Chris could pour him some much-needed wine. 'Gemma is our Finance Director.'

'I know that.'

'You make her sound like a part-time payroll clerk.'

'I didn't mean it like that.' Chris wiped the bottle's rim with a piece of kitchen towel.

'Good. Because she's an integral part of the company. A key player. It's a highly demanding role, in which she excels.'

Chris looked taken aback. 'Well, good.'

'Too right.' Will took a slug of wine, craving the alcohol. 'And Zac is proving himself to be professional, reliable and willing to put in the hours. So don't for a minute think I cut him any slack because he's 'family'. He's expected to work as hard as everyone else, and he does. That's why I hire him, no other reason.'

'Well, that's good.'

'And as for earning a decent salary? Zac's going to be in high demand soon. I'll struggle to afford him.'

Chris looked sceptical. 'Really?'

'Really. Now excuse me, I need to fetch the meat from the kitchen.' Will walked off, incredulous at the cluelessness of his brother-in-law. How the hell his sister put up with such patronising crap, he didn't know.

But his hassles were far from over. His mum collared him in the kitchen the moment he stepped through the doorway.

'Will, love, have you given any more thought to Poppy joining the country club? Your father and I are more than happy to pay for her membership.' She removed a stack of cutlery from the drawer.

Not this again. 'That's a kind offer, Mum, but Poppy isn't keen.'

'We think it would be good for her,' she continued, as if he hadn't spoken. 'They have all sorts of activities for youngsters. Tennis. Horseriding. Badminton. Even dance classes. I'm sure she'd love to do dance. Most girls her age do.'

He opened the fridge door and removed the trays of meat. 'Poppy isn't most girls.'

'And why is that?'

He stopped to look at her. 'I beg your pardon?'

Her expression softened. 'We don't mean to be critical, love. You do a great job with her, but she needs to get out more.' She moved towards him, her expression all motherly and determined. 'You know, socialise with other kids. Not be so introverted.'

He banged the trays onto the kitchen island. 'You think I don't know that?'

'Well, yes, but—'

'But what?' He was tired of everyone constantly offering an opinion.

'Sometimes children need guidance from their parents.'

'Meaning?'

His mum lowered her voice. 'She might need a little push.'

He tried to control the anger brewing inside him. 'I'm not going to force my daughter to do something she doesn't want to do, Mum.'

Her cheeks flushed. 'Oh, dear, I'm not expressing this very well. I didn't mean *force*. I meant, encourage.'

'It's the same thing.' He moved away. They were on opposite sides of the island. Battle lines drawn.

'No, it isn't.' He was subjected to a 'you're being unreasonable' look. 'Poppy didn't want to go on that camp trip, did she? But you managed to persuade her and look how much fun she had.'

Will rubbed his forehead. 'I didn't *persuade* her into going, I just allayed her fears about going. There's a difference. It was her decision to go. Hers alone. And if she hadn't wanted to go, I wouldn't have forced her.'

'Well, maybe in future you need to be more assertive.' His mother moved to his side of the island. 'Bring her along to the country club one Sunday. Show her there's nothing to be afraid of.'

'Mum, I know you mean well, but I know what I'm doing. It would be great if Poppy had better confidence and wanted to do more things, but I'm not going to force her. I'm sure she'll start doing things as she gets older, and when she does, she'll have my full support. Until then, I'm not going to push it. If she says no to something, then no it is.'

'We think you're making a mistake.'

'Who is this "we"?'

'Me, your dad… and Gemma.'

'Great.' He backed away. 'Lovely to have the support of my family.'

'Will, please.' She reached for him. 'Don't take it like that. We're only trying to help.'

'If you want to help, then stop criticising my every decision.'

'We don't, darling. We think you're doing an amazing job…' she trailed off, a silent 'but' hanging in the air.

'But?'

'Well… it's hard for a young girl to be without a mother.'

His anger spilled over. 'You think I don't know that? I'm reminded of it every bloody day.'

'Poppy's a sensitive girl. She's not strong-willed and self-sufficient like you or Gemma were as kids, she needs a guiding hand.'

'And she gets one,' he snapped.

His mum's expression turned disapproving. 'Be honest, love. You work long hours, you're not at home as much as she needs. We do our best to help out with childcare, but it's not ideal.'

He couldn't believe what he was hearing. 'So now I neglect my daughter?'

'Stop twisting my words. You have to work, of course you do, but Poppy needs more in her life. Something to occupy her while you're out earning. Something that will help her grow in confidence and become more sociable.'

His phone rang.

He'd never been more grateful in his life. The interruption prevented him from falling out big time with his mother. Something he really didn't want to do, but was looking increasingly likely.

He headed into the hallway, away from his disappointed-looking mother. 'Will Taylor,' he snapped into the phone.

'Hi, Will. It's Frankie Roberts. Sorry to disturb you on a Sunday.'

'No worries. Is there a problem?' Frankie was one of his project managers. A gregarious woman with big ginger hair and an equally big laugh.

'I've had a call from Nina Munford's husband. She's been taken into hospital. Suspected burst appendix.'

'Christ.' Will closed his study door behind him. 'Is she okay?'

'They hope so, but she's not going to be available for the festival. I thought you should know asap.'

Shit. And they were due to start filming next month. He rubbed his forehead. 'Thanks, Frankie. I appreciate you letting me know.'

'Do you need me to do anything?'

'No, don't worry. I'll find a replacement. Give my love to Nina, if you see her. I hope she makes a speedy recovery.'

'Will do, boss. Sorry to be the bearer of bad news.'

'It's not your fault. I appreciate the call.'

'See you at the prep meeting tomorrow?'

'Looking forward to it.' Will ended the call, struggling to contain his frustration.

Where the bloody hell was he going to find an experienced costume designer at such short notice? Talented designers were booked months in advance. Years, even. There wouldn't be anyone available. He was screwed.

He kicked the wastepaper bin, toppling it over. What a day it was turning out to be. His brother-in-law had accused him of nepotism. His parents and sister thought he was a crap parent. And now he was short of a costume designer for the biggest event of his career.

He slumped into his office chair, letting his head drop onto the desk. What the hell was he going to do?

Could they hire the costumes? No, his whole pitch had been based on recreating historical authenticity and he'd won over the clients with the promise of a set of bespoke designs. One-offs, emulating the couture fashions of the various periods.

And then he sat upright, struck by an idea.

He knew exactly what he was going to do.

He was going to hunt down Lily Monroe and see if he could beg her into helping him out. She was a costume designer, after all. Making one-offs was her speciality.

She might come to his rescue. Save his project and dig him out of a hole.

There was the minor issue of him having lied to her about his personal life, but he could rectify that. He'd come clean and confess the truth.

She'd understand. At least, he hoped she would. They could start afresh and put any misunderstandings behind them.

And besides, this was a business arrangement. It wasn't personal. There was nothing romantic about them working together, he was hiring her expertise. There was

no other motivation for wanting to contact her, just the
need for her professional services.

Right.

Who the hell was he kidding?

Chapter Ten

Six weeks later...

Lily was regretting her decision not to hire a taxi. It had seemed wasteful to pay for a lift when her lodgings were only a ten-minute walk from the station, but what the helpful train guard at Riverside Station had omitted to mention was that the walk was entirely uphill, and involved wheeling her suitcase over bumpy centuries old cobbles.

She stopped to catch her breath and wiped her forehead with her sleeve. It was a warm June day. The bright sunlight added to the trials of dragging her luggage while trying to follow the directions on her phone.

Continue walking past the castle, Google Maps instructed. Castle? What castle?

She glanced up.

Oh, that castle. Where had that sprung from?

Looming above her was Windsor Castle. A huge grey construction with grand turrets and a sweeping lawn where a moat would have once been. It dominated the view, mounted on a hill, overlooking the town below. And to think she'd nearly missed it.

She continued uphill, her shoulders aching from the weight of her rucksack and from struggling to carry the large bin bag filled with her clothes.

Heading for the pedestrian-only area of the town adjacent to the castle, Lily still couldn't believe this was going to be her home for the next two months. It was beyond surreal. A world away from her family home in Haringey.

When she'd finally left the local authority flat, it had looked so forlorn minus her grandparents' belongings. Like all the life had been sucked out of it, leaving only faded wallpaper marks and carpet dents where the furniture had once been. The items she couldn't bear to part with she'd put into storage. The rest had gone to charity shops. All that was left of her life had fitted into a large bin-liner, a rucksack, and one suitcase... which she was currently lugging up a steep hill. Such was her life.

Locking the flat's door for the final time and walking away had been one of the hardest thing she'd ever had to do. It was brutal, like reliving the loss all over again. Feelings which were only magnified by being waved off by her tearful neighbours and handing over the keys to the housing officer.

But it was done now, and hopefully this was the start of phase two of her life.

Lily walked past the giant bronze statue of Queen Victoria guarding the entrance to the castle. The stately monarch looked ominous and foreboding with her stern expression and sceptre held aloft. Then the lanes narrowed and the cobbled stones again made walking hard work. It was the heart of the tourist area, the tall, narrow buildings centuries old and converted into cafes serving cream teas and antique shops selling knick-knacks and royal souvenirs.

Dainty tables and chairs were arranged outside the cafes, squashed full of visitors enjoying a Sunday outing.

Vibrant hanging baskets bursting with colour hung from the period awnings above. It was a fascinating sight.

Lily tried to hear Google Maps above the bustle of the busy lanes as she manoeuvred her luggage through the narrow gaps in the crowd, apologising when her suitcase caught on chair legs.

Finally, the app announced she had *reached her destination*.

She stopped walking and checked the address. *This* was where she was staying?

Ahead was The Crooked House Tea Rooms, an aptly named three-storey building with a definite lean to the left. At street level it housed an olde-worlde cafe with a quaint and welcoming bay window shop front. Above, was a second storey dominated by a sash window, and above that was a small attic window. It looked quirky, charming and very unstable.

But this was her new home for the next two months. How her life had shifted in such a short space of time.

Just six weeks ago, she was still working at Clothing Connexions. That was before she'd dramatically quit her job and announced to her stunned colleagues that she was 'off to seek her fortune'. A move that had felt incredibly foolish in the weeks that had followed.

She'd subsequently registered with numerous film and TV recruitment agencies and sent out her CV to a host of companies, only to be bombarded with a stream of rejections and 'no, thank you' replies. It was disheartening. It wasn't like she was looking to get paid. She just wanted the chance to work alongside an experienced designer to see what the role entailed.

But it turned out a load of other people wanted the same thing. Young designers straight out of college, who'd happily work an unpaid internship if it meant they got their big break. Lily had nothing to offer, other than a decade's worth of experience working in a clothing factory. Not exactly impressive stuff.

All the enthusiasm that had buoyed her to take a leap of faith had deserted her. She now felt idiotic for quitting her job. She should have listened to her colleagues and secured another role first. And although she didn't miss her job, or her draconian boss, she did miss her friends. Life without work or her grandparents had suddenly become a very lonely place.

But just when she'd resigned herself to downgrading her expectations and taking another factory job, she'd received a phone call from one of the recruitment agencies she'd registered with offering her a two-month contract on a small tour guide film soon to begin shooting in Windsor. She couldn't believe it. It was perfect. They needed someone in the wardrobe department urgently, and she happened to be available. Talk about luck. Plus, the job came with accommodation. Double bonus.

She was about to head inside the wonky building, when a woman said, 'Are you part of the festival team?'

She turned to see the woman approaching. 'Err… yes, I am.'

'Excellent. So relieved you found us okay.' The woman extended her hand. 'Frankie Roberts, Senior Designer. Good to meet you.'

Lily dropped the bin bag she was holding and shook the woman's hand. 'Nice to meet you. I'm Lili— *Lily* Monroe,' she said, nearly slipping up. She was *Lily* now. She needed to get into character. And judging by the exuberance of the woman standing in front of her, the sooner she did that, the better.

Frankie Roberts wasn't that tall, but her red platform boots and mass of orange dreadlocked hair spilling from beneath her red trilby hat added to her stance, making her presence seem huge. Her black dress was adorned with embroidered flowers and expanded out from her waist like a spinning top. She looked like a creature from a different world. A mythical being. An advert for how a 'creative type' should look.

And there Lily was. Standing there wearing faded jeans, one of her gran's twin-set cardigans, and carrying her worldly goods in a bin-liner. Talk about humiliating.

Frankie gestured to the building. 'Let's get you checked in. Can I give you a hand with your luggage?'

'That's okay, I can manage.'

But Frankie was already wheeling Lily's suitcase towards the entrance.

Lily hoisted up her bin bag and followed the woman into the tea rooms. It was a cramped space filled with visitors and smelt heavenly of cake.

Frankie lifted Lily's suitcase up the narrow winding staircase as though it weighed nothing and wasn't crammed full of her belongings. 'You don't know how relieved we are to have you on board,' she said, glancing back. 'You saved the day. And I, for one, am extremely grateful. The commission from this project will pay my mortgage for a year.'

Lily was a little confused. How had she saved the day? She was an apprentice. Hardly a key role.

Frankie smiled. 'I love your cardigan. Is it vintage?'

'I guess.' If being decades old and purchased by her grandma counted as 'vintage'.

'You must be quite the savvy shopper. It's in such good condition. You'll have to tell me all your secrets. I'm always on the hunt for a vintage bargain.'

Lily figured the woman was being polite. Although Lily enjoyed making clothes, she didn't follow fashion. She liked period pieces. Fancy dress outfits. Fashions from bygone eras and extravagant costumes created for the stage and screen. But she had no interest in what was 'on trend', as Taye would say. Or what was currently being sported on the runways of Paris. Modern fashion held no appeal.

Maybe that was because unlike Taye, or Ruby from the hair salon, Lily had never worked out what her 'style' was. The closest she'd come to being 'modern' was on holiday when she'd purchased a few coordinating outfits and had used photos from *Vogue* as inspiration to design a couple of evening dresses.

But perhaps it was time to rethink that. After all, if she wanted to be taken seriously as a costume designer – even one starting out – she needed to look the part. And right at that moment, she looked more like a lowly cleaner than a member of a creative wardrobe department.

She followed Frankie up the second set of stairs. It was steeper than the last and lacking a handrail. Precarious stuff.

'You've been allocated the attic room,' Frankie said, seemingly unfazed by the perilous stairway. 'I hope that's okay?'

'It's absolutely fine. I don't mind where I stay.'

Frankie stopped at the top and opened the door. 'Rental prices in this area are astronomical. I'm afraid it's quite basic.'

'Honestly, it's fine. I still can't believe my rent is being covered.'

Frankie looked confused. 'Why wouldn't we cover your rent?'

Lily raised her eyebrows. Err... because she was an apprentice? Working on an unpaid internship?

At least, she assumed it was unpaid. Salary hadn't been mentioned so far, which had to mean she was working for free. But that was okay. She just needed the experience. And if her rent was being covered, then she wouldn't have to dip into her nest egg much. She was more than happy with the arrangement.

Frankie headed into the room. 'Anyway, you might want to check out the room before you get too grateful.'

Lily followed her, figuring anything was better than crashing on a mate's sofa.

And then she saw the space. It was a delightful box room with a slanted ceiling and a wide sash window. A single bed was shoved into the corner, next to a chest of drawers. Net curtains framed the window and vase of yellow sunflowers rested on the window ledge.

'It's perfect,' she said, admiring the soft white walls and low-beamed ceiling.

'It is?'

'Really. It's gorgeous.'

Frankie didn't look convinced. 'Whatever you say.'

Maybe Frankie was used to grander dwellings, but Lily had spent her entire life in a local authority flat. And she'd spent the last week sleeping on Taye's sofa. By comparison, this place was positively palatial. And it overlooked a castle, for goodness sake. How many places could boast that?

'There's a bathroom on the lower floor. Breakfast in the cafe is included in the rent, but no other meals.' Frankie looked apologetic. 'Sorry.'

But Lily wasn't upset. Far from it. She didn't have to pay for breakfast. Result. 'No problem.'

'The landlady will make you up a packed lunch, if you ask, as long as you let her know the night before. We don't get a formal lunchbreak,' she said, heading for the door. 'You know how it is on these projects. Crazy hours.'

Actually, she didn't, but she was here to learn. 'Thanks for the heads-up.'

'I'll leave you to get unpacked. Come and join us at The Carpenters Arms when you're done. It's just across the lane. You can't miss it.'

'What, now?' Lily inwardly cringed. As if she didn't already appear clueless enough, she was now resistant to daytime drinking. But she was exhausted from a week sleeping on a lumpy sofa and she just wanted to rest up and have an early night. 'I hadn't planned on going out tonight. Long journey, and all that. I don't want to risk a hangover on my first day of filming.'

Frankie laughed. 'God, I don't function *without* a hangover. It won't be a late one, I promise. And it'll be good for you to meet the team ahead of tomorrow.' She smiled. 'We can bond over Mojitos. I want to hear all about your design career.'

A conversation that wouldn't take long. Lily's design career had yet to start.

But that was about to change. As of tomorrow, she could officially class herself as an apprentice designer. No longer a lowly pattern-cutter working in factory, but someone working on a real project. It was beyond exciting. And scary. And petrifyingly unknown.

'Okay, one drink.'

'Excellent. See you there.'

Left alone, Lily opened her suitcase and unearthed her sewing machine and the ancient iPad she'd brought with her from Haringey. She didn't have many belongings with her, so the lack of cupboard space wasn't a problem. And it wasn't like she'd be in here much. She was due on set at seven a.m. tomorrow, and she anticipated long days ahead of her.

Not that she minded. This was the start of her dream career. It might be baby steps, but she was headed in the right direction. She didn't even mind what tasks she'd be excepted to do. She was here as an apprentice after all. She'd happily make tea, sew hems, and reattach buttons. Anything, as long as she got to see how it all worked on set. Maybe if she impressed them enough they would offer her a decent reference. Or work on another project.

But she was getting ahead of herself. She needed to keep her head down, work hard, and apply herself. There was no room for pride. Lily was starting at the bottom and she was okay with that.

Half an hour later, she was unpacked. Her clothes were in the chest of drawers, the photos of her grandparents were placed on top, and she'd made up the bed.

She thought about changing outfits, but what would she put on? Her wardrobe consisted of comfortable jeans and simple tops. Not exactly a good advert for a costume designer. Maybe she would knock up a few items during her evenings so she had something more in keeping to wear. Nothing as bold as the outfits she'd worn on holiday, but something a little livelier than her current insipid wardrobe. Good plan.

For now, she brushed her hair and applied lip gloss. Not great, but suitable for an afternoon drink in a pub.

She headed down the two flights of stairs and out through the tea rooms on to the cobbled lane. A few of the souvenir shops had closed for the day, but the cafes were still busy. Behind her, the castle glowed in the late afternoon sunlight, the grey turrets silhouetted against the pale blue sky.

Ahead was The Carpenters Arms, a traditional British pub housed in an attractive period building. The tables outside were full, a bustle of noise and chatter. She couldn't see Frankie, so Lily headed inside. She wasn't likely to miss the woman, not with her abundance of bright orange hair.

Pushing open the door, she was immediately hit by more noise. The interior decor was classy, with wooden flooring, dark grey walls and chandelier lighting. Bodies filled the bar and surrounding tables. It looked like a popular haunt.

She made her way through the crowd, but there was no sign of Frankie.

The doors at the back were open, leading to an enclosed courtyard, surrounded with large potted ferns. The middle was filled with seating and even more drinkers.

She was about to head inside, when a woman shouted, '*Will!*'

Lily instantly flinched.

Memories of her time in the Caribbean came flooding back. Like an unstoppable wave, her brain filled with images of a handsome man with blue-grey eyes and a dimpled chin.

But she shoved the thought away. That was the last thing she needed. She'd made a concerted effort of late to forget all about Will Taylor. He was consigned to the past. No longer a factor in her thinking. He was relegated to the compartment of her brain reserved for 'what might have been'.

Yeah, right. Who was she kidding? He crept into her thoughts all the time, despite her best efforts.

But it wasn't likely to be the same Will, was it? A lot of men had the name 'Will'. It was common enough. The chances of it being him were non-existent.

It didn't stop her turning around, though. Just to be sure. To put her mind at rest.

A man was standing in front of her. The sun was directly behind him, so she couldn't see his face. Even so, something shifted inside her. There was a stirring sense of familiarity.

Or was it foreboding?

Either way, her nerve endings jumped to life, screaming at her to run. Escape. Disappear before…

'Lily…? Is that *you*?'

Oh, hell.

She jerked backwards as if she'd been tasered. Momentum sent her reeling, and she tripped on a chair, toppled backwards and landed with a heavy thud on the courtyard floor.

Pain radiated up her spine and into her elbow, but that paled into insignificance by the torment raging in her head.

Will Taylor was here? In Windsor? At the same pub as her?

It couldn't be. It wasn't logical. Or rational. Or plausible. She'd imagined it. It was a figment of her mind. An hallucination. Brought on by the stress of losing her job, leaving home, and by not sleeping properly.

But then he was there. Right in front of her. His face fully in focus. His light-brown hair moving in the breeze. It was most definitely him.

'Lily, are you okay?' His grey-blue eyes locked on hers, intense and searching. 'Are you hurt? Can you stand?'

She wasn't hurt, but she was far from okay.

And as for standing? Her legs were never likely to work again. She was staring into the eyes of a man she never expected to see again.

Will Taylor.

The man she'd had a holiday fling with.

The man she'd lied to about being a costume designer…

Holy. Crap.

Her brain skidded to a halt as realisation hit.

Oh, God, no. Please, no.

And then she was being lifted up. By a woman at one side, Will the other.

She risked a glance and realised he didn't look anywhere near as surprised to see her as she was to see him. Which set off a whole host of alarm bells in her head.

It was too much to hope this was a crazy coincidence. Serendipity or whatnot. Or just plain bad luck. This was an ambush. Strategic entrapment.

'Wh… what are you doing here?' she managed to say.

'Having a drink with the team before we start filming tomorrow,' he said, holding her steady. 'I wasn't expecting to see you today, though.'

So he was expecting to see her then?

'Have you just arrived?' He studied her face. 'Is your room okay? Can I get you a drink?'

Oh, God. What was happening?

She tried to formulate her thoughts. There was nothing in the brief information she'd been given by the agency to indicate this project had anything to do with Will's events company. If it had, she'd have run a mile.

'I… I was told this was a SmartFilm production,' she said, her voice wavering.

'It is.' He hadn't let go her of arm, the warmth of his touch a distraction she could do without. 'I hired the film company to produce the tour guide film.'

'Right.' She tried to steady her breathing. 'I had no idea you'd be involved.'

He looked sheepish. 'Surprise.'

Surprise…?

She had another word for it.

The woman who'd helped her up was looking at Will in a strange way. 'Is anyone going to introduce me? You clearly know each other, but I've not had the pleasure.'

Will blinked as if he'd forgotten the woman was standing there. 'Right. Sorry, of course.' He smiled. 'Lily, this is my sister, Gemma. She's the company's finance director.'

His sister? This was getting worse by the second.

The woman held out her hand. 'Gemma Hamilton, pleased to meet you.' She exuded confidence, her voice assertive. Her eyes were as intense as her brother's. Added to this was her square jaw, no-nonsense smart-casual jacket and unwavering gaze. All in all, quite an intimidating package.

Lily shook Gemma's hand, trying to hide her wince when her elbow complained. 'You, too.'

'And this is Lily Monroe,' Will said to his sister. 'Our new costume designer.'

Costume designer?

The world stilled.

It took a few seconds for the words to reach her brain.

She was the costume designer? Not an apprentice? Not here on an internship? *She* was expected to be head honcho? The person in charge. Knowledgeable. Experienced... All of which, she most certainly wasn't.

Blood drained from her head faster than a F1 car accelerating from the starting grid.

'Lily's a last-minute replacement for Nina,' Will said to his sister. 'She's a very experienced designer. We were lucky to get her at such short notice.'

The world had gone into a spin.

The potted plants lining the courtyard began to blur, whizzing around as if caught in a sudden whirlwind.

This was a disaster. Worse. It was a catastrophe.

What the hell was she going to do?

'I... I think there's been some misunderstanding,' she said, struggling for breath. 'I didn't realise I was undertaking the role of costume designer for the film.'

Will looked confused. 'You didn't?'

'No... I... I thought I was being taken on as an... as an—' she trailed off.

She could hardly say 'apprentice', could she? She'd told him she was a designer. It wouldn't make sense for her to take an unpaid internship. Not with her supposed experience. Oh, hell.

'As... as an... assistant,' she said, trying to rally her flagging brain.

He laughed, a sound she hadn't heard for several months. 'Well, that would be a waste of your talents, wouldn't it?' The smile on his face was laced with sincerity. 'Don't worry, you're in complete control. The team will support you in any way they can. Frankie is a very experienced project manager. She's overseen this kind of work loads of times.'

Not what she wanted to hear.

There was no way she could get way with this. She'd have to come clean.

But then she'd miss out on her opportunity to gain some work experience.

She needed to think, but her brain was refusing to work.

'So how do you two know each other?' Gemma looked between them, a questioning expression on her face. 'Have you worked together before?'

It was Will's turn to look uncomfortable. He glanced at his feet, unwilling to look his sister in the eye. 'We've not worked together before. We... err... met on holiday.'

Gemma's eyes widened. 'In the Caribbean?'

Will's cheeks coloured. 'We got chatting one night... and Lily mentioned she was a costume designer, so when Nina had to withdraw at short notice, I thought of Lily.'

'Convenient.' Gemma folded her arms.

Will rubbed the back of his neck. 'Luckily, one of the agencies we use had Lily's details on file, so we were able to make contact and see if she was available. And she was.' His voice sounded a little frantic. 'So here we are.'

Gemma nodded. 'Here we are.'

Lily could feel them staring at her.

She wanted the ground to open and swallow her whole.

She needed time to think. To work out a plan. To regroup and work out how she was going to deal with this. And... if she couldn't? Then she needed an escape plan.

'So what other projects have you worked on?' Gemma asked. Her question seemed genuine enough, but Lily's brain wasn't up to coping with an interrogation. Or further lying. Her deception had caused enough problems as it was.

'I'm sorry, but I'm feeling a little faint,' she said, which was entirely true. Her fall was the perfect excuse needed to engineer a way out. And boy, did she need an out.

Will took her arm. 'Why didn't you say? Do you need to see a doctor?'

'No, I'm fine. I just need to go back to my room and lie down.'

'Of course, I'll take you—'

'I'll take her,' Gemma interrupted.

'It's okay, Gemma. I can take her—'

'I've got this.' Gemma glared at her brother. 'You stay and chat to the team. I'll take Lily back to the guesthouse.'

'I'm fine to go by myself.' Lily stepped away, unwilling to be stuck between squabbling siblings. 'I appreciate your kindness, but really, I'm fine.'

'Are you sure?' Will frowned at her.

Her traitorous heart ached at the sight of his concerned expression. So much for getting over him. She was a complete mess.

'Absolutely,' she said, moving away, determined to appear composed and hide the shake in her legs. 'Enjoy the rest of your evening.'

Will watched her go. 'See you tomorrow?' he called after her, sounding to her ears a tad confused.

She couldn't blame him. She was somewhat confused herself.

She managed a weak nod, already dreading the morning.

What the hell had she done?

More importantly, what the hell was she going to do about it?

Chapter Eleven

The start of a new project was always hectic. There was nothing creative about the initial process. It was a case of managing logistics. Or, as Will called it, herding cats. He'd never had to oversee the making of a film before and it was throwing up a whole host of new conundrums. Like where to place the cast trailers? Was there enough room for the contractors? How to fit the crew and the multitude of equipment into the temporary portacabins? And why was there never a decent brew available when he needed one?

They didn't have the luxury of staggering the arrival of everything, either. Film production time was precious, so not a moment could be wasted. Everything had to be on set and ready for the start of filming. Which in this case, was tomorrow. He had one day to finish getting organised.

His phone pinged with a message. The wardrobe trailers were about to arrive. Good. One more thing he could tick off his list.

He glanced over to the portacabin to check Poppy was okay. With workshop and office space in Windsor in short supply as well as costing an arm and a leg, they'd obtained permission from the local authority to erect a temporary work hub within the grounds of Windsor Great Park. It wasn't ideal, as there was no electrical supply, so they'd had to hire generators, but the views made up for any inconvenience. Acres of greenery, with centuries old oak trees and herds of deer huddled together in the distance. Only the solitary tarmacked road cutting through the middle of the vast expanse broke through the spell of being transported back to medieval England.

The work hub was set back from the road, hidden behind a cluster of trees, so as not to blemish the tranquillity of the views. His makeshift office might be the size of a single garage, but it was a lot better than some of the projects he'd worked on. And it was big enough to accommodate his daughter, who wasn't at school today, courtesy of an inset day.

The portacabin door was open, allowing him to see inside. Poppy was hunched over the desk, fully engaged in the art project she was working on.

Satisfied she was safe, Will headed up to meet the wardrobe trailers. The costumes should have been ready by now, but they were still playing catch-up from losing their original designer through sickness.

Being so far behind in the schedule wasn't ideal, but hiccups were only to be expected on a project of this magnitude. His job was to find a solution. Like hiring Lily Monroe as a replacement designer. A solution that came with its own set of sub-issues – namely, admitting to his new designer that he had a daughter. Not something he was particularly looking forward to, but the sooner he came clean the better. He just hoped she'd forgive him for lying to her in the first place.

As he neared the road, he was met by his sister bounding across the grass, looking like Bambi on steroids.

'Ah, here you are. I've been looking for you. We need to talk.'

He kept walking, knowing why she wanted to talk to him, and wanting to avoid the conversation. 'Can't stop. Too busy.'

'Will, wait.' Gemma chased after him. 'You can't keep avoiding me.'

He could bloody well try. 'No time. The wardrobe trailers are arriving.'

'That's what I want to talk to you about.' She caught his arm. 'What's going on?'

He shrugged free from her grip. 'No idea what you mean.'

'Yes, you do.' She blocked his path, placing her hands on his chest. 'Lily Monroe.'

He avoided eye contact. 'What about her?'

'Exactly.' She pinned him with a stare. 'What about her? *Who* is she?'

'You know who she is. She's a costume designer. She came on board last minute to replace Nina. Now, if you'll excuse me.' He removed her hands and continued towards the road.

Gemma followed. 'But we know nothing about her. Or at least, I don't.'

He upped his speed and flagged down the two large white trailers turning into the park. 'What's there to know? She's a designer. We needed a designer. End of.'

'But what are her credentials?' Gemma said, running to keep up with him. 'I can't find anything about her online. There's no website. No LinkedIn profile. Who is she? What productions has she worked on? Does she come recommended? Have you applied for references?'

He glanced at his sister, who was panting in an effort to keep up. 'Jesus, Gemma. I didn't have time to do any of that. We were in a jam and I needed to find someone urgently.' He reached the first trailer and knocked on the cab door, attracting the driver's attention. 'Park in the gravel car park on the right-hand side,' he shouted at the driver, who gave him a thumbs-up and drove off.

Gemma appeared in front of him. 'But you usually vet any new contractors. Obsessively so.'

He shrugged. 'There was no time.'

Ignoring her disapproving glare, he jogged towards the second trailer and gestured for the driver to follow his mate.

Gemma was by his side again, like a persistent terrier. 'What, not even to make a quick phone call? Have you forgotten the magnitude of this project?'

He turned to her. 'Gemma, what's your point? Why are you giving me such a hard time over this?'

Her hands went to her hips. She was dressed in full business mode, a black trouser power suit and crisp white shirt. 'Because you're behaving out of character. We've made last-minute personnel changes before, but you've never skipped on the vetting process.'

'Because I never knew the people concerned before. This time I did.' His phone pinged with another message. The security guard needed clearance for someone without a pass at the front gate. Lily Monroe.

His heartrate sped up, which was immediately dulled by his sister's next comment.

'But not in a professional capacity,' she said, her face etched with concern. 'She was just some random woman you met on holiday.'

'Lily isn't random.' Will turned and walked off, heading for his portacabin.

'No?' Gemma followed him. 'What is she then?'

'She's no one.' His chest contracted with the lie. 'What I mean is… she's a business contact. We met on holiday and hung out a bit. We became friendly. We talked about our careers, and that's how I discovered she was a costume designer. I didn't think anything of it until Nina was taken ill and we needed a replacement, and then…' His eyes flitted about the open expanse of Crown land, his brain searching for a plausible explanation. 'Lily just popped into my head. It seemed like fate.'

'Fate?' Gemma sounded incredulous. 'You don't believe in fate.'

'Luck, then. You know, a solution to a problem.' Who was he trying to kid? He ignored his sister's expression and jumped up the steps to the portacabin and headed inside. 'Hey there, sweetie. You okay?'

Poppy lifted her drawing for him to see. 'It's the Arctic.' She had drawn a penguin standing outside an igloo.

'Cool. Nice work.'

Gemma joined him in the portacabin. 'Nothing more?'

It was too much to hope his sister would shut up. 'Like what, Gemma?'

'Like maybe she's more than a solution to a problem?' she continued, undeterred. 'Like maybe her appointment as costume designer is more about you having a crush on her than her suitability for the position.'

Poppy looked intrigued. 'Who has a crush?'

'Nobody, sweetie. Aunty Gemma is talking rubbish.'

Gemma appeared by his side. 'Then why did you look all mushy-eyed when you saw her yesterday? You haven't smiled like that since...' She lowered her voice. 'Since Sara.'

Like he needed reminding. But the last thing he wanted to do was discuss his love life in front of Poppy. 'I was pleased to see her, that's all. Relieved that she'd accepted the job and bailed us out of a hole.'

'Who were you pleased to see, Daddy?' Poppy's eyes were wide with curiosity. 'A lady?'

Oh, hell. That was all he needed. 'No one, sweetie.' He glared at his sister, wanting to throttle her, and then turned back to his daughter, smiling. 'What are you going to draw next?'

He could feel Gemma studying him. 'Why do I sense there's more to it?'

'Because you're an annoying meddler, that's why.' He kept his focus on Poppy. 'How about a polar bear?'

Gemma punched his arm.

'Ow, bully.' He rubbed his arm and turned to her. 'Look, if it'll make you feel better, I'll apply for references, okay? I'll contact her last job and show due diligence. Satisfied?'

'Better late than never, I suppose.'

'Are we done now?'

She folded her arms across her chest. 'Sure.'

'Big of you.' He checked his watch. 'Now, can you keep an eye on Poppy while I go and deal with Lily?'

Gemma rolled her eyes. 'Sure. Take all the time you need. I mean, I wouldn't want to keep you away from Lily.'

'Who's Lily?' Poppy was no longer focused on her drawing. 'Is she the lady you have a crush on?'

He bit back a curse. 'No, sweetie. She's the new costume designer for the film we're making.'

'Can I meet her?' Poppy sounded excited.

'Maybe another time.' He kissed the top of Poppy's head, figuring there was no way he could spring his daughter on Lily just yet when she was still reeling from seeing *him* again. 'Be good for Aunty Gemma. I won't be long.'

Poppy frowned. 'Why can't I come with you to meet Lily?'

Because Lily doesn't know you exist.

'Because it's work stuff, sweetie. You'd be bored. You stay here with Aunty Gemma. I'll be back soon.'

She looked disappointed. 'Ohhhkaaay.'

'Good girl.' He headed out the door.

'Don't come crying to me if she turns out to be a disaster,' Gemma called after him, as he jumped from the portacabin's steps and started jogging towards the security hut.

'She won't be,' he yelled back, praying he was right.

Up until yesterday, Will had had no doubts about hiring Lily. He was full of excitement at the idea of seeing her again. His head had been filled with romantic ideas about how their reunion would pan out: something like witnessing her initial shocked expression, followed by her joy, and then the pair of them would embrace in a romantic clinch.

An vision that had been shattered when he'd seen the horrified look on her face.

He'd realised that imagining Lily throwing her arms around him and kissing him senseless had been a tad unrealistic. But there hadn't even been a flicker of a smile on her face. No hint of pleasure. Just mortification.

Not exactly what he'd hoped for.

She'd seemed different, too. Less confident. Less sparkly. Like the light in her had been snuffed out. Her face was pale. Her eyes downcast. And the polished, confident appearance she'd worn so easily on holiday was nowhere to be seen.

But then she had just had a shock. She'd also fallen over. Looking a bit peaky was understandable. He was being too harsh, expecting her to greet him with joy and warmth when he'd just ambushed her. She was entitled to be pissed off.

Still, that was yesterday.

Hopefully today she'd be back to her bubbly and engaging self.

A man could hope.

Lily was waiting by the security hut. She was dressed in dark jeans with a white top under a grey V-neck thin sweater. A black rucksack hung mournfully from her back. Her face was devoid of make-up, making her appear younger. The only colour came from her copper-highlighted hair, the bob shape slightly outgrown since their holiday.

His stomach dipped.

Not that she wasn't still attractive, she was, but in the Caribbean she had glowed. Her whole aura had radiated positivity and happiness. He'd been drawn to her, like a hapless moth circling a lightbulb.

Now she fiddled with her hands nervously. She kept glancing behind her, as though she wanted to escape.

Hiding his disappointment, he approached with a smile, hoping to allay her nerves. 'Hey, there, Lily. You made it okay?'

She held out her hand for him to shake. 'Good morning, Mr Taylor.'

Mr Taylor? How formal. 'Will is fine,' he said, taking her hand, noticing the slight shake. 'We're on first name terms here.'

She withdrew her hand. 'Whatever you say.'

Frosty.

Not a good sign.

He pointed to his car parked in the layby. 'Hop in, I'll give you a tour of the festival locations.' Maybe some private time away from prying eyes might relax her a bit. 'And then I'll drop you at the admin office so you can get your security pass made up.'

She followed him over to the car and climbed in, still silent, although her cheeks had gained a hint of colour. She tucked her rucksack behind her legs.

Did she think he was going to nick it?

'You don't want to put it in the back?'

'It's fine where it is.' She stared straight ahead.

This wasn't going well.

The question was why?

'I'm sorry about yesterday,' he said, as he pulled away. Maybe she was still suffering from shock? 'I hope you're not injured from your fall?'

'A bit bruised.' She didn't look at him. She was focused on her surroundings.

'I felt bad for not warning you I'd be there,' he said, wondering if an admission of guilt would soften her frosty exterior. 'Sorry about that.'

For a moment he didn't think she was going to respond. But then she said, 'So, why didn't you tell me?'

Good question. One he wasn't sure he knew the answer to. 'I guess I didn't want to guilt you into taking the job. I thought maybe if you knew it was me you might feel pressurised into accepting the offer.'

She nodded. 'Right.'.

More likely, he was scared the opposite might happen. If she knew it was him she would have declined.

He waited, hoping for reassurance that he wasn't the cause of her distress, but it didn't come.

Not awkward at all.

He drove through The Great Park. 'On your right are the wardrobe trailers,' he said, pointing to the large containers now situated in the car park. 'That's where all the costumes will be made.' And then he cringed. 'Sorry, you'd know that, of course. It's not like you haven't done this before.'

She made an odd sound.

He glanced over, but she didn't say anything.

Maybe she was used to bigger fancier trailers? These weren't tiny, but they weren't as palatial as the big budget films. 'Too small?'

'They look fine,' she managed, her voice a pitch higher than normal.

'They have everything you'll need. Steamers, industrial sewing machines and a fully working kitchen.'

She rubbed her hands on her jeans. 'I'm sure it'll be fine.'

They exited the park and followed the road into town. 'On your right is The Long Walk,' he said, wondering why engaging her in conversation was so hard. On holiday, they'd chatted easily. What had happened?

He glanced at her.

She remained silent.

He tried again. 'That's where the Royal parade will take place on the day of the festival. It starts at The Copper Horse and finishes at the castle.'

She held onto the armrest, her body pressed against the door.

Anyone would think he was trying to kidnap her.

He brought the car to a stop. This was ridiculous. He had to know what was going on. They were parked up next to The Long Walk. The castle loomed ahead, the huge construction proudly guarding the town below. Willow trees lined the walkway, their drooping branches trailing against the grass.

He turned to face her. 'You don't seem very pleased to see me.'

A beat passed. 'I'm still in shock. I wasn't expecting to ever see you again.'

'Me neither. But our costume designer was taken ill, and it seemed like fate was intervening and giving me a reason to contact you again.' He paused. 'I was hoping it'd be a nice surprise.' He hoped to evoke a smile, but none was forthcoming. 'I can see now that I should've warned you. Sorry.'

Bloody hell, this wasn't going well.

He was such a fool. He'd stupidly thought she might have missed him as much as he'd missed her, and would be delighted to see him again. That didn't appear to be the case.

His heart pinched as he looked at her. She was a fraction of the person she'd been in the Caribbean, and yet he still wanted her. He ached to touch her, but she was closed off. Her body language made it clear she felt uncomfortable in his company.

He tried again. 'So, how have you been?'

She stared down at her lap. 'Fine.'

'Busy with work?'

'Not too bad. You?'

'Crazy busy. Getting ready for this.'

She nodded. 'Right.'

Silence followed.

With a sigh, he started the engine and pulled away. It was obvious she didn't want to reconnect. Whatever they'd had, however magical, it was over. That much was clear. It really had just been a holiday fling and he was an idiot for thinking otherwise.

Now all he had to decide was how the hell he was going to deal with seeing her for the next two months. He guessed he needed to be professional and treat her like he would any other contractor. After all, he was paying her a load of money to deliver on costumes. He couldn't afford to be sentimental about work. He was the boss. She was the employee.

Rallying himself into business mode, he continued with the guided tour. 'Up ahead is St. George's Chapel.' He indicated the grand structure situated at the foot of the castle. 'The inside is stunning. We've been given permission to use the main chamber for filming.'

She glanced over. 'I don't actually know anything about the film. The agency didn't have any details.'

That wasn't good. He'd be having words with the agency. 'Sorry about that. Well, it's a tour guide film charting nine hundred years of Royal residency at Windsor Castle. The film will be shown at Madame Tussauds as part of the static exhibition during the day, and then a few of the costumes will be worn by the actors for the Royal parade later in the afternoon.'

'How big is the cast?'

'Not huge. You'll be working with the two lead actors playing the various kings and queens throughout the ages.'

Will continued past the castle. 'To the left is the old railway station.'

She craned her neck to see.

'It's now full of designer boutiques, fancy bars, restaurants. The railway platform is a museum and houses the Madame Tussauds exhibition. That's where most of the filming will take place.'

She seemed to calculate something in her head. 'What about extras?'

'Plenty, but you needn't worry about them, there's a separate team looking after them. All their costumes are hired.'

She looked a little relieved.

Or was it concerned? He couldn't tell.

'I imagine this is a small production compared to what you're used to working on. Sorry if that's a disappointment?'

She shook her head. 'No… it's a relief, actually.'

'Why's that?'

Her cheeks coloured. 'Oh, no reason.' She fiddled with her hands. 'Just nice to have a more low-key commission to work on.'

'I'd hardly call designing bespoke royal costumes low-key.'

She frowned. 'I'm sorry?'

'The agency didn't tell you? All the costumes need to be original designs based on the appropriate period. It's a key element of the film's styling.'

Her mouth dropped open.

'You didn't know that?' He really would be having words with the agency.

Her hand came up to touch her neck. 'Err... no, they didn't mention it. How... how many costumes are we talking about?'

'Six.'

'Right. Six.' She nodded slowly. 'Six bespoke costumes. Needed to be made by when?'

He tried to remember the schedule. 'The first scene is the arrival of Queen Elizabeth and Prince Phillip for a state ball. We're doing preliminary rehearsals this week, so the first dress won't be needed until Monday.'

'Monday?' Her voice shot up an octave. 'Next Monday? As in... a week's time?'

'Is that a problem?'

He prayed she wouldn't say it was. The film crew were booked. The actors were being paid. They had a schedule that needed sticking to. He couldn't afford to get behind on the first week of filming.

Her eyes darted about. 'Of... of course not.'

'Good.' His phone beeped with a message. The additional lighting rig had arrived, which meant he should be getting back to work and not wasting time trying to win over a woman who was no longer interested in him.

He drove by The Royal Windsor Theatre and took the river road back towards The Great Park.

'That's the Thames,' he said, nodding to this right. 'Ahead is Alexandra Park, the main festival site.'

She looked to where he indicated, seemingly interested in her surroundings, even if her response was nonverbal.

He glanced at the river as they drove past. It was lined with a range of boats, from floating cafes to fancy speedboats, a playground for the rich and famous. He was tempted to mention their boat trip in the Caribbean, but somehow he didn't feel it would be a welcome reminder.

Another awkward silence followed.

Her, seemingly lost in thought.

Him, kicking himself for being such an idiot.

At least Will was saved any guilt for not mentioning he had a daughter. What would be the point? It was clear his relationship with Lily was well and truly over.

Five minutes later, they were back in The Great Park and parked up by the admin office. 'Well, that's the tour done,' he said, nodding towards the portacabin. 'Do you want me to wait while you get your pass done?'

She looked puzzled. 'Oh, right. My security pass. No, that's okay.'

'When you're finished, head for the wardrobe trailer. You know where it is.'

'Next car park along. Got it.' She climbed out of the car, appearing a little unsteady on her feet.

He watched her with a growing sense of trepidation. She turned one way, paused, then turned the other, aiming for the portacabin. 'Lily?'

She turned back. 'Yes?'

He reached over for her rucksack. 'Your bag?'

'Oh, right.' She came back and took it from him. 'Bye, then. Thanks for the tour.'

'No problem.' He watched her walk off, her gait shaky and unsure. 'Let me know if you need anything,' he called after her, but she didn't acknowledge him.

Will wasn't sure she'd even heard him. It was like she was in her own world.

And he was left with the sinking feeling that he'd made a catastrophic mistake in hiring Lily Monroe.

God, he hated it when his sister was right.

Chapter Twelve

Lily checked the time on her phone. 7:15 a.m. She was already fifteen minutes late. But it wasn't like she could have left any earlier. She'd been up all night sewing. Just as she had been for the past week, functioning on power naps, strong coffee, and an innate stubbornness to finish the bloody dress. Talk about going down to the wire.

Picking up the heavy bin-liner, she hurried down the narrow guesthouse staircase, trying to avoid tripping over the bag as it became entangled between her legs.

The cafe below was empty. It was not yet open to the public, but the breakfast sitting for the other contractors staying there was finished. Unlike Lily, they would be arriving for work on time, having no doubt enjoyed a restful and uninterrupted night's sleep.

Lily exited The Crooked House Tea Rooms and attempted to run the short distance from the guesthouse down to the old railway station, where they were due to start filming this morning. But she gave up trying to run when the cobbled streets threatened to wreck her ankles. She slowed to an agitated walk.

Following Will's bombshell that she only had a week in which to design and make a bespoke 1950s ballgown, she'd turned up for work last Tuesday full of trepidation.

A feeling that had rapidly descended into full-blown panic as the day had progressed.

Far from being given the space and time to work on the dress, she'd been bombarded with constant interruptions. If it wasn't the film's director, it was someone from the design team wanting to know the colour of the dress, its style, the shape of the cut so they could plan the storyboards – all things she'd yet to work out – and all things that they seemed to have an opinion on. Opinions which differed, clashed, and resulted in her already fragile emotional state reaching close to breaking point.

Her repeated mantra that she was a 'last-minute replacement' and she was 'trying to play catch-up' hadn't bought her any sympathy or space from the team to gather her thoughts. They'd wanted answers, and she didn't have any.

Lily concluded it was only a matter of time before someone realised she was a fraud and wasn't an experienced designer. So in the end, she'd done the only thing she could think of and had locked the wardrobe trailer door, pinning a 'Do Not Disturb' sign to the front.

This radical action hadn't endeared her to Will, who'd reacted to her self-isolation by banging on the door, insisting she open up, and had demanded an explanation.

Blinking back tears, she'd cracked open the door enough to face him. Feigning a confidence she didn't feel, she'd politely reminded him that she'd been told nothing about the project, had received no prior instructions for the costume requirements, but was still expected to produce a miracle in less than a week. Therefore, her actions were wholly reasonable and justified, and he could either accept her request to work uninterrupted, or he could find himself another designer.

Fortunately, he'd backed down, accepted she had a point, and had agreed to her working behind closed doors... which is where she'd been for the last week – researching 1950s couture and designing a ballgown fit for a queen.

Of course, what he hadn't known was that behind the pretence of being a professional and seasoned designer taking charge of a challenging situation, she'd been a complete emotional wreck. She was tired, anxious, and way out of her depth. She felt overwhelmed by the enormity of the task ahead and was bordering on quitting before she'd barely begun. But she'd figured the only possible way of surviving her first week was to hide her tears and work away from prying eyes and constant criticism.

Mostly, she needed distance from Will.

Gone was the laughing and relaxed man she'd met on holiday. Work Will was tetchy, combative, and bloody intimidating. Which had done nothing to ease her agitation. And just when she'd thought it couldn't get any worse, he'd requested a job reference.

Lily had fumbled around for an answer, before mumbling something about not having the details to hand, but that she would get them for him – an action which would immediately expose her lie. Not just because her references would reveal her as a former pattern-cutter and not a designer, but also because she couldn't imagine Darth Vader singing her praises anytime soon. Not when her parting words to Keith Long had included the phrase, 'complete twat'.

Not her finest moment, it had to be said. She was never normally rude to anyone and the one time she had been, it was about to come back and bite her on the bum. Typical.

She jolted when a car horn sounded. She had strayed into the road.

She waved an apology at the driver and hurried across the road.

Windsor was gearing up for a busy day with commuters already on their way to work. The shops had yet to open, but the high street was filled with traffic.

The noise tailed off as she entered the pedestrian area by the old railway station. A huge glass sign decorated the archway above with the words, 'Windsor Royal Shopping'. Below was the House of Windsor crest.

Panting, she hoisted up the bin-liner and continued towards the old station, passing the currently empty Café Rouge and Eat restaurants encased under the glass-domed roof. She passed through the ornate red-brick arches and into the covered section, following the signs for the museum.

It was very grand. The shops were dainty and packed together, all with matching walnut wooden frames and bay windows, designed to appear Victorian, but clearly recently constructed. They ranged from selling designer clothing, to exotic coffee and quirky sweets. The ground beneath was cobbled – although less precarious than up by the castle – and the lighting was atmospheric and industrial. It looked like an expensive film set. She could imagine the tourists loved it.

Picking up speed, Lily hurried towards the museum.

Her destination came into view. Ahead was the grand steam train, the focal point of the exhibition, and the backdrop for the first section of the tour guide film.

'You're late,' Will shouted, appearing in her peripheral vision, making her startle. But his apparent annoyance at her tardiness faded when she turned to face him.

She wasn't sure whether it was the sight of her bedraggled appearance that dispelled his anger, or the deep blue circles beneath her eyes, bloodshot from a lack of sleep. Both, probably.

Whatever it was, his irritation was replaced by a questioning look. 'Are you okay?'

'Fine,' she snapped, feeling anything but. A feeling not helped by Will bloody Taylor standing there looking well rested, smartly dressed in jeans and a blue shirt, and smelling like he'd spent the morning being bathed in exotic spices.

A complete contrast to her stained sweatshirt, crumpled jogging bottoms and uncombed hair. Not that she'd had time to change. Or shower. Or eat, for that matter.

His eyes dipped to the bin-liner. 'Do you have the dress?'

No, I'm lugging this about for the fun of it, she wanted to retort, but bit back the urge to be sarcastic. She opted for, 'Yes, it's here.'

Relief washed over his face. He'd obviously doubted her abilities as much as she had. Understandable, but not great for her self-esteem.

Her head ached from a lack of sleep. Her arms ached from carrying the bag. But most of all, her heart ached at the sight of him standing there.

On holiday she'd felt equal to him, a match for his playful personality and sense of fun. But the scales had tipped in his favour, and whereas he appeared competent and in control, she'd been relegated to the role of 'insignificant underling'.

A feeling compounded when he said, 'I'm still waiting for your reference contact details. Is there a problem?'

His expression was a mixture of part-annoyance and part-disappointment.

It was a world away from how he'd looked at her in the Caribbean. He'd made her feel like the most stunning woman on the planet. Now she felt like a drunken mistake, the woman he'd woken up with the following morning, causing him to instantly regret his decision to get plastered the night before.

'There's no problem,' she said, avoiding eye contact. 'I've just been flat out. I'll get the details to you later today.'

'Please make sure you do. I need them for insurance purposes.'

More likely he needed them because he was questioning his decision to hire her. Her stomach clenched a little tighter. She was on borrowed time.

'Megan's over there,' he said, pointed to a stunningly beautiful woman having her hair fixed. 'Get her in the dress as quickly as possible. The director wants to set the lights, and he's not a fan of being kept waiting.'

She bit her lip. She wasn't a fan of being given a week to design and make a royal ballgown, but she figured pointing this out wouldn't help relieve the tension fizzing between them. 'Fine,' she said, walking off, while trying not to trip over the trailing bin-liner.

Was this what being a designer was like? Unrealistic deadlines? Stroppy bosses? Constant criticism? She'd foolishly thought it would be glamorous and joyous. So far it'd been exhausting and demoralising.

And they'd yet to see her work. They might hate it.

Whether they liked it or not, it was out of her hands. She'd done all she could. She'd carried out extensive research. Studied the gowns worn by other fashionistas of the era, and taken inspiration from the couture designers of the time: Dior, Givenchy and Chanel. The end result was a dress she was extremely proud of.

The question was, would anyone else like it?

She was about to find out.

Megan Lawrence was even more stunning close up than she was at a distance. She had glossy black hair that shone like a mirror. Her blue eyes were wide and cat-like and her lips formed a perfect blood-red bow. She was perfection. A goddess. Like something from a Renaissance painting. No wonder she'd been cast as royalty.

Lily had seen numerous photos of Megan and she knew the woman's measurements intimately. She'd been given a custom-made tailor's dummy especially for the project, but this was their first face-to-face meeting.

Approaching the glamorous actor whilst looking unkempt and scruffy and carrying a large bin-liner wasn't the most professional of introductions. In fact, when Megan Lawrence glanced up and saw Lily approaching, she visibly recoiled, as though Lily was an unstable stalker who'd recently escaped incarceration.

'I'm so sorry to have kept you waiting,' Lily said, hoping her smile would alleviate any concerns the woman had about her mental stability. 'I'm Lily Monroe, costume designer.'

The woman raised a perfectly micro-bladed eyebrow. 'Really?'

'Excuse my appearance, I haven't slept for days. I've been racing to get your dress finished.'

The man tending to Megan's hair turned to Lily. 'Hi, I'm Zac. I'm in charge of hair and make-up.'

'Nice to meet you, Zac. Great hair-do.' She pointed to Megan's sleek chignon, with a hint of beehive. 'It looks amazing.'

Megan flashed Zac a full-watt smile. 'Talented, isn't he?'

Zac's cheeks flushed. He couldn't be more than early twenties. He radiated youth and exuberance, helped by strong cheekbones and startling blue eyes. In fact, with his tall frame and black quaffed hair, he looked like the male equivalent of Megan Lawrence. They made quite a pair… which only made Lily wish she'd stopped for a shower and a change of clothes before leaving the B&B. Still, it was too late now.

'Would you like to try your dress on?' she asked, gesturing to the bin-liner, which in hindsight probably also didn't look very professional. 'I'm hoping it fits.'

'It better fit,' a voice yelled from behind. 'We were ready to start filming an hour ago.' The film's director appeared out of nowhere and tapped his watch. 'Time is money.'

'Well, go away then so I can get changed,' Megan said, pinning him with a glare. 'Or it'll be another hour before I'm ready. Do you want that?'

He clearly didn't, and walked off, tutting.

Megan tutted. 'He's always so stressed.'

Megan Lawrence clearly could stand her ground. No one wanted to offend or alienate the leading lady. But as the costume designer, Lily was learning rapidly that she didn't have anywhere near such sway. At least at Clothing Connexions she'd only had the one draconian boss. Here, she was surrounded by them.

Megan turned to her. 'I'm excited to see the dress.'

Crunch time.

Lily carefully unwrapped the outfit and held it up. 'I hope you like it.'

Megan gasped when she saw it. Her hands covered her mouth. Whether this was through good shock, or horrified shock, was yet to be determined.

Lily held her breath.

Zac let out a low whistle. 'She's going to look stunning.'

Lily breathed out.

Megan squeezed Zac's arm, dazzling him with an enigmatic smile. 'Darling man.'

The colour in Zac's cheeks intensified. The lad had a major crush.

Not that Lily could blame him, she was a bit smitten herself.

Megan's elegant fingers skimmed over the ice-white fabric. 'It must've taken you hours to attach all these crystals.'

Days, more like. But the effort had been worth it.

The dress had a fitted bodice with a sweeping neckline and off-the-shoulder cap sleeves. A full skirt expanded from the narrow waist, and the entire gown was covered in clear Swarovski crystals.

Megan smiled. 'I can't wait to try it on.'

Lily was about to suggest they move to a quiet area without the eyes of the film crew looking on, when Megan untied her satin robe and let it drop to the floor.

The space stilled, as if someone had pressed pause.

With her model physique and nude stiletto heels emphasizing her longs legs, Megan Lawrence made quite the impact standing there in her revealing flesh-coloured corset and sheer hold-ups.

Lily sighed. How wonderful it must be to have that level of confidence in your body. She held open the dress for Megan to step into and slid it up over the woman's slim hips and zipped up the side. It fitted perfectly. Thank goodness.

Megan did a twirl. The dress gently lifted as she did so, making her look like a fairy tale princess. Or rather, the newly appointed Queen of the Commonwealth.

Lily could sense everyone watching.

She felt overcome with relief. Megan liked her dress. No, she *loved* her dress.

And then Lily's attention was drawn to the archways behind. Two men in suits were approaching. One of the men carried a briefcase, handcuffed to his wrist.

A woman shouted something, and then Lily became aware of Frankie Roberts marching towards them with a clipboard. 'Move out the way, please.' She pushed past various film crew. 'Ms Lawrence's jewellery has arrived.'

What followed was a flurry of security checks and the signing of papers, before the briefcase was opened to reveal two glittering diamond necklaces, a matching bracelet, and a pair of clip-on diamond drop earrings. The contents were inspected, before being approved, and then removed from the case.

Frankie pointed to the elegant neck piece designed to look like a waterfall. 'The cascading platinum one, I think.' She held it up for Megan's approval.

Megan nodded her endorsement and turned so that Frankie could fasten the necklace around the woman's slender neck. With the bracelet added to Megan's wrist and the earrings in place, the outfit was complete.

Megan Lawrence sparkled like a precious jewel.

Will came over. He took a long moment to take in the beauty of the tour guide's leading lady, before turning to Lily. 'Nice.'

That was it. One word. Nice.

Still, she was happy to take it as a compliment.

At least her work was done for today. She was exhausted. She just wanted to go home and sleep.

But Will shattered any hope of an early finish when he said, 'What about Isaac's suit?'

She frowned. 'Who's Isaac? And what suit?'

Will looked at her like she'd said, *Who's Father Christmas, and what red suit?*

'Isaac James,' he said, nodding to where a man wearing sunglasses was relaxing against the iron railings. 'The lead actor playing Prince Phillip. Where's his formal suit? Please tell me it's here?' But he could sense by her horrified expression that it wasn't. 'You do know what suit I'm referring to?'

She shook her head.

He rubbed his forehead. 'Didn't you read the brief I sent you?'

'I didn't have time,' she admitted, panic beginning to build. 'I've been working nonstop to make the dress. There's no way I could've made a man's suit as well.'

'You weren't supposed to make it,' Will replied, sounding frustrated. 'You were supposed to hire it.'

Frankie handed Lily the clipboard, pointing at the website details for a vintage suit-hire company in Milton Keynes. 'All the details are here. Sizing. Style. Colour. All that was needed was the order placing. Or at least delegating the job to one of the assistants.'

Lily could feel the anger radiating off Will. 'And I was supposed to do that?'

He frowned. 'You're the costume designer, who else would do it?'

Lily looked at Frankie, hoping for an ally, but she shook her head as if to say, *Don't look at me, it's not my job.*

Lily had messed up. She hadn't read the brief.

Her disguise was unravelling.

She dug out her phone, her hands shaking. 'I'll call them now.'

'Don't worry, I'll do it.' Frankie was already on the phone. 'Mr Patrick? Hi, Frankie Roberts, TaylorMade Events. Sorry to be a pain, but we need an urgent delivery,' she said, retrieving the clipboard from Lily. 'An order should've been placed with you and it wasn't.' She shot Lily a look. 'I know... Apologies... Totally our fault... Very inconvenient... completely understand... But any chance you could help us out of a jam?' She walked off, her annoyance palpable.

Everyone was glaring at Lily. It was like a giant arrow had descended from the sky and was pointing at her, lights flashing, sirens blazing. The guilty party. Exposed for her incompetence.

She felt sick.

The director bellowed through a loudhailer for the actors to take up their starting positions, ready for a lighting check.

'Great.' Will audibly groaned. 'I'd better go and break the news that we're not ready to start.' He walked off, grumbling, 'Our leading man doesn't have a bloody suit.'

Lily realised she was crying.

She wasn't sure whether it was the humiliation, frustration, or a lack of sleep undermining her resolve, but she suddenly needed to sit down, before she fell down.

Trying to keep it together, she ducked through the archways and disappeared into the quiet cobbled section of the closed shopping area.

So much for thinking she'd made progress today.

She might have finished the dress, but she hadn't ordered the suit. Her efforts had been in vain. All that hard work and sleepless nights had been undermined by a schoolgirl error. *She hadn't read the brief.*

Sinking to her knees, Lily buried her face in her hands, and let the tears fall.

She had a lot to learn about being a costume designer, that much was for sure.

The question was, would she be found out before she'd had a chance to prove she had what it took?

And did she even have what it took?

After today, she wasn't so sure.

Chapter Thirteen

Friday, 25 June

Will cursed when a speed camera flashed in his rear-view mirror. That was all he needed, more points on his licence. He was already on six. Last time, he'd avoided further punishment by attending a speed awareness course. But the officer's advice that he needed to 'leave earlier' to avoid running late and risk a further fine, wasn't helpful on days when his kid was poorly.

He glanced over at Poppy. She was wearing her bunny onesie and cuddling the large panda he'd got her for Christmas. 'Tell me if you're going to be sick so I can pull over, okay?'

She nodded, looking forlorn and small as she sunk down into the seat. 'Okay.'

'Okay, as in you'll tell me? Or okay, as in you're going to be sick?'

'I'll tell you.'

That was something.

He turned into Chobham high street, feeling bad for dropping Poppy off with his parents when she was unwell. But it wasn't like he could leave her alone in the house, was it? He was needed on set. He couldn't be in two places at once. So he'd made a few frantic phone calls, and eventually persuaded his mum to cancel her golf lesson and look after Poppy.

He felt guilty for leaving his daughter, guilty for ruining his mum's social life. And guilty for ignoring the multitude of texts he'd received from various work colleagues wanting to know where the hell he was. He was a bad employer.

He was an even worse dad.

Not that Poppy's condition was serious. In fact, he wasn't even sure she was ill. She'd woken up complaining of a tummy ache and a headache. But she had no temperature, no fever, and had eaten her breakfast just fine. He suspected she didn't want to go to school.

Why, he wasn't sure – she normally enjoyed school. Maybe she was being bullied? Or hadn't done her homework? Had she fallen out with a teacher?

All he knew was that his daughter had looked at him with a forlorn expression and begged him to stay at home with her so they could curl up on the sofa and watch a film. Something he would have loved to have done, but something that was an impossibility when he was in the middle of planning such a big event.

He turned off the high street. 'Are you missing anything important at school today?'

'Not really.' She cuddled her panda closer. 'Elliot's mummy is coming into school this afternoon to make lanterns with the class.'

'Seems a shame to miss that. Sounds like fun.'

She sniffed. 'I guess.'

'Maybe if you're feeling better later, Nanny can run you into school, so you don't miss the lesson.'

Poppy gave an imperceptible shrug.

'Wouldn't you like to make a lantern?'

She nodded.

'Then what's the problem?'

She buried her face in the panda. 'The other mummies are coming in to help.'

So that was it.

'And you're sad because you won't have anyone there?' Another nod.

It wasn't the first time this had happened, though it never got any easier to deal with. His daughter wanted something he couldn't give her, and that hurt. For both of them.

He reached over and squeezed her hand. 'Not all the mummies will be there, will they? A lot of them work.'

'I guess.'

'So you wouldn't be the only one without a mummy.'

This didn't seem to appease her.

Why wasn't there a manual for dealing with this kind of crap? He was way out of his depth. But he knew he couldn't ignore the issue. 'Is that why you don't want to go to school?'

She didn't answer, she just fiddled with the ears on her cuddly toy.

'You can't skip school every time an activity involves a parent, sweetie. You'll miss out on so many things. Fun things. And that would be a shame.'

'But it makes me sad.'

'I know, but not joining in with stuff won't make you any less sad. It'll make you feel worse.'

'Can you come into school instead?' She gave him a hopeful look.

Oh, hell. 'I can't today, I'm busy. Sorry, I wish I could.'

Her expression turned quizzical. 'Are you going to see the lady you have a crush on?'

'What?' He nearly crashed the car. Where had that come from? 'No, of course not... I mean, yes, I will be seeing her, but I don't have a crush on her. That was just Aunty Gemma being silly.'

A classic example of why you should never discuss certain topics in front of children. Their memories were far too good. Something he'd be reminding Gemma about later.

'Why did she say it then?'

He rubbed the back of his neck. He hated lying to Poppy, but admitting he'd fallen for someone would not help the current situation regarding her desire for a new mummy. If things had been different, maybe he would have done. If his reunion with Lily had gone as he'd imagined and they'd resumed a relationship, then maybe, just maybe, after a few months of dating, he might have been in a position to introduce her to Poppy. Maybe.

But as it was, Lily and him were barely on speaking terms. The chances of anything happening between them was zero. Inviting speculation about his feelings wouldn't be helpful. Poppy was struggling enough as it was. She didn't need another let down in her life. And neither did he.

He turned into the lane leading to his parents' farmhouse. 'Because that's what sister's do. They like to tease.'

Poppy gazed out of the window. 'I wouldn't know. I don't have a sister... Or a mummy.'

Ouch.

His daughter certainly knew how to push his buttons. 'But you do have a daddy, who loves you very much, and doting grandparents, and lots of extended family who adore you, which is more than a lot of kids have, okay?

So try and focus on what you do have, rather than what you don't.'

Poppy sighed. 'I'll try.'

'Good girl.'

As he pulled into the gravel driveway, his mum appeared in the doorway, smiling and waving. She came over and opened the passenger door. 'I hear somebody's poorly today?'

Poppy nodded mournfully, ramping up the need for sympathy. 'My tummy hurts.'

'Poor baby. Let's get you inside. Bring Panda with you.'

Will passed over Poppy's bag. 'Thanks, Mum. You're a lifesaver. Sorry you had to cancel golf.'

She gave him a tight smile. 'Oh, well, these things happen.'

He leant over and kissed Poppy's cheek. 'Be good for Nanny,' he said, waving her off. 'I'll see you later.'

'Bye, Daddy.'

They headed inside, his mum placing a protective arm around her granddaughter's shoulders.

Hopefully, Poppy's spirits would improve once her nanny had made a fuss of her.

It didn't ease his guilt, though.

Or curb his agitation.

Which is how he ended up speeding through another amber light as he drove away from Chobham. He waited for the flash of a camera, but thankfully luck was on his side this time. He slowed, adhering to the speed limit, and fought his anxiety as he wove through the back lanes towards Windsor.

How the hell was he supposed to cope with his daughter wanting a new mummy? He'd dealt with all manner of difficult phases over the years. Toddler tantrums. A refusal to sleep in her own bed. Chewing her fingernails. Only eating 'dry' food. All of which he'd negotiated, some more smoothly than others. But they'd overcome them and emerged the other side with no obvious psychological issues. Not that he knew of, anyway.

This latest problem was proving trickier to resolve. He'd just have to hope that like all the other phases Poppy had gone through, that she would eventually get over it.

But was it even reasonable to expect a kid to get over not having a mummy? He was a grown adult and he was still struggling to deal with losing Sara. So maybe he was expecting too much from Poppy. But what could he do? He had no idea.

He reached Windsor town centre and swung his car into the private car park they'd been given use of, waving his pass at the security guard as he drove past.

His tires screeched on the tarmac as he skidded to a halt. Then throwing open the driver's door, he ran towards the old railway station museum.

As he entered, Will was met with a blast of noise. Raised voices mingled with the sound of banging as workmen fitted a lighting rig beneath the domed-glass ceiling. The railway platform was filled with extras ready for filming, all kitted out in 1950s eveningwear.

Standing centre stage was the director, a thick-set man with a short fuse. Running late was not the way to impress him. He was jabbing a finger at Frankie Roberts, shouting something about a necklace.

Frankie looked flustered, an unusual sight. Frankie was the epitome of professionalism. Always prepared, always in control, and always super-efficient. Not today. Today she looked like a scolded schoolgirl.

She spotted Will approaching and scurried over in her platform heels. 'We have a problem,' she said, like he hadn't worked that one out himself. 'A continuity error from yesterday's filming.'

He frowned. 'What kind of error?'

'Megan was wearing the wrong necklace.'

'Why?'

She hesitated, her eyes refusing to meet his. 'Err... not sure.'

'I thought all the costumes were supposed to be checked for continuity.'

She nodded. 'They are.'

'Then what happened?'

Frankie wore the expression of someone who knew the answer, but didn't want to admit to it. 'Like I said... I'm not sure.'

'Bollocks. You know exactly what happened. Tell me.' His raised voice made her flinch.

'It was a mistake, that's all. It could happen to anyone.'

Realisation dawned.

He'd worked with Frankie long enough to know she didn't make mistakes. And if she did, she'd admit to it. Her hesitation meant only one thing. She was covering for someone else. And that someone could only be their new costume designer.

'It was Lily, wasn't it?'

Frankie nodded. 'I only spotted the error when Megan arrived on set this morning.'

'But you said there was a problem with yesterday's filming?' Beads of sweat broke out on Will's neck. 'Are you telling me Megan was wearing the wrong necklace for the whole of yesterday's filming?'

Frankie's eyes dipped to the floor. 'Sorry, boss.'

Oh, hell.

'Why didn't you notice the mistake yesterday? That's the whole point of continuity checks?'

Frankie grimaced. 'Normally... yes.'

'Then why didn't anyone spot Megan was wearing the wrong bloody necklace?'

Another hesitation. 'Because... I wasn't here.'

'Where the bloody hell were you?'

Another flinch. Silence followed.

He took a step closer. 'Frankie, where were you yesterday?'

'I was at the wholesalers, picking up the material for Megan's next dress.'

Will ran his hand into his hair. 'Let me guess, material that should have been delivered?'

Frankie shrugged. 'Maybe. I don't know.'

'I admire your loyalty, Frankie, but quit trying to cover for her.' He rubbed his damp hands on his jeans, trying to contain his temper. 'Shit.'

'I'm so sorry, boss.'

'This isn't your fault,' he said, supressing the urge to kick something. 'It's mine.'

Frankie's eyes grew wide. 'How is this your fault?'

'Because I hired her. The buck stops with me.'

He knew it was a mistake not to be here yesterday. He'd been hosting a client meeting, trying to assure the local authority, police, and senior military dignitaries that the project was on schedule, under budget, and hadn't hit any unforeseen hurdles – even though he'd spent the entire morning trying to find a replacement bouncy castle supplier, because the previous one had gone bust. He'd foolishly thought everything would be okay on set, and that the team could cope without him. How wrong he'd been.

He glanced up and saw the director making a beeline in his direction. He didn't look happy. 'Where's Lily now?'

'Back at the trailer, working on the next dress.'

He bit back an expletive. 'And where's the correct necklace?'

'Locked in the trailer's safe.'

'Fine. Tell anyone who asks I've gone to fetch it.'

He ducked away, before the director gave him a bollocking. Even if it would have been a well-deserved bollocking.

This was entirely his fault. He was responsible for ensuring all the departments did what they were supposed to do. And when they didn't, it was his head on the block.

He thumped the double doors leading into the car park, making them swing open and slam behind him as he headed outside.

Why the hell had he hired Lily Monroe? His sister was right. He'd carried out no checks, obtained no references, and had hired her purely on the basis of falling for her on holiday. His stupid lovestruck heart had overruled his normal logical brain.

And boy, was he paying the price.

By the time he'd driven through town and parked up by the large wardrobe trailer in Windsor Great Park, his irritation levels had risen from annoyed to full-blown enraged.

He wasn't sure whom he was madder with – Lily or himself. But right at that moment, it was her error he was focused on. His shortcomings could wait until later.

He jumped up the trailer steps and pushed open the door without knocking, determined to tear strips off the woman inside. '*Lily!*'

He saw her jolt at the sound of his yell. She was crouched down, a tape measure around her neck, a row of pins between her lips. She lost her balance and landed on her bum, dislodging the pins from her mouth.

He marched over, fully intending to let rip, but his anger was interrupted by the sight of the dark red material pinned to the tailor's dummy.

He had a sudden flashback of Lily wearing her clingy red dress in the Caribbean. The way she'd giggled after consuming too many Pina Coladas and pressed against him when they'd danced. It was enough to momentarily derail his anger.

A wash of longing crawled up his insides instead.

Damn it.

Then he remembered this wasn't the same woman he'd met on holiday. This version of Lily was clumsy, tearful, and incompetent. Fun and flirty Lily was long gone.

But even as sadness swept over him at the loss, he fought to hold on to his anger – anger he could deal with, loss he couldn't.

Regaining her balance, she had resumed kneeling. 'Did you want something? Only, the second dress has to be ready by next week and I'm nowhere near finished.' She sounded testy and looked slightly flustered by the intrusion.

She was annoyed? Flaming cheek.

He stared at her. She was wearing skinny black jeans, flowery-patterned plimsolls and a fitted cornflower-blue top. Her hair was tucked behind her ears and there was a hint of colour in her cheeks.

She definitely looked less fragile than last week. Her appearance was more polished, less… dishevelled. Plus, she was wearing lip gloss. He was glad. It meant he could shout at her without feeling like he was kicking an orphaned puppy. 'Forget next week,' he snapped. 'It's this week we have a problem with.'

She looked up at him warily. 'What kind of problem? I mean, everything's done. I know it is. I've checked.' She picked up the wodge of crumpled paper from the floor. 'I've checked your brief a zillion times. I haven't missed anything else.'

'Except for Megan's necklace.'

A look of confusion washed over her. 'What are you on about? She was wearing the necklace when she left here just an hour ago, I put it on her myself.' And then she gasped. 'Oh, no, has it gone missing? Has someone stolen it?' She scrambled to her feet. 'Have you called the police?'

'Calm down.' He raised his hands. 'It hasn't been stolen. It's the wrong necklace.'

'The wrong necklace?' Her frown didn't let up. 'What do you mean, it's the wrong necklace?'

He forced himself to keep cool. 'There were two neck-laces in the case.'

'Well, yes, I know that.' She sounded impatient.

'We used the other one for filming on Tuesday and Wednesday.'

'Again, something I already know.' Her hands went to her hips.

He clenched his fists. 'Then why did she switch to wearing the other necklace yesterday?'

'Because the first one chaffed.'

Had he heard right? 'Excuse me?'

'It gave her a rash. Here.' She touched the side of her neck. His gaze was drawn to Lily's pale skin and exposed collarbone. He looked away. The temptation to kiss her was a distraction he didn't need. 'She asked if she could wear the other necklace instead.'

'And you let her?'

'Why wouldn't I?' She shrugged. 'Both necklaces look exquisite and suit the dress. Why not wear both?'

Seriously? 'Because of continuity.'

A pause. 'Continuity?'

'Yes, so that the same scene being filmed on different days looks identical.'

'Oh... right.' Her bluster faded as she absorbed his words. 'Of course, yes... I knew that.'

'Really? Because at the moment Queen Elizabeth arrives at the state ball wearing one necklace and leaves wearing a completely different one.'

The colour drained from Lily's face. This was followed by her teeth digging into her lower lip... which was oddly distracting.

He cleared his throat. 'Now do you understand?'

She gave an almost imperceptible nod.

'Thanks to you, we've lost a whole day's filming. All yesterday's work will need to be reshot.'

'Oh, goodness. I'm so sorry.' She looked mortified, but that wasn't good enough. It was a costly mistake.

'I don't get it, Lily. You're an experienced designer. This is basic stuff. How did it get missed?'

'I... I don't know.' The colour in her cheeks returned. She was embarrassed. Good, she should be. 'Human error?'

'But that's why there are continuity sheets, so that when the scene is revisited at a later date everything can be checked.'

'Right.' Her eyes darted about the trailer, her hands ringing together. 'Good system.'

Was she for real? 'If people use it, yes. Clearly, you didn't.'

She grimaced. 'It would appear not.'

'And what's worse, you sent Frankie to pick up material you should've already ordered, so there was no one on set overseeing the filming yesterday.' His voice raised in volume, as his annoyance bubbled to the surface. 'How did this happen, Lily?'

No response.

He waited, determined to get to the bottom of her ineptitude, but still nothing was forthcoming.

She was shaking. Tears had pooled in her eyes and she was struggling to swallow.

Once again, he was consumed by guilt. Like he needed to feel guiltier than he already did?

But he quashed the feeling. He was justified in being pissed off. She'd messed up. Again. He had every right to yell at her... So why did he feel so crap about it?

He rubbed his forehead. He was wasting time. He should be on set.

'You know what,' he said, heading over to the wall safe. 'There's no point dwelling. We just need to get it sorted.' He punched in the combination.

She followed him over. 'What can I do?'

'Nothing.'

'But there must be something?'

He removed the jewellery case and turned to face her, his anger lessening at the sight of her tearstained face. 'Just don't do it again.'

She shook her head so hard she made her hooped earrings sway. 'I won't. I promise.'

'Good. Because we can't afford to lose another day's filming.'

She was staring up at him, her close proximity magnified by the cramped conditions. He could see the flecks of gold in her green eyes. Last time she'd been this close, they'd been kissing. 'I'm so sorry, Will,' she said, her voice barely audible. 'I feel terrible.'

He swallowed awkwardly. 'Yep, me too.'

There was a brief drawn-out moment when they just stood there, eyes locked, neither one breathing.

And then he came to his senses and remembered his sister's warning about allowing himself to get distracted by a crush.

He brushed past her and headed for the door. He'd never let anything interfere with the success of his business before. This only served to remind him why that was. 'And I'm still waiting for those reference details,' he said, pushing open the trailer door. 'You assured me I'd have them by Monday. It's now Friday.'

'Sorry, there's been a bit of a hold up. I'll get them to you as soon as possible.'

He turned to her, wondering why he was allowing her to fob him off with a string of excuses. He wouldn't tolerate anyone else behaving this way. But then, no one else had ever affected him this way. He had to at least try and remain professional. If any other contractor had caused him this much grief he'd have sacked them long before now.

And then he remembered the quality of the ballgown she'd produced. Her organisational skills might be severely lacking, but he couldn't fault her creative talent. The dress was exquisite.

Still, she was on thin ice. His patience would only be stretched so far.

'Sorry again for the mix-up,' she said, brushing away tears.

He refused to soften. However hard it was to see her cry.

'Me too,' he said, exiting the trailer. 'I need to go. The director's waiting.' He jumped down the steps onto the gravel.

So what if she was sorry? He was sorry too, more than anyone could imagine.

Sorry that'd he'd ever met Lily bloody Monroe.

Sorry that he'd let his heart rule his head.

And sorry that he'd sullied his professional reputation by allowing himself to be hoodwinked by a woman who clearly didn't want anything to do with him… which was probably the real issue here, if he was honest.

She didn't want him.

And that hurt more than he wanted to admit.

Chapter Fourteen

Saturday, 3 July

Lily had never considered herself to be short-tempered, but she was living in a constant state of stress these days. She wasn't sleeping well, she was working long hours, and she was on edge the whole time. This was definitely not helped by trying to avoid any unnecessary contact with Will Taylor and also waiting for her lie to be exposed. It was no wonder she was exhausted.

She stretched out her back, stiff from sitting cross-legged for so long.

The trailer was blissfully quiet today. During the week, the space was filled with piles of costumes and dressmaking paraphernalia. It was a bustle of noisy interruptions, her 'do not disturb' sign no longer proving effective at keeping interlopers away. If it wasn't actors needing a fitting, it was one of the costume assistants asking for instructions, or someone from the design team wanting to talk through her 'vision' for future scenes. It was hard enough focusing on the current dress, let alone working out what was coming next. But no one seemed to appreciate that.

Realising she was fighting a losing battle, she'd spent yesterday working on the designs for all the remaining costumes, sourcing materials, and placing hire orders for some of the men's pieces – like the ceremonial robes for King Henry VIII. No way was she attempting to make something that complicated and intricate. There wasn't enough time. The festival was in less than a month. Compromise was required, whether Will approved or not.

Consequently, it had been a tiring day, but it meant that she could now answer any number of questions about her designs, so it had been worth it. It also meant she'd lost a day working on the current dress, hence why she was back in the trailer on a Saturday, working while everyone else was enjoying a weekend off.

She went over to the small kitchenette and flicked on the kettle.

She'd thought her job at Clothing Connexions had been hectic. The whir of sewing machines and hot conditions, coupled with a demanding boss who'd set stupidly high targets for output, was a constant challenge. But this had been balanced with the quiet of her home life. Her home had been a peaceful space, in which she'd had time to think and unwind. Unfortunately, the tranquillity of her previous life was long gone. It had been several weeks since she'd had a moment to herself. She was shattered.

Despite her fatigue, she'd agreed to meet up with her former work colleagues Dottie and Taye in Haringey last night for a drink. She'd hoped seeing her old friends would enable her to relax and return to being comfortable 'Lilith' for an evening, instead of pretending to be someone she wasn't. But her admission that she'd won her current job through false pretences hadn't gone down well. They couldn't understand why she didn't just come clean and confess that there'd been a mix-up. But they didn't know about Will, or her holiday fling, so her lame excuse of wanting to 'prove herself', hadn't allayed their concerns that she was 'heading for a fall'. The evening deteriorated when she'd asked Taye for a fake reference. He'd agreed, but she could tell he wasn't at all happy about it.

Consequently, her evening hadn't been as joyful as she'd hoped, and she returned to Windsor feeling even more despondent about her situation than she had before.

No wonder she'd woken up feeling so depressed this morning.

She finished making her tea and carried it over to assess her latest creation. Getting to grips with the logistics of being a costume designer might be causing her no end of stress, but the actual dressmaking part itself was enormous fun.

Gone were the days when she'd had to reuse second-hand castoffs to create her outfits and make do with an ancient sewing machine. This job provided all the mod cons she could ever need, from a proper cutting table, to an industrial sewing machine which didn't snap the needle when dealing with thicker fabric.

And the fabrics? Luxurious expensive handmade silks and quality weaves that didn't stretch when you tacked them, and hung beautifully on the tailor's dummy. It was a dream.

The latest dress was of Tudor design and made from heavy dark red silk, with waterfall sleeves and gold brocade inlets inserted into the front panel of the A-line skirt. The boned bodice was trimmed with gold beading and interspersed with ruby-coloured stones. It was by far the most advanced piece she'd ever worked on and was made up of several metres of fabric and required boning skills and a corset fastening. But the end result was a stunning gown befitting of Queen Elizabeth I.

Sipping her tea, Lily smiled. Whatever happened next, she was incredibly proud of the two dresses she'd made. It was just a shame she had no one to share her joy with – or her problems. What she wouldn't give to have her granddad around, with his wise words of encouragement, or be able to show her grandma the costumes she'd created. As it was, she had no one to talk to. No one to confide in about her subterfuge. And no one to assure her that everything was going to be okay. Was it? She had no idea.

She shook away her sadness.

No point dwelling. She'd made her bed, as her grandma used to say.

The trailer door opened, saving her from dissolving into a teary mess.

Zac's head appeared. 'Okay to come in?'

'Of course. I wasn't expecting to see you here today.' With no filming scheduled, most of the departments were absent, enjoying a well-earned break.

Zac stepped inside the trailer. 'I'm looking after my cousin today. She wanted to see where I worked. I'm giving her the guided tour.' He gestured behind him, where a young girl hovered in the doorway.

She looked about nine or ten, with long light-brown hair and big wary eyes. Her frame was slight, which added to her fragility. All skin and bones, just as Lily had been at that age.

She smiled at the girl, hoping to ease her nervousness. 'Welcome to the wardrobe trailer.'

The girl looked around. She was wearing a pink top, a match for her ballet pumps, and a denim skirt. Quite the contrast to her cousin, who wore his trademark black attire, complete with leather biker jacket, despite the warm weather.

'Come in. Have a look around.' Lily took her mug over to the sink. 'Would you like a drink? We have orange juice. Or diet cola?'

The girl shook her head. 'No, thank you.'

Zac's phoned pinged. He frowned at the screen. 'Sorry, I have to take this.' He headed for the door, pausing to turn back to his charge. 'Wait here, Poppy. I won't be long.'

Poppy looked apprehensive, but did as she was told and stayed put.

Lily went over to the girl. 'I'm named after a flower, too. I'm Lily.'

Her face brightened. 'You're Lily?' She gazed up at Lily as if she'd announced herself as Wonder Woman. 'It's very nice to meet you.'

'It's nice to meet you, too.' Lily sat on the padded bench seat at the front of the trailer, encouraging the girl to do the same. 'My name's actually Lilith, but I shortened it.'

The girl climbed onto the bench seat. 'Why?'

'Good question.' She mulled it over. 'I thought it might make me feel braver. You know, by creating an alter ego. Like they do in the superhero films.'

'Like Wanda in *The Avengers*? She becomes The Scarlet Witch.'

'Exactly like that.' Lily laughed. 'Although "The Scarlet Witch" sounds a lot braver than plain old "Lily". Maybe I should have gone for something bolder.'

Poppy hugged her knees to her chest. 'Did it work? Changing your name? Did it make you feel braver?'

'Some days, yes. Other days, not so much.'

Poppy looked thoughtful.

She climbed off the seat and walked over to the Tudor dress hanging on the tailor's dummy. 'This is pretty.'

'Thank you. I made it.'

'You did?'

'Yep.' Lily joined her by the dummy. 'It's for a film we're making about Royal history.'

Poppy's small hand reached out to touch the material. 'How do you make a dress?'

'Well, to start with, you need a dressmaking pattern. Then you cut out the pattern pieces and sew the pieces together to create a new shape. Like this dress.'

'That sounds hard.'

'It can be, but you wouldn't start with a garment this complicated. You'd start small, using a simple shape. Would you like me to show you?'

The girl nodded. 'Yes, please.'

'Come over here.' Lily went over to the line of drawers. 'I have some offcut pieces of material. Pick out a few bits you like and then we'll sew them together.'

Poppy dropped to her knees, her face as animated as if she was hunting for treasure. 'I like the red and the gold.'

'Excellent choice. Now we need to make a pattern.' Lily opened her pattern book. 'I'm going to draw a simple shape, like a square.'

Poppy leant against her as she watched her draw. Lily could feel the girl's warm breath against her arm. This must have been how her grandma had felt teaching her to sew when she was young.

'Now we cut it out... like so... and then this is our pattern, which we pin to the fabric.' She demonstrated. 'And bingo, we have our first pattern piece.' She removed the pins and held out the pattern paper. 'Would you like a go?'

Poppy nodded. 'Yes, please.'

'Okay, so pin the paper to the fabric... that's right. Now carefully cut around it.' The girl's face was a picture of concentration as she cut. Her hands looked so small holding the large dressmaking scissors. She struggled at first, but soon managed it. 'Brilliant. If we cut out all the pieces then you can take it home with you to finish.'

Her face dropped. 'I don't have any sewing things at home.'

'Maybe you could ask your mummy if she has something you could borrow.'

Poppy averted her eyes. 'I don't have a mummy.'

Lily stilled. 'You don't?'

Poppy shook her head. 'She died when I was little.'

It was a while before Lily could speak. 'I'm sorry to hear that. My mum died when I was little, too.'

Poppy's head tilted in a quizzical fashion. 'She did?'

'Yes. It still makes me sad sometimes.'

'Me too.'

Poor kid.

Poppy pointed to the fabric. 'Can I do the other two?'

'Sure.'

'If we don't have time to finish it today, maybe I can come back another time?'

Lily smiled. 'Maybe.'

When Poppy was done, Lily collected the four squares of material. 'Now we place them face down on the floor like this and pin the edges together.' She lifted the fabric for Poppy to see. 'And here we have our mini patchwork cover.'

Poppy smiled. 'I like it.'

'Clever, isn't it?' She dug out some quilting from the bag. 'Once we've sewn it together, we can add a backing to cover the joins, and then you'll have a little quilt.'

'It's too small for my bed.'

Lily laughed. 'True, but it might be okay for a doll, or an animal. Do you have any pets?'

'Lots. But I don't think Colin the Rabbit would like it, he's too fidgety. But it would be good for Pete the Tortoise. For when he goes into hibernation. Do you have any pets?'

'No. I always wanted one, but they weren't allowed where I lived.'

'Where did you live when you were growing up?'

'In a local authority flat in Haringey with my grandparents.' Lily threaded a needle. 'I'm now tacking the material together to make it easier to sew on the machine.'

'Is that who brought you up after your mummy died?'

'It was.' Lily started to sew, aware of the little girl studying her.

'Do you have any brothers or sisters?'

'Nope, only me.'

'Do you have any children?'

Lily raised an eyebrow. 'No.'

'Do you have a husband?'

'Are you always this inquisitive?' Lily's lips twitched at the girl's determined questioning.

'I guess.' Poppy shrugged. 'Do you have a boyfriend?'

Lily laughed. 'No boyfriend.' She removed the pins. 'Why? Do you have a boyfriend?'

'Yuk, no! I'm only eleven. My daddy says I can start dating when I'm twenty-one. But even then I have to have a chaperone.' Poppy's daddy was clearly the protective type. And who could blame him? 'I don't even know what a chaperone is.' Poppy shifted position, her weight leaning against Lily. 'Do you like children?'

Lily stopped sewing. 'Why do I feel like I'm being interviewed for a dating app?'

Poppy gave an innocent shrug. 'Just curious.'

Zac reappeared in the doorway, rescuing her from further interrogation.

'Sorry about that,' he said, coming over. 'You okay, Poppy?'

Lily was a bit embarrassed to be found on the floor with the girl almost in her lap. She got to her feet and gestured to the mess on the floor. 'Sewing lesson.'

Poppy jumped up. 'The nice lady was helping me make a quilt for Pete the Tortoise.'

'Cool. But we need to go now. Say thank you to Lily.'

Poppy turned to her. 'Thank you for showing me how to make a pattern.'

'You're very welcome. It was lovely to meet you, Poppy.'

'You, too.' Poppy took Zac's hand, waving as she left. 'See you soon!'

Lily leant against the counter, smiling. Cute kid.

Shaking her head, she picked up the discarded material and stuffed it back in the bag. She hadn't been around kids much, but she liked the idea of being a mum one day. But that meant meeting someone. And that wasn't likely to happen any time soon. Not when she was still getting over Will.

Besides which, even if things had worked out with Will, he didn't seem like the paternal type. Too focused on his career.

No sooner had she returned to hemming the Eliza-
bethan dress, than the trailer door opened again. So much
for taking advantage of a quiet Saturday.

'Anyone here?' Megan called.

'Come in,' Lily called back, recognising the actress's
voice.

Megan Lawrence stepped into the trailer. She removed
her designer sunglasses, surrounded by a waft of heady
perfume. 'Any chance you could squeeze me in for a
fitting?'

Lily got up off the floor. 'Sure. Perfect timing. I'm
about to start hemming.'

'My lunch date cancelled, so I thought I'd pop in on
the off-chance you'd be working. I figured you would be.'
Megan studied the dress hanging on the tailor's dummy.
'You certainly have talent,' she said, circling the gown.
'This is a work of art. Can I try it on?'

'Be my guest. Do you want to change in the back?'

But Megan was already stripping off, removing her
sheer top and discarding it on the floor.

'Or not.' Lily raised her eyebrows. She supposed she
should be used to it by now.

'You can't afford to be shy in this industry,' Megan said,
shrugging off her skinny jeans.

'I guess not.' Lily removed the dress from the dummy.
'Bra, on or off?'

'Off.'

Megan unhooked her bra and slung it away.

Of course she had perfect breasts.

Lily waited until Megan had stepped into the opening
of the dress and between them they lifted it up. 'Hold it
in place while I fasten the corset at the back, please.'

Megan shuffled the dress into position. 'High enough?'

'Perfect.' Lily began threading the gold ribbons through the eyelets and tugged the corset together.

'You're new to this, aren't you?'

'What, fastening a corset?' Lily paused. 'Is it too tight?'

'I meant being a costume designer.'

Thankfully, she was facing Megan's back, so her guilty expression remained unseen. 'I don't know what you mean.' She resumed lacing the ribbons.

'It's okay, I won't say anything. But it's clear you've never done this before.'

Oh, God. Lily stopped dead. 'Is it that obvious?'

'Maybe only to me. I've worked with enough costume designers to know how it works.' Megan glanced over her shoulder. 'Keep going. And fasten it tighter. I'd rather look skinny than be able to breathe.'

An advertising slogan if ever there was one.

Lily resumed fastening the corset, slower, her hands shaking. 'Am I that bad?'

'At designing costumes? God, no. You're amazing, these dresses are to die for. I've never worn anything so exquisite in my entire career.'

Well, that was something. 'Thank you.'

'But as for the other stuff?'

'I suck, right?'

'Big time.'

The woman was honest, if nothing else. It was no more than she'd feared, but it still stung having it confirmed.

'Go tighter. I can take it.' Megan sucked in a breath, narrowing her waist even further. 'Can I give you some advice?'

'Please do.'

'You need to be more assertive. You're behaving like a seamstress, not a designer.'

Lily tugged on the corset ribbons. 'What's the difference?'

'Seamstresses tend to be timid creatures, happy to shy away from attention and bury their heads in their sewing machines. They follow orders, never offering an opinion. Whereas costume designers are louder by nature, more confident and vocal. They get involved in discussions, input their opinions, and are more assertive on how things should run on set.'

'And I'm not doing that?'

'No, darling. You're letting everyone bully you. And believe me, no one wants a designer that can't stand up for themselves.'

Lily fastened the ribbons. 'But how can I argue back when I've no idea what I'm doing?'

'But you do know what you're doing. Your costume designs are perfect. They're exactly what the brief requires.' Megan turned to face her. 'Have a little faith, darling. You clearly have talent, and vision, and the right work ethic, so there's no reason why you can't do this. You just need to trust in your abilities.' She placed her hands on Lily's shoulders. 'Trust me. I've been around long enough to know how it all works. And I don't want to see you fired. It would be the end of your career. This is a small industry and word travels fast. You'd never get another shot. You need to make this work, okay?'

Crikey. 'Say it how is it, why don't you?'

'I always do, darling. Now, how do I look?'

'Stunning.'

'I thought as much.'

Her confidence made Lily smile. 'I just need to adjust the sleeve length and pin the hem.' She picked up her pincushion. 'Thank you. I really appreciate your advice.'

'Not at all, darling. Like I say, you're too talented not to make this work. And it's the least I could do after the trouble I caused changing necklace. I rather landed you in it.'

'It wasn't your fault.'

'Oh, it was, darling. I was being a diva. I should have known better. Anyway, apologies.' She glanced down. 'Bloody hell, my cleavage looks fabulous in this.'

Lily laughed.

'I'm commissioning you to make all my gowns from now on. You're a miracle worker.'

'It helps that you have… you know, good assets.'

Megan quirked a brow. 'Good assets? They've never been called that before.' She looked down. 'Hear that, girls? What a fine pair of assets you are.'

'You know what I mean.' Lily flapped a hand, mostly from embarrassment.

She wasn't sure how she felt about having her secret exposed. Relief, partly. It didn't sound as though Megan was about to tell anyone, and she'd given her some invaluable advice. She needed to take heed. It was time to stop apologising and start calling the shots. Could she do that? Only one way to find out. It wasn't like she had anything to lose.

She had just pinned up the length on one sleeve, when there was another knock at the door.

'It's open,' she called out, wondering who else was about to interrupt her.

'Lily, are you in here?' Will marched into the trailer, looking his usual annoyed self.

Oh, good. More yelling. What had she done this time? But despite her indignation at his abrupt tone, the sight of him striding towards her in faded jeans and a soft casual shirt, sent a jolt of electricity coursing through her.

Damn man.

He stopped short when he realised she wasn't alone. 'Oh, hi, Megan. What are you doing here?'

'Baking a cake,' she said, her voice laced with sarcasm. 'What does it look like I'm doing?'

'Right. Well, sorry to interrupt, but I need to speak to Lily.'

'Go ahead.' Megan fluttered her eyelashes. 'Don't mind me.'

Will came over, his face scrunched into a frown. Nothing new there, then.

'Why weren't you at the project meeting?'

Lily returned his frown. 'What project meeting?'

'The one I called yesterday. I sent you a text.'

Oh, hell. She'd been so preoccupied working on the designs she'd forgotten to switch off the 'do not disturb' function on her phone.

Bracing herself for yet another bollocking, Lily turned to Will, intending to apologise for messing up again, when she caught Megan's eye.

Right, yes, be more assertive. Don't succumb to bullying.

'Did you?' she said, aiming for an air of nonchalance as she resumed pinning. 'Sorry, I didn't get it.'

'What do you mean, you didn't get it? Don't you check your phone?'

'Evidently not.' She moved to the other sleeve, using Megan as a physical barrier. So much for being brave.

Will followed her, unwilling to be avoided. 'All departments were required to attend.'

'And I would've done, if I'd known it was happening.' She tugged on the dress sleeve, pulling it straight. 'Twenty-four hours isn't exactly a lot of notice. Lift your arms for me, please.' She hoped the shake in her voice wasn't detectable. 'Thank you.'

'My pleasure.' Megan gave her a discreet wink.

'Everyone else was there.' Will appeared next to her. 'And meetings at short notice are common on a project like this. I would've thought you'd be aware of that. I mean, you have done this before, right?'

For the first time, he'd posed a query about her work experience as a question, rather than stating a fact.

Her cheeks grew hot. Had he also sussed she was lying?

She glanced at Megan, who silently urged her to keep going.

Turning to Will, Lily forced herself to hold his gaze. He stared back, waiting for an answer. His eyes dipped to her mouth, and his expression softened before his frown reappeared and his gaze reverted to her eyes. He looked conflicted. And annoyed. And tormented.

She knew the feeling.

Her exchanges with Will always left her exhausted and flustered. Lily struggled to think clearly and make rational decisions around him. It was infuriating and distracting and made her want him and hate him in equal measures. Which wasn't conducive to stress-free living.

Then she became aware of Megan watching them, of her amused expression darting between them.

Clearing her throat, Lily refocused on adjusting the sleeve length. 'I apologise for missing the meeting. In future, I'll check my phone more regularly.' There, how was that? Polite, professional, and assertive. 'What did I miss?'

'We need an update on the budget, and the director wants to see the designs for the remaining costumes.'

'No problem. I'll ensure that's done.' Thank goodness she'd finished the mock-ups for the other designs yesterday. She moved in front of Megan, but Will blocked her path. She looked at him. 'Excuse me, you're in my way.'

He moved reluctantly. 'And he's amended the timescales for filming. He needs your approval.'

She dropped to her knees to start to pin the hem. 'Send them to me and I'll check them.'

'Assuming you check your phone this time.'

She lifted her gaze. 'Now I know to expect last-minute demands on my time, even on the weekend, I will.'

He opened his mouth to respond, then stopped, and instead simply glared down at her. 'Good.'

They both held the stare, neither one wanting to back down… until Megan coughed and broke the moment.

Will stepped away. 'And he wants the gown for Queen Elizabeth to be blue.'

What did he just say? 'Excuse me?'

'He feels it will give a better contrast to the backdrop at St. George's Chapel.'

Anger bubbled inside her.

She stood up, her hands balling into fists as she turned to him. She had no need to 'fake' being assertive on this occasion, her indignation was genuine. 'I don't care what he feels about the backdrop, the dress is *red*,' she said, pointing to Megan's beautifully tailored dress.

'Can't you change it?' Will said, not even glancing at the dress.

'No, I cannot.'

'But—'

'Will.' She raised her hand. 'It's taken me nearly two weeks to make this dress. Working long days, with late nights and early starts. Filming starts on Thursday. I still have a neck ruffle and breeches to make for Henry's costume. It's impossible to make another bespoke royal gown in four days. So no, I cannot *change* it.' She hoped the warning note in her voice hadn't gone unnoticed.

'What am I going to say to the director?'

'That he's getting a red dress for the scene. Whether he likes it or not. And if he doesn't like it, then I'd suggest he changes the setting.' She turned to Megan, who mouthed, 'Go, girl,' and gave her a thumbs-up.

Lily might be inexperienced and naive when it came to costume designing. And most of the mistakes she'd made she was guilty of. But changing the colour of a bespoke designer gown with less than a week's notice was not okay. Or reasonable. Or fair. There was no way was she going to let anyone get away with that.

Even Darth Vader wouldn't have expected that kind of turnaround on a garment.

There was a long pause, before Will spoke. 'Fine. I'll let him know.'

'Good. You do that.'

Will turned for the door, then paused, as if somehow needing to regain the upper hand. 'And I want those budget and design updates by Monday.'

'You'll have them.'

'And I'm still waiting on those reference details.'

Her hands went to her hips. 'I'm aware of that.'

Megan looked intrigued. 'Reference details? Why would you need a reference for Lily?'

Will barely glanced at her. 'References are required for all new contractors.'

Megan flashed him a smile. 'Darling, you should've asked me. I've heard nothing but good things about this woman. She's a legend in the industry. I'm surprised you've not come across her before.'

Will frowned. 'Funny, because I can't find a single person who's heard of her.'

'Then you're asking the wrong people.' Megan's acting prowess was coming into fruition. 'Besides, look at the quality of this gown. I mean, seriously. Do you really need further endorsement of her talents?'

Will rubbed the back of his neck. 'There's no denying she's talented, but I still need an independent reference. It's protocol.'

'Sounds more like red tape to me.' Megan gave him an amused look.

Lily figured it was time to jump in. Megan coming to her rescue was lovely, but she needed to sort out her own mess. 'I'll text you the reference details this afternoon.' She tried for an assertive tone, hoping that Taye wouldn't let her down. 'Anything else?'

He hesitated. 'No.'

'Good. Now, if you'll excuse me, I have alterations to be getting on with.'

'Bye, Will, darling,' Megan called after him as he headed out the door, as she gave him a little wave.

The door slammed shut behind him.

Lily turned to Megan. 'Thanks for helping out, but you didn't have to lie for me. I don't want you getting in trouble.'

'What's he going to do, fire me? I don't think so.' Megan laughed.

Oh, to be that confident.

'Maybe not, but tarnishing my reputation is one thing, asking you to risk yours is unforgivable.'

'No one asked me to do anything.' Megan rested her hands on Lily's shoulders. 'And tell me, didn't it feel good standing up to him?'

Lily gave a hesitant nod. 'I admit it felt good. I've just got to keep it up now.'

'You do.' Megan winked at her. 'And not just from a work perspective.'

'Meaning?'

'Watching you two spar is very interesting,' she said, smiling knowingly. 'Very interesting indeed.'

Interesting wasn't the word Lily would use. Annoying. Infuriating. Unreasonable. Even downright exasperating, would be better descriptions.

Where was the carefree smiling man she'd met on holiday? The man who was funny and kind and had taken her on romantic dinners and moonlit walks? It was hard to reconcile this grumpy version of Will with the man she'd fallen in love with.

Love, huh? What a mistake that had been.

Well, at least now she knew what he was really like. Whatever they'd once shared, it was well and truly dead in the water. Over. Finished. Kaput.

And she was fine with that.

Happy about it, even.

Not bothered in the slightest.

She glanced at the door, rubbing away a sudden pang of longing in her chest. 'I don't know what you mean. We don't even like each other.'

Megan pursed her lips. 'Since when has that been a factor? Some of my best relationships have been with men

I've constantly argued with. Nothing like a good fight to instigate great sex.'

Lily's blush must have been obvious.

Megan nudged her. 'Don't worry, darling. I know only too well what it's like to fall for the wrong guy.' She sighed. 'The heart wants what the heart wants. Right?'

'Well, my heart does *not* want Will Taylor.'

Megan turned to admire herself in the mirror. 'Whatever you say, darling.'

Chapter Fifteen

Wednesday, 7 July

Will checked his watch. It was 3:15 p.m. He needed to leave to pick up Poppy from school. It was parents' evening and he couldn't be late. Poppy hadn't been happy with him when he'd missed the last one. But how could he leave now when they were trying to film inside St. George's Chapel and no one had thought to cancel choir practice?

The director's temper was already at breaking point, even before the arrival of thirty-two choristers dressed in red and white trailing robes filing into the chapel ready to sing the 'Hallelujah' chorus… or whatever it was they sung.

A heated discussion had followed, whereby the film's director had tried to evict the choir from the building, and the choir master had refused to budge, arguing that they had a recital this coming Saturday and urgently needed to practise.

Will had tried to resolve the dispute, first by mediation, and when that didn't work, by phoning his contact at the castle who dealt with the chapel's hire. When that failed to resolve the issue, he'd resorted to negotiating a compromise, persuading the choir to use the section next to the grand organ, and the director to relocate

filming to the private prayer room. After much delib-
eration, complaining, and disgruntled noises from both
parties, an agreement was reached.

It meant the big procession scene involving all the
extras couldn't be filmed. Hordes of them were lined up
outside, dressed in their Tudor finery, waiting to fill the
vast line of pews in the chapel and celebrate the arrival
of King Henry VIII. Cancelling such a big scene wasn't
ideal, but at least the day wouldn't be completely wasted.
And it meant Will wouldn't be late for parents' evening
and disappoint his daughter, who'd made him promise he
would, 'definitely be there'.

But just when he'd assumed things were sorted, the
director decided to use the prayer room for preliminary
footage of Queen Elizabeth I, so as not to waste the
opportunity.

Changing the schedule last minute caused several rami-
fications. Mainly, there was frantic rushing about by the
styling team to get Megan's hair and make up done, there
was a delay in Will being able to leave Windsor to pick
up his daughter, and multiple failed attempts to get hold
of the wardrobe team to advise them that the Queen
Elizabeth I ceremonial gown was needed a day earlier than
planned.

More specifically, Lily. Who wouldn't be happy. Or be
able to cope with a sudden change in timings. Judging by
past scenarios, she'd get upset, flustered, and try to make
herself invisible, which was not what he wanted from
his costume designer. What he really needed her to do
was rise to the challenge and get the bloody thing done.
That's what a good designer would do. They needed to be
decisive, confident and able to reassure the entire crew that

they had a handle on things. Unfortunately, Lily didn't reassure anyone. Least of all him.

'Where is the bloody costume designer!' the director bellowed across the chapel, causing a slight echo as his voice drifted up to the rafters. 'Queen Elizabeth has no dress!'

'I'm on it,' Will shouted, unearthing his phone.

He tried ringing Lily, but her phone was engaged.

Blast it.

He checked the time. 3:45 p.m.

He backed from the prayer room and headed down the long centre aisle, deafened by the choir belting out a hymn he didn't recognise.

Balancing his phone between his shoulder and ear, he exited the chapel and rang his sister. 'Gemma? I've got a problem,' he said, the moment she answered. 'The filming schedule has changed. Can you pick up Poppy from school for me?'

He heard a disgruntled grunt. 'I'm supposed to be working, Will.'

'I know, and I'm really sorry. I wouldn't ask if it wasn't an emergency.'

'The third emergency this month,' she unhelpfully pointed out. 'This is getting to be a habit. I'm surprised you didn't lumber Zac again.'

He would have done, but Zac was tied up with Megan. 'He's needed on set.'

'Right, but *my* work can be interrupted? These accounts won't balance themselves.'

'I'm sorry, Gemma.' He headed towards the gate. A few of the extras were still milling about on the lush lawns, causing quite a stir with the castle tourists. 'I'd ask Mum, but she's starting her new art class this afternoon. She's already helped me out once this week.'

'You need to make better childcare arrangements.'

'I know, and I will.'

'You can't keep expecting everyone to drop everything and bail you out.'

He bit back an expletive. It didn't happen *that* often. Only when he was tied up with a project. And it wasn't like he didn't try to manage things himself, but life kept conspiring against him. 'I know.'

'We have commitments too, Will.'

He stopped to draw breath. 'I know.'

'And it's not fair on Poppy either. Not being your priority won't help improve her self-confidence.'

He fought back his agitation. Of course Poppy was his priority. But he had to work. What did she expect him to do? Stay at home all day?

He tried to calm his breathing. Losing his rag wouldn't help solve his problems. Although it might help vent a few of his frustrations.

'It's not that we don't want to help out,' Gemma said, her voice softening. 'But you need to get proper childcare arrangements in place.'

'You're right. And I will. But can you help me out this one last time?'

Another sigh. 'Fine. I'll pick up Poppy and then work from home tonight to get the accounts finished.'

If her intention was to make him feel bad then she'd succeeded. 'Thanks, Gemma. I'll pick her up later for parents' evening.'

'Don't be late. You missed the last one because of work.'

Like he needed reminding. 'I won't be late. See you later.'

He ended the call and resumed jogging down Castle Hill. Why was everything so hard? Was it unreasonable to want a meaningful career? Was he expected to work nine-to-five in an office, just so he could be a 'reliable' dad?

Even then, he'd still need to arrange an after-school pick-up. It wasn't like he could work part-time, it wouldn't bring in enough income. And Poppy hated the idea of after-school clubs or staying at a friend's house. She just wanted to be in her own home, with her own toys and pets, and hang out with her dad. But that was an impossibility. So what the hell was he supposed to do?

He tried Lily again. Still engaged.

He phoned Poppy instead as he headed into the busy town centre. It was a sunny day, the sunlight playing tricks with his eyes as it flickered through the castle turrets behind. He should have worn sunglasses.

'Where are you?' she said, picking up on the first ring, sounding breathy and upset.

'I'm sorry, sweetheart. Something came up at work. Aunty Gemma's on her way to pick you up.'

He heard a faint sniff. 'Mrs Beattie isn't happy. The other children have gone home and it's parents' evening tonight.'

'I know, and I'm sorry. But I'll make it up to you, I promise.'

'How?'

His daughter never passed up the opportunity to nego- tiate. 'McDonalds at the weekend?'

'Ohhhkaaay.' She sounded mildly appeased.

He smiled. 'How was school?'

'We had a rehearsal for the end-of-year play.'

He'd almost forgotten about that, Poppy hadn't mentioned it for a while. 'How's it going?' He crossed the road, blocking one ear with his hand so he could hear his daughter above the traffic noise. The pavements were packed full of tourists.

'All right, I think. Mrs Beattie said I'd done well to learn my lines, but I need to be louder. I'm too quiet.'

He could imagine. She hadn't been keen to take part in the play, but the school wanted all of Year 6 to participate. It would be their last activity with the primary school before heading off to 'big school'. 'Keep practising, I'm sure you'll get there. I'm looking forward to seeing the show.'

'Mrs Beattie said to remind you I need a costume.'

He slowed as he entered the old railway station. A costume? 'Right.' This was news to him… or was it? He had a faint recollection of them discussing what kind of hat woodland animals might wear to a tea party. 'Remind me again who you're playing?'

'The Mad Hatter, Daddy.' She sounded exasperated.

'Right. Of course. The Mad Hatter. *Alice in Wonderland*. I knew that.' Even if he'd temporarily forgotten. 'And when do you need your costume by?'

'The end of next week.'

He silently cursed. 'No problem, sweetie. We'll go to the hire shop this weekend.'

No response.

'Poppy?'

More silence.

'Poppy, are you there?'

He could faintly hear breathing so he knew they hadn't lost connection. 'Can't… can't we make it?'

'Make it? What the costume?'

'I don't want to hire one, I want to make one.'

He'd applied himself to all manner of activities over the years, from baking cupcakes to sitting through the *Frozen* film countless times, but so far he'd managed to avoid anything sewing-related. 'Oh, sweetie, I don't know how to make a costume.'

'Everyone else is getting a homemade costume. Their mummy is making it for them.'

And there it was. The constant reminder that his fragile beautiful little daughter didn't have a mummy.

Would there ever come a time when he wouldn't be floored by the impact of losing Sara? It was less acute than it had been. It no longer consumed his every waking thought and, for the most part, he'd moved on. Or at least, he was trying to. But just when he foolishly thought he'd come through the worst and that nothing else could derail him… BANG… another curveball would hit him.

This time it was because of the pain it caused his daughter. No matter how much he tried to compensate for being a lone parent, his daughter was struggling to blossom without a mother. And it broke his heart.

'Tell you what, sweetie. Why don't you ask Nanny when you see her at the weekend? Maybe she can help?' Not that he was being sexist… much. But if he was a better dad he'd be on top of these things. He had zilch ability when it came to sewing.

'Maybe.' She didn't sound convinced. 'Couldn't we ask Lily instead?'

He stopped dead. What did she say…? Maybe he'd misheard. There was no way she could have asked about Lily. She had no idea who Lily was.

'Daddy…? Are you still there?'

'Yes, I'm still here.'

'I said… can't we ask Lily to help?'

So he hadn't misheard. He was hit by another curve-ball. This one very much alive and the current bane of his professional life. 'Lily? Err… who's Lily?' Christ, he'd never make it as an actor.

'The costume lady for the film you're making.'

'And how do you know about her?'

'You and Aunty Gemma were talking about her, remember? Aunty Gemma said you had a crush on her, but you said you didn't.'

Nothing wrong with his daughter's memory, clearly.

How the hell to get out of this one? 'Well… that's right. She's a work colleague, that's all. I barely know her.' Liar.

Or was it? He'd thought he'd known her. He'd foolishly thought himself to be in love with her. Turns out he'd been mistaken. A momentary lapse in judgement that he was still trying to claw his way back from.

'But she works for you, doesn't she? Maybe she could help make a costume?'

'We can't ask her to do that, sweetie.'

'Why not?'

He headed into the car park, glad of a reduction in noise as the doors swung closed behind him. 'Because she's too busy making costumes for the tour guide,' he said, reaching his car. 'She won't have time to make you a costume as well. Sorry.'

'Can't we ask her?'

'No, sweetie. We can't.' He climbed into his car, wondering how his life had become so complicated. 'Please don't worry, we'll get you a costume. I promise. Now, I have to go. Aunty Gemma won't be long. See you later, sweetie.'

'Bye, Daddy.' She sounded dejected, and once again, he felt like a rotten dad.

He started the engine and pulled out of the car park.

He didn't like lying to his daughter. But he didn't want to get her hopes up, either. Poppy was so desperate for a mummy she might get the wrong idea and latch onto the idea of him and Lily. Well, there was no him and Lily. That ship had sailed. Been set alight. Sunk without trace. Covered in rust and was now residing at the bottom of the Caribbean Sea.

Christ, he was being dramatic.

He pulled onto the high street and headed towards The Great Park.

This was why he never mixed his dating life with his home life. He couldn't risk Poppy becoming attached to someone he wasn't serious about, or who wouldn't stick around. It would be cruel. The poor kid had suffered enough. He wasn't about to add to her woes.

He was so distracted by his thoughts, he almost didn't see the figure running up the Kings Road towards him. The sun had temporarily blinded him, blurring his vision and creating deceptive shadows across the road. It was only at the last minute that he realised it was Lily and had to swerve to avoiding hitting her.

Shit! He braked hard and jumped out of the car. 'What the hell?'

She was panting, doubled over trying to catch her breath. 'I might've known this would be my fault.'

He ran over. 'You were in the middle of the road.'

'Hardly the middle,' she said, straightening. 'And where else was I supposed to go? There's no pavement along this section, in case you hadn't noticed.'

'What are you even doing?'

Her eyebrows lifted. 'Seriously?' She lifted the large carry bag she was holding. 'I'm trying to get Megan's dress to her. She texted me and said she needed it urgently for filming.'

He stared at her glowing red face and out-of-breath expression. 'And you thought running it over here was a good idea? All the way from The Great Park?'

'How else was I supposed to get it here? *Fly?*'

He took a step back. Boy, she was riled. Hadn't she heard of a taxi? Somehow he felt pointing this out wouldn't help. 'Why didn't you call me?'

'I *did*. Your phone was engaged.'

'You could've messaged me?'

Her glare intensified. 'And what? Wait around for you to reply?' With an irate toss of her head, she carried on walking up the road.

Was she for real? He jogged after her. 'Better than running here.'

'Christ, you're a pain in the arse.'

'Excuse me?' He caught her arm, stung by her accusation. 'What's that supposed to mean?'

She swung around to face him. 'You yell at me when I mess up, I get that. Deservedly so. But in case you hadn't noticed, I'm trying to help here. I'm not running about carrying a giant bag for my own amusement. The dress wasn't due to be on set until tomorrow morning. I'm not at fault here.' She stepped towards him, her voice increasing in volume. 'This is me trying to be a good team player. Responding to a sudden change in circumstances. Not crumbling at adversity by falling to bits, but rising to the challenge. Isn't that what you're always telling me I need to do?'

'Well… yes.'

'Then stop giving me crap and help me get this flaming dress to Megan.' She shoved the bag at him.

He took the dress, slightly stunned. 'Point well made.'

'Thank you.' She stormed off towards his car.

He waited for her to climb in before laying the dress across the backseat.

She refused to look at him.

He climbed in beside her and turned the car around, wondering if he'd been transported to an alternative universe. One where Lily Monroe wasn't a cowering mess, but a feisty sparring opponent.

He had a sudden flashback of their time in the Caribbean and how Lily had climbed down balconies and thrown herself onto giant inflatables. Maybe the adventurous spirit she'd shown on holiday was finally remerging? He could only hope.

Nevertheless, it was still an awkward journey back into town. Stony silence hung in the air.

He glanced across. She had her arms folded. Her face was set in a scowl.

It wasn't a pleasant feeling, knowing you'd royally pissed someone off, but it was preferable to seeing her tearful and lacking any fight.

'I received your reference yesterday,' he said, waiting for her reaction.

She flinched.

He thought as much. 'Mr Malik had some very nice things to say about you.' Most of which had been spelled incorrectly, leading him to the conclusion that her former employer was either dyslexic or not the 'manager of a leading design house' as he'd purported to be. 'Remind me again of the company's name?'

She gave him a sharp look. 'Are you questioning the validity of my reference?'

'No, but—'

'Is there a problem with the quality of my costumes?'

'No, but—'

'You asked for a reference. I've provided a reference.'

'I know, but—'

'Pull over.' She pointed to a layby. 'It's quicker to walk from here.'

He pulled over. 'Just to clarify, are you refusing to tell me the name of the company you previously worked for?'

She got out of the car and opened the backdoor. 'No, I'm focusing on the task in hand and prioritising my current position over dwelling on irrelevant details concerning my last position.' She hauled the dress out.

'Leave that, I'll do it.'

'I can manage.' She slammed the car door and marched up the hill, weighed down by the bulk of the dress.

Fine. It wasn't like he hadn't offered.

He drove off, puzzled as to whether he should ignore the giant hole in her employment history and risk a lawsuit and his sister's wrath if it all went pear-shaped, or drop the matter and hope things didn't go tits up and leave him with egg on his face.

He'd let the matter go for now. But he'd be revisiting the issue of Lily's unsuitability for the role of costume designer later – when his head wasn't filled with childcare issues, Mad Hatter costumes, or a delay in filming.

Five minutes later, he was parked up back at the chapel.

Ironically, Lily was still lugging the dress up the hill. They arrived at St. George's Chapel at exactly the same time. So not quicker to walk then, after all?

He waited for her to reach the building and then held the chapel door open. 'After you.'

She brushed past him and headed down the centre aisle.

Choral music filled the air. The choir were in full voice, belting out a hymn as though they were performing to a packed congregation and not an empty chapel.

Lily's agitated walk slowed as she took in her surroundings, no doubt struck by the wonder of the architecture and grandeur of the ornate carvings and huge stained-glass windows.

'They're filming in the private chapel,' he said, urging her on. 'This way.'

'Fine,' she snapped. She was still annoyed. Fair enough.

He extended his hand. 'Can I carry the dress for you?'

'No.'

That told him.

But her bluster faded slightly when she stepped into the private chapel and the director bellowed, 'Finally! Nice of you to show up. Maybe we can get some filming done now.'

Will braced himself for her reaction. Tears? Shaking? Turning tail and running from the room?

But she surprised him by walking right up to the director and meeting his disgruntled gaze head-on. 'The dress wasn't scheduled to be ready until tomorrow. Megan's scene wasn't on the listing for today. And yet here it is, ready to go. So how about you stop yelling at me and appreciate the fact that I was able to respond to a sudden change in the schedule.'

The room stilled. Everyone waited with bated breath. Including Will.

The director looked aghast.

Lily lifted her chin. 'No? Nothing? Fine.' She marched over to Megan. 'In that case excuse me, I have an actress to dress.'

Will glanced at the director, wondering how he would react. But far from losing his rag and yelling back, he turned his attentions to the lighting set-up, seemingly unperturbed at being publicly challenged by an underling.

Across the room, a smiling Megan untied her dressing gown and let it drop to the floor. 'You tell him, girl.' She kissed Lily's cheek, leaving a smudge of red lipstick. 'Stand up for yourself.'

'Something I'm rapidly learning to do,' Lily said, sounding miffed.

Will watched on, with fascination. The mouse had roared back. And no one was more surprised than him.

Five minutes later, they were ready to start filming.

The tense atmosphere of earlier finally lifted when the director shouted, 'Beginners!' and turned and saw Megan's dress. He switched from belligerent and grumpy, to gushing and enthused. 'Darling! Exquisite! You're a goddess.'

Will agreed. Megan Lawrence was a class apart. Yet despite her attractiveness, the dress was a thing of beauty in its own right. Whatever her faults, Lily Monroe was an extremely talented designer.

'Well done, young woman,' yelled the director with an approving grin.

Lily stepped forwards, as if introducing herself. 'Lily Monroe,' she said, her chin raised. 'And thank you. I'm glad you approve. I think the dark red works well against the pale gold background, don't you?'

Will held his breath. What the hell was she doing? Why was she bringing that up? Didn't the woman know to quit while she was ahead?

Will braced himself, expecting an explosion, but the director nodded and said, 'Absolutely. Excellent choice.'

Bloody hell.

Lily turned and winked at Will.

Why, the little minx.

He watched her saunter past, a sudden confidence to her walk.

'Nice one,' he said, his gaze drawn to her hypnotic sway.

'You're welcome,' she said, making a point of picking up the continuity sheet lying on a pew. 'Mustn't forget this, must I?'

He couldn't help laughing.

He wasn't entirely sure what had just happened, but it felt like Lily had finally found some of the fire she'd displayed on holiday. And about time too.

Maybe things weren't a complete disaster, after all.

Now all he had to do was ensure nothing else went wrong so he could head off and pick up his daughter for parents' evening.

And then he remembered Poppy needed a costume for her play.

His troubles weren't over yet.

Chapter Sixteen

It had been raining all day. So much so, outdoor filming at Savill Gardens had to be cancelled. Trying to recreate a medieval wedding was challenging enough when the weather was good, but it was impossible when it was chucking it down. It would ruin the costumes for a start, something Lily had been quick to point out to the director, who hadn't wanted to delay the schedule any further. Once she'd explained about the issues of naturally dyed fabrics and the colours bleeding into one another, he'd accepted her point and canned filming for the day.

See? She could do assertive. And she hadn't had to raise her voice once.

In truth, she'd been glad of the extra day to finish the wedding clothes. Not that she'd admit as much. As far as the crew were concerned, she was good to go. Thank heavens for a little rain.

It was now late afternoon, and she was sipping a cup of tea and waiting for her young protégé to arrive.

Further to meeting Poppy last week, Zac had delivered a handwritten note from the young girl asking if Lily would help her make a costume for her school play. She'd offered her two weeks' pocket money to put towards the material and signed the note with a giant heart and several kisses. It was a very sweet note.

Lily had replied to say she'd be delighted to help Poppy with her costume. And thanks to the arrival of bad weather, they'd been able to arrange the visit for today.

Lily didn't mind the interruption to her busy schedule. Plus it seemed Zac was happy to offload his childminding responsibilities onto someone else for a few hours. So everyone was happy. How he'd got roped into looking after Poppy so often, she didn't know. Apparently Poppy's dad was a member of the project team and Zac was being paid extra to look after his kid.

At four p.m. on the dot, Poppy burst through the trailer door splashing rainwater everywhere, remembering at the last moment to wipe her feet before charging inside. 'Hello!' she called, shrugging off her wet coat.

Lily went over and shook the coat outside before hanging it up so it wouldn't soak her latest design with muddy rainwater. Handwoven cream silk could not be put through the washing machine.

'Do you want a drink?' she asked Poppy, who was busy kicking off her school shoes.

'No, thank you,' she said, breathless and red-cheeked. And then she saw the dress on the tailor's dummy. 'Oh, wow! That's soooo pretty.'

'You like it?'

'It's beautiful.' She ran over, shoving her hands behind her back, as if afraid to touch it. 'Who's it for?'

'One of the actresses in the tour guide. It's for a royal medieval wedding.'

Lily watched the little girl scan the floor-length cream dress with a tied bodice, and royal blue overcoat with traditional medieval waterfall sleeves. A narrow belt had been added to the waistband to accentuate Megan's slim frame.

It was the result of more hours of painstaking hard work, leaving Lily with sore eyes, numerous pinpricks and tender fingers. But the result was worth the effort.

Poppy turned to her. 'Is it for Megan?'

Lily raised an eyebrow. 'You know who Megan is?'

'She's the lady Zac goes to see when he thinks I don't know.'

Lily was shocked. Seriously? Megan and Zac...? Then she remembered Megan's comment about falling for the 'wrong guy'. Is that who she was referring to? 'Really?'

Poppy nodded. 'He says he's practising doing her hair and make-up, but I know he's not.' She smiled. 'People underestimate me.'

Lily burst out laughing. 'Well, I'll be sure not to make the same mistake.' Were Megan and Zac really hooking up? It was hard to fathom. And then it dawned on her. 'Is that where Zac is now?'

Poppy nodded. 'He's in her trailer, doing her "hair and make-up".' She made speech marks when she said it, making Lily laugh harder. Poppy reminded her of someone, but she couldn't think who.

Whoever it was, Poppy was a smart kid. She'd have to watch herself around her. 'I've finished designing your costume,' she said, fetching her drawing pad. 'Here we are... The Mad Hatter.'

Poppy's mouth dropped open. 'Oh, wow! It's soooo cool.'

'You like it?'

'I love it.' Her small fingers trailed over the sketch of a cartoon figure wearing a large misshapen pea-green top hat, with matching green bow tie and trousers, and a sunflower-yellow tailcoat with a big collar. 'I love this,' she said, pointing to the 10/6 price tag tucked into the brim of the top hat. 'It's funny.'

'Glad you like it.'

'But I won't be able to make all this.' Her little face creased into a frown. 'It's too difficult. I've only made a bed cover so far, and the show's next week.'

'Don't worry, we'll do it together. You're going to make the bow tie and the sashes for the hat and the waistband, and I'm going to make the trousers and the coat. But first,' she said, leading Poppy to the fold-down table at the back of the trailer. 'We need to make the hat.'

Earlier in the day, she'd popped into the extras trailer and pinched one of the top hats not being used. It was too small for any of the adults, but hopefully perfect for a child.

She placed it on Poppy's head. 'This will be our base. Have you ever made paper mâché?'

Poppy shook her head.

'Then you're in for a treat.' She tied a protective apron around Poppy, so her school uniform was covered. 'Have a seat.' She fetched a roll of wire mesh. 'We'll use this wire to create our shape and then put paper mâché over the top.'

She cut a length of mesh, bending it into an exaggerated elongated cone shape and fixed it to the hat.

'Now for the fun part.' She filled a bucket of water at the sink. 'How was school today?'

'Okay. I had to switch lunch groups, because Riley ate too many sweets and was sick everywhere and they had to clean the canteen, so I didn't get my lunch in the first sitting.'

Lily emptied a bag of flour into the water. 'Boys, huh?'

Poppy was clearly not a fan. 'I didn't like not having my lunch in the first sitting.'

'Not a fan of change, eh?'

Poppy shook her head.

'I'm the same.' She carried the bucket over. 'I think it's because when my mum died life was very uncertain for a while. I didn't know what was going to happen to me, or where I was going to live. Or even who was going to pick me up after school and feed me.'

'That's scary.'

'It was.'

'What happened?'

'Well, as you know, I went to live with my grandparents. It was strange at first, they were very different to my mum. But I soon got used to it. I liked the fact that their lives were very structured. You know, they had their routines. Breakfast was always at eight, dinner at seven. Stuff like that. It made me feel safe.'

She tore the newspaper into strips, thinking back to her childhood. She was only four when her mum had died, so she didn't have many memories of her young life. And what she did remember wasn't great. Snippets of her mum falling ill. A neighbour calling the paramedics. Flashing blue lights. People in uniforms arriving. Staying with a foster carer for a few days until her grandparents could be tracked down and offered permanent guardianship. It was years later before she found out her mum had died of sepsis. A kidney infection that was left untreated until it was too severe to overcome.

'Sometimes change can be a good thing,' she said, coming back to the present. 'Like learning new skills…' She soaked a strip of paper in the glue and laid it across the wire mesh. '… like how to make paper mâché.'

Poppy recoiled. 'It's wet!'

'I know, but it dries hard. So we'll be able to paint it green, like the drawing.'

Poppy didn't look convinced. 'It looks messy.'

'That's why it's so much fun.' She lifted her hands from the bucket, letting the glue drip down. 'You have a go.'

Poppy hesitated.

'I used warm water, so it's not cold. Put your hands in.'

Poppy lowered her hands into the glue. 'Ew, it's disgusting!' But she was laughing.

Lily laughed too. Mostly at Poppy's reaction, a combination of horror and excitement. 'Wipe the excess glue from the paper... that's it... now place it on the mesh.' She guided the girl's hands, their fingers slipping together. 'Fun?'

'Sticky!'

'Can you see how the paper blends together?'

'It's magic!'

'I know, right?' She gestured for Poppy to soak another strip of paper. 'You can make all sorts of things with paper mâché. Christmas decorations, lanterns, bowls, even a face mask.'

Poppy added another strip of paper, her tongue poking out in concentration as she joined the pieces together. 'Who taught you this?'

'My grandma. She was very creative. She taught me all sorts of things. Like how to bake cakes, how to grow tomatoes and how to make greeting cards. Not to mention, how to sew.'

'Did you enjoy learning all those things?'

'I loved it. I was a very shy child. I didn't like socialising much, so I think she saw it as a way of helping me build my confidence. And I liked spending time with her.'

Poppy nodded. 'I like spending time with my daddy.'

Lily smiled. 'That's nice.' She'd never known her own father. He'd disappeared shortly after she was born. They say you can't miss what you've never had, but she didn't think that was true.

She held the hat steady for Poppy. 'What do you like doing with your daddy?'

'Watching films, mostly.' Poppy added more paper to the mesh. 'We cook dinner together and play in the garden with my pets. He lets me practise doing make-up on him, but I know he doesn't like it.'

Lily's heart melted a little. 'But he still lets you do it?'

Poppy nodded.

'Then he's a very nice daddy.'

'He is.' A drop of glue fell from her hand onto the table. She looked mortified. 'Sorry.'

'It's okay, that's why I covered the table in clingfilm. Don't worry about making a mess. It's impossible not to.'

Poppy looked unsure.

'Honestly.' She rubbed her hands on the table, making Poppy giggle. 'See?'

'You're funny.' She returned to soaking more paper. 'Like my daddy.'

Lily fetched a cloth and wiped the table, an effort to keep the mess to a minimum. 'Your daddy makes you laugh?'

'Lots.' Poppy's eyes lit up, but then her face creased into a frown. 'But sometimes he looks sad. I think he misses my mummy.'

Lily rinsed the cloth in the sink. 'Well, that's under-standable. Doesn't he have a girlfriend?'

'No.' She shook her head, making her ponytail sway. 'He's says he hasn't met the right woman yet.'

'That's fair enough.'

'But how do you know when you have? He might have met her and not realised.'

Lily squeezed out the cloth. 'I guess, you just know.' She leant against the sink. 'Knowing someone isn't right is probably easier than knowing that they are, if that makes sense.' Not that she'd had much experience, but she'd certainly felt an instant connection with Will.

Typical. Trust him to pop into her head.

'Have you ever met the right person?' Poppy asked, innocently.

She sighed. 'I thought I had, but it didn't work out.'

'Why not?'

'I guess it became too complicated.' Mostly, thanks to her stupidity in lying about her career. If she'd just been honest, things might have turned out differently. But then, if she'd been honest he wouldn't have wanted her in the first place, would he?

'Why did you think he might be The One?'

Lily quirked an eyebrow. 'That's a very grown-up phrase. Where did you hear that?'

'Prince Edward says it about Giselle in the film *Enchanted*.'

'Right.' Fairy tales had a lot to answer for. 'Well, he made me laugh, for a start. He was very kind and thoughtful. He was good-looking and he made me feel brave. I liked who I was when I was with him.'

'I feel like that about Colin the Rabbit.'

Lily spluttered a surprised laugh. 'Then hold onto him. He sounds like a keeper.'

Poppy sighed, her face a picture of concentration as she smoothed over the glue. 'But if the man you met was that nice, then why did it become complicated?'

No way was Lily about to confess her crime to an eleven-year-old child. She had some dignity. 'I don't know.'

'Adults can be very strange.'

'I don't disagree with you there.' Lily returned to the table and sat down. 'I'm sure your daddy will find someone soon. And until he does, he has you. And it sounds like that's enough for him for the time being.'

'Maybe.' Poppy added more paper to the sides of the hat. She was getting the hang of it. 'It gets a bit lonely sometimes with only the two of us. I see my grandparents a lot, and my Aunty and Zac, but I wish I had a brother or sister to play with.'

'I can relate to that. I always wanted a bigger family. I loved my grandparents, but it didn't stop me feeling lonely. And they were so much older than me. I felt like a square peg in a round hole.' She moved Poppy's ponytail out the way before it landed in the glue. 'Have you told your daddy how you feel?'

'Kind of. He just tells me to play with my friends more, and I don't want to do that.'

'Why not?'

She shrugged. 'I like being at home.'

'Me too.'

She'd lost count of the times people had told her to 'get out more' over the years. But it wasn't that simple. Aside from caring for her grandparents, she hadn't really wanted to. It was the curse of being an introvert.

She shook her thoughts away. 'Right. That's the first layer done. We'll let it dry overnight. It'll probably need two or three layers before we can paint it. Let's clear up and we can make a start on the sashes.'

Her phone started ringing. She glanced at the screen. It was Will. Not that she could answer it, her hands were covered in glue. Thank heavens for small mercies. Whatever he wanted, it would have to wait.

She took Poppy over to the sink and helped her wash off the glue.

Poppy smiled up at her. 'I like coming here.'

For some inexplicable reason, Lily's chest squeezed. 'I like having you here.'

She now understood why her grandma had been so happy to spend all that time with her as a child. There was something rewarding about passing on your skills to the next generation. But there was also another emotion lurking beneath the surface. A longing. A deep-rooted desire to be part of a family again. She missed that.

They'd just finished cleaning up when Zac appeared in the doorway, his black quiff wilted by the rain. 'Having fun?' he said, coming into the trailer.

Poppy ran over. 'I made a hat,' she said, excitedly. 'For the school play. Look. It's made from paper mâché.' She dragged him over to the table.

He eyed it with an approving look. 'Clever girl.'

'It needs more layers, and then we can paint it green.'

'Cool.' He put his arm around her. 'But we have to go now, squirt.'

'Oh.' Her face fell. 'Do we have to?'

'We're going to Nanny's for tea. Don't you want to see them?'

'Yes… but I was about to make a sash.'

Lily intervened. 'We've still got plenty of time. The show isn't until next week. We'll finish everything off next time Zac brings you over. Okay?'

Poppy let out a sigh.

Zac tugged on her ponytail. 'Put your coat on, it's piss… err, I mean, it's raining outside.'

Poppy gave him a reprimanding look. 'You were going to swear.'

Zac grinned. 'Busted.'

Lily laughed. She watched Poppy run off to fetch her coat. 'Smart kid.'

'Tell me about it. Thanks for looking after her. I managed to get to the wholesalers and pick up supplies for next week.'

'Oh…?' Lily tried to keep a straight face. 'Is that where you went?' she asked innocently.

'Err… yeah.' Zak avoided eye contact.

Busted, she thought, as he'd said himself.

Still, who was she to talk? And her lie was a lot bigger than his.

She waved them both off at the door.

'See you soon!' she called, as they ran over to the car, trying not to get drenched.

She was still waving when another car pulled into the car park. The driver wound down his window. 'Taxi for Lily Monroe?'

She frowned. 'I didn't order a taxi.'

'Your boss did. He said to check your phone. He says you never answer it.' The driver smiled. 'I'm happy to wait. No rush.'

Why on earth had Will called her a taxi?

Confused, she headed inside the trailer to check her phone. She'd successfully managed to avoid Will for the past few days, engineering it so that wherever she was, he wasn't. The energy between them had changed of late. It seemed to have switched frequencies, and the previous animosity had now shifted to simultaneous pulses of both desire and displeasure, in equal measures. There was heat in Will's stare, but not necessarily of anger. An unanswered question hanging in the air, waiting for her response. And Lily didn't like it.

As much as she hated arguing with him, it was safer than allowing a friendship to develop. She had too much to hide. Her career was at stake. A career she was finally starting to get the hang of. If she could just get to the end of the project without being outed, then at least if her fabrication was exposed she might be forgiven.

That's what she was banking on, anyway.

She checked her phone. There was a message from Will, asking her to bring all three royal gowns to Madame Tussauds for a photoshoot.

What, now? Was he for real?

He'd added a postscript, reminding her to use the garment bags he'd bought for her. He had handed them over to her silently last week following her exertions trying to lug the Tudor dress up Castle Hill in a bin-liner.

She supposed he was trying to be helpful. The travel bags certainly made for more suitable transportation. Especially in the pouring rain.

With a sigh, she packed up the gowns and headed outside to the waiting taxi. Hopefully, she could drop off the dresses and escape without engaging in conversation.

But her strategy failed when they pulled up at the old railway station and Will was outside waiting for her, sheltering under the domed roof. So much for avoiding him.

He paid the driver and lifted the dresses from the back seat. He then appeared by the passenger window. 'Why aren't you getting out?' he shouted through the glass.

She wound down the window. 'Isn't the driver taking me back to the trailer?'

'No. I need you inside.'

'Why?'

'Come with me and you'll find out.'

Great. Just what she didn't need.

Thanking the driver, she reluctantly climbed out and followed Will into the pedestrian area, past the almost deserted cafes and restaurants. The bad weather had deterred visitors today.

They reached Madame Tussauds. A few tourists milled about, but not the usual throng of people eager to admire the waxwork creations.

Will led her to a small side room, usually set up to depict a drawing room where a waxwork Queen Victoria perched on a sofa being served afternoon tea. The statues had been relocated to the corridor.

Lily glanced around, taking in the traditional dark burgundy carpet, mahogany walls and bronze flock wallpaper behind the fireplace. 'Is Megan here?'

'Just me,' he said, hanging the dresses behind the door.

'I thought you needed the dresses for a photoshoot?'

'I do.' He pointed to the flock wallpaper. 'I thought this would make a nice backdrop.' The space was lit by two spotlights, magnified by surrounding photography umbrellas. 'I promised the company handling our social media a few promo shots of the dresses.' He turned to her. 'I may have mentioned how good they were.'

'Right.' She supposed she should feel flattered. 'But kind of hard to do without Megan. The dresses won't look so impressive on hangers.'

'I tried calling her, but she didn't pick up. I've left a message, but I'm guessing she can't make it. I don't want to waste a free afternoon.' He rubbed the back of his neck. 'Can we use the tailor's dummy instead?'

'Sure, if you want to drive back to the wardrobe trailer and fetch it.'

He moved around her, assessing her.

'What?'

'You're about the same size as Megan.'

'Meaning?'

'You could model them.'

She stepped back. 'No way.'

'Why not?'

Was he for real? 'Several reasons.'

'Such as?'

She threw her arms in the air. 'I'm shorter than her. Paler than her. Less endowed. And not an *actress*.'

'You don't have to be. I just need your body.'

She raised her eyebrows.

'You know what I mean.'

'I do, and you're not having it.'

They both stilled. No doubt the same thought had crossed their minds.

She had given him her body once. The memory of which still had the ability to ignite a hot flush.

'Besides,' she said, covering her embarrassment. 'The colour palette is designed for darker skin, a match for Megan's colouring. Not mine.'

'Bullshit.'

'I beg your pardon?'

He unzipped the red Tudor dress. 'You wore a dress this colour in the Caribbean. You looked stunning in it.'

The faint glow in her cheeks burst into full-blown flames. 'Keep your voice down,' she said, checking the doorway.

'Why? There's no one here.'

'Are you sure?'

'Positive. And why would it matter if there were? I'm not ashamed we… hooked up… are you?' His tone was assertive, but his expression was laced with uncertainty. A beat later, he said, 'Well, are you?'

She folded her arms. 'So you've told everyone about me, have you? About how we met?'

'Well… no, not everyone.'

'Exactly. So don't pretend you're any more okay with this than I am, because you're not.'

'Hey, I'm not the one who's changed. I'm exactly who I was on holiday. You're the one who's had a personality transplant—' She winced. Harsh. '—and I'm still trying to work out why. We had a great time, the best. It was magical. There's no way you faked that.'

She looked away, searching out the flock wallpaper. 'I didn't.'

'Then what happened?'

Lily unhooked the 1950s ballgown from where it was hanging on the door. There was no way she was about to answer that… or model the red Tudor dress, which would require someone to lace it up, and her resolve wasn't up to letting Will Taylor touch her. 'Where can I change?'

The intensity in his unwavering gaze was unnerving. He was obviously reluctant to let go of the conversation. Tough. 'Behind the screen.'

She marched over to the dressing screen and ducked behind it. Anything to avoid further discussion about why she'd been so different on holiday. She yanked her hoodie over her head and threw it on the floor. 'I don't have any suitable shoes.'

'We'll crop the shot so it's just the dress.' He sounded grumpy. Good. It was safer that way.

She wriggled out of her jeans. 'And my make-up isn't strong enough for the lens, so cut my head off too.'

'Don't tempt me,' he mumbled.

Charming. She stepped into the ice-white ballgown and wiggled it over her hips, zipping up the side. 'And my nail varnish isn't the right colour,' she said, emerging from behind the screen.

'It's fine—' Whatever else he was about to say died on his lips.

She stilled. 'What?'

'Like I said, stunning.'

Not a lot you could say to that.

'Come over here,' he said, clearing his throat. 'Stand on this stool.' He was back to barking instructions.

She dutifully obeyed, using his shoulder to lean on as she climbed onto the stool. She could feel the warmth of his skin through the fabric of his shirt. The faint scent of him was enough to invite butterflies to fill her tummy and hold their own private rave. Helpful. Not.

He walked away and picked up a camera, one of those proper photography ones with a zoom lens. 'Face me,' he said, aiming the camera at her.

'What do you want me to do?'

'Nothing. Just stand still, so I can capture the dress.' He moved around her, taking snaps. 'You didn't answer my question.'

'What question?'

'What happened?'

She could plead ignorance and pretend she didn't understand his meaning, but it would only delay the inevitable. 'Reality,' she said, lifting her chin. 'That's what happened.'

'Meaning?'

She sighed. 'We were on a romantic Caribbean island. Everything around us was designed to seduce. The candle-light, the music, the exotic food. It was a film set. A false existence. With no daily chores, no worries, and no challenges to remind us of life back home. And it worked. For two wonderful weeks there was nothing to focus on other than having fun and indulging.'

He caught her gaze. 'You agree it was wonderful?'

Wonderful didn't come close. It had been utter bliss. The most precious two weeks of her life. 'But it wasn't real,' she said, somehow managing to hold eye contact – how, she had no idea.

'It was for me.' He snapped a shot of her face.

'Hey, you said no head shots.'

'No, *you* said no head shots.' He walked off and adjusted an umbrella. 'Can you put on the medieval wedding dress, please.'

She bit her lip. Stay and argue, or comply?

She climbed off the stool and marched over to the door, unhooking the wedding dress.

Feeling flustered and agitated, she removed the ballgown and replaced it on the hanger. A sensible person would keep quiet, or change the topic, but for some reason she felt aggrieved that her character had got such an assassination.

'So you're honestly telling me that was one hundred per cent Will Taylor on holiday?' She unzipped the carry bag and removed the wedding dress. 'There was nothing you edited about your life? No aspect of your history left untold? Everything I saw was the real Will Taylor with no airbrushing whatsoever?'

Stony silence.

'Just as I thought.' She draped the dress over her head, shuffling it down her body. 'And that's what a holiday romance is all about. We present the best version of ourselves, with no dramas or flaws, and omit anything that we dislike.'

She laced the ties at the front, sucking in her breath. Her waistline wasn't as svelte as Megan's. She continued, raising her voice to be heard over the screen, 'I have no qualms in admitting I wasn't entirely honest during that holiday. I was grieving for the recent loss of my granddad, and I needed an escape, so I pretended to be a confident, carefree version of myself, who wasn't afraid of anything. Someone who was up for a laugh, and who was happy to chill and enjoy the attentions of a hot bloke. But it was bullshit, okay?' She wasn't about to admit the full depth of her deception. No way. But maybe partially admitting she'd been 'faking it' might satisfy his need for answers.

Finally, the dress was secured.

She marched out from behind the screen to find Will with his back to her, fiddling with the camera. 'That's why I didn't want it to continue. That's why I was so spooked at seeing you again. Because you'd caught me out in a lie. This is the real me. Inconsistent, lacking in confidence, unglamorous and majorly flawed.' Her hands went to her hips. 'Satisfied?'

He turned. Swore. And fumbledthe camera, nearly dropping it.

Luckily, it was on a neck strap.

She recoiled. 'What?'

But his eyes said it all. He was looking at her like he had on holiday. Full of wanting, longing and tenderness. The kind of look that made you feel like the most stunning woman on the planet. The kind of look that made you want to say sod decorum and remove your underwear.

He removed the camera from around his neck and stepped closer.

Her heart was racing. 'Do you want the overcoat on?'

He glanced at the blue coat still on its hanger before his eyes landed back on her, travelling down the length of her and then up to focus on her eyes. 'I want you… just as you are,' he said, his voice barely a whisper, causing her skin to break out in goosebumps.

The air in her lungs disappeared and for a moment Lily forgot to breathe.

Her brain was screaming, warning her to back off. But her heart was ignoring any objections and giving in to the pull of her body, which was drawn to his like a magnet.

And then he was there. In front of her. His face lowering to hers, his hands sliding around her waist.

A shiver coincided with his lips touching hers, and an explosion went off inside her, as if a tightly wound coil had been unleashed. An unravelling of all the tension she'd held onto for the past four months since they'd last kissed.

It was frantic. Fast. Encompassing every part of her.

It wasn't a question of consent. Or making a rational decision to let this happen. Her body made the decision for her, as it ignored any doubts her brain could muster. Her body went in all guns blazing, entwining itself with his.

And then she was flying, lifted into the air, her legs encircling him as he carried her over to the sofa, their lips still locked together. He pressed against her, his movements fluid, yet driven by an urgency she found startling… but could definitely relate to. Like satisfying a craving. A need like no other.

And then a woman said, 'Whoa! Shit, sorry!'

It was enough to break the moment.

As the fog of lust cleared, frantic uncoupling followed, and both of them resumed an upright position, while adjusting dislodged clothing.

The sight of Megan Lawrence standing in the doorway looking both surprised and amused was like being doused with ice-cold water.

They stumbled away from each other, embarrassed and mortified.

'I'm so sorry,' Megan said, not sounding sorry at all. 'I had no idea. I thought I was needed for a photoshoot. I'll go.'

But it was too late.

Their secret was out.

Chapter Seventeen

Friday, 16 July

It was a glorious sunny day. Almost too sunny. The mass of surrounding woodland was helping to block out the intensity of the burning sun, but the dappled sunlight reflecting off the nearby lake was causing the lighting team a headache.

Despite the technical issues, the scene looked magical. Perfect for a romantic wedding scene.

The grand arbour at The Cow Pond in Savill Gardens had been erected to celebrate the Queen's Diamond Jubilee. It nestled at the edge of the vast forest adjoining Windsor Great Park. The wooden construction had been draped in ivy and an array of pink climbing roses had been wound around the foliage. In front, were several rows of rustic log seating. The centre aisle was decorated with informal displays of pink and white roses and strands of gypsophila which waved about softly in the breeze.

It reminded Will of his own wedding day, years ago. An outdoor ceremony at a small chateau in the Dordogne. It had been a wonderful day, a small affair with close family and friends. Intimate and special. But the memories weren't as fresh as they'd once been. Or as uplifting. And as always, whenever his mind drifted back to happier times, his thoughts inevitably ended up at the same sad place, halted at the tragic conclusion to his all-too-brief marriage.

He closed his eyes and tried to visualise Sara standing next to him at the altar, the pair of them loved-up and gazing dreamily at each other, excited by the promise of a happy life together. It seemed like a lifetime ago now. Like it had happened to a different person.

Not helped by the fact that it wasn't Sara's image that popped into his brain these days, but Lily's. It was her face that he saw now. Not his dead wife's… which was highly disturbing on many levels.

Will shook the thought away.

Dwelling on the memory of kissing Lily on Tuesday wasn't helping him to focus either.

He scanned the rows of extras filling the log seating, all kitted out in their medieval finery. Anything to distract him from thinking about being sprung kissing his costume designer by the tour guide's leading lady.

Too late. He was back there. He was sucked into the reminder of how great it had felt to kiss Lily again. The relief. The flood of endorphins that had overruled his normally rational brain, and the utter bliss of indulging in physical pleasure… until the moment they'd been inter-rupted.

He groaned and rubbed his eyes.

Never before had he acted with such reckless abandon. Not at work, anyway. But something had switched inside him and he'd abandoned caution and had fumbled around like a horny teenager. If Megan had arrived a few moments later, she might have witnessed a hell of a lot more than mere kissing. And there would have been no coming back from that.

Thankfully, as steamy as their encounter had been, they'd remained fully clothed, and his humiliation had been curtailed to mumbled apologies and skimming over the incident as though it had never happened.

Something which Lily had taken to a whole new art form. She wouldn't even look at him. Which was excruciating enough, but was made worse by Megan Lawrence surreptitiously watching them from a distance, a sly knowing smile on her face, as though she was waiting for a repeat performance.

She wasn't the only one.

Because however embarrassing it had been getting caught, it hadn't eradicated how hot it had been at the time. His blood had yet to cool down.

Trying to bring his mind back to work-related issues, Will studied the view ahead. Isaac James was playing the part of a medieval knight. He was standing by the arbour looking dapper in his long black tunic, awaiting the arrival of his princess bride.

All they needed now was for the sunlight to play ball and to wait for the police helicopter circling above to bugger off and stop ruining their take.

Shielding his eyes, he glanced around the congregation, searching out Lily. She was nowhere to be seen.

And then he mentally kicked himself. He wasn't supposed to be thinking about her.

'The director's calmed down,' Gemma said, making him jump.

Jesus, where the hell had she snuck up from?

He turned to his sister. 'He won't stay that way if we don't start filming soon.' He noticed she was holding a coffee carton. 'Is that for me?'

'Nope.' She took a mouthful. 'What's the hold up?'

'Lighting.' He gave her a disgruntled look. 'You didn't think to get me one?'

'Why would I get you one?' There was a warning note in her voice. 'If you want a coffee, get it yourself. I'm not your slave.'

'Someone's grumpy this morning. What's Chris done now, alphabetised your condiment jars again?'

Her cool eyes focused on his. 'Here's an idea. How about you focus on your own family issues, instead of criticising mine?'

He frowned. 'I don't have any family issues.'

Her pale eyebrows lifted in disbelief. 'Then why has my son been acting as a glorified childminder for the past two weeks?'

Not this again. 'Zac doesn't mind looking after Poppy.'

'You're right, he doesn't. Or if he does, he'd never say anything.' She fanned her loose white shirt, trying to get some airflow beneath. 'But I mind.'

'Why? He's getting paid for it.'

'Because you're being hypocritical.'

He turned to her. 'How so?'

'One minute you're telling my husband that Zac is a valued member of the project team—'

'Which he is.'

'—the next, you're treating him like a babysitter.'

An extra walked past, almost poking Will's eye out with her sun-brolly. 'He's helping me out,' he said, ducking out the way.

'But at what cost?' Gemma dabbed her forehead. 'How is Zac supposed to be taken seriously as a hair and make-up designer if the boss keeps dumping his kid on him... Hold that.' She shoved her coffee at him, unearthing a tissue from her trouser pocket. 'You wouldn't ask anyone else on the team to look after Poppy, would you?'

'That's because I don't trust anyone else to look after her. Zac's family. He's responsible. I know she's safe with him.'

'But it's not what he's being paid to do.' She gestured for him to hand over her coffee. 'You're damaging his career… Give me that.'

He held the carton aloft. 'That's not my intention.' He took a swig of coffee, knowing he was being childish. 'And it's just for a few more days, until I can sort out proper childcare arrangements.'

'Something you've been promising to do for months.' His sister snatched her coffee back. 'Years, even. And yet somehow you never quite get around to it.'

'That's not fair. I've explored various options, you know I have, but they never work out.'

He was subjected to a glare. 'So you've registered with an agency, have you? You've advertised for help? You've actively tried to source a suitable childminder for Poppy?'

'Well, no—'

'I rest my case.'

'It's not that simple, Gemma.' Why didn't anyone understand how challenging it was? 'Poppy doesn't like being with strangers. You know how shy she is.'

'And she's not going to get over that if you keep pandering to her insecurities.'

'I do not pander.'

'Yes, you do.'

His agitation kicked up a notch, not helped by the stifling heat. 'It's okay for you, you've always been part of a couple. You've had support looking after Zac.'

'May I remind you we both worked full time. Don't make out our situation was any easier than yours. It wasn't.'

'I know, but Zac was more independent than Poppy.'

'Not at first, he wasn't. He was a painfully shy toddler, or have you forgotten that?' She sipped her coffee, tormenting him. 'But he soon toughened up. Mostly because he had to. We weren't there to mollycoddle him. He had to stand on his own two feet.'

'Model parenting.'

'Better than having a child who's scared of her own shadow.'

'She's not that bad... And will you keep your voice down?' He glanced around, noticing a few people watching them with interest. 'There's no need for the whole team to hear about my parenting inadequacies, thank you very much.'

'You admit you're inadequate?'

'Listen, I do okay,' he said, trying to keep a lid on his temper... and then he remembered he'd yet to source a costume for Poppy's upcoming play. Work had scuppered his plans to take her to a hire shop at the weekend. Indignation switched to guilt. Okay, so maybe he didn't have a handle on everything. Not that he was about to admit as much. Not when Gemma was in such a grump. 'I can't discuss this now. We need to get on with filming.'

'Talking of filming. Have you obtained a reference for Lily Monroe yet?'

'I'm waiting to hear back from the agency she was registered with.'

'They haven't responded?' Gemma frowned. 'What's the hold up?'

He wasn't about to tell his sister that he'd only contacted the agency last week when Lily's reference from

Taye Malik had raised a few concerns. He was well aware something didn't add up, but no way was he about to give Gemma the satisfaction of saying, 'I told you so'. He gave her a half-hearted shrug. 'No idea. I guess they're busy.'

'We're all busy. And the festival's in two weeks,' she said, displaying her dissatisfaction at his lack of professionalism. 'At this rate, the job will be finished before the reference arrives. I'll chase them up.'

'I'm dealing with it, Gemma.'

'Evidently not.'

'Where's Megan Lawrence!?' shouted the director through his loudhailer, making everyone jump. 'I need my leading lady!'

'I'm on it!' Will shouted across the congregation. 'She's in hair and make-up. I'll fetch her.' Anything to avoid dealing with his sister.

'I'm not done talking about this, Will!' Gemma yelled, as he ran off.

'What a surprise!' His returning yell startled a nearby extra. 'Sorry, mate.'

'And hire a bloody childminder!'

He bit back an expletive. What was it with his family? Why couldn't they stay off his back for one moment? As if he wasn't trying his best to be everything Poppy needed.

But maybe that was the problem. He didn't want to share her with anyone else. He wanted to be her everything. And maybe that was the real issue here. But accepting he had insecurity issues when it came to his daughter wasn't something he was ready to deal with. Just as he wasn't ready to deal with the issue of a lack of a reference for Lily. So he headed for the small mobile unit set up to support the location filming and focused on the task in hand.

'Megan? You ready?' he called, knocking on the trailer door.

No reply.

He knocked again. 'Megan? We're about to start filming.'

'She's not in there,' a voice said from behind.

Lily.

He turned, but she'd already hurried away. 'Hey, where are you going?'

'To check on Isaac's costume.'

'Isaac's costume is fine,' he said, jogging after her and catching her arm. 'Wait up.'

'I'm busy. I'm needed on set.'

'You can spare a minute.' He figured interrogating her as to why she'd been avoiding him wouldn't get him anywhere, so he opted for keeping it work-related. 'Do you know where Megan is?'

'Sorry, no.' She slipped from his grasp and walked off, still without looking at him.

This was ridiculous.

He ran after her, moving in front of her so she couldn't escape. 'Lily, will you please stop avoiding me. We need to talk.'

She tried to side-step him. 'No we don't... And certainly not now.'

'When then?'

'Err... how about never?'

'That's a bit immature, don't you think?'

'Probably.' She dodged past him and walked off.

He went after her. 'Wait up, will you!'

But she wasn't slowing down.

'At least help me look for Megan.'

At that, she stopped.

He waited, wondering what she'd do next. He wanted to touch her. To reposition a stray lock of her hair that was dislodged by the breeze, but knew it wouldn't be welcomed. Instead, he waited.

With a resigned sigh, she turned to face him. 'Have you tried the Portaloos?'

'No, just the trailer.'

'Then I'll look there.' She headed in that direction.

'I'll come with you.'

'Hardly appropriate.'

'I'll wait outside, obviously.'

He fell into step beside her, unable to resist glancing at her as they walked. She was wearing a blue top that had slid off one shoulder, revealing the strap of her vest top beneath. It took all his willpower not to trail his fingers over her exposed skin.

Christ, he had it bad.

'So, how have you been?'

She kept walking. 'Fine.'

'You don't seem fine.'

'How do I seem?'

Honesty was the best policy, right? 'Prickly. Embar-rassed… Remorseful.'

She shot him a quick glance. 'And you're not?'

'Not remorseful, no. Embarrassed, yes. But only because Megan interrupted us. Not because I regret what happened… Do you?'

'What do you think?'

'I think you wanted it as much as I did.'

A beat passed before she spoke. 'It was a momentary blip.'

'A blip?'

'Yes. A blip.'

'You didn't enjoy it?'

No response.

Just as he thought.

'It didn't remind you of how great things were on holiday? Or make you think this could be something so much more?'

She made a scoffing sound. 'You got all that from one kiss?'

'Yeah, I did.' He turned her to face him. 'And it would've been a lot more than a kiss if Megan hadn't walked in.'

And wasn't that the truth.

Her face instantly coloured. She'd caught the sun, he noticed, the bridge of her nose was pink.

They held eye contact for a moment. Energy once again beginning to sizzle between them, before she stepped back and broke the spell. 'Well, she did. And maybe that's a good thing.'

'How so?'

Her hand lifted, stopping him moving closer. 'It prevented us from making a huge mistake.'

Despite her words, her hand stayed pressed against his chest. 'I don't see it as a mistake,' he said softly, fascinated by the way the sunlight picked up the colours in her hair.

'You wouldn't.'

He lifted her chin. 'Meaning?'

'It's not your reputation that would be ruined.'

'Jesus, this isn't the eighteenth century, Lily.'

'I meant professional reputation.' She stepped away, shaking her hand as if it was contaminated from having touched him. 'Your career wouldn't be damaged by an… an elicit liaison. Mine would.' She gestured around her. 'Who knows how many people Megan has told. And I have no wish to be the subject of gossip. I don't want this following me around, ruining my chances of making a decent career.'

He was confused. 'But you already have a decent career. You're established in the industry. This won't affect you any more than it would me.'

A look of something undecipherable flashed across her face. Her eyes fluttered closed, and then opened again. 'Right. Of course.'

He rested his hands on her shoulders. 'Lily, please don't beat yourself up over this. It was my fault, not yours. You're right, I behaved unprofessionally, and I'm sorry. But if I'm honest, I don't regret it. It confirmed what I already knew – that there's unfinished business between us. And I for one, would like to explore that further.'

He looked into her enticing green eyes, mesmerised by the way she seemed to glow. There was no other word for it. He was being mushy, he knew that. Sentimental and needy. But it was hard to ignore the effect she had on him. Her cheeks were flushed, her glossy lips parted, and he wasn't sure he'd ever wanted a woman more.

But before he could continue, she said, 'I'd better see if Megan's in here,' and backed away, disappearing inside the Portaloos.

Will kicked at a clump of grass in frustration.

Why was everything in his life so complicated?

Maybe he should go back to enjoying meaningless hook-ups and give up on the idea of a proper relationship. It was certainly easier that way. But was that what he really wanted?

Besides which, he was continuing to ignore the elephant in the room.

Poppy.

He still hadn't mentioned her.

He'd justified not telling Lily about his past on holiday, but continuing to keep his daughter a secret was wrong. He knew that. Especially when on Tuesday Lily had directly asked him if he'd told her everything about his life. Well, no, he hadn't.

But it seemed too big a bombshell to suddenly drop on her now. It certainly wouldn't help convince her to trust him and give them a go as a couple. Yet he couldn't keep denying his life, either. He was a single dad. No getting away from that.

He walked around the temporary Portaloos and into a nearby clearing, needing a moment to himself.

When was the right time to admit he'd been lying? Was there ever a good time? And would it create more of an obstacle between them?

Probably.

Definitely.

He leant against a tree and closed his eyes. It was cooler under the canopy of trees, a welcome respite to the harsh sun. He could hear distant voices coming from the film set and the director yelling through the loudhailer.

Nearby, he could hear the rustle of trees moving in the breeze and the faint sound of crickets in the tall grass.

And then he heard a faint giggle.

He opened his eyes, but there was no one about.

He moved further into the clearing, stepping over a fallen branch.

A flash of cream silk wedding dress disappeared behind a large oak tree.

What the…?

Trying not to make a sound, he moved around the tree, stunned by what he saw there.

Megan Lawrence was kissing his nephew, Zac.

Chapter Eighteen

Tuesday, 20 July

Lily didn't enjoy crowded pubs at the best of times. She wasn't a big drinker, she felt claustrophobic, and she couldn't hear properly above the loud music. An evening spent crammed into The Carpenters Arms along with half of Windsor wasn't her favoured pastime.

She'd rather be back at The Crooked House Tea Rooms, curled up on the bed watching Netflix. Not that anyone else felt that way. The rest of the project team seemed to be having a blast. She was the only one who appeared to be faking having a good time.

When the message had been circulated yesterday inviting everyone to 'let off some steam' after the conclusion of filming today, her initial reaction had been to decline. She wasn't as tired as she had been at the beginning of the project – her body had thankfully adjusted to the hectic schedule of early starts and late finishes – but she'd yet to fully embrace the culture of partying between shifts and rolling up for filming bleary-eyed and smelling of booze. This opportunity might have landed in her lap through a misunderstanding, but it was too precious to blow through misbehaving.

Not that anyone was really misbehaving.

Just 'high jinks' as her grandma used to say.

She watched Frankie dancing with one of the sound engineers. They appeared to be in a trance, lost in the beat of the music and waving their hands in the air – well-practised in the art of raving.

God, she sounded old.

Then again, she'd never been into this kind of thing even as a youngster. Even if her situation had been different and she hadn't been a full-time carer, she doubted this type of evening would have really appealed.

The closest she'd come to a night out clubbing was during her holiday in the Caribbean. Even then it hadn't felt like proper clubbing. The nightclubs on holiday had been more relaxed than in the UK, with a mixture of ages and more of a wedding reception vibe, than hardcore partying. But there was no way this DJ was going to be playing 'Dancing Queen' anytime soon, of that she was certain.

She looked around the room, and smiled when she caught sight of Zac approaching.

He eased himself through the crowd, his tall frame visible above the throng of people. 'Hey there, Lily. Having fun?'

'A blast,' she lied, making a point of lifting her drink. 'You?'

'Music and booze.' He grinned. 'What's not to like?'

He had a point. 'Did you deliver Poppy's costume okay?'

'I dropped it off last night.' He had to raise his voice to be heard above the noise.

'Was she pleased with it?'

'She loved it. She couldn't wait to show it off to her teacher.'

'I'm glad. She's a sweetheart.'

'She is.' He sipped his bottled beer.

'I hope helping her was okay?'

He leant closer so he could hear. 'How do you mean?'

'Was her dad okay about me making her a costume?'

It had only occurred to her at the weekend when Poppy had shown up for her final fitting, that being so familiar with a child without the parent's consent wasn't perhaps entirely appropriate. Zac being okay with it as her temporary guardian was one thing, but maybe she should have obtained permission from the girl's father before agreeing to make the costume. Not being a parent herself, she had no idea what the etiquette was in these situations.

Zac looked sheepish. 'I have a confession. He has no idea. Poppy wanted to keep it a secret and I went along with it.' He gave a half-hearted shrug. 'You know, so I didn't have to explain how come Poppy was making costumes with you when she was supposed to be being looked after by me.'

Oh, dear. That just made her feel worse. She wasn't comfortable being used as an alibi for Zac's romantic liaisons. And she definitely wasn't happy that Poppy's dad was in the dark about his daughter being unloaded onto a stranger without his knowledge. 'Won't he question where she got the costume from?'

'I told him it was hired.'

'Right.' Another lie. Her life seemed to be peppered with them at the moment. Still, it wasn't her place to interfere. 'Are you going to watch the play tomorrow night?'

He took another sip of beer. 'I'd never hear the end of it if I didn't.'

A whistle cut through the noise, drawing Lily's attention across the room. Megan waved her hands above the crowd, beckoning them onto the makeshift dance floor.

She nudged Zac playfully. 'I think you're wanted.'

Zac smiled. 'Joining us?'

She shook her head. 'You go. I'm happy here.'

'If you're sure.' He ambled off.

'Oh… and wish Poppy good luck for me for tomorrow night!' she called after him. 'I hope the play goes well!'

He gave her a thumbs-up, his besotted gaze already fixated on Megan. She met him halfway across the dance-floor and they began moving together. Nothing too intimate or raunchy. They were being discreet, acting like friendly acquaintances rather than secret lovers, but Lily could tell they were smitten. And why not? Megan was single and so was Zac. They got on well and the attraction seemed mutual. Sure, there was a ten-year age gap, but that was hardly the scandal of the century. They were just having a bit of fun.

Hadn't she done the same thing on holiday?

Exactly.

Then she remembered how things had turned out, and how her harmless fling had become a lot more complicated. But that was only because Will had been daft enough to track her down and try to rekindle their affair. If he'd left things as they were, it would have been perfect.

That's what she kept telling herself, anyway.

The truth was, if she hadn't lied on holiday, she'd love nothing more than to rekindle her romance with Will Taylor. Who wouldn't? He was funny and gorgeous and hot. He was also cranky and combative and demanding. But she was hardly without fault, so she couldn't complain. Everyone had their flaws. And she *had* lied. A huge lie that had snowballed and landed her a job that she didn't deserve and wasn't qualified to do. So however much her heart wanted Will Taylor, her head was having to put the brakes on.

The sound of laughter drew her attention to the bar. The lighting lads were congregated there, chatting and drinking, eyeing up a group of girls. The more senior crew were filling the seats around the edge of the bar, not quite up to the task of both standing and drinking.

Sipping her gin and tonic, Lily decided she'd had enough and dumped it on the table, waving away an offer to join various people on the dance floor. She couldn't dance to this music. It was too loud.

Yep, definitely old before her time.

She headed for somewhere quieter.

The Carpenters Arms was usually a serious drinking haunt, but tonight the open courtyard out back had been turned into an amusement area, with gaming tables, a pool table and various slot machines. There was also a cocktail bar, serving garish-looking concoctions that reminded her of being on holiday.

Despite the activities on offer, it was quieter outside. Everyone else was inside the main bar area dancing. She was glad – it gave her the respite she needed.

She approached the empty bar and ordered a virgin Pina Colada. Not the most sophisticated of drinks, but the gin had made her thirsty.

And then she became aware of a man standing next to her. She knew it was Will, even before she turned.

Oh well, she supposed she'd done well to avoid him thus far.

'Let me guess,' he said, sidling up next to her. 'Pina Colada?'

She tried to ignore the frisson of heat his presence evoked. 'Minus the alcohol.'

'I remember how much you liked your cocktails.'

'I'm sure you also remember the state they left me in.'

He grinned. 'Vividly.'

That was what worried her.

She assessed his outfit of black fitted shirt and jeans. 'Where's your box of Milk Tray?'

He rolled his eyes. 'That advert hasn't been on the telly for about thirty years.'

'You still knew what I meant.' She shrugged. 'And you don't need to tell me I'm old-fashioned, I'm painfully aware of the fact.'

He leant on the bar. 'I never said you were old-fashioned.' His eyes travelled over her dress. 'You definitely don't look old-fashioned tonight. Nice dress.'

She glanced down, feeling self-conscious in her knee-length silver-grey skater dress, which she had made quickly last night from an offcut of material ordered for the film. 'Thanks.'

The barman appeared with her drink.

'I'll get this.' Will overrode her attempts to pay and ordered himself a light beer. 'So, having fun, Miss Monroe?'

'Not really, Mr Taylor.'

He laughed and handed her the virgin cocktail, which glowed through the glass like yellow kryptonite. 'Me neither.'

'But you came anyway?'

'I have to, I'm the boss. Plus, it's good for morale. Things have been a bit tense of late. I thought everyone needed to unwind.'

She added a straw to her glass. 'Then it's been a success.'

'But not for you?'

'I'm okay.' She sipped her drink, flinching at the sweetness. 'I'm completely chilled.'

His lips twitched. 'I've seen less tension in a bed spring. You look like you're expecting Armageddon.'

Well, she was. Her secret could be exposed at any moment. Megan had already guessed, it was only a matter of time before everyone else did. 'That's just my natural state.'

The barman handed Will his beer.

He turned to her. 'Cheers.'

'Cheers.' She lifted her glass. 'Thanks for the drink.'

His eyes lingered as he watched her. 'Is it being around me that makes you tense?'

She raised an eyebrow. 'What do you think?'

'I think you weren't this tense on holiday.'

'Nobody's tense on holiday. That's the point of holidays.'

'True.' He took a slug of beer and leant on the bar, fixing her with an intimate gaze. 'So why don't we pretend we're not in a pub in Windsor, but somewhere exotic, like stranded on an isolated island somewhere in the Caribbean.'

She pointed to the amusements. 'That has a Union Jack pool table?'

He grinned. 'Use your imagination.'

'I don't have that much imagination.'

'Sure you do.' He touched her arm. The warmth of his hand connecting with her skin sent a shiver racing up her arm. 'Close your eyes.'

She eyed him suspiciously. 'Why?'

'Humour me.'

'Fine.' With a sigh, she closed her eyes.

His fingers curled around her arm. 'Can you hear the waves?'

'Nope. But I can hear the beeping of slot machines.'

'Concentrate.'

'I'm trying.'

'Can you smell coconut?' He'd moved closer, his voice right by her ear. 'And fresh mango?'

'Do sweaty armpits count?'

'No.'

'And before you ask, I can't hear steel drums either.'

'You're rubbish at role-play.'

She opened her eyes, startled. 'I didn't realise that's what we were doing.'

He smiled. 'I'm trying to get you to relax.'

'It's not working.'

'Clearly.' He stepped away.

It wasn't her fault. How was touching her and whispering in her ear supposed to relax her? Her body was vibrating, every nerve ending on alert, anticipating his next move.

Just when she thought he'd given up, his free hand slipped into hers. 'Come with me.'

She probably should object. After all, past experience had shown she had zero resistance when it came to rejecting his advances. If he kissed her, she was toast. But his hand was warm and smooth and she didn't have the energy to fight him. 'Where are we going?'

'When you were this tense on holiday, only one thing worked.'

'And that was?'

'Physical activity.'

She stopped. 'Excuse me?'

'I didn't mean *that*,' he said, in a hushed voice. 'I meant adventure sports.' But then he paused, as if struck by a thought. 'Although now you come to mention it, sex might also do the trick.'

She pinned him with a look. 'Or not.'

He winked. 'Worth a try.'

'There are no adventure sports here.' She nodded to the various games, anything to avoid looking at him. 'There's nothing risky about trying to hit a pop-up rabbit with a hammer.'

'But it might stop you overthinking.'

'I doubt that.'

Without warning, he bent lower and kissed the side of her neck, his lips trailing up her neck and ending up next to her ear. 'And help you loosen up,' he whispered.

She stepped away. Not because it wasn't nice. But because it was too nice. She only had so much control. 'I doubt that, too.'

He shrugged. 'If nothing else, I get to hang out with you.'

'Which is a puzzle in itself. You don't like this version of me, remember?'

'No, it was timid Lily I didn't warm to. Prickly Lily is just fine.' He steered her towards the basketball game. 'Although I don't think she's the real you, either.'

'Why do you say that?'

He positioned her in front of the hoop. 'Because I've seen beneath the prickly exterior.' He put a pound coin in the slot. 'A happier less defensive Lily lurks within.'

'How do you know she's not the fake? Maybe prickly defensive Lily is the real me.'

'I don't think so.' He handed her a ball. 'Shoot.'

'Why?'

'That's the point of the game.'

'No, I mean why are you so sure prickly Lily isn't the real me?'

A shrug. 'Gut instinct.' He nodded at the hoop. 'And your minute is ticking by.'

'Your instincts are wrong.' She threw the ball. It bounced off the rim and into the gully below.

He handed her another ball. 'What are you hiding?'

'Nothing.' Lying did nothing for her aim. Another miss.

'Something's making you jumpy.' He handed her another ball. 'You look like a fugitive on the run, forever checking over your shoulder, waiting to be found out.'

'Rubbish.' The ball smacked against the backboard and disappeared into the gully.

'Then why are you blushing?'

'It's hot out here.'

'Come on, tell me.' He handed her another ball. 'What evil crime have you committed?'

'Your theory is way off. I'm not hiding anything.' The ball hit the rim again.

'A string of ex-husbands?'

'Never been married.' She snatched the next ball from him.

'Criminal record?'

'Squeaky clean.' She threw the ball. It missed.

'Gambling addiction?'

'Never been in debt.'

He handed her another ball. 'Cheated on your exams?'

She threw the ball. 'So I could obtain C grades? Hardly worth the effort.' The bell rang announcing the end of the game. She'd scored nil points. 'See? Below average. Even at ball games.'

'What then? There is *something* you're not telling me.'

She picked up her drink and took a long sip, wishing he wasn't so astute, and that her drink contained alcohol. But that might loosen her tongue, and she needed to keep her wits about her. 'Are you sure you're not deflecting?'

He frowned. 'How d'you mean? I'm an open book.'

'Really?' She decided it was time to turn the tables. 'There are no skeletons lurking in your closet?'

He broke eye contact immediately.

Interesting.

She studied his face. He looked shifty. 'Now who's blushing.'

He walked off. 'This isn't about me.'

She followed him. Like hell it wasn't. 'Well, maybe it should be.'

He stopped by the air hockey table. 'I've nothing to hide.'

'No?' She picked up a slider. 'So no ex-wives lurking about?'

Whoa! It was like she'd just accused him of murder, or something. He stilled, his face darkening and his brow creased into a frown. He opened his mouth to say something, but closed it again. A beat passed, before he said, 'No ex-wives,' and shoved a pound coin in the machine.

She waited until he was ready and then hit the puck, sending it flying down the table. 'You know, my grandma used to say, "if a man hasn't settled down by the age of thirty, he never will."'

He sent the puck flying back to her. 'Meaning?'

'Some men aren't cut out for commitment.' She swiped at the puck, rattling it down the table. 'They like to play the field. Maybe the chase is more fun than sticking around.'

He hit the puck with force. 'I stick around.'

She had to stretch to reach it. 'How many serious relationships have you had?'

He hit the puck. 'One.'

One? That was a surprise. He seemed like the 'commitment' type. Not that she was an expert. Far from it.

She glanced at the puck, pushing it back to him. 'When did it end?'

'Eight years ago.' He smacked the puck so cleanly she had no chance of returning it. She watched as it fired past her into the waiting goal mouth.

She looked up at him. 'Struck a nerve, have I?'

He set up another game.

So it was okay for him to interrogate her, but not the other way around.

He picked up the slider. 'Ready?'

'Absolutely.'

He slid the puck across to her, with a lot less force than before, some of the fight deserting him.

She returned it, matching his slower pace. 'And there hasn't been anyone since?'

His eyes stayed focused on the table. 'There's been a few.'

'But nothing serious?'

He mis-hit the puck and it disappeared in the goal mouth. 'Damn.'

She placed her slider on the table. 'Then I rest my case.'

He scowled. 'That's not fair,' he said, marching over. 'I've been busy working. And trying to… to…' He trailed off, almost as if he'd been about to admit something, but changed his mind.

'Trying to…?'

He rubbed the back of his neck. 'I haven't had time for romance.'

'I find that hard to believe.'

His eyes locked on hers. 'Meaning?'

It was time to stand her ground. 'Meaning, you have your secrets. I have mine. And neither of us, it seems, feels much like sharing.'

They stayed like that for a good few seconds. Staring down at each other, inches apart. Lily fought the urge to continue fighting, or worse, to cave into the chemistry radiating between them and pick up where they'd left off a week ago.

As it was, the moment was broken by Frankie appearing and informing Will that his services were required to deal with a lighting engineer who'd consumed too much beer.

Lily watched him walk off.

He didn't look back.

She wasn't sure whether she felt relieved… or disappointed.

Chapter Nineteen

Will wasn't sure how he felt about having a free Sunday to himself. He should be glad of the break. The week ahead building up to the festival was going to be manic, no doubt about it. So the chance to relax and savour the good weather and enjoy the ambience of Windsor on a summer's day should be welcome. But his Sundays were usually reserved for Poppy.

Not today.

Today, Poppy had uncharacteristically accepted the offer to attend the country club with her grandparents and have her first ever tennis lesson. And no one was more surprised than him.

'I'm feeling braver,' she'd told him, when he'd dropped her off at her grandparents' house this morning and queried whether she really wanted to go to the club, or whether she was just doing it to please her family.

'Learning new things can be fun,' she'd said, giving him a reprimanding look. 'Maybe you should try doing something new, too… like dating a nice lady who might turn out to be the *one*.' This statement has been accompanied by a knowing look, making her seem a lot older than her tender years.

He hadn't known whether to laugh or cry. He was being given dating advice by his eleven-year-old daughter. But before he could give her his usual spiel about how 'it wasn't that simple', and 'you couldn't force these things', she'd patted his hand and said, 'Why don't you ask Lily on a date?'

Despite never having met the blessed woman, and only ever having heard her name mentioned once, his daughter seemed fixated on the idea of them becoming a couple.

It was insane.

Before he could dismiss the idea, she'd said, 'I know you said you didn't fancy her, but you might never see her again after next weekend.' At this point, she'd climbed out of the car as though she was the adult and he was the kid. 'And wouldn't that be a shame?'

What had happened to his timid little daughter? She'd turned into a dating guru.

Maybe it was the success of being in the school play?

When he'd shown up at the school hall on Wednesday evening expecting to witness a shy and mumbled performance, his daughter had surprised the hell out of him by boldly delivering her lines and not making a single mistake.

It helped that she looked the part. Her Mad Hatter outfit was the standout costume of the show. He had no idea where Zac had managed to find such a quality costume at such short notice, but he would be forever grateful. Partly, for bailing him out of a huge bad parent-shaped hole, but mostly for the confidence wearing it had given Poppy. She'd strutted about the stage like a little diva, completely in character, leaving Will wondering what on earth had happened to evoke such a change.

Whatever the reason, he had to admit she was right about Lily. Time was of the essence. He *did* fancy her, however much he tried to convince his daughter that he didn't. Which is why he'd texted her this morning and asked her to meet him down by the river.

After all, what did he have to lose? Even his twenty-one-year-old nephew was getting more action than he was, and with a hot actress, too. Something he was still trying to get his head around.

Lily arrived bang on time, ambling down the path by the river's edge wearing a white cotton summer dress, flowery plimsolls and a large floppy hat. He had a flash-back to the Caribbean and how she'd dressed on holiday. Stylish, confident, sexy and assured.

It gave him hope. Maybe fun-loving, easy-going Lily was back?

The sunlight made her glow again. The weeping willows trailing along the water added to the serene picture, aided by the fleet of swans floating down the river... It was the perfect backdrop. The ideal setting for a last-ditch attempt to win her over... which she ruined instantly, by saying, 'I assume you have a bloody good reason for getting me out of bed at the crack of dawn on my one day off?'

Not entirely the old Lily, then.

He sighed. 'I do, as a matter of fact. I thought we could go boating.'

Her eyes grew wide. 'Boating?'

'Yes, you know, something fun and relaxing. A chance to enjoy the surroundings and reconnect.'

Her bag slid off her shoulder and hit the ground. 'I thought we'd agreed reconnecting was a bad idea?'

He got up off the bench. 'No, you said the reason we weren't getting on was because we hadn't been our true selves on holiday. And I'm here to prove that's not the case.'

'By boating?'

'By removing the stresses of work and deadlines, and creating a relaxed non-pressurised environment where we can be ourselves.'

'And you think boating will achieve that?'

He picked up her bag. 'As someone recently pointed out to me, in a week's time the festival will be over, and you and I will never have reason to see each other again.'

She glanced away. 'Well, you know... every cloud, and all that.'

'So you're happy to walk away? No regrets?' He took her hand. 'Because that's not what I want.'

She stepped back, dislodging his hand. 'There's no point. It won't work.'

'Why? Because you don't want me? Or because you don't think we have a future?' He lowered his voice. 'Or is it because you think I won't want you if I got to know the real you?'

'Exactly.' She looked exasperated. 'There are things about me you don't know.'

He shrugged. 'That's the same for me, too.'

'Not... good things.'

'You think I don't have flaws? Believe me, I have. But I'm not about to reveal all my failings in one go. Nobody does that. Not any sane person, anyway. Getting to know someone is about learning the good stuff as well as the bad. I don't expect you to tell me all your secrets straight off. That's okay. Can't we spend some time together and just chill.'

She raised her eyebrows. 'Chill?'

'Yeah, you know, enjoy each other's company. No pressure.'

'You mean as… friends?'

'Friends works for me,' he lied. But at that moment he was prepared to accept anything on offer. Sad creature that he was.

She sighed. 'I have a feeling I'm going to regret this.'

'The boats are this way.' He pointed towards the jetty. 'Rowing boat? Or motorboat?'

'Rowing boat.'

'Rowing boat, it is.'

They walked down the path like a regular couple out for a Sunday morning stroll. He had an urge to take her hand but figured that wasn't what a 'friend' would do.

Instead, he tried to enjoy the moment. He'd missed this. Walking with a woman. Taking in the sights of nature. It was such a simple pleasure. 'Pretty, isn't it?'

'Very.'

To their left the pathway was edged with thick shrubbery, lined with rose bushes and trees, masking the road noise beyond. 'Alexandra Park is the other side,' he said, searching for 'friendly' conversation. 'The main festival site for next Saturday.'

She glanced over. 'I remember.'

He pointed to the other side of the Thames. 'That's where the funfair will be set up.'

She shielded her eyes from the sun. 'Funfair?'

'The final event of the festival. They'll be fireworks and all the usual attractions. You know, bumper cars, big dippers. Even a roller coaster.' He was about to add that Poppy was looking forward to experiencing the rides, but stopped himself. He still hadn't mentioned his daughter.

But now wasn't the time for confessing. Things were still too fragile between them. Maybe later.

She looked across the water. 'How do you get to the other side?'

'Eton Bridge.' He gestured behind him. 'Further that way, towards Riverside Station.'

They fell into step.

He glanced at her, trying to assess whether his plan was working.

It wasn't going great so far. She looked tense – conflicted and tentative. She also looked cute in her summer outfit. But the way she kept drawing in deep breaths made it seem like she was at least trying to relax. Maybe there was hope yet?

'How are the festival plans going?' she asked.

At last, conversation.

'Okay, I think. I won't know until Thursday when the contractors arrive and set up the activities. Friday will be a tricky day ahead of the roads being closed. We may have to copy how the military does it, and rehearse the main parade at four in the morning.'

She half-smiled. 'Megan will love that.'

'Isaac too.'

'Luvvies, huh?' Then she started laughing.

'What's so funny?'

'I was just thinking they might say the same about us.'

'I suppose we have had our fair share of tantrums.'

She smiled. 'A right couple of divas.'

They reached the jetty and he arranged for a couple of hours' hire. Probably wishful thinking on his part, but it was a final attempt to convince her they should be together. If he failed, at least he could walk away knowing he'd tried his best.

Having paid the owner, Will went over to one of the blue wooden boats and stepped in. 'Mind your step,' he said, offering Lily his hand.

She accepted his offer and climbed in. 'Thanks.'

The boat rocked as they sat down, making them both laugh nervously, neither one wanting to end up in the water.

He picked up the oars. Unlike when they'd gone kayaking in the Caribbean, they were facing each other, their knees almost touching.

Time to put his plan into action. 'Ready?'

She gripped the sides of the boat. 'As I'll ever be.'

He began to row, awkward at first as they moved away from the jetty, trying to find space with less traffic.

The river was busy. Several large motorboats were moored along the sides. Canoes sped past, the occupants in competition training kits, making it look easy. In amongst the boats were pristine-white swans and noisy ducks, taking off and landing, creating splashes in the water.

Lily sat rigidly, her bag tucked behind her, her expression tentative. 'No shipwrecks here, I'm guessing?'

'None that I know of.' He pulled on the oars. 'Although I imagine there's a few sunken treasures below.'

'Discarded toasters and bicycles, you mean?'

'There might be the odd casket of stolen gold lying somewhere.'

'More likely, a few dead bodies.' She held onto her hat when the breeze threatened to dislodge it.

'Dead bodies?'

'There's bound to be a few,' she said, glancing over the side. 'Victims of the Royal Windsor Mafia.'

He continued rowing. 'I can't imagine Windsor having a mafia.'

'You'd be surprised. Posh people are way more sinister than poor people.'

'How do you figure that?'

'Lord Lucan was from a titled family.'

'Well, the Krays weren't. They definitely weren't posh.'

'True.' She shrugged. 'They were from my neck of the woods. Just a few miles down the road.'

'Really? Was crime a problem where you grew up?'

'In Haringey?' She shook her head. 'Not really. The usual stuff, nothing notorious or newsworthy. You?'

'House break-ins, mostly. I think someone stole a horse once.'

She smiled. 'Like a racehorse?'

'No, a regular horse. The thief used it as getaway transport.'

She burst out laughing. 'That's so posh. See? I rest my case.' She shook her head. 'So where did you grow up?'

'Chobham. A small village in Surrey.'

'Ah, rural country. Well, we Londoners are made from tougher stuff.' She squealed when the boat rocked. 'Most of the time.'

It was his turn to laugh.

He continued rowing down the river, smiling, despite the ache in his shoulders. He didn't care. At some point over the last week, any remaining doubt he'd had about wanting another relationship had vanished. Despite the arguing and disagreements, the misunderstandings and strains of working together, he'd felt more alive and invigorated than he'd done in the past eight years.

He was finally ready to make that leap. To venture into the world of being in a relationship. Now all he had to do was convince Lily.

A gondola sailed past, it's eight-man crew dressed in straw boaters and striped blue tops. They were singing, waving at the other boaters as they passed by.

Lily waved back. 'That's not something you see every day.'

'Eton boys, probably. Eccentric lot.'

She twisted her body, watching them sail away down the river. 'Fancy having to wear top hats and tails to classes.'

'What were you like at school?'

'Me?' She tilted her head. 'Nondescript, I guess. Quiet. Well-behaved. Punctual.'

'The model student.'

'C grades, remember?' She smiled and took a long breath, seeming to relax another notch as she turned her face up to the sun. 'What about you? What were your school days like? Probably captain of the sports team, and voted most likely to succeed, I imagine.'

'Not even close. Regular detentions, lazy at revision, and outshone by my very-clever-and-annoying-teacher's-pet sister.'

She smiled. 'Jealousy is not an attractive quality.'

'Neither is gloating over better exam results.'

'I sense tension between you and your sister.'

'Very astute.'

She studied him. 'Let me guess? The transition from annoying younger brother to being her boss hasn't resulted in a harmonious working relationship?'

'Correct.'

'Then why work together?'

Good question. 'It's not that we don't get on. We do. And she's amazing at what she does. I haven't got a clue about quarterly accounts or fiscal percentages.'

He thought back to their childhood and their numerous squabbles. Maybe they wouldn't have ended up working together if Sara hadn't died. That was the thing about death. It shifted things. Changed the dynamics. Altered life's journey.

And not just for those directly affected. Some relationships were destroyed by it, others strengthened. Their joint couple friends had drifted away, feeling too uncomfortable to deal with the awkwardness of Will's grief. But his sister had been his rock. She'd stepped up to the plate and kept him sane. He'd be forever grateful. And indebted... which is probably what caused the tension.

'I guess we're just pre-programmed to fight,' he said, slowing his stroke rhythm. 'Can't be together, can't be apart.' His arms were feeling the strain. He let the boat float towards a secluded inlet. 'Aren't you like that with your siblings?'

'Don't have any.'

He brushed away the trailing weeping willows as the boat disappeared under the trees. 'What about your parents?'

'Don't have any of those, either.' She said it in such a matter-of-fact way, he almost didn't register her words.

'You don't have any parents?'

'Nope. Dad left soon after I was born. Mum died when I was four.'

'Shit.' He had to duck under a branch.

Why hadn't he known this? But then, why should he? They'd never discussed their personal lives on holiday – something he'd been extremely grateful for at the time.

He was now realising how little he actually knew about her.

Lily removed her sunhat and fanned her face. 'I was brought up by my grandparents.'

'That's a blow. Sorry.'

''Tis what it is.' She trailed her fingers in the water. 'Fortunately, my grandparents were lovely people.'

'I remember you saying you cared for them.'

'My grandma died a while back, but I looked after my granddad for more than ten years. He died last December.'

He pulled the oars into the boat, letting the boat rest against the bank. 'That must've been hard, trying to build your career and care for someone at the same time?'

As he knew only too well. It was bloody exhausting. And he'd had help. His family had rallied to his aid. He couldn't have done it without them. He certainly couldn't imagine doing it alone.

She looked away. 'You could say that.'

'Do you have any other family?'

'Nope. Just me.' She didn't sound upset, just resigned.

She pummelled her bag into a cushion and lay back, resting her head on it. 'This is nice,' she said, closing her eyes. 'You were right, boating is very relaxing.'

For a moment, all he could do was watch her. The dappled sunlight flickered across her face. Her breathing slowed and she was the picture of tranquillity. 'I feel bad now for moaning about my sister.'

'You weren't to know. And fighting with your siblings is normal.' She opened one eye. 'At least, so I'm told.'

'So you had a good relationship with your grandparents?'

'The best. I was very lucky.'

She didn't sound lucky. She sounded like she'd had an awful upbringing. If he'd been her, he would've felt highly aggrieved at the unfairness of it all. 'Don't you feel angry?'

'What for?'

'For… I don't know, being cheated out of the life you should've had.'

She shifted position. 'Who's to say life with my mum would've been any better? It might've been harder. More challenging. Less fun. Maybe I would've been happier with her, maybe not.' She shrugged. 'All I know is that I was loved and cared for. My grandparents did everything in their power to give me a stable and fulfilling life. They never punished me. Never put pressure on me to do better at school. And they always supported and encouraged me to do the things that made me happy. That's more than a lot of people have.'

She made a good point. 'I feel suitably chastised.'

Lily wriggled onto her elbows. 'Why? There's no need to be. I'm just saying that life is a series of crossroads. No one knows how taking a different route will have turned out. You can only follow the road you've taken… or been shoved down, in my case,' she said, shrugging. 'No one intentionally chooses an unhappy path in life. But sometimes you just have to make the best of the situation you find yourself in.'

Is that what he'd done? Made the best of a crappy situation? Or had he spent the last eight years dwelling on how unlucky he'd been and focusing on what he'd lost, rather than what he had to be grateful for? Like having Poppy in his life.

Suddenly, he wasn't so sure.

She tilted her head. 'Your turn. Parents?'

Right. His turn. 'Diane and Bobby, retired school teacher and police chief, respectively.'

'Do you get on with them?'

'I do. We're a close-knit family.'

She smiled. 'That's nice. Any other siblings?'

'No, just Gemma.'

She reached out to touch a trailing willow branch. 'What about love? I know you've never been married, you said so the other night.'

He flinched. What he'd actually said was, he didn't have an ex-wife. Not that he'd never been married. There was a difference. But before he could correct her, she said, 'Kids?' And he was hit by another wave of guilt for not mentioning Poppy earlier.

Sure, he had his reasons. And they were justified. He didn't have to apologise for not divulging everything about his personal life sooner. But however much he could defend his previous behaviour, now was the opportune moment to confess all.

But before he could open his mouth, she said, 'Forget that. Silly question,' and started laughing. 'Of course you don't have kids. Not the commitment type, right?' She raised herself onto her elbows, smiling. 'Although you did tell me you once had a serious relationship. It ended… what… eight years ago? So what happened? Or am I being too intrusive?'

He'd been gifted a second opportunity to reveal the truth. It should be easy enough to say the words. They weren't hard. All he had to do was take a deep breath, clear his throat, and admit that, actually… he *had* been married and he *did* have a daughter, but his wife had died… But somehow, he couldn't get his mouth to work. The words just rolled around his brain, trying to escape, but failed to form themselves into a sentence.

Lily raised her hand. 'You're right, none of my business. We're supposed to be chilling, right? No heavy topics, just fun and relaxation.' She let her head drop back.

Oh, crap. He was losing the moment.

Speak, you idiot. Tell her the truth. You can't expect the woman to agree to a relationship with you if she doesn't know about Sara and Poppy.

But the words wouldn't come.

Why?

Good question.

Was he scared she might not want him? Or ask too many awkward questions?

Probably.

Was he worried he might not be able to hold it together when talking about his past and would dissolve in a puddle of tears?

Most certainly.

He'd never been a fan of public outpourings. He preferred to keep his anguish hidden. But there was no bypassing the situation. He couldn't expect to say silent on the subject. She deserved to know the truth. He owed her that much. And if Poppy had found the courage to act in her school play, then the least her dad could do was act like a grown man for once.

He needed to admit that he'd omitted sections of his life and reveal his true self. The unedited version. The real Will Taylor. He cleared his throat. 'So, the thing is—'

A bird flew out of the tree above and startled Lily.

She jolted, sending the boat into a rock and drifting away from the bank, dislodging one of the oars.

'Oh, crikey,' she yelped, trying to stand up, making the boat even more unstable. 'Grab the oar!' She was giggling, stumbling about, losing her balance.

'Stop moving,' he said, laughing at her attempts to rescue the oar.

Old Lily was back. Smiling, uninhibited, uncoordinated... and about to fall into the water if she didn't stop moving.

'Take my hand,' he said, trying to steady himself.

But she was too off balance. She stumbled backwards, caught her foot on the remaining oar and disappeared off the back off the boat.

Shit.

She landed with an almighty splash in the Thames.

His first instinct was to laugh. But then he remembered she wasn't a strong swimmer. He dropped to his knees, searching for her in the water. 'Lily...? Lily?'

Why hadn't she resurfaced?

He searched each side of the boat. No sign of her. Where was she?

He kicked off his trainers, ripped off his T-shirt and jumped into the water. It was cold, murky and filled with algae. The dense foliage under the water caught in his legs, entangling in his arms and feet as he searched for her.

His knee hit something solid. He ducked under the water, trying to see, but it was too cloudy. And then a flash of white. He grabbed at her dress, tugging on it, kicking his way to the surface.

She weighed a ton. Why wasn't she helping? Because she couldn't, he realised. She was out cold.

Christ, was she dead?

He dragged her to the bank, taking what felt like an age to push her from the water onto the grassy bank.

His limbs felt like lead. His lungs couldn't take in enough air. He'd lost all his strength. Only sheer will-power and determination pushed him on, as he dragged her from the water and pulled her to safety.

And that's when he saw the blood.

Lots of it.

Covering his hands, her dress, gushing from her head.

She'd hit her head.

She had a head injury.

She'd hit her head.

Images filled his brain. Flashes from his past.

He was gripped by a pain so acute he wanted to scream.

Not again. Please, not again.

'Help me!' he yelled, hoping someone would hear.

He was paralysed. Stunned into a panic and too traumatised to act.

He forced himself to think.

Breathing. Was she breathing?

He lowered his face to her chest, looking for signs of life. He had no idea whether she was breathing or not.

'Lily…? Lily! Can you hear me?' He rolled her onto her side, rubbing her back, willing her to answer him.

A man on a pushbike stopped on the path above. 'You all right, mate?'

'I need help! An ambulance. She's hit her head. She's unconscious. I don't know if she's breathing.'

The man jumped off the bike. 'I'll call 999.'

'Please hurry.' Will rubbed her back harder. 'Come on, Lily! Breathe, for Christ's sake.'

And just then she began coughing, retching up water, spluttering as she tried to catch her breath.

'It's okay… you're okay,' he assured her, stroking her hair, his hands covered in blood. 'You'll be okay.' *Please be okay.*

Will was shaking, sobbing like a baby and unable to comfort her. A useless specimen of a human being. He felt even more redundant when a couple appeared on the pathway by the man on the bike and rushed over.

'I'm a paramedic,' the woman said, dropping to her knees. 'Let me see her. What's her name?'

'Lily,' he managed to say, before he staggered away and threw up everywhere.

He left the woman to deal with her. He couldn't do this again. He couldn't lose someone else he loved.

Why did he think he was ready for a relationship?

Love hurt.

It led to loss. Pain. Endless grief.

He couldn't deal with that again. Not now. Not ever.

He threw up again.

And then he passed out.

Chapter Twenty

Lily was already feeling warm, despite the early hour. Her cream linen dress was helping to keep the heat at bay, but she knew it wouldn't last for long. The sun was slowly burning through the early morning mist, building up to be another scorcher. The sky was a powder blue, sprinkled with wispy clouds, taking their time to disperse, with no breeze to move them on.

From her vantage point high on the hill, the view down The Long Walk was stunning. The lawns either side were a lush green, the trees in full bloom, the central pathway drawing her eye to where Windsor Castle dominated the skyline. Other than a couple of joggers out exercising, the project team and actors were the only people milling about, taking advantage of a quiet time to rehearse before tomorrow's grand parade.

As adjustments were currently being made to Queen Victoria's carriage, Lily took advantage of a lull in proceedings to duck behind The Copper Horse statue and take some painkillers. Having assured everyone that she was fit for work, it wouldn't do to be seen knocking back the drugs.

She opened the nearly empty packet of ibuprofen and washed down a couple of maxi-strength tablets with a swig of water.

The gallant-looking George III statue above stared down at her disapprovingly.

'What are you looking at?' she said, wiping her mouth. 'You'd be popping pills too if you'd had a week like mine.'

His stare continued, his arm raised in battle, the once copper horse beneath him now a tarnished blue-grey, but he refrained from comment... which was just as well. If he'd answered back she might have suspected her concussion hadn't abated. She'd never had concussion before. She hoped to never have it again.

She'd left Wexham Park Hospital on Monday morning with the gash on her head glued together, a splitting headache, and the promise to return to A&E if the nausea didn't let up within forty-eight hours. Confined to bedrest for two days, she'd foolishly thought she could ignore the advice, override the dizziness, and complete the final dress for the festival as planned. But her concussion had won over and she'd resigned herself to resting up.

Consequently, the tour guide filming had to be concluded with a frontal-only view of Queen Victoria, so no one could see the array of pins securing the back section of her gown.

Thankfully, by yesterday Lily's symptoms had started to ease and she'd managed to finish most of the alterations. All that was required today was a tidy up of the hem and adding the lace shawl, which she had completed in the early hours of this morning ready for the parade.

Finishing the bottle of water, she re-emerged from behind the statue, fixed a smile in place, and returned to helping dress the actors.

'There you are,' Megan said, looking both relieved and regal in her sapphire-blue ballgown. 'I thought you'd collapsed somewhere.'

She lifted her water bottle. 'Just being a good girl and keeping my fluid levels up.'

'How's your head?'

'Peachy.'

'Liar.'

'At least I can function now. And once this dress is finished, I can relax.' She knelt down, searching out her needle in the mass of heavy silk fabric. 'Hold still so I can finish the hem.'

Megan glanced down. 'Aren't you sticking around for the festival tomorrow?'

'Of course. My contract doesn't officially end until Sunday, but other than a few alterations, my work here is done.'

'You did it, then. You completed the project without being exposed.'

Lily sat back. 'I suppose I did.'

The culmination of six weeks hard work had been completing the Queen Victoria ballgown, a replica of the dress the young queen had worn to welcome Napoleon to Windsor Castle in 1855. Luckily this was at a time when Queen Victoria had still enjoyed wearing colour, before Albert's death, when her wardrobe had switched to mourning-black.

Lily felt her life was being played out in reverse. Unlike Victoria, she'd spent her early adult life in permanent mourning, grieving for the loss of a stable home life. It was only in recent months that she felt she'd escaped the confines of grief and was finally emerging onto the other side, ready to start phase two of her life. But what that would look like was anyone's guess.

'Why aren't you happier about it?' Megan asked, looking perplexed.

'I'm not sure,' she answered honestly, resuming sewing.

'You should be ecstatic. You've designed a set of exquisite costumes and fulfilled the brief without your embellishments being found out. You're in the clear.'

'I guess.' But it didn't feel that way. The weight of her lie was curtailing any pleasure Lily might feel at her supposed 'success'.

Megan bent down. 'It also means you can pursue 'you know who' without fear of being fired. He's no longer your boss. You're on an equal footing.'

At the mention of Will, Lily glanced over to where he was in animated discussion with Frankie, as they busily tried to manoeuvre the extras into position along the walkway. 'Slight issue.'

'Which is?'

'He's avoiding me.'

'Avoiding you? Why?'

She shrugged. 'No idea. We were getting along great. We'd had a really lovely time on Sunday boating up the river…' until she'd decided to go for an unscheduled swim and cracked her head open, '…but since then, he can barely look at me.'

'Didn't he visit you in hospital?'

'Briefly, but I was too busy throwing up.'

Megan frowned. 'And since then?'

She moved to the back of the dress, using sewing as a buffer for the hurt she felt. 'Get well flowers delivered to my lodgings. The occasional text asking how I was. And an assurance that I wasn't required on set until I was fully recovered.'

'Hmmm, interesting.'

Confusing, more like. One minute the wretched man was trying to persuade her into resuming their fling, the next he was acting like he barely knew her name.

Megan twisted her head to look at her. 'How was he yesterday?'

'I hardly saw him.'

'The man is kind of busy.'

'True.' Lily glanced over again. He was rubbing the back of his neck, something she noticed he did when he was agitated.

'So what's your plan?'

Lily searched around for her scissors. 'Plan?'

'How are you going to get things back on track? I'm assuming you want to?'

Strangely, she did. 'Yes, I want to.'

Even a week ago she'd have given a different response, but something had shifted during their excursion on Sunday. It was the comment he'd made about them both having flaws and secrets, and how they needed to accept each other's failings if they were to explore the possibility of a relationship. She'd realised that the only thing standing in the way of being with Will was her lie. There was nothing else holding her back.

She liked being with him. She was attracted to him. She wanted to kiss him… along with several other things. And the thought of never seeing him again made her feel physically sick.

She'd suffered enough loss in her life. It was time to evoke some joy. All she had to do was admit to fabricating her career, explain about the mix-up, apologise, and hope that in time they'd laugh about it and see the funny side.

But the idea of confessing filled her with dread. There was a good chance Will would be so disgusted with her falsehood that he'd lose interest. But wasn't it worth the risk? Wouldn't it be better to know for certain than always wonder 'what if?'

This was the conclusion she'd reached as she'd lain in bed for two days, nursing her battered skull. She was going to tell Will the truth.

It would mean admitting to falsifying a reference, but if she stood any chance of a 'happy ever after' then she needed to admit her crimes.

But having reached this decision, it appeared that the man in question was now avoiding her, which was kind of making it hard to confess.

Megan nudged her. 'Quick, go now. He's on his own. Before it's too late.'

Oh, heavens. Was she really going to do this?

She cut though the cotton with her teeth and jumped up, stuffing her sewing kit in her bag.

'Leave that, I'll do it,' Megan said, almost shoving her in Will's direction. 'Go. Be brave.'

Brave. Right. She could do brave.

She jogged over to Will, adopting a casual air. 'Hi. How's the rehearsal going?'

He turned at the sound of her voice, but immediately turned away again. 'Terrible.'

Not a great start.

And then he walked off.

An even worse start.

She followed him. 'Problems?'

He glanced back, his expression one of stone. 'The bouncy castle is stuck on the M1. The Windsor Eye has a malfunction, and the local council are pissed off because the funfair trucks have churned up the grass on Brocas Green.'

'Anything I can do to help?' she said, struggling to keep up with him, which wasn't helping her headache.

'No.'

His abruptness shocked her.

But then he stopped and turned to face her.

She nearly smacked straight into him.

'I meant, no thanks. It's my mess. I'll deal with it.' His expression softened a fraction. 'How's your head?'

'Better. How are you? I mean, apart from being stressed about the festival.'

'Fine.' He didn't sound fine. Or look it. He looked… pained. Tired. And conflicted.

She tried again. 'The paramedic said you passed out on Sunday?'

He looked away. 'Only for a second… too much blood.'

'Right, yes. I remember you saying you weren't a fan.' She tried for a smile.

No response.

Okay, time to quit with the niceties and jump to her confession. 'I haven't had a chance to properly thank you for getting me out of the river.'

'It was no big deal.'

'Are you kidding me? I would've drowned.'

'Luckily, you didn't.'

'Thanks to you.'

'Like I said, it's no big deal.' He turned to leave. 'I need to go. It's crazy busy.'

Well, that went well. And then she realised it might be her last chance to talk to him. 'But you know, maybe once the festival is over and everything isn't so manic, I could… perhaps… take you out for a drink. To… you know… say thank you.'

'No need.'

Crikey this was hard.

'Well, maybe a drink for some other reason. Like… perhaps a date?'

His face fell.

Not quite the response she was hoping for.

She forced herself to continue. 'Which is something I wasn't sure was a good idea… but now I am.'

If she'd hoped this admission would soften his frosty manner, she was wrong.

He closed his eyes as if silently cursing… and then rubbed the back of his neck.

Not a good sign.

Oh, well, in for a penny, in for a pound, as her grandma used to say. 'But before we do, there's something I need to tell you.'

'You really don't.'

'Actually, I do. It's kind of a big thing… which I'm hoping won't be such a big thing once I explain… although I'm aware at first it will definitely seem like a big thing.' She paused. 'Am I making any sense?'

'No.' He glanced over to where the extras were becoming fractious, no doubt hot in their Victorian costumes.

'Right. Well, the thing is, I—'

'Will! We have a problem!' Frankie scuttled over, her wedged shoes unsteady on the grass. 'The Household Cavalry are about to practise their display for tomorrow. We need to clear The Long Walk.'

He frowned. 'But we haven't finished rehearsing.'

'I know. I tried to explain, but it seems they have to be ready for Changing of the Guard at eleven.'

'Christ. Who's in charge?' he said, walking off to where the military horses were congregated.

'The main blokey over there,' Frankie said, running after him. 'The one with the fancy hat.'

'That hardly narrows it down,' he said, disappearing at speed.

'Catch you later, then,' Lily called after him. 'Good chat!'

Not.

Well, if nothing else, she hadn't been imagining the change in his behaviour. He definitely did not want to go on a date with her. And she had no idea why.

Feeling despondent, she returned to Megan.

'How did it go?'

'It couldn't have been more disastrous.'

'How so?'

'I'm not sure which was worse. The fact that we were interrupted before I could confess, or his total disinterest in going on a date with me.'

Megan frowned. 'But the man is besotted with you. Anyone can see that.'

'Obviously not.'

Megan took her hand. 'He's probably just preoccupied with the festival. You'll see. Come Sunday he'll be eager as anything to hook up.'

Somehow Lily doubted it. 'He seemed distant. Like he couldn't even look at me.'

'Leave it for today. Regroup and try again once this is over, okay?' Megan gave one of her trademark winks. 'Trust me, I know men.'

'Thanks, Megan.' Talking of men. 'How's it going with Zac?'

A moony expression appeared. 'Darling, not to rub it in, but goodness me, the boy has stamina. The delights of youth,' she said, looking over to where Zac was touching up an extra's make-up.

Lily was glad someone was making progress. Unlike the rehearsal, which was rapidly falling apart.

Despite Will's protestations with the head of the Household Cavalry, the rehearsal had to be cut short and everyone was sent home with a view to regrouping later.

Lily didn't mind. She could do with a brew and a lie down. Her head hurt. Plus, it would allow her time to recover from the humiliation of being rejected.

She packed up her things and took a slow amble back to the guesthouse.

She'd be sad to leave Windsor. It was a beautiful town. She'd enjoyed her stay. But a new plan was required. A revamp of her CV and the search for another job.

At least she had genuine design experience now. She'd just have to hope Will would give her a decent reference. The irony wasn't lost on her.

An hour later, she was back at The Crooked House Tea Rooms and enjoying a Danish pastry and cup of tea in the cafe, nursing her bruises... both internal and external... when the bell above the door tinkled.

Zac appeared with Poppy.

He searched the room. His face lit up with relief when he saw her. 'Any chance you could look after Poppy for an hour or so?' he said, coming over to her table.

She blinked up at him. 'Well, sure, but—'

'Thanks, you're a lifesaver.' He kissed the top of Poppy's head. 'Be good. Back soon.' And with that, he headed for the door.

'Yes, but, Zac…' She scrambled after him, dodging around the other packed tables. 'Does her dad know she'll be with me?'

He dismissed her concerns. 'He'll be fine about it.'

She caught his arm. 'Are you sure? Shouldn't we tell him?'

'I'll only be a short while. No point interrupting him. He's busy with the project.'

Whoever 'he' was.

'Where are you going?' As if she needed to ask. 'Supposing there's an emergency?'

'I need to do a practise run on Megan's hair and make-up before tomorrow.'

Fibber. Her hair and make-up looked fine this morning. She glanced back to check Poppy was okay. She'd seated herself at the vacant table by the window. 'I'm not happy about her dad not knowing where she is.'

'This is the last time, I promise.' He crossed his heart. 'You're a star, Lily. I owe you big time.'

He certainly did.

At least he was right about one thing. This was definitely the last time. After tomorrow there would be no reason to see Poppy again… which strangely enough, made her feel incredibly sad. It would be hard saying goodbye to another person she'd grown close to.

She returned to Poppy. 'Sorry about that. It's not that I don't enjoy your company, but I'd be happier if your daddy knew where you were.' She sat down.

'I get it. You're being a responsible adult.'

Lily laughed. 'Why, thank you, young lady.'

'I'm a big responsibility, I know.' The kid pulled a dramatic face. 'If only I had a mummy. It's very saaaaad, you know, being all alone in the world.'

'Wow, someone's been practising their Oscars speech.'

Poppy grinned. 'How'd I do?'

'A tad overkill on the woe-me routine. You'll have someone calling Social Services.'

Her grin widened. 'Please may I have some cake?'

'You may. What would you like?'

'A scone with jam and cream, please.'

'Drink?'

'Tea. Like you.'

'Coming right up.' She ordered another pot of tea, and Poppy a scone, and carried the tray over to the table. 'Here we go. Tea for two. So… how did the play go? Tell me all about it.'

That was all the encouragement Poppy needed. For the next twenty minutes, she regaled Lily with details of the play and how much everyone had admired her costume, and how she'd watched all the episodes of The Great British Sewing Bee during her stay with her Nanny over the school holidays.

Lily listened, content to sip her tea, and wondering if it was too soon to down another couple of pain killers.

Poppy concluded with, 'I'm asking daddy for a sewing machine for Christmas, so I can make all my own costumes at big school.'

'Sounds good.' Lily passed Poppy a napkin. 'You have jam on your chin. But you know we need to come clean and tell him I made the costume, don't you?'

Poppy wiped her mouth. 'That's okay, it's all part of my plan.'

'Your plan?'

She nodded. 'That was a very nice scone. Thank you.'

'Good. What plan?'

She had a mischievous glint in her eye. 'You'll find out soon.'

That was what worried her.

Poppy took a gulp of tea. 'My daddy is up at the castle.'

Lily paused, teacup halfway to her mouth. 'What, right now?'

Poppy placed her napkin on the table. 'I think it's time we went to meet him, don't you?'

'Err… yes, I guess so.' Not that she was entirely sure it was a good idea. But if Poppy wanted to be with her daddy, then so be it. And it meant Lily could stop feeling guilty for being the 'anonymous' childminder. 'Will he be okay about you being with me, do you think?'

'Oh, yes. He'll be delighted.'

Somehow Lily doubted that. And she didn't want to get Zac in trouble. But maybe her dad was one of those laid-back parents? Happy for his daughter to be looked after by strangers. Raised by the whole village, and all that. It seemed unlikely.

They left the tea rooms and headed onto the cobbled streets towards the castle.

Poppy slipped her hand into Lily's, looking up at her with such an adoring smile, that it seemed cruel to let go.

The pair of them wandered up to the castle, hand in hand, chatting about Poppy's plans for the summer holidays now school had broken up, and admiring the displays in the shop windows.

As they neared Queen Victoria's statue, Poppy said, 'How's your head?'

'My head?'

'Yes, you hurt it. Can I see?'

Lily lifted her hair, showing Poppy the shaved patch with a bloody glued-together gash. 'Impressive, huh?'

'Yucky.'

'Very yucky. How did you know about my head injury? Did Zac tell you?'

'No, I overheard Daddy telling Aunty Gemma.'

Aunty Gemma? Something niggled in Lily's brain. 'Aunty Gemma…? As in, the woman who looks after the project finances?'

Poppy swung her arm. 'Yes.'

She slowed. 'She's Zac's mum?'

'That's right.'

Which meant… Pennies started to drop. They tumbled like hailstones from the sky. Each one sharp and painful.

Information flickered through her brain, fighting for its place, like a complex jigsaw with a key piece missing. 'Poppy… what's your surname?'

'Taylor.'

She stopped dead. No… surely not?

The ache in her head swelled to a throb, the pain fuelled by an increase in her heart rate. 'Which would make your daddy's name…?'

'Will Taylor.'

Oh, holy hell.

She staggered sideways and collapsed onto the low wall surrounding the castle. 'Your dad is Will Taylor?'

Poppy nodded.

Maybe there were two Will Taylors?

No point panicking until she absolutely had to. 'As in… Will Taylor, owner of TaylorMade Events?'

'Yes. Didn't you know that?'

'I most certainly did not know that.'

The time for panicking had officially arrived.

She dropped her head in her hands, trying to control her breathing, wishing the pain in her skull would stop.

'Poppy?' The approaching familiar sound of Will's voice only added to her torment.

Lily forced herself to stand up and face him.

He appeared at the castle gate, pausing when he saw who was with his daughter, as if his brain wasn't computing what he was seeing.

She knew the feeling.

His startled gaze switched between them. 'Poppy? What are you doing with Lily?'

Poppy beamed, unaware of what was looming. 'She's looking after me.'

His face clouded over. 'Where's Zac?'

'Having a playdate with Megan.'

In any other circumstances, Lily might have laughed. But the thunderous look on Will's face killed any hope of her finding it funny.

'Get over here now,' he snapped, beckoning Poppy over.

The little girl ran over. Her gleeful expression was now worried. And rightly so.

'What have I said about going off with strangers?'

'Lily isn't a stranger. She's my friend. She made the costume for my school play.'

Lily groaned.

'She did *what*?' The look he gave her could stop traffic. Fury. Outrage. And indignation mixed in with utter disbelief.

For some reason this annoyed her. He was angry with *her*? *Bloody cheek*. If anyone had the right to be angry, it was her.

Poppy was Will's *daughter*?

He had a *kid*?

He was a *father*?

Which meant he'd lied. And not just a little white lie. But a great big fat stinker.

He told her he'd never been married. That he'd only had one serious relationship. That he had 'no commitments'.

And all this time he'd been hiding the fact that he had a bloody daughter, whilst giving her grief about not being her 'true' self!

Bastard!

She pinned him with the most venomous glare she could muster.

'Hello, *Dad*,' she said, walking right up to him. 'Care to explain?'

Chapter Twenty-one

Will had woken with a splitting headache. It had been too hot to sleep. Not helped by worrying about the festival today and stressing over the events of yesterday. The sight of his daughter with Lily had launched a curveball at him so huge it could have knocked him all the way across Windsor and into the Thames. He wasn't sure which had been the dominant emotion: guilt, embarrassment, or fear. But it had been rage that had surfaced first. The primal instinct of a parent when their precious offspring is found wandering the streets with a supposed 'stranger'.

The fact that Lily wasn't a stranger was semantics. She was as far as Poppy was concerned. And as for his nephew... well, that was a fight yet to have. As it was, Lily had taken the brunt of his anger. Will had marched off with his daughter morosely in tow, refusing to offer an explanation as to how come he had a kid.

To say he wasn't proud of his actions would be an understatement.

But he wasn't the one in the wrong. Well, he was, but he wasn't about to let his part in this debacle derail him from feeling aggrieved. He was owed an explanation.

Shielding his eyes, Will looked across the expanse of Alexandra Gardens, the open green space dappled in bright sunlight. Despite a few hitches, the festival had officially opened. The roads in the town centre were closed to traffic, the participating stalls were set up and the visitors were arriving in droves. The Windsor Eye had been repaired and the bouncy castle already had a queue of kids lined up waiting to exhaust themselves.

His phoned pinged with a text. His parents had arrived with Poppy. She'd stayed with her grandparents last night, which was probably just as well. A reprimand of his daughter was needed, but not whilst he'd been in the mood he was in last night.

He walked over to the main gate to wait for them.

He phoned Frankie while he waited. 'Any problems your end?' he asked when she picked up.

'No, boss. All running smoothly here. Ticket sales for Madame Tussauds are good. The actors are engaged in a meet-and-greet with the punters and all the exhibitor stalls have opened.'

'Is the tour guide film running?'

'Yep, all working a treat. Feedback so far is excellent. The costumes in particular are getting a lot of interest.'

He wasn't surprised. Even if he didn't need the reminder of Lily. 'Is she there? Lily, I mean?'

'Yep, she's got everything under control. A few final costume adjustments, but nothing major. Zac's got a handle on hair and make-up, so it's all good. How's it your end?'

'No dramas so far.' He spotted his parents approaching with Poppy and waved.

'You want me to stay here, boss?'

'Only until the actors leave for the procession. Go with them to The Long Walk. That way I'll know everything's in safe hands.'

'Copy that. Speak later.'

'Thanks, Frankie.'

His parents arrived all smiles and relaxed, ready for their day out.

Poppy lingered a few steps behind, her eyes downcast.

'Hi, Mum. Hi, Dad. Did you find a parking space okay?'

'Just about.' His dad was already red-cheeked from the heat. 'It's getting busy out there. I thought I was going to have to beg a favour from the boys in blue and park at the police station.'

Will smiled. 'I think a lot of people have opted for the park and ride.'

His mum was frowning. 'Aren't you going to give your daddy a hug?' she said, sensing her granddaughter's reluctance to approach her daddy. Poppy was normally such a hugger.

'Daddy isn't very happy with me,' Poppy said, kicking the grass with her trainers.

His mum looked alarmed. 'What happened?'

'Nothing that needs discussing now.' Will had no desire to get his parents involved. He went over and hugged Poppy. 'Come here, sweetie. Did you have a nice time with Nanny and Granddad last night?'

She nodded.

'Did you enjoy your homemade pizza?'

Another nod, this one without much conviction.

'I'm sorry, Daddy,' she whispered, her words barely audible.

She looked so forlorn he knew they had to clear the air. Making her wait wasn't fair.

'What's going on?' his mum said, concern furrowing her brow. 'What's Poppy got to be sorry about?'

'I need a moment with my daughter,' he said, pointing to the tea tent. 'Why don't you go and have a cuppa. We'll join you in a couple of minutes.'

He could tell his mum wasn't happy about being shooed away, but his dad took the hint and led her towards the tea tent. 'Come and find us when you're done,' he said, dragging his wife away.

Will waited until they were out of earshot, before crouching down to eye level with his daughter. 'Do you understand why I'm upset with you?'

'Because Lily made me a costume.'

'No, because you lied to me.' Her eyes filled with tears. 'You never told me you'd met Lily, did you? Or that you were spending time with her? And when I asked you about the costume, you told me it was from a hire shop.'

Although to be fair, the real guilty party here was Zac. Poppy wouldn't have lied without an accomplice.

'You must know that's not right?'

She nodded.

'Then why did you do it?'

'I... I... wanted to get to know Lily for myself.'

'Why would you want to do that?'

'To see if she'd make a good mummy.'

Holy crap. He should've realised this might happen. She'd dropped enough hints.

Her big eyes filled with tears. 'And I think she would. She's very kind and funny, like you. And she teaches me all sorts of things, like paper mâché and dressmaking, and she smells nice. Like strawberries. And I think Pete the Tortoise would like her—'

'Poppy—'

'—and she knows what it's like not to have a mummy, and I feel more braver since I met her... and...'

'Poppy, sweetie. Stop.' For his sake, if nothing else.

His agitation levels were beginning to rise again. How dare Lily do all those things with his daughter? Certainly not without checking with him first. It was his job to educate and enlighten his daughter, no one else's.

Boy, was he going to give her a piece of his mind when he saw her.

'I'm sure you enjoyed spending time with Lily, but I've told you before, you can't pick out a new mummy like she's a piece of furniture. It doesn't work like that.'

'I thought I was helping.'

'How?'

'Well, you never let me meet any of your girlfriends. And I thought maybe it was because you thought they might not like me. Or I wouldn't like them. So I thought if I met Lily on my own, we could see if we liked each other, and then you wouldn't have to worry about whether we'd get on.'

He stared at his eleven-year-old daughter. At least, he was pretty certain she was only eleven. Sometimes she seemed younger, like when she played with her dolls. Other times, like right now, she exercised more logic than he did at thirty-four.

He had no idea how to respond. But then, he couldn't speak even if he wanted to. So much for protecting her.

'I did the wrong thing, Daddy. I'm sorry.' Tears streaked down her face.

He felt like hell on earth.

'I know you meant well,' he managed to say, pulling her into his arms. 'But it's not your responsibility to vet the women I date. Okay?'

How could he tell her that most women he'd met didn't want a man who already had a kid? And that even less of them wanted to take on the role of 'substitute mummy'.

So even if he had met someone he liked, there was no way he was going to invite her into his life if it meant pushing Poppy aside. His daughter came first, always. And from what he'd learnt about women, not many of them were prepared play second fiddle to a man's affections.

But maybe that was his fault. He'd hardly dated women looking for a serious relationship, had he? He'd deliberately avoided anyone who wanted anything other than a casual hook-up, so was it surprising they didn't want any baggage?

Until Lily.

He'd let his guard slip with her. He'd allowed himself to focus on his own needs and desires and not put his daughter's interests first. Big mistake.

He realised in hindsight that's why he was so reluctant to tell her about Poppy. He hadn't wanted to frighten her off. Or for her to be suspicious of his motives. He hadn't wanted to find out Lily wasn't willing to take on a 'ready-made' family. Who would blame her?

As it happened, it was his own heart that had needed protecting. Reacting as he had last Sunday to her fall had brought him to his senses. He wasn't ready to be with someone. More specifically, he wasn't ready to risk losing them.

He doubted he ever would be. He couldn't cope with the constant fear. It was too draining.

'Let's get some ice-cream,' he said, kissing Poppy's cheek.

'Am I forgiven?'

'Yes, sweetie. I'm sorry I yelled at you. You know I love you very much, don't you?'

She nodded. 'I love you too, Daddy.'

He stood up and took her hand, fighting back tears. 'So, do you want to go on the bouncy castle later?'

'Yes, please… and the Windsor Eye… and the carousel… and have my face painted.' She was back to being a little kid again. 'And I'm excited about the funfair tonight.'

'You've checked out the website, have you?'

'Nanny showed me.' She looked up at him. 'Are there really magicians here?'

'There are. Let's go find Nanny and Granddad and see if they'll take you to find one.' He squeezed her hand. 'You know I won't be able to spend all day with you, don't you? I have to work.'

'I know.' She let out a long sigh, making him smile.

'Mr Whippy?'

Her face broke into a mischievous grin. 'With a chocolate flake?'

'Of course.' And just like that, everything was back to normal.

For his daughter, anyway. He on the other hand was a complete mess.

Having reunited Poppy with her grandparents and arranged to meet up with them later for the grand parade at The Long Walk, he spent the next two hours visiting each venue site to check there were no problems.

The Queen was in residence at Windsor Castle, so security was paramount. The police were out in force, but being discreet in their behaviour, chatting to the festival visitors and offering the tourists directions for the various events taking place.

He walked the perimeter of Alexandra Gardens, checking in with the stall holders and festival participants. All of the activities were proving popular, from the remote-control boats on the pond, to the stilt-walkers entertaining the kids with their off-balance antics.

There were queues of people lined up for The Windsor Eye and the picnic area was packed with families enjoying a day out. The bandstand was attracting an older crowd, with numerous couples waltzing along to the swing band sounds of The Grenadier Guards, rather than jumping around to the pop music blaring out from the bouncy castle and spinning carousel.

Everything was going to plan.

But it was too soon to relax. The next big event was the grand parade, the scale of which terrified him. They hadn't managed to rehearse the whole event, only sections, so combining all the floats, mounted regiments, and historical re-enactment groups was going to be a logistical nightmare. Not to mention the security issues of having thousands of people lining The Long Walk, waving flags and cheering – at least, he hoped so. It would be rather a flat affair if no one turned up.

Satisfied everything was under control at Alexandra Gardens, he made his way across town and headed for The Long Walk.

He texted Frankie, checking the actors were congregated where they should be. She replied with a thumbs-up emoji.

He texted Gemma, who was overseeing the musical recital later this afternoon at St. Georges Chapel. Her reply stated that 'all was good' and that she'd 'meet him at The Copper Horse later'.

He walked past King Edwards Hospital towards The Great Park. Walking around Windsor was a necessity when most of the roads were closed. He didn't mind. It gave him breathing space to clear his head.

His phone pinged.

An email from the recruitment agency. Finally, Lily's reference had arrived.

He paused before clicking on the link, wondering if perhaps it would be better to let sleeping dogs lie. What did it matter now whether her credentials were genuine or not? The job was done. Not without its hiccups, but completed nonetheless, and the costumes were certainly a hit.

But there was more at stake here. His professional reputation. He needed to know whether his judgement was sound or skewered. Had he been right to offer Lily a job? Or was he a lovestruck fool who had been hoodwinked by her charms?

He opened the reference.

It was short. Factual. And contained confirmation of employment dates. Attendance record. And salary... All from one employer. Not a varied and comprehensive career designing for the stage and screen as she'd stated, but more than a decade working for the same clothing factory... cutting patterns.

It was official. He was a mug.

And Lily...? Well, she was a brazen liar.

He guessed he should feel aggrieved, wounded by the discovery, hurt that she'd misled him. But in truth? He was relieved.

Why?

Because he no longer had to feel guilty for having lied to her about Poppy.

He no longer had to regret yelling at her and pointing out her mistakes and failings while working on the project. And he no longer had to question his decision not to pursue a relationship with her.

She wasn't who he thought she was. She wasn't the enigmatic confident and accomplished Lily he'd met on holiday. She was… actually, he had no idea who she was.

And he didn't care.

Well, he did.

But he was going to do everything in his power to get over that and reassure himself that far from her being 'the one' he'd just experienced a lucky escape.

Ignoring the knot in the pit of his stomach and the ache in his chest, he crossed the road, and flashed his pass to the security guard manning the gate.

The Long Walk was filling up with spectators eager to secure their place at the front of the crowds. Barriers had been erected along the sides, ensuring everyone's safety.

Will headed past the fast-food vans and first aid tents and reached The Copper Horse, where he encountered more chaos. Hordes of participants were in costume milling about waiting to take part in the parade. There were fourteen floats in total. Two for each century, decorated to represent the relevant eras. Various groups had been invited to participate, from the Scouts to the Women's Institute. The Household Cavalry would lead the parade, complete with gun carriages and mounted rides, and the parade would conclude with Queen Victoria in her horse-drawn carriage, waving at the crowds.

He scanned the area and spotted Gemma approaching. 'Where's Poppy?' she said, shielding her eyes from the sun.

'With Mum and Dad. Where's Zac?'

'Where he should be I guess, working.'

'Don't count on it,' he snapped and walked off, searching out the actors.

Gemma followed him. 'What's that supposed to mean?'

'Let's just say, I'm not very happy with him.'

'Why, what's he done?'

He stopped and turned. 'Did you know he's been leaving Poppy with Lily when he was supposed to be minding her himself?'

Gemma's eyes grew wide. 'No, I didn't.'

'Right. Well, he has been.' He walked off again, too mad to stay still for any length of time.

Gemma jogged after him, slaloming her way around various groups of people seated on the grass. 'But then, I wasn't happy about you dumping Poppy on him in the first place when he should be working. I'm not surprised he needed help looking after her.'

Will raised his hand. 'Trust me, he didn't dump Poppy with Lily because of work.'

'What then?'

They reached the other side of the statue.

The extras were congregated in a group by the refreshment tent. The main actors were standing by the carriage under large umbrellas, their assistants lumbered with the thankless task of keeping them cool.

Zac was a few feet away, rolling up his brushes bag.

Will marched over.

Gemma was hot on his heels.

Zac glanced up as they approached, smiling with all the carefree abandon of someone who didn't know they'd been busted. 'The actors are ready for the parade. They're looking good.'

Will didn't return his nephew's smile. 'Megan included?'

Zac's eyes automatically searched out the actress, who was surreptitiously looking over. 'Megan, too. She looks amazing in the dress Lily made.'

But Will wasn't in the mood to allow thoughts of Lily into his head.

Not in the mood at all.

What did it matter if she'd made a few nice dresses? She'd lied about being a seasoned designer.

He pinned Zac with a stare. 'Any problems looking after Poppy yesterday?'

Zac's eyes darted about. 'Err... no. She was fine. As always.'

Will folded his arms. 'As always?'

When he'd texted Zac to tell him Poppy was with him at the castle, he hadn't mentioned it was Lily who had dropped her off. He wanted to see if his nephew would confess. He hadn't.

Zac looked wary. 'I don't get what you mean.'

'Quit with the cryptic remarks,' Gemma said, nudging Will's arm. 'Just tell him you know Lily's been helping him look after Poppy and get it over with.'

Zac closed his eyes. 'Shit. You know about that?'

'Your uncle just told me.' Gemma went over to her son. 'He's not happy. And neither am I.'

Zac looked at Will. 'I was going to tell you.'

'Oh, you were going to tell me, were you? Not ask me? Or get my consent before handing over my daughter to a stranger? You were going to *tell* me?'

Zac cowered. 'It wasn't like that.'

'No?' Will moved closer, his anger making him almost vibrate. 'What was it like then? Because all I know is that for weeks I've been trusting you with my daughter, and last night I discovered she hasn't been with you at all.'

'She has been with me,' Zac said on a rush. 'Just… not all the time. Poppy really likes Lily… and Lily was teaching her to sew, so it seemed harmless to leave them together.'

'Harmless?'

Zac looked at his mum, hoping for an ally. 'Err… I didn't think you'd mind.'

'Oh, you didn't think I'd mind?' Will was struggling to keep his voice down. A few people looked over, including Megan. Tough. 'Then why didn't you tell me? If you thought I'd be so okay with it, why not mention it?'

Gemma intervened. 'He probably didn't want to admit looking after Poppy was an inconvenience, Will.'

Will turned to face her. 'An inconvenience?'

Gemma's hands went to her hips. 'He was supposed to be working, or have you forgotten that?'

'I haven't forgotten anything. But Zac wasn't using Lily to childmind so he could work.'

'Well, why else would he leave Poppy with her?'

Will glared at his sister. 'Why don't you ask him.'

Gemma turned to Zac. 'What's he on about?'

Zac stared at his feet, looking much younger than his twenty-one years. 'I may have met up with a girl a few times.'

'A girl?' Gemma looked shocked. 'What girl?'

Will raised an eyebrow. 'I'd hardly call her a girl.'

Zac lifted his hands. 'Okay, woman, then.'

'Woman?' Gemma looked even more stunned. 'What woman?'

'It wasn't like Poppy saw anything,' Zac said, trying to backtrack. 'I made sure she didn't know anything.'

'But she cottoned on anyway,' Will barked, pointing a finger at Zac. 'Do you know where she told me you were yesterday?'

Zac shook his head.

'On a *playdate* with Megan.'

Zac groaned.

Gemma gasped. 'Megan?' Her hand went to her chest. 'As in, Megan Lawrence? You've been seeing Megan Lawrence?'

'Calm down, Mum. It's just casual.' Zac glanced around, fearful of people overhearing.

'I don't care what it is… the woman's ten years older than you.'

'Keep your voice down.' Zac looked over at Megan. 'And so what if there's an age gap?'

Gemma frowned. 'Well… she's clearly not a good influence, is she?'

'How d'you figure that?'

'If she's happy to sneak around when you're supposed to be working, then I'd say that's not being a good influence.'

Zac looked affronted. 'It was never when I was supposed to be working.'

'No, it was when you were supposed to be looking after Poppy,' barked Will, advancing on Zac.

Gemma blocked his path. 'Something he shouldn't have been doing in the first place,' she snapped back.

'So now you're on his side?'

'I'm not on anyone's side. But this would never have been an issue if you'd just organised proper childcare like we've been asking you to do for months.'

'That's irrelevant – this is about Zac letting me down.'

Zac cringed.

'And you think you haven't let him down? Using him to look after Poppy? Treating him like a babysitter, rather than a valued employee?'

'Fine.' Will felt the lid on his temper lifting. 'Maybe I shouldn't have done that. But it doesn't alter the fact that he shouldn't have left Poppy with an unsuitable child-minder.'

'Lily isn't unsuitable,' Zac said, jumping in. 'Honestly, she's not. She's great. And Poppy adores her. She's completely trustworthy.'

'Trustworthy?'

Lily was a lot of things, trustworthy wasn't one them.

'So you know for a fact she hasn't got a criminal record, do you? That she's not on the child sex offender register? You did a background check on her, did you?' His accusations were overboard and completely unwarranted, but he needed to make a point.

'Well... no.'

Gemma tapped his shoulder. 'Will.'

'Exactly. So without asking me, or telling anyone else what you were doing, you left my eleven-year-old daughter unsupervised with a woman who couldn't organise a piss-up in a brewery let alone look after a child.' Using Lily as a vent for his anger was cruel, but Will was too mad to be rational. He'd always suspected she was hiding something. And it turned out he was right. Humiliation was preventing him from acting reasonably.

Gemma tugged his arm. 'Will.'

'A woman who's unprofessional... unorganised... completely inept—'

'Will!' Gemma tugged harder.

'—and who it turns out is nothing but a liar... a fraud... and isn't even who she bloody says she is!'

'*Will!*' Gemma yanked on his arm.

He spun around. '*What!?*'

She pointed behind him.

Standing just a few feet away was Lily.

Shit!

Chapter Twenty-two

Saturday, 31 July

On any other occasion, Lily would be enjoying the opportunity to attend a choral music recital at a stunning venue with amazing acoustics. But try as she might, she couldn't focus on the haunting melodies or dramatic organ music filling St. George's Chapel. Her mind was too absorbed by anger and resentment.

She watched the choir belt out Handel's 'Messiah', desperate to appreciate the magical surroundings. But the constant ache in her chest prevented her from savouring the moment, or relishing the way the early evening sunlight lit up the stained-glass windows hanging above the altar.

All she could do was stare at the carved ceiling and try to make sense of her messy and twisted life.

A year ago everything had been so simple. Painful, but simple. She'd been a carer. She'd had a steady job. And although her life was mundane, and sad, and limiting, she'd known who she was, what she was doing, and how she fitted into the world.

Fast forward twelve months, and her life was a chaotic shambles.

She had no family. Only a few close friends. She'd blown her one chance to create a meaningful career, and the only man she'd ever loved... hated her.

Why else would he have said those things about her?

He'd called her a liar and a fraud… which she accepted was true… but the implication that she couldn't be trusted around children was grossly unfair. And cruel. And incredibly damaging.

Who would trust her now?

It wasn't like he was without fault. She might have lied about being a costume designer, but he'd kept hidden the fact that he had a *child*. His crime was way worse than hers. Yet somehow she'd been the one whose character had been completely and utterly annihilated. Publicly, too!

Tears slid down her cheeks. Lily had never missed her grandparents more. She missed having someone in her corner. Someone to defend her and comfort her and assure her she wasn't a bad person. Someone to put their arm around her and promise her that the pain would fade, the humiliation would subside, and that she would move on from this. Stronger, wiser. More resilient.

Because right at that moment, she felt so useless and insignificant, that all she wanted to do was curl up in a ball and sob.

Maybe that's what she needed to do. It wasn't like she had to be here any more. Her job was done… such as it was. No one would miss her. Maybe the best thing for everyone would be to return to the guesthouse, pack up her bags and leave tonight.

With any luck, Taye would let her crash on his sofa for an extra couple of nights. She was due to arrive back there on Monday anyway. He'd forgiven her for the whole reference debacle and offered to put her up until she could work out her next move. Not that she had any idea what that might be. Her future looked bleak. An endless black hole, waiting to suck her into the abyss.

Her grandma's voice popped into her head, reminding her that feeling sorry for herself wasn't going to achieve anything. Maybe not, but feeling positive and motivated about her future wasn't within her abilities right at that moment.

Lily waited for the famous oratorio to conclude and the chapel to erupt with applause before she escaped the packed pew and made her way to the exit.

It was time to leave Windsor. To escape the disaster of her own making and work out what the hell she was going to do next.

She drew in the warm evening air as she skipped down the steps onto the grass, knowing she wasn't in the right frame of mind to solve any conundrums tonight. Tomorrow was a new day. She might feel better after a good night's sleep. Problems always seem less drastic in the morning, right?

But as she turned the corner, she smacked into a man's chest. Her forehead connected with his chin, and they both groaned as they bounced apart.

The man rubbed his chin and glared at her. 'Seriously?'

Of course it was Will.

The way her luck was panning out, it couldn't have been anyone else.

She glared back, not in the mood to accept responsibility for their collision. She wasn't always the one in the wrong. 'Oh, so this is my fault, is it?'

'You were the one not looking where you were going.'

'And you were the one running.'

'I wasn't expecting anyone to be leaving the chapel mid-concert.'

'And I wasn't expecting a character assassination this afternoon, so I guess we both get to be aggrieved.'

He stilled. 'I didn't say anything that wasn't true.'

She pointed a finger at him. 'You implied I might be a child molester.'

He flinched. 'No, I reprimanded Zac for not checking you *weren't* a child molester.'

'Which implies that I might be one!' She lifted her hands, enraged by the assumption. How dare he. 'And on the subject of telling the truth,' she said, advancing on him. 'May I remind you, it was you who kept hidden the fact that you had a daughter.'

'A daughter whose head you filled with inappropriate ideas.'

Was he for real? 'I did no such thing. And I had no idea who she was, did I?' Her hands laced into her hair, and gripped hold, until the pain of her gash throbbed so hard she was in danger of removing the glue. 'At no point did anyone… including you… tell me Poppy was your daughter.'

He adopted a righteous expression. 'But she was someone's daughter, wasn't she?'

'What's that supposed to mean?'

'It wasn't your place to look after her, or teach her to sew, or… or do whatever it is you did with her, without gaining parental consent. Any parent knows that. It's the basic rule of parenting.'

'Well, I'm not a parent, am I?' she said, folding her arms, trying to dispel the crippling urge to thump him. 'Unlike you, Will Taylor. Who seems to think he's parent of the year and can lecture me on the etiquette of raising a child, when for the last five months he's been hiding the fact that he has one! Hardly model parenting, is it?'

He glanced away. 'I had my reasons for not telling you.'

'And I had my reasons for not telling you I was looking after her. Namely, that I had no idea she was yours. I was simply doing Zac a favour, minding his charge for a few hours, and foolishly thinking I was helping. Keeping the girl entertained, keeping her amused, and trying to be a responsible adult. Pardon me for trying to do the right thing.' She shoved him in the chest. She couldn't help it. He was pushing her buttons.

'The right thing? Like lying about being a costume designer?'

Ah, so he *had* found out.

It was inevitable, really. But the shock still knocked some of the fight out of her. She felt her lungs contract, like a sail denied of wind.

He on the other hand hadn't lost any of his anger. He was on the offensive, as he took the moral high ground, happy to shove it down her throat. 'Imagine my surprise,' he said. 'When I received an email from the recruitment agency this afternoon telling me that far from being an experienced costume designer, you've been working in a clothing factory for the past decade!'

There was no point denying it. It still stung though. She'd hoped it wouldn't matter now the job was done. How naive was that?

'You're right. I lied,' she said, her voice tight from the effort of not crying. 'I fabricated my career history. But instead of confronting me about it in private, you chose to announce the fact to half of Windsor and publicly humiliate me.'

If she expected him to feel remorse, she was wrong. He looked incredulous. 'And you think you haven't publicly humiliated me? I took a chance on you. I overrode my professional instincts and hired you, believing all that crap you gave me on holiday about being an experienced designer.'

'The same holiday whereby you omitted to mention the fact that you had a daughter.'

'The same holiday where you pretended to be...'

'To be... what?'

His hand came up to rub the back of his neck.

'Go on, say it. I pretended to be what? A nice person? Confident? Happy? Not— how did you phrase it?— incompetent... inept... and a complete *fraud*!'

He looked away. 'I'm not the one who lied about their career.'

'And I'm not the one who lied about never having been *married*.'

He paled, suitably abashed. Good.

She swallowed back the lump in her throat. 'Looks like we've both been pretending to be someone we're not.' She walked off, unable to stop the tears falling. 'And don't bother telling me I'm fired. I know!'

'I'm glad we agree on something!' Will called after her, his voice cracking.

But she wasn't about to let that derail her. He wasn't the only one who was upset.

She sped towards the guesthouse, head down, tears streaming down her cheeks. Her feet slipped on the uneven cobbled stones, her vision clouded from crying.

The town centre was packed and it was an effort to push through the crowds. Most people didn't even notice her. The few who did gave her an odd look.

Lily didn't care. She just needed to get to the sanctity of her room and succumb to the hurt she felt. The remorse, the humiliation, the inadequacy. Most of all, the rejection.

She'd been found out, and found wanting. As a costume designer, as a person and as a lover. Even as a childminder. It was quite crushing to discover you sucked at so many things.

She wondered if there was a competition for people who'd stuffed up their life? Like the Darwin Awards. If so, she had a shot at the Gold Medal position. She defied anyone to have made such a mess of their life in such a short space of time.

Stumbling into the tea rooms, she ran for the stairs, ignoring startled looks from the punters enjoying a festival special cream tea.

She was being dramatic, she knew that. Indulging in self-pity and feeling sorry for herself. But she didn't care. Tomorrow she would regroup, pull herself together and move on, lesson learnt. For now, she just wanted to wallow in self-loathing.

She flopped onto the bed face down and let the tears fall, expelling her grief. For her granddad, for the loss of her family, for her home in Haringey, even her old crappy job.

Mostly she cried because she'd been dumped. Both as an employee and as a girlfriend. Not that her and Will had ever been a couple, but they might have been. They could have been. She'd wanted them to be. But she'd blown it. And so had he.

The deep sobs morphed into a pathetic whimper, followed by drifting into a fitful sleep, which was abruptly ended by a loud knock on the door.

She blinked and rolled over. What time was it? How long had she been asleep?

Another knock. 'Lily…? Lily, are you in there?' It was Zac.

She sat up and stretched, stiff from lying face down. It was dusk outside, the daylight replaced by evening twilight.

'Lily? Open up, it's urgent.' Zac banged on the door.

'Okay, okay, I'm coming.' She crossed the room and opened the door. 'What's the emergency?'

'Poppy's missing.'

'Missing…? What do you mean missing?'

'She's run off.' Zac looked frantic. 'One minute she was there, the next she was gone.'

'Why would she run off?'

'She overheard you and Will arguing.'

'What do you mean, she overheard us arguing?' The implication that this was somehow her fault *again* smarted. 'How did she overhear us?'

'We were on our way to meet Will after the concert finished, but we arrived early. Me, my grandparents and Poppy, when we saw you guys arguing.'

'I didn't see you.'

'You were kind of busy. We hung around the side of the building, out of sight.'

Just when she'd foolishly thought her humiliation couldn't get any worse. 'And you thought it was okay to listen in?'

'No, but by the time we realised what you were rowing about, it was too late.'

'Too late for what?'

'To stop Poppy running off. One minute she was there, the next she'd vanished. We couldn't keep up with her, there were too many people about. We've looked everywhere. We can't find her. I thought she might've come here.'

'Well, she hasn't.' Poppy had run off? Lily rubbed her chest. This was not a good situation. 'Have you called the police?'

'Will called them. They're out looking for her.'

'Well, good. I hope they find her.'

'I hope so too. Will's frantic.' She could imagine. Zac continued, 'I kind of feel responsible. You know, for involving you. Sorry.' He looked ashamed and vulnerable, and like any young person who'd learnt the hard way that they weren't invincible. 'I had no idea it would blow up like this. I feel like shit.'

He wasn't the only one. 'Is there anything I can do?'

'Not really, I just wanted to check she wasn't here. I'll keep looking.' He turned to leave.

'I hope you find her,' she called after him as he disappeared downstairs.

She went over and sat on the bed pondering what to do.

Should she join in the search? Will wouldn't be happy about her involvement, he'd made it clear he wanted her to stay away from his daughter.

But Poppy had run off because she'd heard them arguing, so she was partly to blame. She'd never forgive herself if something happened to the girl.

Grabbing a cardigan, she ran from the guesthouse, shoving her arms into the garment as she raced downstairs. The more people out searching for Poppy, the better. And if Will didn't like that, then tough. She no longer cared what he thought... or at least, she was trying very hard not to.

Lily exited her lodgings and scanned the cobbled streets, checking the pubs, the cafes and the empty doorways. No sign of her.

She headed up to the castle, but the gates were closed for the evening, so she then made her way to the old railway station, and began searching the packed restaurants and bars, asking on repeat if, 'Anyone had seen a little girl in a red dress?' hoping it might jog a few memories. No one recalled seeing her.

Where next?

Lily ran down the hill towards Alexandra Gardens, but the venue was closed. Only a few workers moseyed around collecting litter and checking the grounds for lost property. But there was no Poppy to be seen.

The last place she could think of was the funfair.

Would Poppy have gone there? She had no idea.

By the time Lily reached the Thames and crossed Eton Bridge, her legs were like jelly. Her lungs were devoid of air and she was in danger of getting cramp. She was seriously out of condition. She stopped for a moment to catch her breath, resting her hands on her knees.

Partially recovered, she resumed her search, checking the side streets, the crowds, asking anyone and everyone on the way if they'd seen a little girl in a red dress. No one had.

Reaching Brocas Green, the site of the funfair, Lily was hit by the noise first, a cacophony of machines, fairground music and the whir and bang of mechanical rides.

The ferris wheel dominated the view, a huge construction lit up with red and green flashing lights. There were stalls selling candyfloss and toffee apples. Fishing and shooting games seduced punters with the promise of winning a goldfish or a giant teddy bear.

She could hear screams from the riders on the nearby rollercoaster and bumper cars, as well as yelps from the people being thrown from the mechanical bull ride, and threats of 'I'm going to be sick' from those being spun around on the waltzer and spinning teacups.

The place was packed. How on earth was she going to find Poppy amongst the crowds? That was if she was even here. Where would an eleven-year-old girl run off to?

Lily tried to think back to being that young. Where would she have sought refuge?

Her bedroom.

Well, Poppy wasn't likely to be there, was she? Or if she was, then hopefully Will or the police would locate her.

Unwilling to admit defeat, Lily continued searching, more from a sense of needing to do something, than believing she'd find the girl. It was better than returning to the guesthouse and spending the night worrying.

Flashing red lights drew her attention to the love ride. It was advertised for 'couples only', attracting a load of loved-up teenagers queuing outside. Lily checked the line, but Poppy wasn't among them.

And then a flash of red caught her eye.

Someone was sitting on the steps of the magical gypsy caravan. The person was small, hunched over, and hugging their knees, their long fair hair hanging lose.

Poppy.

Thank goodness!

Lily ran over... but then slowed, realising she needed to approach with caution and not frighten the girl. 'Hey, there, Poppy,' she called, trying for a casual tone.

Poppy glanced up. Her face was tearstained and wretched with misery.

It broke Lily's heart.

She gestured to the wooden steps. 'Okay if I sit down?'

Poppy nodded.

Lily perched next to her. 'What are you doing here?'

Poppy shrugged. 'Hiding, I guess.'

'A lot of people are looking for you.' She put her arm around her. 'Your daddy's really worried.'

No response.

She rubbed the girl's shoulder, figuring she needed comforting. 'Come on, talk to me. What's up?'

'He didn't tell you about me,' she said, so quietly Lily barely heard her.

Lily stilled. Oh, hell. 'Is that why you ran off?'

She nodded. 'And because he yelled at you.'

'Well, I deserved it.'

She looked up, her eyes wide. 'You did? What did you do?'

Lily had no idea what the right thing was to do here. As Will had unhelpfully pointed out, she wasn't a parent. But as lying hadn't worked for her so far, maybe the truth was needed.

'I'm afraid I lied to him. I pretended to be a qualified costume designer to get the job on the festival project. That was a very bad thing to do. He was right to be angry with me when he found out.'

'Why did you lie?'

'Well, to start with, it was a mix-up. I thought your daddy knew I wasn't an experienced designer when his company hired me. By the time I realised there'd been a mistake, I was too cowardly to confess.' She tried to look contrite. 'I've always wanted to be a costume designer, you see, and I thought I could pretend to be one and not get found out. Silly, huh?'

'But you do design costumes. You made my Mad Hatter costume. It was beautiful. Everyone said so.'

'Aw, thank you. I'm glad it went down well.' She hugged the girl closer. 'But it turns out that making costumes isn't the same as being the lead designer on a project like this.' She gestured to the enormity of the event surrounding them. 'There were lots of things I didn't know how to do, and I made lots of mistakes.'

Poppy stared at her hands. 'Is that why Daddy got mad?'

'Yes. This project is very important to him, and I nearly messed it up for him. I feel very bad about that.'

Poppy's forehead creased into a frown. 'But why are you mad at him? You were yelling, too.'

'That's true.' Crikey, how much to reveal? Telling the truth seemed to be working so far. 'Your daddy was upset that he didn't know you were spending time with me, he thought you were with your cousin. Which is fair enough. But you see, I didn't know you were his daughter. Not until yesterday, so I was angry that he hadn't told me about you.'

'Why didn't he tell you about me?'

Bloody good question. Something she'd like to know the answer to herself. 'You'll have to talk to him about that. But I think it's because he's very protective of you. He needs to know a person is completely trustworthy before he allows them into your life. I get that.' And she did. Will had something incredibly precious to protect. She understood that now.

Poppy rested her head against Lily's shoulder. 'I wondered if he regretted having me.'

Oh, hell.

Lily knew she needed to tread carefully. 'Why on earth would you think that?'

'I overheard my friend's mum saying that his life would be a lot easier if he hadn't had me.'

Crikey. Nice woman. 'My grandma always used to say, it's better to trust what you know to be true, than listen to what other people imagine to be true.'

Poppy raised her head. 'What's does that mean?'

'It means, trust what's in your heart.' She gazed into Poppy's huge grey eyes. 'Let me ask you this... do you think your daddy loves you?'

Poppy nodded.

'And do you think he'd be happier or sadder if you weren't in his life?'

Poppy mulled it over. 'Sadder.'

'Exactly. I don't know your daddy very well, but one thing I do know for certain is that he definitely loves you. He adores you, in fact. Why else do you think he was so angry yesterday when he discovered you weren't with Zac like you were supposed to be? You gave him a fright. If something had happened to you, he wouldn't have known where you were, or who you were with. That scared him.'

'But I make his life hard sometimes.'

She smiled. 'You also make it wonderful for him. Do you know how I know this?'

Poppy shook her head.

'Because I know what it's like to be in his position. I don't have a child to look after, but I did care for my poorly granddad for a very long time. It wasn't always easy. He was sick and confused and it upset me a lot to see him that way, but I never regretted for one second looking after him. I loved him very much. He was my family. I would've done anything for him and that's how I know your daddy feels the same way about you.'

Poppy let out a long sigh. 'I guess.'

'He's had to be both a mummy and a daddy to you. That must have been hard at times, but it doesn't mean he doesn't want you. It just means things aren't always easy, or as straightforward as when you have two parents.'

Poppy sat up straighter. 'That's why I've been trying to find a new mummy. So he wouldn't have to do it all alone, and he could be happy again.'

Lily's chest contracted. For a moment, she couldn't speak.

'I thought… maybe… you could be my new mummy?'

Lily closed her eyes. Oh, if only.

But it wouldn't do to share her feelings with the girl. The poor thing was upset enough as it was. She didn't need another disappointment. Or for her dad to be portrayed as the 'baddie' in the situation. And admitting Will 'didn't want her' any more to an eleven-year-old was a humiliation too far.

She mustered a smile. 'Well, that's the nicest thing anyone has ever said to me. If I'm lucky enough to ever have a daughter, I hope she's as lovely as you.' She kissed Poppy's forehead. 'But I'm afraid your daddy and I are never going to be girlfriend and boyfriend. We're just not compatible. We want different things. I'm sorry.'

Poppy buried her head in Lily's shoulder, 'Ohhhkaaay.'

It was now time to return Poppy to her rightful owner… before Lily became even more attached than she already was. Staying wasn't an option, sadly.

'Now, being the numpty that I am, I didn't pick up my phone before I left the guesthouse, so I can't call your daddy and let him know you're okay. Dumb, huh?' She lifted Poppy's chin. 'So shall we head off and see if we can find a policeman to call him for us?'

Poppy nodded.

'Good girl.' Lily stood and offered Poppy her hand. 'Your daddy will be worried sick.' She pulled Poppy upright and they wandered off hand in hand in search of assistance.

As it happened, they didn't need the police. As they reached the exit, Will appeared, running towards them. He looked frantic, tearful and close to exploding.

Gemma was behind him, struggling to keep up.

'Over here!' Lily waved to catch his attention. 'Poppy's here. She's safe!'

Will screeched to a halt, his face crumpling into relieved agony as he raced over. 'Sweetie, you gave me such a fright. Where have you been?' He dropped to his knees and pulled her into a crushing hug. 'I've been so worried.'

'Sorry, Daddy,' she mumbled, her face squashed into his shoulder.

'Don't ever run off like that again! You've taken years off me.' He held her at arm's length. 'If I upset you, tell me, okay? Yell at me, even. But *don't* run off. My heart can't take it. I couldn't bear to lose you. You're my world.'

She nodded. 'I know.'

He gave a shaky laugh. 'Well, I'm glad that's cleared up.'

'Lily told me.'

'Lily?' He reluctantly turned to look at his daughter's rescuer properly. 'Lily, right. Err… thanks for finding her.'

Wow, could he sound any more begrudging? 'No problem,' she said, trying to sound gracious, but knowing that she sounded peevish. 'I'm glad she's safe.'

'Where did you find her?' Gemma joining the group, panting. 'We looked everywhere.'

'I found her sitting on some steps by one of the rides.'

'Thank God nothing's happened to her.' Gemma offered her a grateful smile. 'Thanks for looking after her until we could get here,' she said, with a lot more sincerity than her brother. 'I'm sure Will's very grateful.'

And Lily was sure he wasn't.

But it didn't matter. Poppy was safe, that was all that mattered. She could cope being in Will's bad books.

She touched Poppy's shoulder. 'Take care, Poppy. Good luck with the sewing. It's been a pleasure getting to know you.'

Poppy broke free from Will's clasp and flung her arms around Lily. 'I'll miss you.'

It was an effort for Lily to swallow. *Hold it together*, she told herself. *Don't lose it now.* Just a couple more minutes. For Poppy's sake.

'I'll miss you, too,' she said, stoking the girl's hair. 'Be good for your daddy, okay?' And with that, she extricated herself from Poppy's impossibly tight hug and walked off, unable to contain her emotions any longer.

However much she wanted to fall apart, she was determined not to collapse until she was out of sight. She refused to give Will Taylor the satisfaction of seeing her cry.

'Thanks again for finding her,' he called after her, just as the first firework exploded into the night sky. 'I really appreciate it!'

But Lily didn't respond. She couldn't.

She kept on walking. Away from Will Taylor. Away from his gorgeous daughter. And away from her time in Windsor.

Bloody hell, it hurt.

Chapter Twenty-three

Six months later...

Lily took a deep breath and closed her eyes, relishing the feeling of warm sun on her skin. She could smell coconut and fresh mango, and she could hear the rhythmic sound of nearby crickets. Soft reggae music drifted in and out of earshot, playing at the bar further down the beach. The gentle breeze lifted her hair, a welcome respite against the burning sun. The lap of the waves lulled her into oblivion as she trailed her fingers through the warm sand beneath.

It was bliss. Utter bliss.

She smiled, still unable to get her head around the joy of being back in the Caribbean.

Who would have thought it? Her second holiday in less than a year. But then, not a lot surprised her these days. Life had been a series of twists and turns. She was getting used to the rollercoaster of living life on the edge, rather than relying on the security of a regular routine. It still scared her, but she was certainly never bored.

The low point had been last July, after the festival, when she'd left Windsor feeling heartbroken and a complete failure, with both her personal and professional lives lying in tatters. She'd moved in with her friend Taye for a couple of weeks, fully intending to accept defeat and apply for a regular job. But an unexpected offer had landed in her lap.

Taye's uncle had announced he was retiring from running his tailor's shop in Richmond, and rather than selling, he'd offered Taye the business at no cost. Taye had jumped at the chance to leave Clothing Connexions and escape the wrath of Darth Vader, and had accepted his uncle's offer. He'd then asked Lily to go into business with him.

She hadn't hesitated. It was the stuff of dreams. A chance to make something of herself. Even better, she'd been offered tenancy of the small bedsit above the premises. It was perfect.

And so, three months later, Malik & Monroe had opened, a bespoke boutique with a quirky purple and gold shopfront, offering tailormade clothing at affordable prices. Lily had moved into her new pad, and life had been a chaotic whirlwind of orders and deadlines ever since.

She couldn't be happier.

Well, she could, but at least her professional life was on the up. Her personal life was still lacking, but there wasn't much she could do about that. She'd been coerced into going on a few dates by her friends, but she'd yet to meet anyone she'd liked as much as Will. She still missed him… which was nonsensical, infuriating, and hugely depressing in equal measures. But such was life.

At least her friendship circle had increased.

'Do you realise how embarrassing it is asking for a virgin Pina Colada?' Megan said, appearing with their drinks. Her sheer sarong flapped in the breeze, revealing bronzed shapely legs that nearly caused the man next to them to spill his beer. 'The barman looked at me like I had a screw loose.' She handed Lily her mocktail and settled on the sunlounger next to her. 'So, have you heard anything yet?'

'I haven't checked.' Lily sipped her drink. It was sickly sweet and delicious.

Megan rolled her eyes. 'How can you be so relaxed? This could be your big break.'

'I don't want to get my hopes up.'

'Where's your phone?' Megan delved into Lily's bag, unearthing her phone. 'Right, let's see.' She scrolled through her emails. 'It's here!' She grabbed Lily's arm. 'Do you want me to open it?'

Lily nearly spilled her drink. 'Go on then. Put me out of my misery.'

Megan opened the email, and took forever to read it, her expression giving nothing away.

'It's a no… isn't it?'

'Patience, woman. Let me read it.'

'Just tell me. Is it a yes, or a no?'

Megan looked up, serious at first… and then smiled. 'You did it. You landed the job.'

'Seriously? Let me see.' She snatched her phone from Megan and scanned the email. 'Thank you for attending the recent meeting… blah blah blah… impressed by your portfolio of ideas… after careful consideration… and a glowing endorsement from your previous project… we're delighted to offer you the position of head costume designer.' She squealed with delight. 'Oh, my, God. I did it. I actually did it!'

Megan launched herself at Lily and hugged her. The man next to them got an eyeful of the back of her friend's bikini briefs. He didn't look unhappy about it.

'Well, of course you did. I knew you would.' Megan squeezed her so tightly Lily almost couldn't breathe. 'We get to work together again. Yippee! And I get to wear your gorgeous costumes.'

And then something clicked in Lily's brain.

'Wait a sec.' She extricated herself from Megan's clasp and reread the email. 'Glowing endorsement from my previous project…? *Will Taylor* gave me a reference?'

Megan avoided eye contact. 'That's nice.'

'But how did he even know I'd gone for the job?'

'A little birdie must've told him.'

'And you've no idea who this little birdie might be?'

Megan avoided eye contact. 'Look, what does it matter? You've got the job. This is a massive deal. Your first feature film. The exposure will do wonders for your career.'

But Lily wasn't letting her friend off the hook that easily. 'You haven't answered my question.'

Megan ignored her. 'If you think you're busy with orders now, just wait until after the film. You'll be inundated. My friends can't get enough of your designs as it is.'

'You're not going to tell me, are you?'

'Tell you what?' Megan feigned innocence, fluttering her long eyelashes. 'Maybe he heard through the grapevine? Or maybe Zac told him? Or maybe he saw the error of his ways and wanted to make amends…'

'Or maybe you coerced him into giving me a reference,' Lily concluded, hating the idea of Will doing her any favours. Then she had an awful thought. 'Please tell me you didn't fake it? I've only just recovered from the mess of my last forged reference.'

'As if I'd do such a thing.' Megan's attempt at being 'affronted' fell a little short. Especially for an actress. 'What kind of friend would that make me?'

'The interfering type. Which is a waste of effort when it comes to Will Taylor. The man hates me.'

'He does not hate you.'

'He called me a child-molesting incompetent fraud.'

Megan grimaced. 'Yes, that was rather unfortunate. Still, nobody's perfect.' She stood up. 'Come on, finish your drink, we need to get ready for tonight.'

'It's only five o'clock. What's the rush?'

Megan's hands went to her hips. 'I have a full evening planned. Our first night in the Caribbean needs to be memorable.'

'Should I be worried?'

'Of course.' Megan pulled Lily to her feet. 'You know me. Now, come on.'

'Wait… let me get my drink.' Lily stretched for her half-finished mocktail, before allowing Megan to drag her up the beach. 'This is supposed to be a relaxing holiday.'

Megan linked arms with her. 'Relaxing days. Party nights… And proper cocktails,' she said, looking disdainfully at Lily's drink. 'I have my reputation to protect.'

Lily laughed. 'Idiot.'

'Now, what are you wearing tonight?'

'No idea.'

'Did you bring that gorgeous red dress with you?'

'The one I made last year? Yes, why?' Lily stopped walking. 'Hang on, how do you know about that dress?'

'Err… I must've seen a photo?' Megan said, trying to sound innocent, but not achieving it. 'Anyway, the point is, wear it.'

Lily resumed walking, suspecting something was afoot.

Megan patted her hand. 'Trust me. We need to go all out to impress.'

'Why? You have a boyfriend, remember?'

'Yes, but you don't, darling.' Megan kissed her cheek. 'Meet you in The Olive Bar at seven. Look gorgeous.'

'I'll do my best.' Lily would still pale into insignificance next to her stunning and exotic friend. Not that she minded, she was content with how she looked. She'd finally found her groove, so to speak. 'See you later.'

'Don't be late!' Megan called, disappearing into her room, blowing kisses.

Smiling, Lily returned to her own room. Who'd have thought she'd end up friends with Megan Lawrence. They'd met up for a drink shortly after leaving Windsor and realised they enjoyed each other's company, and things had developed from there. Life really was strange.

She flopped onto the bed and flicked on the air conditioning. She needed to cool down before getting ready for their girls night out.

Digging out her phone, Lily reread the email from the producer of the film. She could hardly believe it. She'd been offered the role of head costume designer on a big budget film. Two months based in Prague. Working on the set of a fantasy extravaganza, the costumes on a par with *Game of Thrones*. It was beyond exciting.

And as Megan had said, it would give her design business a massive boost.

When she'd agreed to go into business with Taye, she'd fully intended to give up the idea of working in films, but Taye had been in total favour of her juggling the two. He said the publicity would put them on the map. She hoped he was right. She'd be leaving him to run the business solo when she was off filming, so he needed to be on board with it.

When she'd previously met with the film's producer, he'd been impressed by her proposed designs for the costumes, but he'd expressed concerns about her lack of experience. She hadn't been foolish enough to lie twice about her career, so she'd been brutally honest. So much so, she feared she'd talked him out of offering her the job. Had Will's reference swayed him?

At the reminder of Will, she hauled herself off the bed and headed for the shower, hoping a dose of cold water would shock some sense into her and stop her pining after a man she couldn't have. And shouldn't want... but did. Such was life.

At seven p.m. on the dot, she was dressed ready for a night clubbing. Her recently highlighted hair was scrunch-dried, her lips were painted red and she was perfumed and ready to go.

At Megan's request, she'd opted for the long clingy red dress with the split up one leg, and teamed it with jewelled flip-flops rather than heels, knowing otherwise her feet couldn't withstand a night partying with Megan. She'd been dragged to enough events over recent months to know hours of relentless dancing lay ahead. She needed to be prepared.

Lily exited the chalet and walked past the infinity pool, now minus any swimmers and lit with soft lighting. The palm trees swayed in the warm breeze. The crickets were in full voice, amplified by the stillness of the night. The indigo sky above was clear, the stars out in force.

It was an enchanting evening. She stopped for a moment to absorb her surroundings, closing her eyes and filling her lungs with warm air, focusing on her breathing.

This time last year she'd been mourning the loss of her granddad. Fast forward twelve months and she was the joint owner of a small business, enjoyed a colourful social life, and was about to embark on her first film. It was almost perfect.

Almost.

She glanced at her reflection in the water. Last year she'd faked being a costume designer. She'd pretended to be happy and confident, with the promise of being a 'new version' of herself. A pretence that had crumbled under the scrutiny of the man she'd fallen in love with and also when challenged by the reality of working on a demanding project. She'd floundered her way through those months, experiencing failure and heartbreak, but she had emerged bruised, yet more resilient, and certainly less naive.

She crouched down and trailed her fingers through the water. The image reflected back now was a hybrid version of 'Lily'. Here was a woman who'd found her calling, was proud of her achievements so far and was ready to be challenged by the next adventure.

All that was missing was a family.

But what would be, would be, as her grandma used to say. Sometimes you couldn't have it all.

'Nice dress,' a man said behind her. He gave her such a shock that she lost her balance... and fell face-first into the pool.

It wasn't even an elegant landing. She ended up sinking to the bottom, her dress dragging over her head, her new underwear unattractively wedged up her bum and both boobs unleashed, floating about like a couple of untethered life rafts.

Consequently, by the time she was rescued and dragged to the surface coughing and spluttering, she was beyond fearing for her life, and was more concerned with rearranging her clothing. Thankfully, they were in the shallow end and she could stand up.

'I'm so sorry,' the man said, sounding scarily familiar. 'Are you okay?'

'Am I okay?' She wiped wet hair from her face. 'No, I am not okay!' she yelled, shoving a wayward boob back into her dress.

And then his face came into focus.

Will bloody Taylor.

Of course it was.

Why was she even surprised?

She groaned. What had she ever done to deserve this? She was a good person. A hard-working person. Caring and loyal. She just wanted to live a quiet life. Fly under the radar, with no desire to be the centre of attention. But for some reason whenever Will Taylor was around she ended up soaking wet!

And then she realised he was smiling.

'Oh, you think this is funny, do you?' She tried to sound outraged. 'I'm drenched.'

'Me, too.' His hair was flat against his head, yet somehow he still managed to look desirable. Damned man. 'I hadn't planned on an evening swim either.'

'Then you shouldn't have given me a shock.'

'You're right, I shouldn't have.'

She viewed him suspiciously. 'Why are you agreeing with me? You never agree with me.'

'On this occasion I am.'

Then Megan appeared from the bar. 'What on earth are you doing in the pool?'

Lily rolled her eyes. 'Swimming.'

Megan came running over – an impressive feat in her skyscraper heels. 'Why?'

'Oh, you know, it seemed like a good idea at the time.'

Will's sheepish grin widened. 'Need a hand getting out?'

'I'm fine,' she snapped, shaking him off and making a right palaver of getting out of the pool. Her red dress clung to her body, weighing her down, the neckline sagging so low she had to hold the material in place to prevent flashing a member of hotel staff who was fast approaching.

'No night swimming,' the manager scolded, wagging his finger. 'Pool closed.'

'Oh, you think?' Lily realised she'd lost a flip-flop. 'Tell him that,' she said, pointing at Will. 'It was his fault.'

But Will had returned to the pool to retrieve her shoe. 'Yours, I believe, Cinderella.'

She snatched her flip-flop from him. 'Thank you. But you are no Prince Charming.'

'No more swimming,' the manager said, making a slicing motion across his neck. 'Too dangerous. Not good mix with alcohol.'

'Oh, she's not drunk,' Will said, ringing water from his shirt. 'Just clumsy.'

'I was startled,' she said, indignantly. 'And can you blame me? I mean, what are you even doing here?'

He gave her an embarrassed grin. 'Surprise!'

'Surprise?' That was one word for it.

And then Zac appeared from The Olive Bar, holding a beer bottle. 'Why's everyone wet?' he said, looking confused.

Lily's night was getting stranger by the second. 'Zac…? What are you doing here?'

He slung his arm around Megan's shoulders. 'Couples holiday,' he said, wincing when Megan elbowed him in the ribs. 'What? What did I say?'

'I haven't told her yet,' hushed Megan, glaring at him.

'Told me what?' Lily looked between three very guilty looking faces. 'What the hell is going on?'

'Okay, timeout.' Megan marched over and took Lily's arm. 'Let's get you dried off and then we can try again.'

'Try what again?' she said as she was being dragged towards the hotel. 'Will someone please tell me what's going on?'

'We'll reconvene on the beach as soon as I've got Lily dried off,' Megan called back to Will and Zac.

Lily squelched her way back to her room, hampered by her dress sticking to her legs. 'I've got mascara in my ears. How is that even possible?'

Megan carried her bag for her. 'Well, that didn't go quite according to plan, did it?'

Lily stopped. Realisation dawning. 'You knew he was going to be here, didn't you?'

Megan tugged on her arm. 'Keep walking. Time is of the essence.'

'I'm not done yelling.'

'Then yell while you walk.'

'You planned this, didn't you?' She was torn between wanting to rip her best friend's head off and needing more information. 'This isn't a random coincidence. You engineered this.'

They had reached Lily's room. Megan shrugged, 'Now, are you going to keep yelling at me and waste more time, or are you going to get changed and meet Will on the beach for a romantic evening?' She pushed Lily's wet hair away from her face. 'The choice is yours.'

'Romantic?'

Megan smiled. 'Well, he's not flown halfway across the globe to talk about the weather, has he?'

Lily quashed the glimmer of hope flickering inside her. 'I'm not sure this is such a good idea. It didn't work out well the last time, did it?'

'So now's the chance to try again.' Megan suggested. 'At least hear what the man has to say. If you don't want to see him again after tonight, we'll move to a different hotel, okay? Promise.'

'He's staying here?'

Megan grinned. 'What have you got to lose?'

'I would say my dignity, but that boat's already sailed.'

'Good choice.' Megan kissed her cheek. 'See you later. Have fun!'

Fun…?

How was she expected to have fun?

She was about to meet up with the man who'd humiliated her, made her fall for him, not once, but twice, and then had unceremoniously dumped her. That was not her definition of *fun*.

But curiosity won through, and three-quarters of an hour later, she was wearing her second dress of the evening – this one a lot less provocative – and experiencing a sense of déjà vu as she left her chalet and headed for the beach… giving the pool a wide berth this time.

She was greeted by a waiter. 'Miss Monroe? This way, please.'

He led her away from the bar and down a bamboo-matted walkway onto the beach. The pathway took them to where the open-sided wicker pods floated above the sea. She had a flashback to her holiday from last year when

Will and her had dined at a similar venue and had ended up getting a little frisky after drinking too much.

She would not be making that mistake tonight. Sobriety was called for.

Will was waiting for her inside the pod. He stood up as she neared, his hair still damp from his unscheduled shower. He brushed it away from his annoyingly handsome face.

'Champagne?' he said, offering her a flute.

The waiter lifted the bottle from the ice bucket. 'Would you like me to serve?'

'That's okay, we can do it ourselves.' Will tipped the waiter, who discreetly disappeared into the night.

Lily remained standing, still unsure whether she should stay or run back to her room. This man had the ability to bring out the best and worst in her. 'No Megan and Zac?'

'They're up at the bar.' Will poured two glasses of champagne and handed her one. 'We can meet them later, if you'd like.'

So much for not drinking.

He lifted his glass. 'Shall we raise a toast?'

She viewed him suspiciously. 'What are we toasting?'

'I hear congratulations are in order. You've landed your first big film. I think that deserves celebrating, don't you?'

'Fair enough.' She clinked glasses with him. 'Thanks for the reference. I'm guessing Megan had to twist your arm.'

'Not in the slightest. I offered. I figured it was the least I could do.' He rubbed the back of his neck. 'It was only fair. The costumes you made for the festival were amazing. You worked incredibly hard. Providing a reference was no less than you deserved.'

Okay, who was this man, and what had he done with Will Taylor?

He gestured to the wicker seating. 'Shall we?'

She joined him, leaving a safe gap. She wasn't ready to risk touching him.

'Megan tells me you've started your own business.'

She sipped her champagne. 'That's right, designing bespoke dresses. Unusual designs with a theatrical twist.'

'Sounds right up your street.'

She fiddled with her glass, unsettled by the way Will was watching her. 'I'm hoping to combine film and stage projects with running the shop. I figure it should keep me busy and provide a regular income. The business is a joint venture with my friend Taye.'

'Ah, yes… Taye, the creator of the fake reference.'

She felt her cheeks colour. 'So, about that…'

'I was teasing.' He closed the gap between them. 'You don't have to explain.'

'Actually, I do.' She took a large gulp of champagne and edged further away. She couldn't form proper sentences when he was gazing at her mouth like that. 'When we met on holiday last year, I was still grieving and trying to make sense of my life. Being a carer meant I'd never been able to fulfil my own dreams to become a proper designer. When you told me you ran an events company, I was a little intimidated by your success. That's why I fibbed. I didn't want to admit to working in a factory…'

'It wouldn't have made a difference,' he said, looking at her so tenderly she felt a shiver run up her spine. 'I would've understood. And besides, you'd been caring for your granddad. It's understandable that your career took a back seat.'

'Maybe, but I was feeling bruised at the time. Inventing a more successful persona seemed easier and more... I don't know... appealing. It made me feel more confident. Like I could do anything and be anyone. It gave me a glimpse of what my future might look like.' She gave a small shrug. 'I never imagined my lie would come back to bite me on the bum.'

'Tell me about it.'

'Anyway, then there was the mix-up with the recruitment agency – I honestly thought I was being hired as an apprentice for your project. Not that I knew it was your company in the first instance. But instead of coming clean, I stupidly thought I could blag my way through the event and get away with it... Dumb, huh?'

'A bit.' He smiled. 'But I admire your tenacity.'

Lily raised an eyebrow. 'You didn't feel that way at the time.'

'Hindsight is a wonderful thing.'

'Anyway, the rest sort of snowballed from there, and... Well, sorry for lying. And sorry for putting the festival in jeopardy. That was very unprofessional of me.' She took another mouthful of fizz, needing something to dampen the overexuberant butterflies in her stomach.

'Don't apologise.' Will shifted closer. 'I didn't behave very professionally myself. I only offered you the job so I could increase the odds of getting you into bed again.'

Lily spurted champagne everywhere.

He reached for a napkin. 'Too honest?'

'A bit.' She dabbed her mouth, aware of him watching her. Perhaps they needed to switch to a safer topic. 'How's Poppy?'

His expression softened, his eyes turning misty. 'Good, thanks. New neighbours moved in next door in August and Poppy has made friends with the daughter. The girls spent the rest of the summer cutting up clothes and making new outfits for their collective pets. They're both in the same school year, so it's been a godsend in terms of childcare. Poppy's over there now most days after school.'

Lily smiled. She liked the idea of Poppy continuing to sew.

'The pair of them started secondary school last September,' he continued, looking proud as he spoke about his daughter.

Who could blame him? She was an adorable kid.

'Textiles is their favourite subject. They both asked for sewing machines for Christmas. Since then I've been dressed up in all manner of odd costumes, including several dresses.' He pulled a face. 'You've created a monster. She'll be after a job with you soon.'

Lily giggled. 'There's one there waiting for her whenever she wants it.'

'If I tell her that she'll be on the phone to you next week.' He downed his drink. 'She still talks about you, you know.' Will reached for her hand. 'You made quite an impression on her.'

'Likewise.' When his fingers entwined with hers Lily felt a little jolt of electricity.

'On me, too.'

The heat radiating off him mixed with his woody after-shave was a heady combination. It made it hard for her to breathe, let alone think straight. She needed to retain some control before she did something really stupid… like kiss him. 'Will, I—'

'You were right,' he said on a rush.

She paused. 'I was? What about?'

'When you said I presented an edited version of myself on holiday last year. That's exactly what I did.' His intense gaze was unwavering. His blue-grey eyes locked on hers. 'So here goes with the unedited version.' He cleared his throat. 'Hello... My name's Will Taylor. I'm a widowed father of an eleven-year-old daughter.'

'You don't have to—'

'I was married at twenty-three. To a woman called Sara. We met at university. Poppy was born a year later. We had three blissful years together before Sara died in a freak skiing accident.'

Lily flinched.

His gaze didn't let up. 'She... she hit her head.'

Poor man.

Poor *woman*.

And then it dawned on her. 'Oh, goodness. Is that why you...?'

'Freaked out when you hit your head when you fell out of the boat?' He nodded. 'It brought it all back.'

'I'm so sorry.'

'Wasn't your fault. You weren't to know. How could you? I never told you.' He stood up and moved to the other side of the pod. 'And that was the problem. I never told you anything, and yet I got frustrated when you didn't understand. But, again, how could you?'

Behind him the waves lapped the sand, offering a soothing backdrop to the sadness in his voice.

He leant against the pod. 'After Sara's death, I focused my energies on my company and raising Poppy. I didn't want any help. I didn't think I needed it. I stubbornly thought I could do it all myself. Be everything my daughter needed. Be a successful businessman and the perfect parent.' He sighed. 'A normal reaction to death, according to the grief counsellor. But naive, nonetheless. I ended up trying too hard and overcompensating for Poppy's loss.' He glanced over. 'Mine, too.'

'Understandable.' Lily was glad he'd had counselling. Someone to help him through the grief. She knew only too well how crippling it could be. 'It's an awful thing to happen, whatever the circumstances. No one comes through something like that unscathed. Trust me, I know.'

He gave her a half-smile. 'Anyway, unsurprisingly I exhausted myself. I reached breaking point and I needed a respite.' He opened his hands. 'Hence the Caribbean holiday last year.'

All was becoming clear. 'No wonder you were reluctant to talk about your life.'

'I didn't want to dwell on my problems,' he said, looking uncharacteristically vulnerable. 'Or talk about my feelings. I just wanted to have a laugh and forget my troubles.' His angst softened into a smile. 'Meeting you was the perfect tonic. We had such a blast – it was great. It was just what I needed.' His expression turned sad. 'It's just... well, I never expected to fall for you. And I certainly never expected to still be pining after you two months later.'

He slumped onto the wicker seating next to her and dropped his head in his hands.

Oh, crikey. What to do now?

Silence filled the air, broken only by the sound of the waves. Lily considered patting his back, but decided to wait it out. She figured he wasn't done.

She was right.

He sat up. 'I swear to God I was going to tell you about Poppy when we met up for the festival events. But when you weren't happy to see me, I didn't think there was any point.' He shrugged. 'And then there never seemed like the right time. I did try, but—'

'The longer it goes on, the harder it is to confess, right?' She knew that feeling only too well.

'Exactly. But then you found out.' He shook his head. 'Christ, I felt guilty. But instead of coming clean, I lashed out. I called you all those names.' He looked tortured, and helpless, and her resistance to him melted another few degrees. 'I have no defence. It was inexcusable. But I was already so freaked out by you almost drowning that I… I panicked. I couldn't bear the thought of losing another person I cared about. So, I… you know…'

'Pushed me away?'

His shoulders slumped. 'I was such an idiot. Especially having tried so hard to convince you to give us a chance, I bottled it.'

At least she knew why now.

Will leant back against the seating. 'I was so sure walking away was the right thing to do. I even convinced myself I was the aggrieved party, that you were wholly to blame. But it was bollocks. I was just scared. A coward. Too afraid to admit how I felt. Too afraid of committing to another person in case I lost them.'

'So what changed?' Lily placed her empty flute on the table. 'I mean… I'm assuming something changed, and you didn't come all this way just to push me in a swimming pool.'

He laughed. 'Christ, I've missed you.'

She'd missed him too, but she wasn't about to relax her guard just yet. 'You haven't answered my question,' she said, adopting a serious tone. She needed to know where they stood. And how he felt about her. Apologies and hashing over the past were all very well, but it was the here and now that mattered. Were they a lost cause… or was there still some hope lying amongst the ashes of their spectacular burnout?

'What changed?' he said, looking up at the stars as if searching for inspiration. 'Well, nothing dramatic. I reversed my car into a tree.'

Not what she'd expected. 'Were you hurt?'

'Just shaken. But as I sat there, covered in a smashed windscreen, I started crying. I mean, like really uncontrollable crying.' He shook his head. 'Thank God no one saw me.' He moved to sit beside her. 'I realised what an idiot I'd been. I was miserable, I missed you. I couldn't stop thinking about you and I knew life without you was a hell of a lot more painful than the fear of losing you. I guess I had what you'd call an epiphany.'

The butterflies in her tummy went berserk. 'Uh huh,' she managed, and then cringed. Not the most eloquent of responses, but she was a little shell-shocked.

'I love you,' he said matter-of-factly, and the air left her lungs with a whoosh.

He loved her?

'You make me laugh. When I'm with you, I feel… I don't know… joyful. Like I'm a whole person and don't have a piece of me missing. You… complete me,' he said, and then groaned, 'Shit. That's a line from a film, isn't it?'

Lily's lips twitched. 'And you were doing so well up until that moment.'

Will gave her a wry smile. 'This isn't easy, you know… talking about all this feelings bollocks.'

'Beautifully put.'

He shifted closer. Close enough that she could see her reflection in his irises. 'So… what do you say?'

'What do I say about what?'

'About being with me. Forgiving me. Putting up with all my insecurities and crap, and letting me… love you.'

Oh, good heavens.

She blinked away her surprise. 'What do I say? Well, I say… you had me at hello.'

He stilled. 'That's another line from a film, right?'

She shrugged. 'It was all I could think of, sorry.'

He started laughing. 'Christ, here I am, opening up my heart to you, laying out all my feelings like a right bloody wuss… and you decide to take the piss—'

Lily placed her finger over his mouth. 'Shut up and listen for a moment.' She gave him what she hoped was an intimidating stare, trying not to be distracted by the feel of his warm lips against her finger and the dimple in his chin. 'I'm not the one who secretly colluded with my best friend to book a couples holiday.'

His expression turned sheepish. Too bloody right.

'Nobody does that for a woman they once called… what was it again? …Oh, that's right… an incompetent *fraud*… unless that person is incredibly stupid… or incredibly sure that the woman in question is going to surrender her grievance, forgive the man, forget his damning words and end up rolling around his bed with him, all hot and sweaty.'

His eyes grew wide. 'Hot and sweaty?'

'Disgustingly so.' She removed her finger. 'But first… I'm owed some payback.' She leant in… so close her lips almost touched his. Almost.

He let out a soft groan. 'You're going to make me suffer, aren't you?'

Lily pushed him back against the seat and straddled him. 'Oh, you have no idea.'

He grinned up at her. 'Do you at least love me?'

'Love you?' She tried to sound incredulous, her expression turning thoughtful as she chewed on her lower lip, knowing it would torment him. 'Do I love you?' She pretended to mull it over, feeling him shiver beneath her. 'That's a very good question,' she said, lowering her mouth to his ear. 'I think that's for me to know, and for you to find out,' she whispered.

Who knew she had it in her to be so assertive?

What else was she about to discover about herself, Lily wondered, as she bit softly on his ear, making him groan and pull her close.

Whatever lay ahead, she was finally ready to leave behind her old life and venture into the world as her true self.

Lily Monroe.

Optimistic. Inspired. Hopeful and innately clumsy.

Part gifted, part flawed. But no longer afraid to show it all.

She was a costume designer.

A lover.

A friend.

And with any luck… a soon-to-be step-mummy.

World, look out.

Acknowledgements

Thank you so much for reading *Someone Like You*! I sincerely hope you enjoyed the story of Lily & Will as much as I enjoyed writing it.

The majority of this story was written pre-pandemic – hence the lack of face masks and social distancing – so although I appreciate the idea of heading off on holiday to an exotic Caribbean island has been out of reach for most of us over this past year, I hope this story provides a little sunshine during these bleak times.

I'd like to thank a few people for their help and support during the writing of this book. Firstly, Julia Knight, a very talented costume designer working in TV and theatre, who kindly shared some of her experiences with me. In particular, the curse of the continuity error! Some of her stories really made me laugh and sparked the idea for the necklace scene in the book. Apparently these things really happen. Not great for the poor TV execs, but wonderful material when writing a book.

The book is dedicated to my grandparents, and the opening Elvis song mix-up scene is a true account of Granny Dorothy's funeral back in 1996. The vicar really did play 'Jailhouse Rock' and 'Return to Sender', before finally selecting the correct song – 'The Wonder of You'. As painful as it was at the time, it was hilarious too, and

I've always wanted to include it in a book. And now I have. Thanks, Granny!

As always, a huge thank you to my agent, Tina Betts, who has stuck by me through the ups and downs and always encourages me to keep writing. It's hugely appreciated. And a big thank you to my lovely editor, Emily Bedford, who has given me such constructive and helpful feedback on this book, enabling me to make it the best it can be. Thank you!

Finally, thank you to all the fabulous readers, bloggers and fellow authors for supporting my journey, sharing posts, posting reviews and generally being wonderful people. Thank you.

If you'd like to follow me on social media or make contact then I'd love to hear from you:

Twitter: @tracyacorbett
Facebook: @tracyacorbettauthor
Instagram: tracyacorbett
Website: tracycorbettauthor.co.uk